PRAISE FOR CREED

"Susan May Warren's *Creed* redefines what it means to be a hero. If you love action and suspense . . . all mixed in with love and faith and grace and lessons learned, then Creed is the book for you."

— AMY, GOODREADS

"Wow! What an epic ending to this latest series by Susan May Warren! This one ties up all the stories with so much action, suspense, drama, and romance. In true Susan May Warren style, it has you gripping the edge of your seat while trying to breathe. Her books lead me on an adventure and never let me stop until the last page."

— MARYLIN, GOODREADS

"The action is almost non-stop so buckle your seatbelts and hang on. You'll keep turning the pages to see what happens next."

— LISA, GOODREADS

"Warning! This book is an adrenaline rush!!! I started it one evening and stayed up till I finished it! I could NOT put it down! The story plays like a fantastic action movie in my mind, full of twists and turns, romance and just good old fashioned story telling!!!"

— STEPHANIE, GOODREADS

CREED

THE MINNESOTA MARSHALLS

BOOK FIVE

SUSAN MAY WARREN

CREED

THE MINNESOTA MARSHALLS

ONE

They'd called him a hero so many times, Creed had actually started to believe it.

Even now, as he stood at the top of the stairs, again, the dream so familiar he wanted to shout—*stop!*

But no, in this dream, his legs worked, his body juiced with adrenaline as he watched beautiful Princess Imani of Lauchtenland on the dance floor.

In the arms of Prince Xavier Neville of Keswick.

The jerk.

But Creed's focus wasn't on the couple waltzing around the crowded dance floor but on a man in the wings, dark hair, dressed in black, a gun leveled at Imani.

Fredrik Ferguson, former protection officer from Her Majesty's Security Detail turned traitor.

Turned *murderer.*

And it seemed only Creed saw him.

"Stop!" He started down the stairs—

And that's when the dream turned on him. Again, he tripped, started falling.

Again, he grabbed for the rail and found only air.

Again, he plunged forward.

Again, his legs had vanished. Both of them, whittling away to nothing right before his eyes.

And again, he tumbled headfirst, the pain blinding as he careened down the massive staircase.

His shout lifted, jerked him out of the nightmare.

Breathe. He blinked awake. Sweat coated his body, his good leg tangled in the sheets, the other still in a brace. His breaths fell over each other even as he blinked, orienting himself.

"That one was louder," said a voice, soft, from the doorway.

He glanced over.

Jonas. He stood, arms folded, his hair mussed, still in his pajama bottoms, wearing a Vortex.com T-shirt. He'd grown a beard since returning to Minnesota from Slovenia, like a man trying to figure out his life.

"Sorry."

"I was awake, little bro." He walked into the room. "Same dream?" He reached for the pain meds on Creed's beside table.

"Yes. And no meds. I'm trying to stay clean."

"You're clearly hurting."

Creed had grunted while sitting up. He leaned his head back on the headboard. "It's not terrible."

Jonas made a noise and set the container back on the table. "Define terrible."

"Shards of glass shooting up my leg, a constant hammer on my bone, and sharp, stomach-churning flares of agony when I move the wrong way."

"Fun."

"It's a blast. Especially in the morning when my thigh muscles contract, flushing out all the toxins gathered during the night." Even now he drew in a long breath, waiting for his muscles to release.

Finally, he exhaled and swung his legs over the edge of the bed, easing the injured one down to the floor. "At least I can walk. Sorta." He reached for the crutches.

"You'll get there," Jonas said. "You're getting stronger every day. Tell me about the dream."

Creed stood up, balanced, then walked to the window. Outside, the sun layered red along the horizon, dark clouds cluttering the sky. Crystalline white snow covered their dormant vineyard, little puffs whisking from the tops of the sleeping vines in a bully wind.

"Looks like a storm is headed this way."

"Mm-hmm."

Jonas wore his curious, scientist, tell-me-everything expression.

"It was just a dream."

"I know." His brother's gaze didn't waver. Because, of course, he knew the story.

"Fine. It might be a premonition." His mouth tightened. "Probably not."

"Tell me."

Creed sighed. "I'm at some fancy event. Wearing a suit. Fraser is there too."

Jonas raised an eyebrow.

"Imani is dancing with a guy. That prince she's been writing to."

"She's been writing to a prince?"

"Yes—no. Sort of. He's a friend of her stepfather's, and she met him during her gap year world tour. Apparently, he's some distant cousin of Prince John."

"Aren't all the royals around the world distant cousins?"

"I don't know. Maybe. But Imani is adopted, so it doesn't matter. But her stepdad did write to her and asked her to go to some Christmas ball with the prince, so—"

"That's what the fight was about."

"You heard that?"

"The entire house heard that, Creed. For cryin' out loud— fish or cut bait, man. You can't tell Imani who she can correspond with if you're not going to ask her out."

Creed just stared at him, his chest rising and falling. "It's complicated."

"What's complicated? You like her—she likes you—"

"She's a princess!" He shook his head and crutched over to his dresser. Pulled out a fresh T-shirt.

Silence.

Creed pulled it on, one-handed. Glanced at Jonas. "It can't work."

"Fine. Tell me about the dream."

Creed pushed past him to the bathroom down the hall. "It's stupid."

Jonas clearly didn't get the hint and followed him. Stood outside the door as Creed brushed his teeth. "Why is it stupid?"

Creed stared at himself. He hadn't shaved in a week, dark whiskers grazing his chin. He looked wrecked, tired, in pain, and frankly, didn't love the view.

He'd never been a victim, thank you.

So he opened the door, gave Jonas a look. "Someone is about to shoot Imani, and instead of saving her life, I fall down the stairs."

Jonas just blinked at him.

"My legs vanish."

His eyebrow rose.

"It's just a stupid dream!" He pressed past Jonas and headed toward the stairs.

He gripped the stairs, then he hopped on the railing.

"What on earth are you doing?"

"I saw it on YouTube. It's parkour, and I figure if I can't go down the stairs the regular way, I'll slide."

"Great idea. Break your head as well as your leg."

Yeah, well, Jonas had two working legs.

Creed slid halfway, balancing, then stopped himself at the bottom and lowered himself down, holding in a grunt. The tantalizing smell of cooking bacon, eggs, and flapjacks, not to

4

mention the sound of laughter from the Marshall family brood, urged him into the kitchen-slash-great room.

He spotted Fraser sitting at the long kitchen island, eating eggs over easy, bacon, and some flapjacks. He nursed a cup of coffee. His oldest, former-SEAL brother still wore a cast on his hand, but he worked his fingers against the granite countertop. But that was Fraser—always moving.

Now he looked up and lifted his cup to Creed. Invalids-in-arms, maybe.

His mother turned from the big six-burner stove. She looked better today, wearing an apron over her jeans, her blonde hair back, although still tired. Her collapse in the kitchen a week ago had scared everyone. But she'd gotten an all-clear from her cancer fear. Still, Creed couldn't help but feel something wasn't right.

"Morning, son," she said, and slid him a plate with scrambled eggs.

"Thanks, Ma." He reached for a couple flapjacks from the big plate in the center.

Jonas had followed him downstairs. "Can I get one of those?"

His mother winked at him. "Runny eggs for you?"

Jonas nodded and sat next to Iris. She wore her blonde hair back and an oversized Vienna Vikings sweatshirt—probably on loan from football boyfriend Hudson Bly. The big wide receiver sat next to her, also finishing off eggs. He dwarfed the Marshall boys, which was saying something, but Creed liked the Aussie. Hud might be the one man who could stand up to Iris.

The only sibling missing was Ned, but he was off on his honeymoon, so no one really expected him for Thanksgiving.

Weird that Imani and Pippa weren't eating breakfast too.

"Is Pippa watching the perimeter?" Creed asked as he slid onto a stool.

"Nope," Fraser said, sort of snippy even.

Creed frowned at him. "Did I do something?"

"You tell me," Fraser said, now holding his coffee.

"Apparently, you read Imani's mail?" He cocked his head at Creed.

Creed glanced at Jonas.

"Told you that you can't tell Imani who she can write to," Jonas said, accepting a plate of eggs from his mother. He grabbed toast from a platter.

Swell. "Yes. I just read the email. She was sitting on the sofa, right there next to me. It wasn't like I unlocked her computer and went snooping. I mean, we practically lived on the sofa for the last two months. She read a lot of my mail too."

"Even reading over someone's shoulder is a violation of privacy," Iris said. "Is that what you were fighting about last night? Hud and I could hear you from the kitchen when we got in."

"Yeah, I know. Listen, she was upset, and so I read it. Whatever." He didn't know his sister well, but clearly his memory of her bossiness wasn't wrong. "And yeah, we got into a fight. What would you do if the father of the girl you liked suggested she date someone else?" He pushed his plate away, suddenly not hungry. "So what he's the future king of Lauchtenland? Doesn't mean he gets to pick her husband. The days of arranged marriages are over."

"Not for royals," Fraser said. "Pippa said this guy is a lesser prince but still in a royal line. And according to her, the email was just a suggestion from her father that Imani attend some charity ball with him. Not marry him."

Creed picked at his eggs. "I know."

"Pippa said that there is some unrest in the country over a possible American in the royal line of succession, so maybe this was a gesture from her father."

"Stepfather."

"The future king of Lauchtenland," Fraser said.

And he didn't know why Fraser's words just sat in his chest like a shard of glass. Maybe because Fraser had been there to witness how hard he'd fallen for her.

It wasn't every day that he helped a princess escape a murderer. Or took her home to Minnesota to hide in his parents' home-slash-winery while his brother and her bodyguard, Pippa Butler, stood guard.

Wasn't every day that he got shot trying to protect her.

And it was probably only Fraser who really knew how Imani had found her way inside his heart. Made him fall for her laughter, her smile. Made him feel like they belonged together. A couple of refugee kids.

Probably because Fraser had fallen for Pippa.

But Fraser wasn't Creed. And that, maybe, burned him the most. He leveled a look at Fraser. "So this was the king's attempt to keep up appearances that his princess stepdaughter not marry an American kid from the streets."

Silence, and even his mother turned.

After a second, "You're a Marshall, Creed. Full stop. Your past is not you. Not anymore."

He hated the sudden thickness in his throat. "Whatever."

"And I don't think for a second that's what Imani cares about." She gave him a smile.

Fine.

She turned down the heat on the stove. "Besides, you don't know the whole story. Don't take offense at something that wasn't meant to harm you."

He picked up the syrup. Swallowed. "Problem is, it wasn't her first email from this guy. Xavier. In fact, they've been emailing for months." He swamped his pancakes in the syrup. Set it back on the counter. "Apparently, we're not exclusive."

"Are you two even *dating*?" Iris said. She picked up her coffee cup. "Because, like you pointed out, it sort of looked like you were sitting on the sofa playing video games."

He stared at his sister. "I was shot in the leg! I have pins holding my freakin' bones together. What do you suggest I do, go outside and play a little one-on-one with her?"

Iris raised an eyebrow. "Just calling it how I see it."

7

"For your information, we were...dating. I think. And we kissed, not that it's any of your business, but it's not like it's a secret. Fraser and Pippa caught us and nearly came unglued. Try 'dating'"—and he finger-quoted the word—"with your spec ops brother and her overzealous bodyguard watching your every move."

Fraser rolled his eyes.

"Believe me, no one wants to get back on his feet faster than me."

"Of course you do, Creed." This from his mother. "You've always been the guy who goes after what he wants. Ever since you joined our family, you've been the fighter. Remember how you kept those kids alive in the school after the tornado?"

"I was just one of many, Mom. The teacher was there—"

"But you were the captain. You led the team, you found water. You kept their spirits up as we searched. And even your track scholarship—"

"Please don't talk about track," he said, reaching for the orange juice. "I'll be lucky if I walk again."

"Oh, I've met you. You'll walk again," Fraser said. "Run, even."

He didn't know why those words seeded inside him, filled his throat. "Yeah, well, not anytime soon. And I understand Imani getting sick of waiting for the guy who saved her in Europe to get off the sofa. *I'm* ready to get off the sofa."

"Please," Fraser said. "I drive you to physical therapy every other day. I watch you sweat and fight and try not to howl. So that's not why Imani left."

He stared at Fraser. "Wait. *What?*"

"Imani and Pippa left about four hours ago," Iris said quietly.

A punch to the solar plexus taking out his breath would have had less effect. "No, that can't be..." He slid off the chair and headed up the stairs. His stupid brace made it hard to take the steps at any impassioned pace. Still, he made it to the top, then crutched his way down the hall to her room—Iris's old room.

Empty. The morning sun shining across the stripped and remade beds, the sheets in a tumble on the floor.

Gone.

The floor creaked behind him. Fraser had followed him up. Now he folded his arms, drew in a breath.

"You just let them go?" Creed said, wanting to push him back. Or punch something. Or—run.

Just run.

Wow, he missed running. The freedom, the power of pushing his body. The sense of not being helpless but in control.

Not falling down stairs.

Fraser held up his hands. "Listen. Pippa says that Lauchtenland wants her back. She's been putting it off now for weeks. Especially now that the assassin is in custody—"

"We don't know that!" Creed shook his head, pushed past him to his room, formerly Jonas's, and picked up his cell phone. He depressed her number, holding his phone to his ear even as Fraser came to stand in the doorway. "She could be in danger right now."

"Dude. Pippa is with her—"

"Pippa nearly let an assassin find her—pick up, Imani!"

But his call went to voice mail. He pressed End and dialed again. "They found our house. They can find them."

"And since then, we've had no attacks, nothing to make us think she's in danger," Fraser said quietly. "It seems, based on Gunner Ferguson's investigation, she's out of danger."

"What does he know?" Still not picking up. He hung up.

Fraser was giving him a look. "Right. He's only the captain of the guard in Lauchtenland. What could he possibly know—"

"He didn't believe her—*us*—when we told him she was being stalked. If it was up to him, she'd be dead already." He tossed the phone on the bed, went to the closet. Pulled out his duffel bag.

"Bro. What are you doing?"

"Going after her."

"On crutches?"

Oh, if he could have gotten to him, Creed would have. Just launched himself over the bed, taken his way-too-smug brother down. Probably would have managed a couple good hits before Fraser shut him down.

But yeah, he was *on crutches*. And yes, sometimes pain meds. He couldn't even drive, so that was super-duper convenient and totally helped him make good on his impassioned statement.

He stared at the bag. "I can't believe she just...left. Just...*left*?" And he wasn't going to do something stupid and cry, but his chest tightened, and he crutched over to the window, stared out at the snow and ice and the barren, frigid world, the oncoming storm.

Gritted his jaw.

So, clearly he'd been right.

He meant nothing to Imani at all if she could just leave him without a word.

He closed his eyes and refused to let the past take a run at him.

"Sorry," Fraser said softly.

Creed drew in a breath. "Good thing I never told her I loved her."

Silence.

Another beat, then, "Yeah, good thing."

Creed swallowed past the terrible burn blocking his throat.

"Pippa said she'd check in every twelve hours. I promise I'll keep you updated. But maybe this is a good thing."

Creed turned then, narrowed his eyes at him.

Fraser was looking at his hand, still in a cast. He wiggled his fingers.

"Maybe you double down on your PT. Get yourself back in fighting shape." He looked up at Creed.

It wasn't until this moment that Creed realized that when Imani left him...Pippa had also left Fraser. So maybe the words weren't just for him.

"Are you...are you going after Pippa?"

Fraser's mouth tightened around the edges. "Not sure exactly how I fit in her world either."

Creed had nothing.

Finally, Fraser lifted a shoulder and walked away.

Creed followed him downstairs. Heated up his plate of food. In the adjoining room, a football game played. Iris was already on the sofa, criticizing the refs.

"This will be a loud day," Hudson said, grinning.

Anything to drown out the terrible shouting inside that said somehow, he'd blown it. Caused someone to abandon him again.

And he hadn't a clue how to win back the heart of a princess of Lauchtenland.

Or if he should even try.

SHE SHOULDN'T HAVE RUN.

But apparently, running was what Imani did best.

"I still don't understand why you call this comfort food. It's messy and I burned the roof of my mouth." Pippa set down the piece of pepperoni pizza. "I'll take a steamy shepherd's pie from the Clemency Pub in Port Fressa."

"They do have good fries. But nobody beats Angelo's for New York-style pizza." Imani tried a smile, failed, and then set her gaze on Justin Whittaker, playing his guitar, singing a sad country love song across the room.

"Blue looks good on the sky…"

An old Keith Urban cover, and Justin knew just how to croon it out, with twang and soul and everything he needed to make it big in the country music capital of Nashville, just down the road. He looked cute, too, wearing a baseball cap backward over his curly brown hair, those blue eyes warm, his jeans faded, his white T-shirt tight across his basketball-player chest.

SUSAN MAY WARREN

Almost exactly like she'd left him three years ago when she'd moved to Lauchtenland to become a *princess*.

What. Ever.

She'd almost bought into the fairytale.

Around her, locals and others from Hearts Bend ate pizza or calzones, a few families at the long table with the checkered tablecloths, the lantern centerpieces. She didn't recognize any of the current waitstaff, but when she'd seen Justin's name on the sandwich board as they drove down main street, she'd made Pippa pull over.

Justin had been in the middle of a set, so he'd just nodded at her when she came in, but warmth still flushed through her. See, that's what she needed—a familiar face.

Family.

The place where she belonged.

Justin finished his song as she sat down.

He tipped his hat to her and started a new song, a cover by Brett Young. "I can't count the times I almost said what's on my mind..."

"You and this cowboy have a thing?" Pippa said. "Is that why we're here in Hearts Bend?"

"No. Yes. I don't know. He's with my friend Penny now, so... it doesn't matter." She took a sip of her coke. "I'm here to spend Thanksgiving with Memaw and Pops. That's it."

"Mm-hmm. And hiding."

"Not hiding."

"Running?"

"Thinking."

Pippa folded her arms. Leaned back onto the red leather seats, considering her. "This was a bad idea. I should have never let you talk me into it. I could lose my job—I didn't even check in with Gunner."

"Didn't you tell Fraser where we were going?"

"Yes, and I said I'd call every day. It's just...I have this feeling in my gut."

"That's just the pizza."

Pippa cocked her head. "It's the same feeling I had at the club when you ditched me."

Imani held up her hands. "I promise, no more ditching."

"Please. I'm smarter than that. Now, at least. I'm on you like Velcro, honey."

"Velcro?"

"Fraser says that."

"Mm-hmm."

Justin's song wheedled between them. "You don't need that guy..." Justin flashed her a smile across the room, his gaze connecting with hers. She smiled back.

And her heart gave a tiny, painful squeeze.

"Thinking of Creed?"

She glanced at Pippa. "What, now you can read minds?"

Pippa set down her pizza. "Yeah, that one was really tricky. You sure you don't want to call him?"

No. Not at all.

In fact, calling Creed was just about the *only* thing on her mind since she and Pippa had boarded a plane this morning and flown to Nashville. And maybe she would have if her phone hadn't died.

"Maybe after my phone is done charging."

"You can use mine." Pippa handed over her phone. "His number is in my saved contacts."

Imani raised an eyebrow.

"Just in case you and he decide to go walkabout again."

"You're hilarious. You here all week?"

Pippa sat back, smiling. "I'm on to you."

"I'm surprised you haven't embedded a tracking device on me."

Pippa waggled her eyebrows.

A patron came in, bringing in the cold night air with him. Barely any snow on the ground in Tennessee; still, Imani shivered.

Darling, I'd like you to consider allowing Prince Xavier Neville from the Kingdom of Keswick to take you to the annual Dickens Christmas ball in Port Fressa. He says you two are friends...

She wrapped her hands around her arms. Sighed.

"Are you coming down with something?" Pippa said.

She ground her jaw. "A case of idiocy. I should have never let Creed read that email."

"Oh, I see. Yes, he did not take the invitation well."

"No, it wasn't Prince John's suggestion—even I was a little undone by that. No, it was the fact that Xavier and I have been texting occasionally. We met in Peru, remember? He was climbing Machu Picchu?"

"Oh, I remember. I told you he had a thing for you."

"No. We're just friends."

"But you texted with him."

"As *friends*."

"And you didn't tell Creed."

"Am I supposed to tell him everyone I talk to?" She pushed the pizza away, no longer hungry. "He was overreacting. And jealous."

"Of course he was. He was—*is*—crazy about you."

Imani made a noise. "Hardly. We had one kiss. One."

"Maybe he was trying to respect you."

"Maybe *you* scared him off with all your hovering."

"He tried to save your life."

Yes, there was that. Her voice fell. "Maybe *I* scared him off."

"Hardly. He's a Marshall."

"He's adopted, like me."

"And like you, he's exactly like the family he belongs with. He's a Marshall. You're a royal."

"Please stop."

"I'm just saying that maybe don't assume he doesn't want you—"

"Like Fraser wants you?"

Pippa blinked at her. "What?"

Aw. "See, I'm sorry. That wasn't—I'm sorry, Pippa. I think

I'm just angry for you too. You got about as much commitment from Fraser as I got from Creed."

Pippa looked back at her. "My commitment is to *you*. And Fraser knows that." She sighed. "But yes, I sort of thought, maybe...but he has to get his hand back in shape, and then who knows?" She gave a smile, and it resembled Imani's from earlier.

"Oh, we're a pair."

"Indeed we are, Your Royal Highness."

"Oh, please, not here. If you care about me at all."

"Okay...Imani. But know in my heart, I'm adding *Your Royal Highness* and *Princess* to everything I say."

"Noted." She leaned back. "You're right. This was a bad idea. I'm not sure what I'm even doing here."

"Eating turkey with your grandparents tomorrow?"

"No, I mean—I'm supposed to go back to Lauchtenland and then what? College?"

"I suppose."

She sighed. "I don't want to go."

"You're just missing Creed, and it's hard to see the future when you keep looking at what you've lost."

Her words felt like a slap. "I've lost him?"

Pippa's eyes widened. "Well, you...walked out on him. Without saying goodbye. At dawn's early light. I think...yes."

Perfect. Because Pippa was right. *Shoot!* Imani hung her face in her hands.

The front door jangled. Then, "Are you kidding me? *Imani*?"

Imani spread her fingers to see Penny Wilkes walking across the restaurant, her brown hair longer, dressed in jeans, a TSU sweatshirt, and a pair of high-top converse.

"Hey." Imani slid out of the booth to catch Penny's hug.

"Seriously? What are you doing back?" Penny let her go, held her away. "Hmm, you still look pretty normal. Where's your tiara?"

"You two need to get an act," Imani said, pointing at Pippa then Penny.

15

Pippa raised an eyebrow but held out her hand to Penny. "Pippa Butler. Her Majesty's Security Detail."

Penny took her hand but looked at Imani. "You have a bodyguard? Cool."

"She's more like a friend," Imani said, and Pippa smiled. Whatever. "After you spend a year touring the road together for a gap year, you get to know each other pretty well." Never mind the crazy last two months sharing a bedroom at the Marshalls' house. Yeah, Pippa was a friend. A big sister, maybe.

Who would kill anyone who tried to hurt her, so there was that too.

Imani scooted into her booth, and Penny joined her, glancing at Justin. He looked over at her in the middle of his song and winked.

"So, you two are still together?"

Penny shrugged, grinned. "He's the one."

"How do you know? You guys grew up together. Maybe—"

"Oh, I know. It's the way he makes me feel—like the sun rises inside me, into a new day. When I'm scared or alone or even angry, he's the one I want to talk to. He believes in me, and around him I'm braver, bolder, smarter, prettier...yeah, he's the one."

No, she would not think of Creed. Not—

"Did you bring your boyfriend? Last time we texted, you—"

"No. That's..." Imani sighed. "That's over. I just came to visit my grandparents."

Penny's eyes widened.

"What?"

"Oh...um...well, I can't believe they didn't tell you."

Imani stilled. "They're okay, right?"

Penny gave a laugh. "Yeah, they are. They won a cruise from the Publishers Clearing House sweepstakes. Too bad they didn't win the million, but they made the paper and everything. They left two days ago for a nine-day cruise to the Bahamas."

Of course they did. "So much for surprising them. I guess

we'll have to pick up some bread from Haven's Bakery and make peanut butter sandwiches."

"What*ever*," Penny said. "You're coming to the cabin with me."

"What cabin?"

"Buck Mathews has a cabin in the mountains. Justin and some other friends and I from TSU are leaving tonight for the weekend. I think Buck is coming on Friday. Come with us."

"Where is it?"

"Daniel Boone National Forest. The cabin has a hot tub and a lake, and a big fireplace. There are about a thousand bedrooms, and even Justin's parents are coming up. We'll play games, and Justin and his buddies will jam, and it'll be ridiculous." She looped her arm through Imani's. "C'mon, it'll be just like old times."

Imani set her head on her friend's shoulder. Maybe coming back wasn't such a terrible idea.

Justin's set ended, and he came over to the table. "Hey, Princess. How's your jump shot?"

"Better than yours." She got up and gave him a hug. "You sound good. But you should play your own songs."

"We'll see. This pizza up for grabs?"

"Knock yourself out." She joined Pippa on her side of the table while Justin scooted in with Penny.

Justin reached out for a piece of pizza, and his arm hit Imani's soda. The glass tipped, flooding the table.

"Oh!" Imani leaped up to get away from the flood as Penny grabbed napkins and threw them on the glass.

Coke dripped off the side of the table.

Justin grabbed the pizza and held it aloft.

Penny grabbed the cup, put it upright.

Pippa followed Imani out of the booth, her jeans wet. "My cell!" She grabbed it off the table, now dripping with soda. "Aw."

Penny handed her some napkins, but even as she wiped it, she shook her head. "It's dead."

17

"Sorry," Justin said. He'd put the pizza down on a nearby table and grabbed napkins.

"Maybe it'll dry out," Imani said as she took the napkins from Justin and wiped the booth seat.

"Maybe," Pippa said and pocketed the phone. She also helped wipe the booth.

A waitress came by. "I'll get you more soda." She left a tray for the soggy napkins.

They wadded them up, put them on the tray, and slid into the sticky booth.

The waitress brought more soda and some waters for Justin and Penny.

Justin retrieved the pizza. "That was a close call. Could have lost a perfectly decent pizza."

"Priorities," Penny said, shaking her head.

"That's right, girl." Justin grinned and reached for a piece.

Pippa was wiping off her phone.

Imani looked at Justin. "How's the old farm? I haven't driven by it. Any improvements?"

Justin took a bite of his pizza, then set it down. "Yeah. Your grandparents remodeled the old house. It looks nice."

She didn't know why his words fell like a stone inside her, sitting in her chest, her heart.

Or maybe she did.

They'd all moved on. Justin with his music. Penny at TSU, both of them finding their happily-ever-after while she...what? Ran from an assassin? Hid from...life?

Princess, shmincess.

"Yeah. We'll go to the cabin," Imani said, and next to her, Pippa winced. Imani put a hand on her arm. "Hey. I promise, no one is going to find us in the middle of the mountains of Kentucky."

"Why, are you in danger?" Justin said. He'd moved his arm over Penny's shoulder. She'd tucked in next to him.

"Yes," said Pippa.

18

"No," said Imani. She made a face. "Only from my stepdad trying to marry me off." She shook her head.

"Really? Is that a thing?"

"No," Pippa said and looked at her. "Lauchtenland is not a country of arranged marriages. You should know—our Princess Gemma is your Hearts Bend Gemma Stone, right?"

"And the prince's sister, Scotty, lives here too," said Justin. "So if trouble were looking for you, I guess Hearts Bend might be the first place they'd check."

Next to her, Pippa froze.

Please. Imani looked at her. "He was kidding."

Pippa raised an eyebrow. Shook her head. "I don't know, Imani. Maybe we just keep going, back to Lauchtenland."

She was right. The last thing she wanted was to bring trouble to Hearts Bend.

"Aw, c'mon, she just got here," Justin said.

"Yeah." Penny reached out and took her hand. "Just the gang, having fun, one more time. Before you go back to the castle and your fairy godmother."

Laugh. Smile. But Penny's words crashed through Imani, dragging up the truth. She just wanted the fairytale to end. For everything to get back to normal.

Whatever that was.

Two

He was never going to walk again.

Okay, maybe that was just Creed being melodramatic, and not a little grumpy this early in the morning, but sweat ran down his chest, and everything, from his head to his foot, burned as he rested between squats.

He'd finally turned up the music on his Airpods so he couldn't hear himself grunt or roar or shout as the pain lit him up.

The sun poured into the high windows in the extra garage-turned-workout room. It'd once housed his father's old silver Airstream, the family bicycles, and a worn out vintage Alfa Romeo spider convertible, half the engine in pieces on drop cloths.

Now it contained, on a padded floor, a weight set with a bench press, various dead lift weights in racks, a pull-up bar, a stationary bike, numerous stretching bands, a tire, ropes, and a slanted sit-up board. Fraser's doing, back when he returned from Nigeria, worked up and antsy, needing a good morning sweat. He'd also installed speakers, but they remained silent this early in the morning.

A few space heaters made a decent attempt at warmth, but Creed worked up his own heat. He'd already logged pull-ups and some shoulder presses. Managed a few sit-ups, but he'd never realized how much he used his thighs in that exercise.

Really, never realized how much of his thigh muscle he used for *everything*.

Now, he picked up the long pole benching bar secured to the base of the bench press, loaded with a ten pound weight, blew out a breath, and lowered himself down. Fire shot into his knees, his hips, but he held it for a count of ten, then stood back up, his body shaking.

Sweat burned down his face.

"What is that, son?"

He looked over to see his father standing in the door, bundled up in a flannel jacket, jeans, boots, a wool hat, tugging on his gloves.

"Just...trying to get my life back." Every time Garrett Marshall used the word *son*, it did something to him, even now, six years after he'd been adopted. "Stupid leg won't let me bear any weight on it."

"No, that contraption you've rigged up."

"It's a lumberjack press. I saw it on YouTube. Thought I'd give it a try."

"Don't hurt yourself." His father walked into the garage. "You know better than anyone that it takes time for the body to heal. You worked your way out of a broken ankle. This, too, you'll overcome."

"I don't know, Dad. This time I have a metal bar in my leg. Pins. I don't think track is in my future." Which meant his scholarship was gone too.

His dad walked over to the outer door. "You don't know what God has for you, Creed. Don't look ahead and despair. Look up and trust." He gave him a wink. "Maybe I should join you later and work off the turkey." He slapped his stomach. "Your mom sure knows how to feed us Marshall men."

Creed gave him a thumbs-up, the words landing. *Us Marshall men.*

Someday, he might feel those words in his bones. For now, they landed, skidded off.

He picked up the bar, lowered, held, breathed. Managed to power back to a stand. "Forty-two." He might actually throw up.

The door to the garage opened again, and this time it was Fraser who came out. Dressed in a sweatshirt, a pair of workout shorts, tennis shoes. He glanced at Creed. "Mornin'."

"Yep," Creed said and gritted his teeth, lowered, breathed. He shook as he stood.

"That's a fancy little rig you got there."

"I don't have a leg press. I figured this would do."

"Creed, leave it to you to rig up something you saw on the internet."

"Hey. I spent what felt like thousands of hours on the sofa. What else am I going to do but watch DIY shows?"

"I might rewatch the entire season of *The Last Kingdom*." Fraser lay on the board, his arms crossed, and started to sit up.

"Uhtred, son of Uhtred. You *would* like that show," Creed said. Why did Fraser always have to be so impressive? Show-off.

"I'm thinking of growing my hair out, shaving it, and making a Viking braid."

"Pippa would love that."

Fraser said nothing. Oops. Walked into that one.

Creed turned up his workout music, hip-hop punctuated by motivational quotes. *Remember, the pain you feel today is replaced by the strength you need tomorrow. The harder the battle, the sweeter the victory! You will make it through the hardship if you put all your heart in. You didn't come this far to quit!*

Fraser was a freakin' machine on the sit-ups board, and Creed couldn't watch as his brother knocked them out.

He focused on the lumberjack lift. Forty-four. Forty-five.

Clapping came from the doorway, and Creed glanced over to see Hudson entering the now crowded gym. He stood about six foot gigantic and took up pretty much all the extra air in the room, so to see him reach down for a palm slap from Creed had him a little nonplussed.

Creed pulled out his Airpods. "The props are for me?"

"I've been in rehab more than once. Not fun." Hud pointed at Fraser, now climbing off the sit-up bench and moving to the stationary bike. "Anytime you want a challenge, let me know."

Fraser grinned. "You prissy athletes can't handle the SEAL workout."

"Really."

"We'd eat you up and spit you out for breakfast." He got on the bike, braced himself with one hand on the bar, and started to spin.

Hud pulled off his sweatshirt and picked up a jump rope, bringing it out to the cement floor of the garage.

"When are you guys heading back to Austria?"

"Sunday," Hud said. "At least, I am. I think Iris is going to Italy. We'll meet in Lauchtenland in a couple weeks for the game." He was working up a sweat now, huffing hard as the rope hit in rhythm. "Are you going to be there?"

Fraser leaned over, breathing hard now. "I don't know... probably not. Pippa has an entire security team there and..." He made a face. "I'm not sure she wants me tagging along."

Hud gave him a look.

Even Creed frowned. "What's going on?"

"It's just—she said she'd call. And she hasn't. And maybe it's a message. Like...it was great, pal, but this is reality. Besides, I'm not going to force myself into her life."

Yep, what he said.

Laughter from the big guy with the jump rope. "Seriously. This from the guy who flew over the ocean to chase down his kid brother?"

Fraser glanced at Creed. "He was in trouble."

"And you—you're just going to let Imani walk out of your life?"

Creed sat up. "When did I get roped into this fight?"

"I'm just saying—I've met you Marshalls. You don't sit still when someone you love is in trouble—and don't tell me for a second you two aren't in love with those ladies."

"They're not in trouble. They walked out that front door of their own volition, no looking back." Fraser sat up, slowing down, and grabbed a towel. Wiped it over his face.

Huh. So big bro was a little more upset than he'd let on.

Fraser tossed the towel away.

"It doesn't bother you that Pippa said that she'd call—and she hasn't?" Hudson slowed his jumping.

Fraser looked at Creed, back to Hud.

"Iris didn't call for three days, and five of you got on a plane to Paris. Just sayin'."

"It think it was more than three," Fraser said.

"A plane. To *Paris*."

Hud dropped the rope into a bin, then went over and chose a couple forty-pound hand weights. He started some bicep curls. "Not a bad setup here for a weekend workout."

From the bench, Fraser's phone rang. He glanced at Creed as he got off the bike, and Creed read the relief in his expression.

Fraser looped the towel around his neck, picked up his phone, then walked over near the door, looking out the window, and answered.

Creed picked up the bar. Forty-six. Forty-seven. Creed just needed fifty.

"Are you serious?" Fraser ran his hand behind his neck.

Hud glanced at Creed.

"Fine. Yes. I'll be in touch." Fraser hung up. Stalked back to the mat. Creed was hunched over, grabbing his knees, breathing hard. "Do you know where they went?"

Creed looked up. "Wasn't that Pippa?"

"Nope." He just stared at Creed.

Silence.

"Um, I think so. Before Thanksgiving, Imani mentioned wanting to see her grandparents. They live in Hearts Bend,

Tennessee, so if they're not in Lauchtenland, that's my best guess."

"Right." Fraser headed inside.

A beat. "So, should you be packing?" Hud finished his reps, then went to lunges.

Forty-eight. "Me?"

"You're going to let Fraser go alone?"

"What am I going to do? I'm on crutches."

"So?" Hud had the legs of an oak, his arms bigger than Creed's. "You love this girl or not?"

"She doesn't love me."

"Seriously."

"She was texting a different guy this entire time. A prince. How am I supposed to compete with that?"

"Hey. Don't look at the competition. Look at you. You were the one who stuck with her in Europe, saved her countless times. You were the one who got shot protecting her. You were the one she hung with over the past two months. You were the one she kissed—"

"Once."

Hud raised an eyebrow.

"Really."

"So was the one kiss enough to make you run after her again?"

"I can't run."

"You can...in here." He thumped his chest.

"What. Ever." Creed picked up the pole. Forty-nine.

"You want something, you go after it—"

Creed pushed himself up. "She *abandoned* me, okay? Walked out the front door without even saying goodbye. That is all I need to know."

Forget fifty. Creed reached for a towel.

"Aw, I see. Your lies get to win today."

He stared at Hud. "What?"

"Iris told me about your past—the fact that you were adopted after going into foster care. How your sister was killed by a drive-by shooting, your brother in prison. Your mom died of an overdose—yep, I can imagine you have all sorts of abandonment issues."

"Hey. Back off. I'm not a case, okay? I'm fine. Over it."

Hud held up a hand. "Hey. Sorry. I wasn't trying to start a fight. I'm just saying—you get to choose whether or not you are offended. Whether or not you're hurt. You decide not to be harmed, you're not harmed. And if you're not harmed, you can think clearly, without the past screwing it up. So, I ask again, you want this girl?"

Creed stared at him. Nodded.

"Then go pack. Because I guarantee you that Fraser—"

The door opened. Fraser stuck his head in. "I'm leaving in thirty for Hearts Bend. Just letting you know."

Creed glanced at Hud, back to Fraser. "I'm coming with you."

Fraser's mouth tightened a little around the edges, but he nodded. "Don't slow me down."

Creed looked at him, then, aw... He picked up the bar with a growl. Blew out and lowered himself into a squat. Held for ten and then powered back up. Dropped the bar on the mat. "Fifty."

Fraser looked at Hud and smiled.

Creed grabbed his crutches, got up, and headed toward the door. Pushed past Fraser. "Try and keep up."

Jonas stood in the hallway, barefoot, T-shirt and jeans, holding a cup of coffee. "What did I miss?"

RUN!

The thought pulsed with every heartbeat, hitting her chest, rushing over Imani. *Run!*

A look behind her, and yes, he was following. A shape, a face.

A gunshot rang through her mind, a bullet pinged against a nearby tree.

She cut into the woods. Branches smacked her face, stinging.

Help!

She stumbled, nearly fell, caught herself on a tree, and hung on, her breaths razors in her throat.

Don't stop. Don't think.

She pushed away from the tree, took off.

Help!

Footsteps behind her, crunching—

No, this wasn't right. Something—

She burst out into the open. Ahead of her, moonlight scattered upon water. No slowing. She leaped into the cold.

It sucked her under, and she gasped. Water filled her throat, even as she kicked to the surface.

Help!

She thrashed, her clothing weighing her down. Water burned her nose, her eyes, black casting over her.

Wait—Creed. Where was Creed?

She coughed, choking. *Creed!*

Water closed over her—no, not like this—

"Imani! Wake up!"

She opened her eyes. Blinked into the darkness. Breathed.

Pippa stood over her, Penny behind her, both dressed in their pajamas.

What—

"You were having a nightmare," Pippa said. "You were calling for help."

"Is Creed the guy you left behind?" This from Penny.

Imani looked at Pippa. "I was running in Geneva. And then I was in the lake. And it was freezing—"

"Yeah, well, this house is freezing. Someone should tell Mr. Country Music to turn up the heat," Pippa said, standing up and reaching for a blanket on her nearby single bed. "I knew I should have stayed up."

Imani sat up, also drawing the blanket around her. They all bunked in the same room—Pippa in the twin bed, she and Penny in the bunk beds. Moonlight glazed the wooden floor of the cabin, and outside, turned the surface of the lake to shiny pewter.

"Maybe it's too big to heat," Penny said, also grabbing a blanket. "I mean, when he said cabin, I thought cozy little three bedroom hut in the woods." She walked to the window, looked down. "I didn't realize *cabin* in Buck Mathews-speak means 'massive complex of timber-framed houses in the woods.'"

Imani joined her at the window. "What time is it? There's a light on in the great room."

"Midnight," Pippa said.

"I'm going in search of a snack," Penny said, and walked out into the hallway.

Pippa turned to Imani. "You okay?"

No. "Yeah."

"It's been a while since you had a nightmare of that magnitude." Pippa was also looking out the window.

"What are you looking for? Bigfoot?"

"What's that?" Pippa glanced at her. "That big dog we saw?"

"Seriously? No, his name is Elvis. You haven't heard about the legend of a tall, hairy man who roams these forests?"

Pippa raised an eyebrow. "Is that like the skinny man?"

"The thin man? No. This guy is like, I dunno, half bear, half human. Or a Neanderthal or something. It's just a story to scare kids, I think."

"Yes, I'm looking for Bigfeet."

"Foot." Imani laughed. "I'm going to get some food too." She headed down the hallway, past pictures of Buck and his illustrious music career. Pictures taken with country stars she recognized—Garth Brooks, Tim McGraw, Randy Travis, Ben King. A few women—Reba, Shania. And some younger guys she didn't recognize, some with signed pictures—Brett Young and a group, Rascal Flatts.

Crazy.

A grand flight of stairs led to a massive great room with a tall stone fireplace, a fire in the hearth, and she spotted Justin sitting on the sofa, his guitar over his lap, laughing and talking with Buck Mathews himself.

Elvis the bloodhound lay in front of the fireplace, his big floppy ears puddled onto the floor.

Penny walked through the room, stopped by Justin and kissed him.

Sweet, but Imani's heart gave a twinge.

Yes, she should call Creed, but even though she'd charged her phone, the remote cabin didn't have cell service. Or Internet.

But maybe it was designed to be remote, a getaway from the media and phone calls and the world telling you who you were and who you should date, even marry.

Yes, marry. Because yesterday, when Penny went to town for supplies, she'd returned with an article saved on her phone.

Is the American princess suited to marry a prince? Sources close to the palace suggest that American Princess Imani is secretly seeing Prince Xavier Neville from the tiny kingdom of Keswick. She's clearly recovered from her harrowing adventure in Europe. What do you think about this royal union? Give us your comments!

Maddy from Madeline & Hyacinth Live!

Oh, Imani had wanted to leave a comment, but Penny had yanked the phone from her hand.

But first thing Imani would do when she returned to Lauchtenland was track down the palace leak and...and...

Probably nothing. Because a princess was supposed to be seen —no opinions, no waves. And that was about the most ridiculous thing she'd ever heard.

She met Penny in the massive kitchen, where she stood staring at the contents of the fridge. "There's leftover pizza, some yogurt, fruit—yuck—and some milk. Cereal it is." She grabbed the milk,

SUSAN MAY WARREN

and Imani headed to a walk-in pantry stocked with cereal, cans of
fruit and vegetables, dry goods, chips, and cookies. She grabbed a
box of Lucky Charms and headed back to the counter, where
Penny had found a couple bowls.

Penny poured them cereal and milk and pushed over a bowl
to Imani, who got them spoons.

"So, Creed. Not so much over, I think." Penny dug into her
cereal. "Not when a girl cries out for him in her sleep."

"It was just a dream. Or rather, a memory. And in the original
version, he was in it."

"What kind of memory has you screaming?" Penny raised an
eyebrow.

"Yeah. I never really told you what happened in Geneva."

Penny set down her spoon. "What happened in Geneva? With
you...and Creed."

"Creed saved my life."

A beat. "What?"

"I saw a murder."

Penny pushed the cereal away. "Are you serious?"

"Yeah. This guy got shot right before my eyes, and I just
started screaming and ran, and that might have been the stupidest
thing to do, but it was all I could think of. So of course, the killer
ran after me, and then suddenly, out of the darkness, Creed
showed up."

"Just like that?"

"Okay, not exactly. We met earlier, on a gondola ride over
Mont Blanc, and then he invited me out to a club with his friends.
I suggested we go for gelato, and then I ditched Pippa."

"You ditched your bodyguard?"

"Yeah, she did," Pippa said, now coming down, her bathrobe
latched tight around her, her hair down. She almost looked like a
normal person. Except, of course, for the dark look she gave
Imani.

"Admittedly a bad idea. I was on my way to the gelato place
when I saw the murder. And so was Creed."

"Which is how he found you."

"Caught me, hid me, and we jumped into Lake Geneva together."

"And then went on the run through Europe." Pippa closed the fridge. "Any tea in that pantry?" She headed inside.

"You and Creed ran away together?" Penny reached for the cereal. "This part I like."

"We were trying to get to my parents' yacht, in Italy. Which we did—right about the time Pippa and Fraser, Creed's brother, showed up."

"Creed's *brother.*" Penny stirred her cereal. "Is he cute, like Creed?"

"Very. A former Navy SEAL. Muscles and blue eyes and mean protective skills. He and Pippa had a—"

"Joint interest in protecting Her Royal Highness." Pippa stood outside the pantry, holding a box of tea like it might be a grenade.

Right.

Penny raised an eyebrow, glanced at Pippa. "Mm-hmm."

"So how did you end up at the Marshall family home in Minnesota instead of on the royal yacht?"

"It felt like the right move at the time."

"We weren't sure who to trust," Pippa said. "As it turned out, we had a mole inside Her Majesty's Security Detail." She filled a pot with water.

"A mole?"

"He tracked us to Minnesota and shot Creed, and Fraser," Imani said.

"He's the brother of Gunner Ferguson, the head of Her Majesty's Security Detail," Pippa said, setting the pot on the stove. "He was part of a political party that opposes the monarchy." She folded her arms over her bathrobe. "Fredrik and I were actually friends. It's hard to imagine someone turning on everything they've sworn to defend."

Penny just stared at her.

On the stove, the teakettle began to simmer.

"And since then, we've been holing up at the Marshall family winery."

"'Holing up.'" Penny finger-quoted the words.

"Stop." But Imani smiled. And then... "I walked out on him."

"Because of that prince."

She stared at Penny.

"I mean, it's not hard to figure out. I saw that article. What's up with the prince?"

"Nothing! We met in Peru—he started texting me. It's just a few texts—"

"From a *prince*."

"I didn't even know he was royalty until my stepdad emailed me. It's not a big deal."

"Not a big—seriously. You're emailing with a prince." Penny put her arm to her forehead. "Oh, the tragedy. I've been invited to the ball by a prince. Whatever shall I wear?"

Imani gave her a look.

Penny returned a smile. "I'm sorry, but cry me a river. You're a *princess*. With a bodyguard, and parents with a yacht, and a castle, and probably an endless shoe collection. Please tell me how you're suffering here."

"It's not that I'm suffering, Penny, but...I went from a nobody in a small town, shooting hoops and eating pizza on Saturday nights, to...to the subject of talk shows and headlines and social media commentaries and—no one even knows me, and they all have an opinion on my life." She shook her head. "Maybe I don't even know myself anymore. I used to think this was fun. What I wanted. Now...I just..."

"You want the boy in Minnesota."

A beat, then, "I don't know. Creed is more than I ever thought. He totally swept me away in Europe, but that was...we were on the run. It wasn't real life. And then he got shot, and things got hard. I'm not sure he doesn't blame me for everything that happened. Maybe he's glad I left."

"I doubt that."

"Maybe I'm too much trouble for him. He didn't even try and kiss me after he came home from the hospital." She shook her head. "Not that he should—he was in a lot of pain. I just...I think that changed things for us. Maybe it freaked him out. I mean, who wants to be with a girl who needs twenty-four-seven protection."

From the stove, Pippa's teapot began to sing just as Elvis's deep barks thundered through the house. He hit his feet, barking, heading to the front door.

Pippa turned off the kettle, then walked over and grabbed Imani.

"Hey!"

"Sorry, Your Royal Highness, but..." She pushed her into the pantry.

"Wait—"

"You too," she said to Penny, whose eyes widened.

"What? I'm not a princess—"

"But you're a friend to the princess, and that makes you a liability. Into the pantry."

Penny slid off the stool and, eyes on Pippa, walked into the pantry.

Pippa closed the door.

"She's a little scary. Even in her bathrobe."

"Oh, you have no idea. See how much fun it is to be a princess?"

PIPPA KNEW THIS HAD BEEN A BAD IDEA. THE WORDS from Justin just kept swirling around her head. *So if trouble were looking for you, I guess Hearts Bend might be the first place they'd check.*

They should have just kept going, all the way to

Lauchtenland.

See, this was what happened when you camped out, away from the world for too long. You started to believe in the happy ending.

"Lights off!" She strode into the great room and did the favor for them. "Stay put, and if you hear shooting, or even my shout, you get down, okay?"

She said this to Justin and his country music star friend, Buck, who clearly should have way more security on this place. Sure, the massive home was tucked away in a dense forest, off a long, windy dirt road. But other than the less-than-menacing bloodhound and a couple motion-sensing porch lights, the house had all the security of the common square in Port Fressa.

And of course, since she'd been on a commercial flight, she couldn't conceal and carry. Which meant she was weaponless. Although she did have a taser. And her wits.

Letting herself out of the side door, Pippa palmed her taser and stepped onto the wooden porch.

Elvis was still lit up inside the house, freaking out.

Breathe. She spotted the dome lights of an SUV in the driveway down the hill from the house click off. Probably, an assassin wouldn't park in the drive, but again, that's how people got killed—by assuming.

She edged around toward the front of the house and spotted two figures heading up to the wide front steps. Stopping short of activating the porch motion lights, she pressed herself against the side of the house.

So, this would be interesting. Next time, she slept in her clothes, so she wouldn't be running around the forest in her bathrobe and pajamas, barefoot.

Breathe.

Footsteps on the boards of the porch, scuffing, the boards creaking.

She'd wait until the lights popped on, then do a meet and

greet, her weapon out. Because common sense said anyone approaching the front door also didn't have nefarious intent.

Then again, there she went assuming.

And not for the first time, she wished Fraser were here, watching on camera, his low voice in her ear, thrumming through her, steadying her.

She'd come to depend on him way too much, clearly. Because he hadn't even suggested he go with her when she told him that she and Imani were leaving.

Just a swallow, a nod, and a grim smile. *Take care of yourself.*

She'd felt a little punched by his lack of response. Not even a kiss goodbye. Like whatever they'd had meant nothing.

So she'd walked away before he could see hurt in her eyes, before the heat in her throat could make it out. Yeah, she'd been a fool to think that they might have something beyond their hideout.

Footsteps on the deck...

Breathe.

The light over the door flickered on.

She swung around the edge of the house, her taser out. "Stop."

Her eyes hadn't totally adjusted to the brightness, so it took a second for her to recognize the men standing at the door. They wore canvas jackets, one oversized, and baseball hats, and one held what looked like a shotgun—

The first one stepped forward and, just like that, disarmed her. Simply grabbed the taser out of her hand.

Oh!

She responded with a jab to his throat, but he dodged, her jab hitting air. "*Pippa!*"

The voice stilled her, and she blinked. "Fraser?"

He looked good, albeit a little tired, his blue eyes framed in fatigue, whiskers along his chin. "Is it always going to be like this? I'll come home with groceries, and you'll try and tase me?"

Her mouth opened.

"Nice bathrobe, by the way." Then he slipped his hand around her neck, leaned down, and kissed her.

Not a gentle kiss, but one of possession, almost frustration. Quick, but thorough, and it took her a full second to catch up. Didn't quite have her feet under her when he pulled away.

His eyes held hers. "That was the kiss I should have given you when you left."

Her mouth opened again.

"And this one is hello. Wow, I missed you." Then he lowered his mouth again, this time softer, sweeter, his lips caressing hers and igniting everything inside her.

Oh, hello.

She touched his jacket, then grabbed his lapel, holding on for dear life when he tried to pull away. He tasted sweet and familiar and everything she'd longed for, her heart slowing to a deep, languid thump.

Fraser.

She finally let him go. Met his blue eyes.

He smiled. "Okay then. I think we settled that."

Settled...maybe so. Still, "What are you doing here? Please don't tell me this is because I didn't call you for three days."

"Not entirely. But you *didn't* call me for three days."

"My phone got soaked in soda. It's still drying out. And there's no service up here." She made a face, then glanced behind him. "Creed?"

"Hey, Pippa."

So, not a gun, but a cane that he leaned hard on.

"Let's get you inside," she said and motioned them around the side of the house, back into the darkness. "The front door is locked."

"Whose place is this?" Fraser asked, handing her back her taser.

"Buck Mathews. He's a country music singer."

"I know who Buck Mathews is. Seriously—how did you—"

"He's a friend of a friend. It's a long story that I'm not sure I completely understand." She stopped at the side door. "How did you find us?"

"Coco still has Imani's GPS tracked on her phone. It works even when you're out of service area."

Right. She'd forgotten about his cousin, the super hacker who worked for some clandestine, off-books super-spy group Fraser was connected to.

Inside, Elvis was losing his mind, his barks turning to braying.

"Are we going to get torn limb from limb?" Fraser asked.

"Stay behind me," Pippa said and pushed the door open. "Friendlies!"

"Elvis, c'mere!" Buck said.

She turned on the lights as she came in.

Buck and Justin were crouched behind the sofa, both holding their guitars. Now, Buck got up. A handsome man, he was broad-shouldered and fit, dark hair, sturdy. Not exactly a weakling beside Fraser, but Pippa couldn't help the comparison.

"Buck, this is Fraser Marshall. He's a former SEAL, and he's part of our security detail for Princess Imani."

Fraser, even one handed, still bespoke a warrior as he reached out to shake Buck's hand.

Creed, too, appeared as if something had changed inside him since she'd left them, his brown eyes sparking, his mouth tight.

"Where's Imani?"

"Pantry."

He spiked an eyebrow, then headed to the kitchen.

She couldn't help but watch as he opened the door.

It took a second, during which Fraser slipped his hand into hers, then Imani launched herself from the pantry into Creed's arms.

He stumbled a second, but righted himself, his hand against the island even as she wrapped her arms around his neck.

Just a hug, but he dropped his cane and wrapped his arm around her waist, closed his eyes, lowered his head into her shoulder.

Prince Xavier didn't have a chance.

Elvis had stopped barking and now began wiggling, pawing at Fraser to kneel and greet him. He did, using his good hand to massage the dog's floppy ears.

Buck's wife came out of the lower level master bedroom, tightening a bathrobe around her growing waist. "What's happening?"

"Just some more guests, JoJo," Buck said.

"Sorry to barge in," Fraser said, "but I really needed to track down Pippa."

Now he had her attention. "So this wasn't one of those Marshall family panic moves where the entire family decides to hop a plane—"

"We drove."

"From Minnesota?"

"We listened to a book on tape."

Oh, *that* made all the difference. She still couldn't get used to people driving for more than three hours to get to a destination. Lauchtenland was barely three hours top to bottom by train.

"But no, this wasn't because you hadn't called. Okay, not entirely." He gave her a look.

"Sorry."

"You get to do that once," he said. "But no. I came because of this." He pulled his phone from his jacket pocket, opened it, and scrolled until he came to an image. Then he held it up to show her. "It's an article from *News Leader*."

She read the headline, and slowly everything inside her emptied.

Possible Traitor to the Monarchy, Fredrik Ferguson, Dead.

"What—" She took the phone, tried to scroll.

"It's just an image," he said. "I tried to text it to you, but it was never read, so I thought...well, I had a number of thoughts, actually. Most of them induced the aforementioned panic. At the very least, I thought you should see it."

"Poor Gunner."

"Yeah. He called me, looking for you. I told him I'd find you. Even if his brother was a traitor..." He glanced at Creed. "Family is family."

Her eyes filled. "I still can't believe Fredrik turned on the monarchy. We were friends, and now... How did this happen?"

He took the phone back. "According to the article, they found him poisoned in his cell at the Port Fressa jail. No suspects yet, but he was going to be arraigned, publicly, this week. I texted Logan Thorne, with the Caleb Group, and he says that the back channel conversation is that Fredrik wasn't working alone—which of course, we know, given the guy who came after us in Minnesota, Konrad Vogel. And recently, the assassination attempt of my sister by Vogel's brother, in Germany. So...clearly, there is still a plot in play they want shut down."

She glanced at Imani. "And that plot could include wanting Imani dead."

"She can still testify to seeing Vogel kill Gerwig Buchen, the nuclear physicist shot in Geneva."

"Which remains a mystery. Why kill a nuclear physicist?"

"Other than his remote connection to stolen nuclear material from a reactor in Lausanne?"

This from Creed, who walked over and eased himself onto the sofa.

She gave him a pointed look. "Thank you for sharing that with the class."

He gave her a wide grin.

Imani sat next to him. Took Creed's hand.

A silence fell into the room.

Then, "We need to return to Lauchtenland," Pippa finally said. "I need to talk to Gunner, and as much as I appreciate the Marshall stronghold, we need Imani under Her Majesty's protection, from the entire complement of security."

"Except, if there is another traitor—"

"I'll vet everyone," Pippa said.

"I'm not going anywhere without Creed," Imani said.

Pippa closed her eyes, pinched the bridge of her nose.

"I'd feel better watching both your backs," Fraser said.

Of course he would. Even one-handed.

Pippa opened her eyes. "We have a full team, Fraser."

And right then, the chill—or maybe hurt—she'd seen from him in Minnesota entered his heartbreaking blue eyes.

"What about the prince?" The voice came from Penny, also released from the pantry.

Imani looked at her. "What about the prince?"

"If Creed goes with you, are you still going to the ball with the prince?"

Even Pippa could see Creed stiffen.

Imani's golden-brown eyes sparked. "I'm going to the ball with *Creed*."

Creed raised an eyebrow.

Pippa started to shake her head—

"All of Lauchtenland thinks you're dating the prince," Penny said.

"I don't know who leaked that, but it's not true." She looked at Creed. "It's not true."

"I know, babe. But I don't know about me going to Lauchtenland—have you seen me? I can barely walk. I don't know about dancing."

"It's not about dancing. It's a royal ball. It's a statement."

Exactly. Pippa shook her head. "Imani—um, I don't think Prince John—"

"I don't care what Prince John says. It's my life. I can take who I want."

Oh boy. Pippa cleared her throat. "Creed, I'm sorry, but you can't go to Lauchtenland. You still have charges pending against you for kidnapping the princess."

All the air seemed to leave the room.

"I didn't—"

"He didn't—"

Pippa held up her hand. "I know. But that's not what the press thinks. To our countrymen, Creed, you tried to kidnap Imani. If you try and enter the country, you'll be arrested. And with the current mood, I'm not sure you'll get a fair trial."

"Trial?" Fraser said.

"I'm not sure the queen will pardon you. Not with all the details still top secret."

"But that will come out during any trial."

"Not if it's postponed...indefinitely."

More air out of the room.

"You mean I could be arrested and, what? Sent to the dungeon—"

"Tower."

His eyes widened. "For how long?"

Pippa made a face.

Silence. Pippa looked at Fraser, who looked stricken.

"Am *I* in danger of being arrested?" Fraser said quietly.

She looked at him. "I'm not sure. But possibly."

He blinked at her.

"I'm sorry. But like I said, I think we have to do this without the Marshall family protection service," Pippa said.

His mouth tightened. "One hint of trouble, and I don't care what happens, Pippa. I'm on a plane."

She would expect nothing less. "We'll be fine. What's going to happen? A terrorist showing up in Lauchtenland? That's about as likely as us being overtaken by dinosaurs. I promise—we'll be just fine."

Now, if she could just say it enough, she might believe it.

THREE

"I hate this with everything inside me." Imani stood in the gate area, dressed in a white wool coat, a red scarf around her neck, the wind catching her curly dark hair, her beautiful eyes glossy.

Heat filled the back of his throat, and if Creed weren't careful, he might stupidly tear up too.

Behind her, on the tarmac where the private Gulfstream sat, ready to fire up, Pippa stood with Fraser, probably having a similar conversation. Even the sky seemed to agree, dour and gray, snow in its countenance, the trees stiff with cold.

"It's no big deal," Creed said, but his voice said something else.

Her jaw tightened, and she looked away.

"Imani—"

"If you don't think this is a—"

"It's a big deal, okay?" He took her hand, and she turned back to him. And for a second, he was back in the kitchen, her full gaze on him as he opened that pantry door. Right before she'd full-on leaped at him, her arms, her legs around him, and ho-boy, if that wasn't a signal, then he needed his gray matter checked.

But he wasn't stupid, either. "You have to go back. And I can't go with you. I get it." Sort of.

Okay, not at all.

"But you didn't kidnap me!" She pressed a hand against his cheek.

Exactly. He covered her hand with his and pulled it from his face, then wove his hand into hers. "Listen, as soon as all this dies down, I'll come over."

Her mouth pinched, and again she looked away. Took a breath. "I don't want to go back."

"Imani—"

"I don't belong there." Her eyes flashed. "I belong—okay, maybe not here either. I don't know." She shook her head. "I just...I'm not a princess, despite what you and Pippa and everyone else says."

"You are—"

"Fine. Yes, I am. Whatever. But I don't know what that *means*." She sighed. "I thought it meant freedom—but clearly not. And then maybe I thought it meant fun, but that feels wrong too. So I guess I don't know..."

"It means you get to go to a ball."

She narrowed her eyes at him. "You do know that I'm only going because my stepdad asked me to."

He did, and he nodded, but it didn't help that she was going with someone else. Or rather, a someone else who was an actual prince.

"Imani!"

Pippa had stuck her head into the small waiting room for the private flights. No one else occupied the room, thanks to Pippa's instructions, but still it felt too open, too visible.

Or maybe it was simply the sense that it was now...or never.

Because despite Imani throwing herself into his arms, he hadn't...well...

"I know! I'll be right there." She closed her eyes, almost in pain.

43

"Imani. I...I'm not like...I don't...listen. The last two months have been amazing. And fun and..." He hadn't expected this to be this hard. Before they'd been having fun. Flirting. And yeah, he'd kissed her, but this...

"I..."

"Don't."

His eyes widened even as she put her mittened hand to his mouth.

"Don't say it until you really mean it. Until it matters." Her gaze blazed into his. "I don't know how to thank you for everything you did from—well, from that moment on the mountain in Switzerland when you kept me from getting hurt in the gondola to actually saving my life in Geneva. And then...this." She looked down, at his leg, the brace, the cane. Back up. "You were right. Your life is wrecked because of me, and I can't get it back for you."

"Imani, my life isn't wrecked—"

"It sort of is."

He drew in a breath. Oh, he needed something, because her eyes filled again—

"Listen, my dad says that...there's a plan for everything, so—"

She kissed him. Just lifted herself up, her hands in the lapels of his jacket, and pressed her lips to his.

And he was right there, ready, trying to figure out how to kiss her anyway, so he put his arms around her and kissed her back. She tasted of adventure and laughter and so much like everything he'd ever wanted that he teared up too.

This couldn't be over. Wouldn't be over.

No matter what his heart told him.

So, when he let her go, he forced a smile. Nodded. "Try not to get into trouble."

She backed away and again ran her mitten over her cheek. Picked up her backpack. "Not without you, I promise."

He laughed, and it sounded wretched, so he followed her to the door. Held it open as she walked through. He stood at the glass as she met Pippa on the tarmac then climbed the stairs to the jet, turned, and waved.

He lifted his hand, his chest so tight he couldn't breathe.

Then she was inside, Pippa behind her, leaving Fraser on the tarmac as the wind whipped his jacket, his hands shoved into his pockets.

He finally joined Creed in the waiting room, and they watched the plane taxi out to the runway. Stood in silence as it took off.

Neither moved until it disappeared into the clouds.

And barely spoke during the entire twelve-hour drive home.

Fraser drove, such a darkness in his eyes that Creed couldn't look at him.

Probably he wore the same look.

No, definitely wore the same look, because four days later, the mug that stared back at him in the mirror looked wrecked, his whiskers dark and rough on his face, his eyes bloodshot.

Stupid nightmares.

Stupid Instagram that posted Imani's return to Lauchtenland like she might be Sleeping Beauty, back from her years of hiding.

Never mind that she hadn't called. Or texted.

Whatever.

He had showered and now ran a towel over his hair, then hung it on the hook, pulled on jeans and a T-shirt, and headed downstairs. His leg hurt from this morning's workout, but he had PT later today.

Just trying to move on with his life.

He took the banister down—he was starting to get it—to the kitchen. Empty. His mother had left fresh muffins on the island. Outside he spotted Jonas and his father in the vineyard, hats on, working on the vines. Probably he should join them—

"Creed, is that you?"

He looked up to see his mother emerge from the den-slash-former security HQ. Fraser had spent the past three days dismantling the operation and returning the den to his parents' office.

His mother wore a sweatshirt, her blonde hair down, and something about her seemed...no, it was just his fears.

He'd already lost one mother. Losing Jenny—he couldn't even think it.

"Hey, Ma."

She slid onto a stool, breathing a little hard.

"You okay?"

She looked up. Her eyes seemed almost yellow. "Yeah, I'm fine."

"Yeah, I'm not buying that."

"I'm just tired. All the fuss of Thanksgiving. It's nice to have a break before Christmas."

Sure.

"You have mail." She pointed to a pile on the island.

"Hopefully it's from the University of Minnesota."

She said nothing.

He tried to ignore the fist in his gut as he reached for the pile.

"Or it could be from the athletic department, cutting off my scholarship."

Still nothing, and he found the envelope.

Department of Corrections, from the State of Minnesota.

He looked up at her.

"You want me to leave you alone?"

He thought he shook his head as he opened the envelope. She probably read over his shoulder, so he didn't need to sum up, but even so, as he set the letter down, he couldn't help but breathe it out.

"It's from my brother. He's getting out of jail. And wants to see me." He looked at her. "How did he even get my address?"

She opened her mouth, but he shook his head. "I don't want to see him."

"Why not?"

"Spider is going to ask questions. Like what happened to Apollo. And if I've heard from my dad."

"You were ten, son. And you had no choices."

"He made me promise that I'd watch over Apollo—"

"Your brother made his choices. You can't pay for those. But maybe you should see him. Make peace between you two."

"There'll never be peace between us. Not after what he did." He drew in a breath. "I keep having the dream."

Silence, then he looked at her. She was definitely sick, her face drawn, her eyes a little tired, dull, but she gave him a hard nod. "The one with your sister."

"No. It's with Imani this time."

"Oh. I see."

"We're at a party, and I know someone is going to shoot her, or poison her, or hurt her in some way, but I can't get to her. I'm standing at the top of these stairs, and my legs just...dissolve. And then I fall. And I just keep falling until I wake myself up."

"How long have you had these?"

"Before Imani left. But it's worse now. Every night. Sometimes even after I go back to sleep."

"She's in good hands with Pippa."

He nodded, sighed, folded up the letter. Picked up the envelope. "It's happening again."

"You couldn't have known, Creed."

"I can't help but think it was a premonition. Like God, maybe, was trying to tell me. Warn me."

"That your sister was going to be shot in a drive-by shooting?"

"I saw it, Mom!" He closed his eyes, the envelope twisting in his hand. Breathed out and schooled his voice. Looked at her. She didn't blink. "I saw it happen. Over and over again until it did. Right before my eyes."

"I read your case file, Creed—you know that. There'd been drive-by shootings around your neighborhood all summer long. Of course it was on your mind, in your head—in your nightmares."

"It happened exactly the way my dream showed me—we were playing in the sandbox, and I hear the car. And I leap at her because I know—I *know*. But I'm too late, and she stands up and screams and then—" He shook his head, his throat tightening. "I'll never forget watching her just—the bullets took her right off her feet. She hit this toy slide we had in the yard and slid down it, all bloody and wide-eyed." He ran his hands down his face. "So much blood. And my mom, screaming. And my dad, chasing the car down the street, then turning on Spider. He..." He shook his head. "The cops had to pry Janelle out of my mom's arms. She was dead before she hit the slide, but Ma just...she was never okay after that."

"I'm sure not."

A hand on his back yanked him from the memory. From the memory of his sister's dirty jeans, blood in the sand, the sounds of more shots shattering the air. The squeal of tires.

"It's not your fault—"

"I know." He turned to her now, almost shaking. "It's Spider's fault. They were after him and got Janelle instead." He looked at the envelope. Then picked it up and ripped it in half. Then again. And again.

Dropped the litter on the island.

"I'm a Marshall now."

"Yes, you are, son. But you might want to think about that when you consider Spider."

He had no idea what she meant by that. He looked at the pile of debris, then scooped it up and carried it to the trash bin. Dropped it in.

Then he turned.

"I just can't shake the idea that something bad is going to happen to Imani. What if this is another premonition? What if she's in trouble, and I can't get there because...because I'm a criminal, just like Spider?"

"Son. You're hardly like Spider."

His mouth pursed. "Not according to the Lauchtenland government."

She slid off the stool. Walked over to him. Caught his face. "Son whom I love. You are not a criminal."

"What if it's in my genes, Mom? What if...I'm like my dad? Or Spider?"

"Creed. When I say that you're a Marshall now, I mean it. Your destiny isn't the street anymore. And your relationships are not broken. Adopting you into our family means that we gave you the rights and responsibilities of a full member of the family. You deserve to be here because you are a Marshall. Not because of anything you've done or will do. You no longer need to ask *Who am I?* You can now ask *Whose am I?*" She stepped up to him. "You are my son, and Garrett's son, and Fraser and Jonas and Ned and Iris's brother. And the son we always wanted, before we even knew it."

He met her eyes, the words fighting to find soil.

"And for the record, I think you're a hero."

Aw. He pulled her into his arms, hating how she felt almost breakable. "I do wish you'd stop saying that."

She pushed away. "Don't you know that all heroes are just reflections of Christ? Embrace it." She walked away from him. "And if you feel like you need to follow Imani to Lauchtenland... then you probably have a brother who might be willing to help you get there." She pointed outside.

Fraser stood in the middle of a line of vines, staring out into the pewter-gray sky. Yeah, that was the last thing Fraser needed— his kid brother asking him to sneak him into a country, maybe commit a half dozen more international crimes.

Besides, Imani was just fine.

Just. Fine.

Really.

SHE WAS GOING TO DIE.

Or at least suffocate. "Mom. I can't wear this. It's...like from the Victorian Era." Imani stood on a dais, three mirrors circled around her as a seamstress measured the hem of a brand new, but terribly archaic, dress.

"It's a Victorian ball, honey," Gemma said. She sat on a chair in Imani's sitting room, where the team had assembled— apparently it took a team to make her fit for a royal ball. "Of course it feels ancient."

"And it's heavy."

"It's velvet."

"It's like eighty pounds."

"You're just jet-lagged, and I promise, it's not eighty pounds." Gemma leaned back in the chair, closing her eyes.

So not like her. "Mom, are you okay?"

"I'm fine, Imani. I just...please like the dress." She didn't open her eyes.

Strange. "Okay, fine. It's pretty." And maybe it was. Royal blue, with sparkles on the gown, and it sat tight around her waist, falling off the shoulders. But it was the lacing up the back that had her unable to breathe. "For cryin' in the sink, I'm not a size two."

Problem was, the entire return had felt...off. She'd expected her mom to grab her up, maybe suggest a movie night with popcorn while she peppered her with questions about Hearts Bend and how Jeb was taking care of Herc and Silver and Whinny on the farm. Their farm, the one Gemma had promised they'd visit in the summers. And then, possibly, she'd get to Creed, although Imani had kept her updated on her life at the Marshall winery.

Except, her mom didn't know about the kiss. And not the one on the basketball court so many months ago that felt stolen, but the *real* kiss.

The one where Creed wrapped his arms around her and made her feel, for a moment, like he'd never let go. Like he didn't want her to leave.

Maybe he *was* a criminal, because in that moment, he'd stolen her heart right out of her chest.

In this old castle, she had just about the worst cell reception on the planet. She'd texted Creed at least five times and was yet to get an answer. What she wanted was to call him. But the paparazzi had her trapped.

Because apparently, she was a *princess*. *Sheesh*.

Frankly, she didn't recognize herself in the mirror, even as a seamstress named Hollis tidied up the hem and Effie, her mother's stylist, fussed at her hair.

She belonged in jeans and a T-shirt, barefoot in the cool Tennessee grass. Or maybe in Uggs, curled up in a flannel shirt in front of a fire...in the Marshall family home.

"By the way, after the ball this weekend up at Hadsby, I've arranged for an interview with you at Haxton. It's really a formality, but it's a requirement."

"How about a weave, Your Highness?" Effie had brought in a portable dresser, and now opened drawers to pull out weaves.

"Haxton?"

"It's the University in Lauchtenland."

"I thought I was going to ETSU. Or...I don't know. Anywhere in America."

Effie held up a breaded weave to her head.

She looked at it, sighed. "Maybe something curly? Like my own hair?"

Effie set the weave down and picked up something long and shimmery.

"I know you want to go to America, but right now, we can't spare the security. Not with Prince John's travels and the recent threats—we need you on safe soil."

"Tennessee is safe soil!"

Her mother ran her fingers against her eyes.

Effie held up a long weave, straight hair that hit to her waist.

"Sure. Whatever."

"Prince Xavier won't know what hit him." Effie smiled,

shrugged. "He's quite well proportioned, if I do say so myself. Even if he is a few years younger than me."

"He's a decade younger than you, darlin'," Hollis said through her pins. "But a few years older than our princess, so he'd better mind his p's and q's." She fluffed out the dress, then measured the hem up again.

"I saw him on *Madeline & Hyacinth Live!*" Effie said. "He was talking about the charity game coming up between the two football teams. He's in charge of the event—at least the International Children's Cancer Fund that they're raisin' the fundin' for. He is dishy. All that dark hair, that chiseled jawline—"

"I have a boyfriend."

She didn't know where it came from, but Imani just... couldn't, okay, maybe— "I'm not—we're not...Prince Xavier and I are just friends. And barely that."

Hollis glanced at Effie, who raised an eyebrow.

"Okay, what is that look?" Imani asked.

"Oh, nothin'," said Effie. "We'll need to straighten your hair for this, but I think it could work."

"I like the curly one," said Hollis, pins back in her mouth.

Imani looked at Effie. She wore her hair up in a handkerchief, thick dark braids trailing out the back. "Tell me."

She just stared at her, then sighed. "According to Prince Xavier, you two have been corresponding since you met in Peru."

"Yes, we have—"

"And he said, and I quote, 'that he has special plans for a very special American.'" Effie's eyes widened.

As did Imani's.

"The *News Leader*, page six, has you practically engaged. There, it's all hemmed." Hollis scooted back. "It's breathtaking on you, Princess."

Imani just stared into the mirror, into the eyes of her mother, who had opened them on Hollis's words.

"Thank you, ladies," said her mother. "I think maybe I need a moment alone with Princess Imani."

Effie helped Hollis from the floor, and they dropped their supplies, curtsied, and backed out of the room.

The door closed.

"Seriously."

"The House of Blue already issued a statement saying that you had no comment."

"I have a comment."

"Imani—"

"Mom, no." She rounded, the dress hushing around her. "It's not right that Creed isn't here."

"I know. But your little getaway to America is still on the DL, and frankly, having Creed here would raise all sorts of questions that might jeopardize national security. He will be cleared of all charges, I promise. We just need to make sure that any threat against the crown is snuffed out. And the truth is, you going to the ball with Xavier does help us get past this stuff with the RECO party."

Imani gathered up the dress. "What stuff with the RECO party?"

"Oh, the PM, Hamish Fickle, has dusted off an old law that says that any royal heir has to be the direct issue of the ruling family."

It took a second, even as her mother looked out the window.

"Direct issue. As in you and Prince John need to have a baby."

"Apparently."

"And if you don't?"

Gemma's eyes brightened.

"Mom?"

"I'm sorry, Imani. I just..." She turned to her. "It's not right, I say. This law. You're my daughter, and you're John's daughter—or will be as soon as the papers are finalized in America—and the fact is, they'd be lucky to have you as their future queen."

Imani froze. "No. No. Mom. Please. Never say that again. I don't *want* to be queen. That is...no."

Her mother blinked, and a tear crested. Oh, wow—

"Mom. What's going on? Are you okay?"

Gemma nodded, then shook her head, then nodded again and—

Imani moved off the dais, took two steps, and put her arms around her waist. "I love you. Please tell me what's going on."

Her mother's arms encircled her. "I know. I...I should have told you. Prince John took us away on the yacht because...I had a miscarriage."

Imani froze. Looked up at her. "You did? And you didn't tell me?"

"It was...new. And we hadn't told anyone we were pregnant, so...and you were running from a murderer. So...no, I didn't say anything. But now, I...what if we can't get pregnant again? Or what if—"

"Mom. Stop." Imani turned her, gripped her arms. "What are you really afraid of?"

Her mother frowned at her.

"It's something Pippa did. When I was scared—especially after Creed was shot. I'd be freaking out and she'd say, 'What are you really afraid of?' And that helped me get to the real fear. So, what are you afraid of? Not getting pregnant?"

"I suppose...that I'll fail Prince John. He needs an heir."

"And then what?"

Her mom smiled. "I get what you're doing."

"Just...stay with me. Remember when you came back from Lauchtenland, after the Prince proposed and after the video came out?"

"Imani—"

"You thought that it was over. You'd lost the farm and Prince John...and then a miracle happened. You realized that God had a plan for it all along, right? The feather?"

Gemma sighed. "Yes, the feather. From heaven. But that was after I put on the wedding dress."

"The magical dress."

"The magical wedding dress. I stepped into it and it changed me. I saw myself...different. Healed." She looked at Imani. "I saw myself as God saw me."

"Yeah. And then Prince John proposed again, and you said yes. Because even though Prince John had lost his wife, you were the next perfect ending. And you told me when you adopted me that God made us a family. And that nothing could separate us. Nothing is going to stop Prince John from loving you either. You're his princess."

"And you're mine," she said, and pulled Imani close. Held her. "So, a gap year globetrotting and you come back a wise old woman."

"It's hanging around the Marshall family. Jenny Marshall. She says stuff like that all the time." Imani pushed away. "Seriously, Mom. This dress?"

"It's gorgeous on you."

"I just...I can't." She faced the mirror. "I want to find my own dress—like RJ."

"RJ Marshall—I remember her. She and York got married in Hadsby Castle right before the Rosendans this summer. Wait—is she related to Creed. Your *boyfriend*?"

"Yeah, they're cousins, I think. And okay, maybe we're not official yet, but..." She sighed. "I don't want him thinking I ran off into the arms of some prince." She lifted her hair. "Unzip me."

"Oh, honey, I'm afraid. Hollis would murder me if I messed up her pins." She winked, then stepped out and called for Hollis, standing in the hallway.

Hollis helped her out of the dress, and Imani reached for her jeans. As she pulled them on, she addressed Hollis. "Ever heard of a dress store in Hadsby that sells vintage gowns?"

"The Vintage Shop, in Centre Street in Old Dalholm," Hollis said.

"That's the one," Imani said. She turned to her mother. "I want a dress from there."

Her mother glanced at Hollis, who took a breath.

Imani turned to her. "Oh, Hollis. I'm sorry. Your dress is gorgeous, for sure. And if I don't find something, I'll wear it. I just...I need to find something that is...me." And even as she said it, it sort of resounded through her.

Maybe she could figure out this princess thing if she could find her own footing. And it started with this stupid dress.

And ended, please, with Creed. But maybe that was pushing the House of Blue too far.

Gemma sighed. "Fine. I'll arrange for the royal train to take you up there. And then maybe you can go to Hadsby Castle and oversee the decorations."

"Sure. Okay."

"I'll bring the weaves, Your Highness," Effie said as she packed them up. Hollis wrapped the dress in paper.

Imani looked at her mother. "What I wouldn't give for a barn, a soft bed of hay, and the sound of old Herc snuffing around."

"Yeah, me too." She walked over. Put her arm around her daughter and turned her to the view of gothic cathedrals amidst shiny skyscrapers—the skyline of Port Fressa. "How about I order us a pizza. I think it's time for a movie night." She leaned close. "And then you can tell me all about the handsome and adventurous *Creed*."

Okay, so she might not die quite yet.

She'd wait until the night of the ball.

It wasn't the worst way to pry his mind off Pippa.

Fraser raised his fist amidst the crowd's raucous cheering as Wyatt Marshall, goaltender for the Minnesota Blue Ox, mitted another attempt on goal by the Colorado Sting.

He high-fived Coco, dressed in an oversized hockey sweater with Wyatt's name and number on the back. Then he bumped fists with Mikka, their son—he thought he might be about ten years old—also wearing his father's jersey, albeit miniature.

Wyatt threw the puck back out onto the ice, where the ref grabbed it for a face-off, and Fraser sat back down. The air in the St. Paul arena bore a chill, but the crowd was rowdy and hot, and there had already been one fight on the ice.

Two minutes left on the clock. He hadn't thought about Pippa for at least, okay, maybe five minutes, given the excitement on the ice. So, that might be a step in the right direction.

As soon as we get this situation with the princess sorted, we'll figure this out, Fraser.

Her words to him on the tarmac, before she climbed a plane back to Lauchtenland.

He'd nodded, agreeing with her, because what else was he going to do? But in her eyes he saw the same thing that probably lingered in his own.

Denial.

"So, the princess and her bodyguard have gone back to Lauchtenland. And you didn't go with them?" Coco looked over at him.

"Nope," he said.

Pippa dreamed of being on Her Majesty The Queen's protection detail, and yes, she'd turned the offer down once to protect Imani, but Fraser had no doubt that the offer would circle back around.

No way could he let her turn it down. Not for...what? Because as soon as he could get back into the game, he planned on rejoining Ham's Jones, Inc. private security team.

No. Their lives were mutually exclusive, despite what he wanted.

So, living in denial seemed the best option all around.

The Blue Ox had taken the puck down the ice into Sting territory, fighting it out in the last minute of play.

"Why not?" Coco said. She clapped her mittened hands. "C'mon, boys, put the puck in!" Turning back to Fraser. "I thought maybe you two had a little thing going."

More than a little thing. Fact was, she'd left a gaping hole where his heart used to be when she left. "Yeah. It was...we..."

"Oh boy," Coco said. "That sounds pretty serious."

"We live in different worlds."

"Agreed." She sighed. "So did Wyatt and I. But we made it work."

He didn't know the full story—just that Coco had lived in Russia in hiding for a few years before Wyatt went searching for her. He wasn't sure where Mikka fit into that story, as they'd only been married for a couple years, but he didn't ask.

"I don't know how. Especially since Creed and I are supposedly on Lauchtenland's blacklist. We set foot into the country, we're arrested."

"Seriously?"

The buzzer sounded, and the crowd erupted with the win for the Blue Ox, two goals to nothing. He hugged Coco, then double fist-bumped Mikka, and finally saluted Wyatt, who came out of the crease and waved to them, sitting in the family section.

Coco picked up her bag, grabbed Mikka's hand. "Arrested?"

He followed her out of the row. "Yeah. Since I helped Creed escape from the royal yacht after his arrest, I'm on the watch list. At least until they get this threat with the princess sorted."

They started up the stairs. "By the way, thanks for your help getting into Werner Vogel's phone."

"Did the information help?"

"Yeah. It all circled back to the original, um, *event* that set Imani running. His brother was the guy in Geneva, same guy who shot Creed."

"Who attacked you at your house."

"Yep. And they're connected to the RECO party in Lauchtenland, so it's on Gunner's turf now."

They reached a private tunnel, and she flashed her family pass.

"And how's Ned?"

He glanced at her.

"Please. I'm a member of the Caleb Group. Logan knows your brother's team is on the hunt for the missing, um..." She raised an eyebrow.

Right. Because they shouldn't be taking about top secret trouble in the middle of a crowd.

He lowered his voice. "Yeah. They recovered the materials that Ned, um, liberated. But apparently there's still a rogue package on the loose. But Ned is on his honeymoon."

"Seriously?" Coco flashed her pass again, allowing her into the family waiting area of the arena. "Wyatt usually comes out pretty quickly."

"He and Shae eloped a week or so ago."

"I should hope so after everything he—and you—did to find her. I'd put a tracking device on her."

He laughed. "I'm sure that's not far from Ned's mind, if he could get away with it. She did text us, though, and said she'd see us in Lauchtenland for the game, so I'm not sure what's going on with them. I should get going." He checked his watch. Nearly midnight.

"Wyatt will want to say hi to his cousin. Not every day we get the famous Fraser Marshall at one of his games. And it's his last season, so I'm glad you got to see him play." She sat on a sofa while Mikka went to get hot cocoa from a nearby machine.

"He's the poster boy. I'm just under the radar—"

"Keeping the world a safer place. How's the hand?"

He lifted it, wiggled his fingers. "Better. I have feeling again in my fingers. Doc says with more PT I'll have full use. Got my cast off a couple days ago. Dad used it as an excuse to get me into the vineyard, pruning the vines."

Mikka came back with the hot chocolate. Blew on it. Good kid. He'd had leukemia for the first two years he was in America—his mother had apprised Fraser a couple times. Now Mikka seemed to be in remission, his dark hair long and tumbling out of his cap, not unlike his hockey-player father.

"So, why did Pippa and the princess go back? Is the threat neutralized?"

"We think so." He dropped his voice. "The man who tried to eliminate Imani was recently, um, benched. Permanently." He flicked a gaze at Mikka, but the kid was stirring his hot chocolate. "It was time for Imani to go home."

"Gunner?"

"Captain of Her Majesty's Security Detail. He used to be Prince John's personal bodyguard."

"Right. I think I remember York talking about him."

"How is York. And RJ?"

"RJ is pregnant. About six months now. And you know, they're adopting a little girl from Russia. So she's busy. Still working for Logan, however. Mostly analysis."

"And York?"

"Home a lot, for now." She stood up and pushed past Fraser, heading toward the door.

He spotted her throwing her arms around her freshly showered, wet-haired husband. Wyatt was a big man, wide athletic shoulders, lean body, and now scooped his petite wife up with one arm, kissing her.

"Papa!" Mikka left the bench, and Fraser just righted the hot chocolate, still in a Styrofoam cup, as he launched himself at his dad.

Wyatt dropped his duffel and caught up his son.

Fraser didn't know why a lump formed in his throat. But he swallowed it back down just as Wyatt set Mikka down.

"Couz!" Wyatt said, holding out his hand. Fraser met it, but Wyatt pulled him in for a back slap. "It's about time."

"Great game. Lots of epic snatches."

"Thanks." Wyatt picked up the duffel. "We need to get together, slap around the puck. I have an ice rink in my backyard."

"Of course you do. I'll talk to my brothers, see if we can put together a little face-off."

"They're in town?"

"Not Ned, but Jonas is here. For a bit."

"Still chasing storms?"

"Always." He held out a fist. "I gotta get back. It's late."

"I'll start hounding you," Wyatt said, bumping his fist.

Fraser headed outside and into the dark parking lot, beeped on the lights to his truck. Got in.

Overhead, the stars scattered across the sky, a perfect, chilly December night. He ran the truck a moment, waiting for the heater to kick on.

We made it work.

Sometimes, if he closed his eyes, he could be right back there on the tarmac, or maybe his own home, in the den-slash-security HQ with her, and, when the house was ultra quiet and the monitors humming, he'd pull her up, back her against the wall, meet her eyes, and kiss her.

And in that moment, the world would stop whirring, the constant knot in his chest would loosen, and he'd let himself dream. Of a home. Family. A wife who made him laugh and feel as if he didn't have to apologize for being himself.

He loved her.

He swallowed, opened his eyes, and took a breath.

Yeah, it would take a miracle.

And frankly, maybe she thought so too, because she hadn't called him. Not once in five days since returning to Lauchtenland.

So much for getting his mind off her.

Traffic was light as he left St. Paul, driving west out of the city, through Minneapolis, then out toward Waconia. He'd left the city behind, tooling along country roads just a few miles out of the town of Chester, near his family's winery, when the call came in through his Bluetooth.

Identity-blocked number. But anything this time of night had

SUSAN MAY WARREN

his chest tightening. He pressed it on via his steering wheel. "Hello?"

He tapped the brakes and pulled over. Around him, snow-dusted fields glowed a deep silver.

"Seriously." In a moment, the video call came through, and Pippa's face filled the screen.

For a second, he couldn't breathe, just seeing her there. He'd forgotten how beautiful—oh, he was turning into a sap.

Still, "You look good." She wore a white parka and makeup, her long, dark hair back in a sleek ponytail.

"We're back on duty here. Paparazzi around every corner." She sat in what looked like a high-end subway, or maybe—

"Are you on a train?"

"Yes. The royal coach. Heading up to Dalholm. What time is it there?"

"After midnight."

She made a face. "Sorry. I didn't check. Bother. I'm sorry it's taken so long to check in. I haven't had a moment to think since we got back. So much to debrief Gunner on, catch up on activities...but I miss you."

He could make out the coach, just barely, and spotted Imani behind her, seated on a creamy white sofa. The landscape moved in the window behind them, mostly sky.

"I miss you too. And it's okay. I'm driving home from a hockey game. My cousin Wyatt."

"Fun. Everyone in Lauchtenland is about the upcoming football game here in a week between the Minnesota Vikings and the Vienna Vikings. I'm hoping to connect with Iris and Hud while they're here, but we'll see what's on Princess Imani's agenda. She's restless. I think she misses Creed."

"Creed misses her. She hasn't called either—"

"Blimey. Of course. The palace in Fressa is ancient and it has these thick walls, and it's terrible for cell reception. Again, I'm so sorry—I should have stepped out or found a landline, but I

62

thought it might not be a good look to trace a call from the switchboard out to a known criminal." She smiled.

"You think that's funny?"

She wrinkled her nose. "Listen, Captain America. I promise, everything is sorted here. We're fine. Going to do some shopping today, and then heading to Hadsby Castle for the ball this weekend."

"She's still going with the prince?"

"Yes. But not happy about it. Apparently, the prince has been alluding to a romance between them."

"So that's what has Creed in a knot."

She glanced behind her. "Actually, it looks like they're chatting." She turned the phone toward Imani. "Say hi to Fraser."

Imani lifted her hand, then turned her phone. Indeed, Creed's face lit up the screen, his beard a little longer, his hair tousled—clearly she'd woken him up. "Hey, bro," Fraser said.

Creed lifted his chin, and Imani turned him back around, putting in her ear pods.

"So...how are things there? Everything okay with Gunner?"

"Yeah. He's turned the investigation largely over to the Lauchtenland Investigative Service. Gunner's turned his attention to the security for the game. They built a bulletproof box for the royals—long overdue, in my opinion. And he's beefed up security for the queen, as well as Princess Gemma and Prince John, Prince Gus and Princess Daffy."

"What we need is motivation for why the RECO party Fredrik belonged to would want to assassinate Prince John."

"He's the next in line to the throne. And recently, Hamish Fickle, the PM, has been throwing around the Writ of Succession—it's an old law that says that the successor to the crown must be the direct issue of the ruling family. So Imani is not in the line of succession."

"What about Gus and Daffy. Didn't they just have a child?"

"Yes. And precautions are being taken for them also."

She moved aside as a male porter came into the coach,

trolleying a cart. Fraser spotted him—he wore a white uniform, clean-shaven, a pullman's cap over his short, dark hair, gloves. He left the cart, with a shiny teapot and a French press with coffee, in the room. "Thank you," Pippa said as he left, and he stopped by the door, where Imani was sitting, and nodded.

Imani thanked him also, and he left.

Pippa set the phone down on a table, propping it up as she went to pour tea.

"So, are you going home for Christmas?"

"I don't know. Mum and Basil are pretty busy. There's talk of them going skiing in the Haskells, on the north side of the country. There's already snow in the high mountains, and the resort is open."

He'd sort of hoped she'd suggest visiting him. "Sounds fun."

She was making herself tea, and he had a decent view of the cart. On the bottom sat a duffel bag. Something about it... "Hey, Pip, what's in that bag?"

She glanced at the phone, then at the bag. Set her cup down. Pulled it out and set it on the bench. Opened it.

He could only see her face, but the way it blanched white— "What is it?"

She picked up the phone and turned it to the open bag.

All the air left his lungs. "Is that—"

"Yes."

A very simple but clearly lethal IED, with two white pipes encased in duct tape, a timer affixed to the outside, and wires attached to terminals at the top.

A beat, and he reached for his phone. "Don't move." He took a screen grab. Then, "Get rid of it."

"It could be a training device," she said.

"Get rid of it!"

"We're over the sound! I'll have to throw it out the window." She looked up. "Imani—get out, now!"

Fraser went flying as Pippa dropped the phone. He landed on

the floor, staring up at the ceiling, and only got bits of movement as Pippa grabbed the bag. "Imani, I mean it—get out!"

Then, a terrible rushing sound as the window opened. Pippa stumbled back. The duffel in her hands, a second before she threw it—

The screen lit up, a flash of light and flame, the blast deafening through the phone.

Then everything went black.

"Pippa!" He pressed redial, but the call cut off, unable to connect.

The phone landed on the seat next to him as he put the truck into drive. He slammed his hand on the steering wheel as he peeled out onto the highway.

He picked up the phone, palming it, yelling at it to ring as he floored it, fishtailing into his driveway, skidding as he slammed on the brakes.

He nearly fell from the truck, scrambling to the house.

He threw open the door. "Creed! Creed!"

"I'm here, man." Creed stood in the kitchen, dressed in his pajama bottoms, a T-shirt.

"Please tell me you've still got Imani."

But Creed's eyes were huge, his hand also fisting his phone, and Fraser's stomach wanted to empty when he shook his head.

"What happened?" he whispered. "Pippa was shouting, and Imani was trying to open the door of the car—"

"A bomb. It was left by the porter—it went off, I think." He closed his eyes, pressed his hands to his face, still holding his phone.

No. No. No—

When he lowered his hand, Creed still stood there, but the expression had turned from horror to something of anger. And a fierceness had entered his voice, low and dark. "Don't just stand there, bro. Figure out a way to get us into Lauchtenland."

FOUR

"I cannot believe the House of Blue is still going through with the ball. Seriously." Imani stood in front of the flatscreen in her bedroom in Hadsby Castle, dressed in yoga pants and a T-shirt—the attire of a prisoner, thanks—staring down her mother.

Who was not attending the ball.

"I know, Imani, and the protection detail is doubling their staff and their precautions, but the Dickens ball is an annual charity event for the House of Blue, and it's too close to the event to cancel. We have dignitaries from around the world attending—"

"Except you. You're not attending."

"Gus and Daffy will be there in our stead. But we have...some other things to attend to." Her mother wore a deep-royal blue dress with a mock turtle collar and a gold necklace, looking very, overwhelmingly royal as she sat on a chair in her office, a massive picture of herself and Prince John in their wedding attire on the wall behind her, an oil painting from the original photograph. Sometimes—like today—Imani didn't even recognize the woman who'd adopted her while living on a farm for rescued animals in Hearts Bend, Tennessee.

The woman who'd preferred, at least once upon a time, a pair of jeans, flip-flops, and a T-shirt.

"Like what things."

Gemma drew in a breath. "Like a doctor's appointment."

Oh. *Oh.* "Are you—"

"No. This is just...well, we're doing some testing. But we need it to be on the sly, while the press is occupied."

"I see."

She gave a tight-lipped smile. "I need you there. Besides, I think you really will have fun."

Imani nodded, climbing onto the plush king-sized bed, dressed for the season with a green velvet cover and white pillows. A tree decorated with gold balls and white lights brightened the corner of the room. "Fine. I just..." She looked away.

"Are you sure you're okay?"

"Yes. I'm really fine, Mom. It was Pippa who was hurt."

"How is she?"

"Fine. Just bruised. And she had stitches, but she's like a dog with a bone with the LIS, trying to track down that porter."

"You still don't remember him?"

"No. He was in and out so fast. And I was talking to Creed, so...no, I wasn't paying attention. Not until Pippa shouted at me to get out."

Her mother shook her head, pressed her hand to her mouth, her eyes speaking for her.

"Really, I'm fine. It all happened so fast, and Pippa was there to protect me."

"It's good she's such a fast thinker. If the bomb hadn't detonated outside—"

"I know. I told you she's good." She drew up one knee. "I just wish..." She shook her head.

"Does Creed know you're okay?"

"My phone was destroyed, but I did get a phone to call his house and leave a voice mail. I'm going to try him later today, after Pippa brings me my new phone."

Her mother sighed. "Maybe it is too much to ask of you to go to the ball—"

"No. Mom. I got this. Besides, Hollis is dying for me to wear the blue dress, so..." She lifted a shoulder.

"No Vintage Shop for you?"

"I'm a prisoner in my own castle. Or your castle."

"The queen's castle. But I get it." She made a face. "I know we promised you that we'd spend time in Hearts Bend. I never knew that royal responsibilities would take up so much time, especially with the queen's health so precarious. I will make it up to you."

"Mom. Seriously. I've spent the past year touring the world. I get to go to a ball. I have a bedroom the size of a football field and a closet the size of a locker room, not to mention so many shoes I feel like I should start a donation center. So...kill the apologies. Cinderella will survive the ball. If I *have* to." She smiled and added a wink.

"That's my girl. Thank you, Imani. Love you."

"Love you too." She hung up on her phone, and the cast died on the screen. Then she flopped back on the bed, staring at the chandelier that dripped from the ceiling.

If she closed her eyes, she might be back on the train, hearing Pippa scream at her. Ten seconds of delay and, yeah, maybe they both wouldn't be here. But she'd obeyed—clearly the last three months had taught her something—and bolted out of the car just as Pippa threw herself at her.

After, of course, hurtling the duffel bag bomb from the train.

It ignited, but they were already in the other compartment, Pippa's body over hers, protecting her with her life as glass shattered around them from the concussion.

Could have been so much worse. Like the train derailing. Or—yeah, Pippa or her getting firebombed.

Pippa was clearly shaken—angry mostly—but she'd refused to leave Imani until they were safe at Hadsby, the ancient castle on the outskirts of the old city of Dalholm, under the shadow of the Highcrest Mountains.

It was built like a castle from ancient days, with the fortress on a hill, a walled courtyard surrounded by tall walls cordoning off a dry moat turned flower garden, but she'd never felt more like a kept princess than the moment when Pippa shut the door to her room and asked—but really sort of ordered—her not to leave the grounds. Or her room.

Given the bloody bandage on Pippa's arm and the way she carried herself, as if she might really be hurting, Imani just nodded.

Pippa had sent in staff—an attendant to run her a bath, another to take her food order. Yet another with a phone that she used to call Creed. Then later, herself, tidied up, her expression tight and fierce, to ask her what she remembered.

"Sorry I'm not more help," she'd said after Pippa walked her through every moment.

"That's what I'm here for," Pippa said. "I'm sorry I didn't vet the porter. It was a stupid mistake, and—"

"It was on our private car. The staff should have already been vetted," Imani had said, weirdly wanting to comfort her bodyguard.

"Still. If it weren't for Fraser seeing it..." She'd run her finger and thumb into her eyes. Taken a breath. Looked at Imani. "You okay, or do you want me to stay?"

And that's when Imani did take her hand. "What I want is for you to decompress. I'm fine. I'm safe. And you can stop worrying about me for the next eight hours and get some sleep, okay?"

Pippa's mouth tightened. "You call if you need anything." And that's when she'd pressed into Imani's hand the necklace, a new brooch with a panic button to replace the one lost in her run across Europe so many months ago.

Right.

But she'd taken it, put it around her neck, and nodded. And only then had Pippa left.

Now, some twelve hours later, please, let her have gotten some sleep.

The old castle, built of stone and marble, bore a chill that the modern furnace couldn't nip. In the summer, like when she'd been here for the Rosendans, the place harbored the cool breath of the sea, just behind the high cliffs to the east. Now the cold stone floors were covered with thick plush rugs, and heat was being cast out of the inserts in the ancient hearths that graced every room. Her own room, on the second floor, hosted a sitting room with a smaller hearth and a bookcase, not to mention the massive closet. But the place smelled of age, now that the windows were closed and the lavender scent from the gardens below had died under the glistening snow.

Imani got up and walked to the window, staring at her world. The castle was bigger than it looked, with three stories, ten guest rooms, three apartments, a theater, an indoor lap pool, offices, a massive library, family rooms on each floor, receiving rooms, and a gorgeous ballroom with a wooden floor and a hearth big enough to push two sofas on either side of the frame. Balconies and terraces surrounded the entire estate, and in the summer, gardens flowered with gorgeous English roses and peonies and hydrangeas and larkspur and, okay, she liked the place.

Usually.

But for Pete's sake, it was something right out of a Hans Christian Andersen fairytale.

Of the two wings cast off the main structure, the wing opposite her window, across the inner courtyard, was reserved for Gus and Daffy, the royalty who officially resided at Hadsby. She leaned her head on the leaded pane and gazed through the main gate. It led to a cobblestone, now wintery road that led down to Old Dalholm.

She would have liked a trip to the Vintage Shop. During yesterday's quick trip through Dalholm she'd spotted the old town decked out with greenery on the lampposts, and along the quaint and old Centre Street, twinkle lights on the trees.

Snow capped the red-tile roofs and laced the tall gothic steeple of the town church. When she'd first arrived, in the early days of her mother's marriage, she had toured the town, instantly falling in love with that too.

Beyond Dalholm, the Highcrest Mountains rose, a fortification between Dalholm and the high country to the Haskells in the north. Now, snow layered the peaks and fell into the granite fissures, an imposing barrier to escape.

Not that she was going to run. She'd made promises, but...

A knock. "Enter."

One of the attendants—Maude, she thought. Middle-aged, she worked on staff at the castle, maybe as one of the secretaries. "Ma'am, you have a guest in the receiving hall."

She frowned. And for a terrible, dangerous moment— "Is it an American?"

"No, ma'am. It's Prince Xavier from Keswick."

Right. Because Creed was a fugitive here.

She looked at herself in her yoga pants and Buck Mathews tour T-shirt. "I'll be down in a moment."

"Very good, Your Royal Highness."

She nodded and headed to her closet-slash-second home and found a pair of black jeans and a white cashmere sweater—not sure who'd put those in her closet, but it felt...royalish? Then she tied a handkerchief around her mind-of-its-own hair. Glanced in the mirror. Hazel-green eyes, no makeup, but she grabbed some lipstick as she went through the bathroom.

Good grief, her mother was rubbing off on her. Still, he was a bona fide prince...

And she was...well, whatever.

She slipped out of her room, down the hallway, through the gallery with the ancestors watching, down the circular staircase to the main level, across the travertine foyer with the tower of poinsettias on a massive round mahogany table, and stopped at the closed doors of the reception room.

Calm. Down. She knew Xavier. Had spent the day with him in Peru, hiking Machu Picchu. He was handsome and sweet, and maybe the tabloids had made everything up.

She'd simply set the record straight. *I have a boyfriend.*

The man standing in the stripe of sunlight casting into the room was not the dusty boy she'd left behind at a cafe in Peru, drinking a bottle of Sanpellegrino.

He wore a blue suit—perfectly cut to enhance his shoulders, his six-foot-plus athletic frame, and his strong legs—dress shoes, and a hint of a tan on his neck under that white shirt. He'd shaven, although she remembered liking the dark spray of whiskers, and cut his curly black hair short, just above his ears.

"Holy smokes, you clean up."

He smiled, and for a second, a flash, she was hiking beside him up a million steps, the sun hot on their shoulders, laughing as he teased her about her useless Incan knowledge. Oh, she'd liked him, probably more than she should.

Now he walked toward her, his hands behind his back. "Eye-eee-anch-ooo."

Oh, she'd forgotten his blue eyes too. "Eye-eee-anch-ooo to you too."

"I remembered." He tapped his head.

"I see that."

"That's all I got, though. *Hello, how are you?* in Quechuan." He'd closed the gap between them and now held out his hand.

He even smelled good. Aftershave. She took it.

He bowed. "Your Royal Highness."

"Oh...Prince Xavier—"

"X. Just X, remember?"

She sighed. "Yes. And you might have mentioned you were a prince before you texted me."

"I thought it was only fair since you didn't mention you were a princess."

Right. There was that. "Sorry."

"I get it. I like to go incognito also." He stepped back. "But you clean up too."

"I was in yoga pants about five minutes ago."

"Would have looked just as amazing on you."

That was sweet. "Thanks. Um, you should know that—"

"Me first." He held up a hand. "I know I made it awkward. I didn't mean to say what I said to the tabloids—I got sort of flustered on Maddy and Hy. I just meant that I had a gift for you." He reached into his pocket and pulled out a small cufflet bracelet. Silver, and inlaid with stones and mother-of-pearl, it shone in the light.

"You found my bracelet."

"No, it's not the original. But I remembered you buying it in the marketplace, and I hated that you lost it, so I swung by the market after you left and got another one." He held it out to her.

She took it, examined the stones. "This is a lot nicer than the one I bought."

He lifted a shoulder.

"That's so thoughtful, but I can't accept it." She held it out.

"You can. You lost yours because you were reaching down to grab my hand and I flicked it off. I felt sick watching it bounce down the mountain."

"Yes, and then you offered to give me your watch. The one your dad gave you for your birthday."

"Indeed, that was...panic. But this is redemption, so you have to take it. Otherwise, I'll be burdened with guilt forever."

She gave him a look. He winked.

Oh boy. "Thank you." She slipped it on.

"I also have this." He looked past her to a steward standing there—she'd barely noticed him when she entered—who then left the room. She glanced at X. He looked at her, waggled his eyebrows. Yes, he was handsome, in a regal sort of way.

Prince, indeed. The man should have *Charming* after his name.

The door reopened, and the steward returned with a spray of lavender roses so large it hid his face. He walked up to her, then bowed and presented her with the array.

"Seriously?"

"Lavender is our state color."

"I don't even..." She held out her arms to collect them. "How many are here?"

"Four dozen, for the four months since I last saw you."

"X—" She smelled them. "Okay, this is so nice. But you need to know, I'm...dating someone."

He drew in a breath, raised an eyebrow, but even in that, didn't lose his smile. "A lucky man. Will I meet him at the ball?"

"No. He's...American."

One eye narrowed. "Not the lad that kidnapped you in Europe—"

"Not kidnapped, and it's complicated, but yes. His name is Creed."

"I will duel him for your hand—"

"X!"

"Kidding! Sheesh. No, that's wonderful, Your Highness. Of course. I'll be glad to stand in his stead at the ball." He bowed slightly.

She looked at the roses. "This is really sweet. And it's Imani."

"I wanted to put you at ease. I know the paparazzi will be there, and I wanted us to have a real conversation before we walked in with the world's eyes on us. Just a couple of hikers, dressed up for a night out, okay?"

She nodded. "No proposals of marriage or declarations of true love."

"There you go, boxing me in—"

"Xavier."

"X, and again, playing with you, love. I've got your back. You're safe in my hands, I promise."

She didn't know why, but the deep knot inside her somehow loosened, the sense that she might even like the look in his eyes when he saw her in the blue gown.

As he stood in for the man she loved.

Yep.

"Thank you."

"Very good. Now, I believe that we have a pending duel of Kings in the Corner that needs settling?"

She laughed. So maybe her mother was right.

Maybe she would have fun.

IF HE WASN'T A CRIMINAL BEFORE, SURELY CREED HAD broken enough laws to be behind bars for the better part of his young-adult life.

"Seriously, Fraser. This isn't going to work. When I said cook up a plan, I didn't mean let's take over a country."

Fraser stood before him in the Queen Charlotte Inn, which was not an inn at all but a shiny high-rise on the shores of Dalholm Harbor. Their suite, on the tenth floor, just happened to adjoin the suite of one Duke of Porto, or rather his father, Duarte Pio, Grand Duke of Portugal.

Which made it easy for Fraser to poach the man's Victorian costume, delivered by a steward while said grand duke was out sightseeing with the other royal guests.

"I'm not Portuguese. I'm Hispanic."

The suite spanned two rooms, with gold brocade draperies and white plush carpet and a crest on the pillows. He'd felt a little royal, just walking in.

That, or like a thief, because he'd also stolen the name in his passport. Christofer Bento. Whoever that was. But it was the only way through customs, according to Coco, and Fraser traveled as his mate, one Fletcher Monroe.

So they were both a couple of criminals. Maybe if they got caught together, they could share a cell. Although he'd let Fraser go first on the executioner's block.

"I get it, bro, but fact is, according to Coco, you are the height and weight of Crispin, Duke of Porto, son of the heir to the

Portuguese throne, and while Crispin isn't here, his father is, and that puts you on the guest list. I can't tie this stupid thing."

Creed pushed away his hands and stepped up to the mirror. "She's going to recognize me."

"Not with that suit, those mutton chops, and the top hat. You look like Pip."

"Philip Pirrip. The orphan of *Great Expectations*. Thanks for that."

"It was a compliment. I, however, look like I belong in *Downton Abbey*."

"You make a tidy footman." He wore a full-on livery—blue velvet jacket, silver vest, ascot, breeches, white socks, black shoes, and was clean-shaven, as opposed to Creed's Wolverine mutton chops.

"Lose the bad British accent. Crispin studied in America, at Yale, so you're American, mate."

"I just want to know, am I in line for the throne?"

"Not a chance." He smoothed out Creed's suit. "Grab your cane. Let's see you walk."

He'd managed to ditch the crutches and had taken off his brace in America, but he still leaned hard on his cane. Now, as he strode across the room, the limp was mostly—well, a little better.

"Just don't ask anyone to dance."

"I just need to see Imani. Get her alone, find out that she's okay."

"And I need a face-to-face with Pippa. Same, and I need to know what Gunner has found out."

"Any word from Sibba or Jonas?" He watched as Fraser popped an earwig into his ear canal, then went over to Creed and handed him one.

Creed put it in while Fraser activated a hidden lapel mic. He held up a finger, then went into the next room and shut the door.

"Not since he and Sibba met with Logan. Speak."

"Good thing you caught that photo. Of the bomb."

"Maybe. I wish I could remember what the porter looked like."

"Me too. I saw him look back at Pippa through Imani's phone. Dark hair, and he had a scar on his neck, but that's all I remember."

Fraser opened the door. "At least you remember the scar."

He pulled down the cuffs of his shirt, then stepped up to the mirror and donned a white wig over his short hair.

"That wig looks ridiculous," Creed said. "Here." He pulled it off. "What you really need is a wig cap."

Fraser looked at him.

"What? Imani is into wigs." He turned the wig inside out. "These are temple tabs. And these are the combs. You use these to attach these to your head."

"Give that to me."

Creed yanked it out of his reach. "You want to feel secure that your wig won't go anywhere?"

"Not even a little. You watch too much YouTube."

"You try breaking your leg and sitting on the sofa for two months. Turn around and sit."

Fraser rolled his eyes, faced the mirror. Creed flipped it over his head, then reached around in back and pulled the tabs in the back, tightening it down. "If you had a wig cap, I could put the comb under it."

"If I had a wig cap, I'd jump off a bridge."

Creed shifted the wig so it sat right on Fraser's head, then flattened the temple tabs into his hair.

"You do know that we can never talk about this again. Ever," Fraser said.

"Get comfortable being uncomfortable."

"No. You don't get to use a SEAL quote on me."

Creed grinned, stepped back. "Where's my carriage?"

"I'm about to make you walk." He got up. "Here's how this is going down. As soon as the grand duke gets back, I lock him in, and we go down with the other royals and get on the transport to the castle. They're taking us in sleighs, in groups. If your name isn't on the list, say that you came in lieu of your father."

"Why not. What's one more lie?"

"You want to see Imani or not?"

"At least we didn't have to drug the guy."

Fraser smiled.

"You didn't."

"Just messin' with you. No. But he doesn't have a costume, so by the time the duke is out of his room and raises a fuss and gets a replacement—if there is one—we'll be at the palace and..."

"Hopefully not arrested."

"Yep."

"I'm trusting you, bro. Don't get me shot." He held out a fist. Fraser bumped it. Then, "You look ridiculous."

"I hate you."

Next door, voices rose. Fraser pressed a finger to his lips, then nodded.

The doors were electric, but Coco had delivered a scramble key that would intercept the key code, and now Fraser slipped out and pressed the key card to the lock on the duke's door. In a moment, the lock turned red, and he pulled it away and nodded down the hall.

And so it began.

His life of crime.

Or rather, continued, because Creed had nearly lost the pitiful snack from the plane when he'd landed in Port Fressa and stood in passport control. How many years did a guy get for identity theft on a passport? Or of a duke?

They got into the elevator.

"You're a duke. Act like it. Ignore me, expect me to wait on you, and act like you belong here."

He nodded at Fraser's words as the doors opened. He moved aside for the two women, one mid-fifties, the other in her twenties, along with an older gentleman.

They all wore the Victorian regalia, the older woman in a

deep-red hoop skirt with layers and a V-neck, the younger in a blue dress with lace ruffles. The man wore a short-waisted tuxedo, not unlike his, black brocade, with a rich tapestry vest and a lacy ascot and ruffles around the wrists. At least the duke had better taste. No lace for him—gold vest, black ascot, and he'd scored a top hat.

And a cane.

He smiled, gave a nod. Was he supposed to bow? No—no, he was the royal here.

This was going to be a fiasco.

The lobby was full of a bygone era, managed by modern-day security. Victorian footmen and a slew of horse-drawn sleighs pulled up at the front, most of them on wheels.

He got in line with Fraser but ignored him, and when he made it to a steward with an iPad, he gave his name.

Twice. The first time sounded a bit like he'd eaten something bitter.

The second was better. Or maybe too loud. "Crispin." Oh brother, he rolled his *r*. But that felt weirdly right. "In the stead of my father, Grand Duke Duarte Pio of Portugal."

"Of Braganza."

He glanced at Fraser, who stood head down, hands clasped, but nodded once.

"If you must."

"Very good, sir." He directed him to a cluster of other guests waiting to board, and in a moment, he was seated next to a Prince Sébastien of Luxembourg and his date, along with Prince Stephen and Princess Corina from Brighton Kingdom.

He sat facing the rear, Fraser on the jump seat with another footman.

Creed had nothing as the others talked about the North Sea Summit, the recent wedding of some crown prince of Jordan or whatever Middle Eastern state. Creed just nodded, smiled, and prayed no one talked to him.

Except they did, and when he introduced himself to Prince

Sébastien, the man frowned, then nodded. "So, your father is still claiming the throne of Portugal."

He swallowed. "Indeed. Heir of King Manuel the Third, from the Constitutional Charter of 1826. He represents the people of Portugal with pride. As do I. Not unlike your father, Grand Duke Henri."

Sébastien raised an eyebrow.

"Is he here?"

"No." Sébastien drew in a breath, put his arm around his date. "You certainly got spunkier since I last saw you."

"Sorry, I don't remember that." He met Sébastien's eyes.

"Yes, well, you were three, so..." He lifted a shoulder.

"A wedding. I remember now."

Sébastien laughed. "My brother Louis, and Tessyy, his wife. That's impressive."

Even Fraser, from where he sat in the back, glanced over his shoulder halfway and nodded.

Hello, he'd only spent all thirteen hours over the ocean watching YouTube and studying the various royals in the Lauchtenland circles, preparing, clearly, for his life of crime.

While Fraser snoozed next to him.

But there went his stomach, having a thought or two about said crimes.

They rode through the city, exiting the newer area into older Dalholm, the streets turning to cobble, the streetlamps here festive with garland and red bows, the light puddling the wintry streets. Shoppes from a bygone era lined Centre Street, names stenciled on the glass fronts, icicle lights dangling across the rooflines.

Grand draft horses pulled the sleighs, two to a sleigh, the driver clucking to them as their hooves hit the ground, bells jingling.

And then on a hill above the town rose Hadsby Castle. A real castle, with towers at the corners of a massive palisade, with parapets at the top, each flying the royal standard. Light was cast on the massive building from the courtyard, turning the place a royal blue, probably for the House of Blue—he didn't have to think hard for that one.

They rode through a grand gate, the massive wooden doors standing open. Soldiers dressed in deep-blue jackets, white pants, and helmets with tiny crosses at the peak held very real-looking weapons as they stared past them into nowhere.

He swallowed, met the thin smile of Prince Stefen, who frankly looked like he belonged with the men at the door, a military bearing around him, and then turned his attention to the castle entrance.

The guests disembarked, then entered a main hallway flanked on the outside by grand torches, lit and flickering into the night.

When Lauchtenland put on a party, they meant it. Holy cannoli.

He got out and followed his fellow royals inside.

A line formed along the gallery, twisting around into another room.

Fraser joined him, standing just behind his shoulder.

Creed glanced at him. Fraser stepped away, walked down the hallway a bit, then stood, staring through windows into an adjoining room.

"It looks like the line winds into the audience room where royals are greeting guests."

He smiled, nodded.

"Imani is with them, standing next to some guy."

Prince Xavier. And he managed to keep his smile, not grind his teeth into dust.

Of course the prince was standing beside her. Because he was a *prince*, thank you.

Not a fake duke in a stolen costume, in the country illegally.

He should leave.

"I'm going to find Pippa."

Fraser turned and headed his direction. Creed couldn't help but reach out, catch him. Smiled, but leaned in.

"And what am I supposed to do? Clearly..."

"Yes." Fraser smiled at someone—probably Prince Stephen standing behind Creed. "Come with me."

Creed turned out of line and simply followed Fraser, as if he might be summoned somewhere important and not in a full-out run.

Fraser rounded the end of the gallery, turned as if he knew where he, too, was going, and strode right down the hall. Opened a door and stepped inside.

Creed followed him. "What. Are you *doing*?"

"Regrouping. Listen, I memorized the layout of this place. This is the library."

"Really? What gave it away—the gazillions of books in floor-to-ceiling shelving? The ladder that runs around the room? Maybe the leather chairs—"

"Stop babbling. You're freaking out."

"I'm not—" He took a breath. "I'm just not used to sneaking around and lying—"

Fraser put a hand over his mouth. "Breathe. You're a duke. Be a duke. In here." He patted his chest. Then he unhanded Creed's mouth. "Listen. There's no difference between you and these royals except money, and maybe lineage. But they all hurt and worry and love and fear and die just like the rest of us."

"They just do it without worrying about where their next meal comes from."

"Yeah, but we don't worry about being shot at, having illicit pictures taken of us while we're at the beach, or having our children kidnapped either, so there's that."

Huh.

"Okay. I'm a duke."

"A hot, rich duke. And you're going to walk into the ballroom and get something to eat. Preferably one of those little hotdogs in a biscuit."

"I highly doubt they're serving pigs in a blanket here."

"Fine. I'd settle for caviar."

"I'll bet."

"In the meantime, I'm going to find Pippa."

"Oh, so we're going right to the arrest, then. Skip the dancing? What about the caviar?"

"She won't turn me in."

Creed narrowed his eyes.

"I trust her."

And what could he do with that? "Okay. Well, I guess I'll just...wait for...what?"

"I don't know, genius. You were the one who said, 'Please, Fraser, get me into Lauchtenland.' You're here, pal. Play ball."

Music sounded through the double doors. Creed pointed at them. "Was that a metaphor?"

"Maybe." He tapped his ear. "Stay frosty."

Creed rolled his eyes.

"After you, Your Dukeness," Fraser said and turned him toward the door.

Here went nothing.

He took a breath, then pulled the door open.

Nearly knocked over a guard.

The man stepped back. "This is off-limits."

He held up his hands. "Sorry. I got lost."

The man cast a look across the room, where the receiving line dumped out onto the dance floor.

"I've already met the princess, mate," Creed said. Then he winked and slapped a hand on his shoulder. "Trust me, I'm here for the food."

There he went, rolling his *r*'s again, but it seemed to work. He walked away and didn't glance back. Very duke of him, if he thought so himself.

The ballroom sported a massive evergreen to one side, bedazzled with gold and silver ornaments, tinsel, and red bows. A chamber orchestra played a waltz, although no one was dancing, and a balcony circled the room, with fresh garland looping the balustrades.

Thick brocade drapes framed the doors to the patio, and as he watched, a steward opened one of the doors, then stepped outside and turned on one of the massive patio heaters, probably hoping to entice a few guests outside to enjoy the star-strewn night.

Not a bad party to crash.

He spotted a server and caught up, lifting a glass of champagne off her tray. "Thank you."

She bowed her head, then kept circulating.

He glanced toward the reception room and spotted Prince Stephen and Princess Corina come through. The line hadn't been much longer past them.

A few people mingled on the dance floor.

"Did you find the food?"

No answer.

He glanced back. No Fraser.

Of course.

Drawing in a breath, he searched the room, now more than half full with guests, all of them in vibrant Victorian wear. He would have liked to see Imani—he'd bet...

He stilled as he spotted Fraser, moving against the far wall. Leaning now against it. Casing the joint.

The guy had *former SEAL* and *current operator* written all over him, even in that ridiculous wig and tight livery.

Fraser stood up. Turned toward the wall. And that's when he spotted the royals coming through the door. First Prince Gus and Princess Daffy, then Imani, her hand on the arm of her prince.

Creed couldn't breathe, and he reached out to brace himself on one of the corner columns.

If he'd ever doubted Imani was regal, fit to be a princess, the thought vanished at the sight of her in the royal blue velvet dress. She practically floated across the floor behind her aunt and uncle, smiling, her hair long and shimmery, pinned back and up into a small tiara and then down her back, nearly to her waist. She wore her dress off the shoulders, a simple diamond choker at her neck, and yep, he was a criminal to the bone, because all he wanted to do was swoop her up and steal her away.

Or maybe he should just run. Because clearly, clearly he was out of his league.

She glided to the dance floor, and the crowd parted as the prince took her in his arms. Then the hosts of the party, the royal family of the House of Blue, led the first dance.

Creed couldn't watch, not the way she smiled up at her stupid prince, so he searched for Fraser.

Of course he found him standing behind Pippa, who was positioned near the door, her gaze on Imani.

Oh... "Fraser, don't make a scene!"

Fraser didn't respond.

Then Creed watched as Fraser leaned up behind her and spoke into her ear.

A hand clamped on his shoulder. "Sir?"

He turned and met the guard he'd walked by earlier. "Can I help you?"

"We just need to talk to you a moment."

We? He looked past the man to another, this one not in regalia, wearing a dark suit, earwig attached, bulky and official and headed his direction.

Aw—he'd just known this wasn't going to work.

An explosion ripped across the patio.

It shattered glass and sent fire screaming up the thick brocade drapes.

The crowd turned to chaos, running past him, toward doors.

He turned, spotted Imani still in the middle of the room, and started running.

AND TO THINK FIVE MINUTES EARLIER PIPPA HAD thought Imani might actually have a perfect night. That HMSD hadn't missed anything.

The royals were somehow safe.

In fact, Gunner had just whispered into her earwig, "We have eyes on Imani. You can take fifteen."

Which, considering she still ached from the bruising tackle on the train and the wound in her shoulder from the shattered glass, Pippa didn't hate. Besides, they'd vetted everyone, with double security starting at the hotel all the way to the castle. No one got in without being checked and rechecked.

And they hadn't employed outside staff this time either, unlike last summer when a caterer had had an assassin on the payroll—one who then tried to kill one of their American guests.

So, yeah, when Pippa saw Imani take to the dance floor, she actually let out a breath. Oh, her princess looked gorgeous, too. And happy, maybe, the way she smiled up at Prince Xavier. Clearly the man had charm, what with his visit to Imani two days ago, the gift of the bracelet, the purple roses—Imani had put them in a massive vase in her room and suddenly stopped complaining about the event.

Had started cooperating, even, sitting for hours this morning as Effie wove in her extensions then did her hair and makeup.

She'd done the House of Blue proud as she'd greeted guests.

She deserved this moment, this dance with a handsome prince, even if it wasn't *her* prince.

No, her prince was back in Minnesota, and Pippa just had to shake that sadness away. She'd make a point to call Fraser later. She hadn't talked to him since after the explosion, a short text to tell him she was okay, and he'd sent her the picture of the bomb.

"Pippa, do you have eyes on the Duke of Porto, eleven o'clock from you, across the ballroom?" Gunner in her ear.

She scanned the crowd and her gaze landed on a man standing near a column, one hand bracing it, watching Imani dance.

Wait—

"We need to talk."

The voice, not in her earwig but at her neck—a soft breath, a familiar tone—made her freeze. She turned.

It took a second. A long, unbelievable second as her gaze took him in—so handsome under his livery costume that only accentuated his shoulders. He'd shaved and wore a silly white wig, but she'd recognize that get-me-in-trouble smile anywhere.

"What are—"

He grabbed her arm and pulled her away from the crowd, into the reception room, now empty. Closed the doors.

She stared at him, mouth wide.

And then he simply advanced on her, two steps, slid his hand around her neck, and kissed her. Bam, just like that, his mouth was on hers, and right then, right there, she forgot.

Forgot who she was, forgot Imani, forgot the ball, forgot the frustration of the last two days, the terror of the train bombing, even the fact that the man she was kissing was clearly breaking too many laws for her to count.

Fraser, *here*. She wrapped her arms around his neck and let him back her against the wall, and kissed him back.

His touch was surprise and safety and power and danger and even a little desperation, and she kissed him back with the same, holding him so tightly that when she left her feet, she didn't even realize it.

Just his arm around her waist, the other braced on the wall as he leaned into her.

She didn't know how long they kissed before he finally leaned back, his beautiful eyes in hers, and took a long breath.

"There," he said softly.

She just blinked at him.

"I just needed to know that you were really okay."

"Not even a little," she whispered. "But I might be mending."

He smiled then, and her heart was lost. Oh, this man—

Only then did she realize that he'd pulled out her earwig.

Oh, he was good. She put her hands on his silly costume and pushed him away. "What. Are you doing. Here?" She cut her voice low. "Did you sneak into Lauchtenland?"

His eyes narrowed. "Define *sneak*. We took a plane. Walked right in."

"You did not."

He winked then. "I had some help from Coco."

Her mouth opened. "Oh, this is...I am...you are..."

"You missed me." Then he leaned down and kissed her again. Maybe not quite so desperately, but sweetly, perfectly, that infuriating tease.

But yes, she'd missed him. Desperately.

He lifted his head again, and his smile faded. "Actually, aside from wanting to make sure you were okay, I did come bearing news about the bomb—"

An explosion rattled the closed doors, and right behind it, screaming.

"What the—" She pushed him away, but he was already heading toward the room. He flung the doors open.

Black smoke billowed against the ceiling, the draperies near one door on fire. Guests pushed past her, running hard, and she dodged them, searching for Imani, shoving her earwig back in.

"Gunner, do your guys have eyes on Imani?"

No answer, but Fraser's hand gripped hers, and he took the lead, shoving through the crowd. Security had grabbed fire extinguishers, fighting the flames, and the orchestra was evacuating. It wouldn't be long before the sprinkler system splashed on.

"The fire is outside!" Fraser yelled.

"Where's Imani—" There. She spotted the princess with Prince Xavier and another man. Both had their arms around her, heading toward the opposite side of the ballroom.

The other man limped.

She jerked Fraser's hand and pointed, and he nodded, and she clamored past people, fighting toward the trio.

They'd nearly reached the door to the library when they caught up.

"Creed!"

The man froze, turned.

Oh, she was going to kill them both.

Creed's eyes widened. "Pippa—"

She ignored him and grabbed Imani. She seemed undone, but Pippa found her eyes. "Go in the library and stay there until I come to get you."

Imani nodded.

She glanced at Prince Xavier, who nodded, then to Creed. Pointed to him. "You."

Creed slid his hand into Imani's, his mouth a thin line. But she recognized a fierceness in his eyes and just nodded.

Okay. Still—

Maybe Prince Xavier saw her hesitate, because, "My security is right behind me."

She glanced over, and indeed, a man stood behind the prince, wearing the same fierce expression. Right. The prince had brought his own team, albeit small, and they'd helped secure the grounds over the past two days. She'd even met a couple of them.

"Okay," she said to the man. "Don't let her out of your sight."

"Never, ma'am."

"She's not going anywhere without me," Creed said as he opened the door and pulled Imani into the library.

Clearly not. But she'd deal with the trespassers later. She turned to Fraser. "Let's find out what's going on."

Fraser still gripped her hand and now wove them through the crowd, toward the fire. Security had tamed the flames of the draperies, but Fraser led her out a side door onto the balcony.

Two men were spraying down a tall outside heater, now charred and smoking, a few flames licking out of the propane tank at the bottom.

More security cordoned off the terrace area, now void of guests.

"Sir, you'll have to leave," said one of the men to Fraser— Pippa recognized him as one of Gunner's team, a newer guy named Oliver.

"He's with me," she said. "He's part of our undercover

security." She opened her jacket and flashed her creds, just in case he'd forgotten.

"Very good, ma'am," he said. "Just stay away from the heaters. We're not sure if they're all rigged or just this one."

"Rigged?" Fraser said.

He glanced over to the fire area, where another man with gloves was bagging pieces of charred metal. "We found pieces of a Raspberry Pi in the debris."

Pippa frowned. "Raspberry Pi?"

"It's a small computer that can be used for all sorts of purposes. Even turned into a cell phone receiver to activate, say, an igniter," Fraser said as they walked over to the man.

"Can I see that?" Pippa said, and he handed her the plastic bag. Inside was a box, half destroyed, about the size of a matchbox, maybe a little larger. The metal was singed and warped, but the remnants of a motherboard remained, also charred.

"There's more of them," said Oliver, calling from another nearby heater. He reached for it, but Fraser took two steps and grabbed his arm.

"Could be booby trapped."

Oliver yanked his arm from Fraser's grip but nodded. Spoke into his walkie. "I think we need you down here, sir."

Pippa looked at him. "Why the walkie?" Funny, her earwig still didn't work.

"Communications went down during the fire."

She narrowed her eyes at him. But, "So, are we under attack?"

"I don't know, ma'am—"

"Pippa. Where's Her Royal Highness?"

Gunner was beelining for her.

"In the library, sir, with Prince Xavier's detail."

Gunner's gaze fell past her then, and he frowned. "Who are you?"

"Security for the Duke of Porto—"

"Oh, for the love—it's Fraser, Gunner. Fraser Marshall."

Gunner didn't blink, didn't move. Then, "Of course it is." He held out his hand. "We'll talk about this later."

Fraser shook it.

That was *it*?

No arrest? No—

"But don't go anywhere, mate. You're not off the radar yet."

Okay then.

Gunner turned then to Oliver. "What do we have?"

"Raspberry Pi sir. On this heater, and I think at least three others." He flashed his light on the device, attached to the propane tank assembly.

Gunner crouched, shined his torch on it also. Then he picked up his walkie. "Bring her down here." He stood up and addressed Oliver. "I need to talk to the staff who placed these heaters."

Oliver stepped aside to relay the message.

"How could this happen? We had only our staff here the last two days," Pippa said.

Gunner shook his head, then walked over to the charred heater. A security officer still held the extinguisher. "Arthur, was this the only one lit?"

"Yes. It was getting chilly, and the room warm, so staff asked us if they could open the doors. I radioed in to ask, but the steward opened them, then lit the heater. It ignited a minute or so after being lit."

"You weren't burned?"

"No, sir. I grabbed the fire extinguisher."

"What happened to the steward?"

"I don't know, sir. He disappeared."

"Find him."

"Yes, sir." Arthur set the canister down and lifted his walkie, moving away.

"You think the Raspberry Pi set it off?" Fraser said.

"I don't know. If so, why didn't the others ignite?"

"This one was the only one lit," said Pippa. "Maybe it ignited on its own."

Gunner looked at her. "Everyone off the terrace, *now.*"

Fraser grabbed her arm, tugged her into the empty ballroom.

"Mr. Ferguson, I need your attention for a moment." This from the head steward of the house, a Mr. Lewis. "What are we going to do with the guests? They are all in the reception rooms and the gallery."

Gunner's jaw tightened, and she was seeing the headlines from six months ago. *Castle Security Baffled by Attack.*

This was bad.

He drew in a breath. "I need another sweep of the ballroom. How long until dinner?"

"The kitchen is nearly ready, sir, but some people are asking to leave."

"Indeed. Okay, then, tell the valets to provide sleighs for the guests who want to vacate. As for the rest, I'll have my team sweep the dining room." He drew in a breath. "The last thing the House of Blue needs is another scandal about security. These state events are vastly important for tourism and influence. If my team deems it safe, let's continue with dinner."

"Very good, sir. I'll inform Their Royal Highnesses." He left, and Pippa cast a look at the library door.

"I should check on Princess Imani," she said.

Gunner glanced at her, nodded, then looked past her. "Good. You're here."

Pippa turned. Stilled, her eyes widening. "Sibba?" The Slovenian EOD expert wore a pair of black pants, a jacket, her long brown hair back in a loose bun, her dark-brown eyes hard, even angry.

"Hey, Pippa," she said, as if it might be a Monday, just another day at work.

"What—"

And that's when she also spotted Jonas. Of course. Because Marshall men didn't go anywhere without the women they loved.

"That's what I needed to tell you," Fraser said. "That bomb in the duffel bag—I showed the picture of it to Sibba. Who recognized it as the same bomb structure as the one that blew up Jonas's weather dirigible in Slovenia. Whoever built that bomb might have also built the one on the train."

She just stared at him. "Wait. I thought the Russian mob— the Petrov Bratva—was behind that adventure in Slovenia."

"Yes."

Gunner shook Sibba's hand. "Thanks for coming. I think we have a terror attack in the works."

"Show me," she said as a knife went through Pippa's chest.

Pippa turned to Fraser. "Catch me up later." Then she headed for the library.

She didn't know why, but she couldn't help but feel that the lines seemed to be pointed straight back to Imani.

Someone was still after her princess.

She reached the door, flung it open. "Your Royal Highness, we need to move."

Except Imani didn't rise to her words, Creed beside her, or even Prince Xavier to tag along.

The room was empty.

"Oh no," she growled. "Not again."

FIVE

I mani didn't know where the bad ideas stopped and the good ideas began.

Or if there were any good ideas.

"No, we can't—Pippa will *murder* me!" Imani stood in the hot kitchen on the far end of the house, the smells churning her already upset stomach. Besides, she couldn't breathe in this stupid dress.

The kitchen staff kept looking at her like she might have the plague or some incurable disease, worry etched into their faces. The head chef looked up with not a little alarm from where he was directing the plating of some one hundred and fifty Cornish game hens when Xavier pushed her into the room.

That was after, of course, their rousing argument in the library, where he told her that his security said they were under a terrorist attack.

What?

She just wanted to rewind to that moment when, just as her world had exploded, the fire ripping into the beautiful ballroom, she heard his voice.

"Imani!"

No, it couldn't be. She'd pushed away from Xavier, who had pulled her close after the initial explosion, and spotted him.

Running, sort of, maybe—okay, she'd call it a skip-hop-grimace-fast limp, leaning hard on his cane—straight for her. Pushing aside costumed Victorian women, tuxedoed men, and liveried stewards all rushing for the exit.

For a second, she just stood there, staring, trying to wrap her mind around—

Creed?

In a short-waisted tuxedo, a vest, long pants, and a top hat?

Heavens, he was hot, even with those silly sideburns. And she would have recognized him anywhere with the ferocity of his gaze, the way he burned his way through the crowd to get to her.

What on *earth*?

Xavier turned and must have spotted him coming, because he grabbed her arm, made to pull her behind him, even put out his hand—

"It's Creed!" she'd shouted and pushed past him.

She threw herself into the arms of her crazy boyfriend—she'd called him that to Xavier, and frankly, the sight of him here only made her double down on that distinction in her mind. Yes, *boyfriend*.

Creed caught her up and crushed her to himself, breathing hard. "Are you okay? Are you okay?" His hand ran over her hair, and he dropped his cane, wrapping the other arm around her. His heart thundered against hers, her arms around his neck.

"What are you doing here?" She leaned back, met his eyes. Those beautiful brown eyes.

Nothing of indecision in them now. Oh my. This was the guy who'd stolen her heart back in Switzerland when he'd promised her he'd keep her safe.

Yeah, Hero Creed was back, and how.

"I'm here because I should have never let you go."

Then he leaned down and kissed her. Something purposeful and honest, but over way too quickly. "Let's get you out of here."

Right. Fire. Screaming. And not least of the people shouting was Xavier. "C'mon!" She looked at him, and if he felt slighted by Creed, he didn't let on. Just wore worry in his blue eyes as he put his hand on her back, looking around for an escape.

"The library," said Creed, and took her hand. He swiped up his cane and leaned hard on it as they fled-slash-limped through the crowd running the opposite direction back to the reception hall.

She didn't know where Pippa might be, and that was just the first time she thought it—*wait for Pippa.*

Creed reached the door, put his hand on the handle—

"Creed!"

Oops. Pippa had found her. And Creed's wide eyes only confirmed it.

Pippa looked completely unraveled, her hair loosened from her tight bun. Fraser stormed up behind her, looking ridiculous in a cockeyed white wig.

No wonder Pippa hadn't shown up immediately when the...*bomb?* detonated.

Maybe not a bomb, but she didn't know what else to think.

"Pippa," Creed started, but Pippa grabbed Imani by her shoulders.

Imani froze, a little shaken by Pippa's intensity. "Go into the library and stay there until I come to get you."

Right. Yes. She managed to nod.

Pippa glanced at Xavier, then turned her gaze to Creed. He met it.

"You."

Creed took her hand, so warm, so solid.

Xavier said something about his security, but all Imani could think was...Creed. Here? In Lauchtenland? *At Hadsby Castle?*

Pippa said something to Xavier, then turned back to Imani. Beside her, however, she heard Creed. *She's not going anywhere without me.*

Apparently not. Hallelujah and fist bump.

Then he pulled her into the library.

The silence in the room muffled the shouting in the hall. Xavier's man locked the door behind them while Xavier headed to the other door. Locked it also.

But Creed turned her, caught her face in his hands. Looked her over, then let her go and stepped back.

"I'm fine."

"You're breathtaking."

Oh.

Silence dropped between them, his chest rising and falling. A swallow. Then, "I don't care."

She blinked at him. "You don't care?"

He took a step toward her. "You're worth every day in the tower."

Then he closed the gap, slid his hand behind her neck, and kissed her.

Not so desperate this time, but something sweet, deliberate and sure, and yes, Creed was back, and she'd follow him anywhere.

She kissed him back, her eyes closed, lost in the fact that he'd sneaked into a country for her. Dressed up like Charles Dickens for her.

Run through a crowd on a broken leg for her.

He smelled good, too, like aftershave and the night air, and maybe tasted like champagne, so that was a surprise. But she liked it, and when he finally let her go, she'd forgotten that—

"You're in such big trouble."

She looked over at the voice. Xavier stood across the room, his arms folded, his expression dark. But the words didn't sound like a threat or a warning but concern. He flicked a glance at his security detail. "Can you get us out of here?"

Wait.

"I'll find a way," said the man.

"X. I don't think that's a good idea."

"Listen. Your boy here is persona non grata in Lauchtenland. If the press finds out he's here—"

"Okay, okay. Let me think." She looked at Creed. "Pippa knows you're here, so it won't be long before Gunner finds out. But my guess is that he'll only detain you. X is right—if the press finds out, they'll barbecue you. Gunner will have no choice but to turn you over to state police, and then...I'm not sure even the queen can pardon you. It might be up to the PM—"

"And Hamish Fickle might be RECO, but he's savvy," Xavier said. "He knows the royals are beloved, even if Imani is an American. Someone threatening her life won't go over well. There will be consequences."

She looked at Creed. "You need to leave."

"Not without you."

She closed her eyes. "Okay. Maybe...we could hide him in my apartment. It's on the second floor, across the gallery, in the west wing."

Xavier considered her. "How do we get there?"

"From here? Out the back door, down the hallway between the formal dining room and private dining room, then take a right and go up the stairs to the sunroom. There's another stairway to the tower, but on the opposite side of the room, the sunroom opens to a private hallway to Gus and Daffy's apartments. There's a gallery there that leads to my wing."

Xavier had raised an eyebrow. "I think I need a GPS."

"It's not that hard—just follow me." She took Creed's hand. Glanced at him. "I'm not going to let you end up in the tower."

He grinned, one side of his mouth twitching up, and it was everything she could do not to curl back into his arms.

Xavier's guard went first, then X, and finally she and Creed. Shouting sounded from the ballroom. Maybe they were still fighting the fire. They crept down the hallway.

"Take a right at the corner," she whispered.

Xavier and his detail, however, stopped, pressing back to the wall.

"What?"

"There's security in the gallery, right by the sunroom stairs," Xavier whispered.

Perfect.

"Can you distract him?"

Xavier looked at her. "What am I, James Bond?"

She grinned. He might not be her boyfriend, but he could still make her laugh. "Fine. Let's hole up in the kitchen."

Which was how they ended up bursting into the kitchen, to the alarm of the head chef and his sous staff, and found refuge near the massive kitchen cooler.

Now, she leaned against the tile wall, her arms folded against the oh-so-hot velvet dress, a sweat breaking out across her brow, her hair sticky against her neck, shaking her head at Xavier's crazy idea. "We can't *leave*. Pippa would murder me. Like really, I'd be dead."

"Tell her, Griff."

His bodyguard—big guy, dark hair, chiseled jaw, wore a few scars like he wasn't unused to fighting—leaned in and said, "They're saying it might be a terrorist attack. They called in a bomb expert."

She looked at Xavier. "Who's saying?"

"My people are hooked into the comms, of course. So I would guess it's your people. What's his name—Ferguson?"

She blew out a breath. "I need to talk to Pippa."

"We'll call her as soon as we get in the car, I promise. Besides, you're with me." He smiled.

Creed's mouth tightened, but probably Xavier was right. He had his own security, and frankly, if Pippa could choose, she'd probably pick X and his team.

"Fine. Where's your car?"

He turned to Griff, and the man nodded and pushed through the kitchen, out the back entrance.

"Griff will bring it 'round."

Oh man. Imani looked at Creed. He met her gaze. "It's probably for the best."

"I cannot believe I'm ditching her, again. I just..." She pressed her hands to her face. "I am a terrible person."

"Oh please. You're not a terrible person. And I think you *are* in danger. Fraser had a picture of the bomb that went off in the train—not sure where he got it, but he showed it to Sibba, and she recognized it as something the Russian mob uses."

Next to her, Xavier was frowning, shaking his head.

"Fraser thinks that there is something more going on, bigger than just something with RECO supporters who want to get rid of the monarchy. He thinks it might be a threat against Lauchtenland."

"Oh, don't be absurd. The country has been in turmoil since you absconded with our princess. This is on you, chap." Xavier kept his voice low, but his eyes blazed.

Creed drew in a breath. Nodded.

"Well, then it's up to me to make sure that nothing happens to their princess." He locked eyes with Xavier, and for a moment, she felt like she should step between them.

Then Xavier nodded. "Very good. Let's make it so." Then he strode through the kitchen, stopping to talk to the head chef. "Thank you, sir. We are sorry to barge in."

Creed glanced at Imani, an eyebrow up, then followed him, tugging her along. He, too, stopped at the head chef. "Sorry we can't stay for dinner. Smells awesome."

What was going on?

She gave the chef a wan smile, then followed them outside. Griff had pulled up a black Range Rover, and Xavier stood by the open passenger door, like a valet.

Creed stopped by the door, and she gathered up her crazy dress, the cold air raising gooseflesh. Creed helped her up on the running boards, then inside, tucking her dress in, and then shut her door.

Walked around to the other side and got in behind the driver.

Xavier took the front.

Griff locked the doors, and she pulled on her seatbelt, feeling sick.

"Where are we going?"

"I have a cabin in the Haskells. We'll go there for the time being."

She looked out the window, the starry sky partially blotted by the smoke still lifting from the back terrace.

Bad, bad, Imani.

But as they pulled away around the side entrance of the castle, then out onto the wintery road that bypassed Dalholm, Creed took her hand.

And just like before, she held on and escaped into the night.

"I HAVE HALF THE ROYALS FROM AROUND THE GLOBE IN my dining room—I do not have time to figure out what is going on. I just need to know the guests are safe." Gunner Ferguson bore the look and tone of Fraser's good friend Hamilton Jones, with the addition of a British accent, and Fraser simply stayed out of his way.

Regardless of the thousands of questions rattling through his brain.

At least Pippa had stopped freaking out, in her scary, non-freaking-out way. He didn't know what she would have done if Imani hadn't called from Prince Xavier's bulletproof Range Rover on their way to the prince's secret Batcave in the mountains. She'd let slip, too—probably in case they were on speaker phone, which they were—that Prince Xavier had also brought along the Duke of Porto.

Creed, you dog. He'd known the guy would find Imani.

"How'd the duke get here?" one of the security guys said quietly. "I thought he was still at the hotel."

SUSAN MAY WARREN

Whoops.

But Gunner didn't seem to notice, his gaze on the dozen or so monitors, each one displaying four angles of various rooms. He stood, arms akimbo, legs planted, scanning each one, barking into his comms, which were up and running on a different channel.

Fraser didn't want to suggest that the comms glitch might have been part one of the terrorist attack. Probably Gunner already knew that.

Just like Fraser knew that this wasn't over. And if he were in charge, every single Bob Cratchit and Ebeneezer Scrooge would be sent packing, back to the safety of the Queen Charlotte Inn.

Or maybe even out of Lauchtenland.

"Fine. Okay, tell the staff to open the doors and let in the guests. Let me talk to Mr. Lewis."

He looked at Fraser, pointing as he headed into his office. "Don't go anywhere."

Fraser held up his hands.

Gunner closed the door, pacing his office as he spoke, gesturing.

The security room was located in the southwest tower of the castle, with a good view of the courtyard. Fraser had watched earlier as not a few sleighs carried terrorized guests away from the castle. About half of the guests had stayed, however, so maybe the night wasn't a bust. More pigs in a blanket for the staff, maybe.

"What are you grinning about?" Pippa came up to him, her arms folded, and stood beside him.

"Nothing. I'm hungry."

"You're always hungry." She glanced at him. "Too bad we can't go into the kitchen and grab a sandwich."

"Why not? They've got a kitchen here, right?"

She gave him a look. Then sighed and closed her eyes. Oh, with everything inside him he wanted to reach out and pull her against him, tell her that everything was going to be fine. But not with her fellow officers watching.

And besides, they were a long way from fine.

"The EOD expert has finished with the last device." This from one of the techs, watching the patio through the screen.

Fraser had turned away, unable to watch—he'd left that to Jonas, whose gaze was glued on Sibba disarming the Raspberry Pi devices, cutting off their power after checking for trip wires.

He'd put up a little fight when she'd asked him to stay in a secure area. "I can't focus if I know you could get hurt."

Fraser got that. He'd had nothing on his mind but Pippa and her injuries the entire flight over, and frankly, had Coco not suggested going to the ball in disguise, he might have attempted to just sneak in, track down Pippa.

Although, then he might have ended up facedown on the wooden floor, mistaken for a terrorist. As it was, he itched everywhere and probably should have gotten the livery laundered prior to renting it in Minneapolis.

He had, however, taken off the wig. He ran a hand through his hair. Good thing he wasn't wearing a wig cap.

"Okay, that's sorted." Gunner exited the office. "Listen, I want every eye on that monitor. Anything twitches wrong, you send it down to the lads in the hall." He looked wrung out too, fatigue in the lines around his eyes. Fraser put him in his late thirties, early forties, maybe—again, a British version of Ham.

Jonas stepped away from the monitor just as Sibba knocked, then entered the room. "The Raspberry Pi are secured, disabled, and the outside heaters also secured." She had stripped off the helmet, now carried it under her arm. "I'm not sure who last wore this, but I need a shower, and probably this entire kit needs to be burned."

A beat, and then Gunner sighed. Shook his head, glanced over at Fraser, then Pippa. "What trouble did you bring me?"

"Sir—"

He held up his hand. "Just being cheeky, Pip. All good." He folded his arms. "Brief me."

Fraser looked at Jonas, then back to Gunner. "Do you have a whiteboard?"

Gunner raised an eyebrow. Then he motioned back to his office.

Fraser followed him, along with Sibba, Jonas, and Pippa. The office wasn't huge, but it had curved walls and views of the mountains to the north, the jagged outline just barely visible against a star-strewn sky.

"No whiteboard, but I'm pretty sharp. I'll try and keep up."

Fraser wasn't sure if he was kidding or not, and it didn't help that he felt a fool in his costume. But the whole thing seemed like a Tom Clancy plot, and he really didn't know how it all fit together, so maybe it would all come out crazy anyway.

"Let's start in Geneva, with Imani seeing the murder of nuclear physicist Gerwig Buchen," Fraser said.

"I'd prefer to start with the bomb that nearly killed my princess two days ago." Gunner leaned against the front edge of his desk, holding on to the lip with each hand.

"Yes, sir. Then we need to start in Slovenia, with the bomb that took down my brother's weather dirigibles."

"His what?" He looked at Jonas.

Jonas and Sibba had taken the only other seats, leather chairs that sat on a Turkish carpet. It sat on a red bricked floor, on which also sat Gunner's large desk, which hosted three computer screens. Behind him, two flatscreens showed live shots of the outside of the castle—one of the courtyards, the other behind the castle, looking out to the vast North Sea, now almost black despite the stars.

A picture of Gunner and a team of bravados sat on his credenza behind the desk. And a Lauchtenland flag hung on the rounded wall.

It felt suddenly, creepily, like the tower cell Creed dreaded.

"Weather balloons," Jonas said. "I was tracking storms across Slovenia when one of them went down in the northern mountainous area. We tracked it down and discovered it had been taken, rigged with a bomb, and then detonated to deploy nuclear waste into the atmosphere."

He had Gunner's attention.

Yeah, Fraser had had that same reaction when he'd first heard Jonas's story after his brother had returned from Slovenia, wounded and broken-hearted. Now, Jonas slid his hand into Sibba's, his wounds healed. "We tracked down the material—with the help of my brother's SEAL team—"

Gunner looked at Fraser, who shook his head. "Different brother. Ned."

An eyebrow went up, but he turned his gaze again to Jonas.

"And discovered that the Russian mob—the Petrov Bratva, to be exact—had stolen the waste from the Swiss Federal Institute of Technology in Lausanne."

"Which happens to have a sister relationship with the University of Haxton," Pippa said.

Gunner frowned.

"Which brings us back to Imani and the man she saw murdered in Geneva," said Fraser. "One Gerwig Buchen, who ran the Lausanne research reactor."

"I'm trying here, guys," Gunner said. "What does this have to do with a bomb on my train in Lauchtenland?"

"Right. So, the guy who killed Buchen was—"

"Konrad Vogel, the son of Bernd Vogel," Pippa said. She'd gone to lean against the windowsill.

"What?"

"Yes, the man who killed my father—"

"Who tried to assassinate the king consort," Gunner said.

"Yes. He's with the RECO party."

"I know." He drew in a breath.

"As was your brother," Fraser said quietly.

"Yes." Gunnar said. "Poisoned in his cell. We don't know who did it." Fraser met Pippa's eyes. "Maybe we do. Poison was used to kill a football official on my sister Iris's team."

"Someone tried to kill your *sister*?"

"Twice, actually," Jonas said. "The first time was a man named Werner Vogel. Brother to Konrad. The second was an attempt by the Russian Bratva to poison her through her water bottle at a football game."

"How do you know—"

"The woman Ned caught was a Russian actor—a woman who was being coerced by the Petrovs. Her name was Vikka, and Ned only caught her because she was in the same labor camp as my sister-in-law."

Gunner narrowed his eyes.

"Long story. Ned had to go to Siberia to find her—"

"And had to steal the nuclear material back from his own SEAL team after they liberated it from the Petrovs in Slovenia," Pippa said.

"Maybe I do need a whiteboard."

"Actually, my sister Iris had three attempts on her life—the first was in Greece, when someone tried to blow up the boat she was on. There was a hit taken out on her, and it traced back to a rogue CIA agent named Alan Martin," Fraser said quietly.

Gunner looked up. "I know him. He was involved in some plot to kill your president last summer."

The room turned quiet.

"I don't know anything about that," Fraser said.

"Wait—are you...are you related to RJ Marshall?"

"She's our cousin," Jonas said. "Why?"

"We need a travel ban on anyone named Marshall. Okay, so again, how does this connect with *a bomb on my train*?"

Pippa held up her hand. "The reason Alan Martin wanted her dead is because she had a key to a locker that held incriminating evidence against him."

Silence from Gunner.

"Okay, so the key was for a locker in a German train station, and inside was the map and the itinerary that I sent you a couple weeks ago."

"The map of Lauchtenland's Titus Stadium, and the private itinerary of Their Royal Highnesses Prince John and Princess Gemma."

"That one," Pippa said.

"How'd it get there? And how did she have the key?"

"That's a long story. But we think that whoever was supposed to pick it up was killed before he could retrieve it."

"He?"

"We were thinking maybe Konrad Vogel?" Fraser said.

Gunner nodded.

"When did Iris drop it off?" Sibba suddenly asked. She had leaned forward, her hands on her forehead, as if it might be overheating.

He sort of felt like doing the same.

"I think it was the weekend of Creed's international meet," Fraser said. "She was at the meet, and then Creed met Imani, and then we went to her house in Italy to find him—thinking he'd gone there—and...yes, she told me she was in Germany. And then, a week or so later, she met Martin and told him she was out."

Gunner opened his mouth, then closed it and shook his head.

"And then she saw Hudson on the bridge, and he fought with someone, right?" Sibba leaned up. "I remember her telling us about it over Thanksgiving." She looked at Pippa. "Right? You were there. We were upstairs, talking about the guys—"

"Yep," Pippa said, and didn't look at Fraser.

Interesting.

"She said that she saw Hudson fight someone and they...they went over the bridge."

"Who's Hudson? Another relative?" Gunner asked.

"Not yet." Fraser smirked.

"Who did he fight?"

"She didn't know."

Fraser leaned up from where he'd found a place against the wall. "I think that's worth finding out."

Gunner nodded. "I'll do some checking. In the meantime, one final time—what does this have to do with a bomb on my train? Or someone trying to kill Imani? I thought this all was about Prince John and an assassin at the upcoming football game. We spent, well, a lot of money reinforcing their booth, making it bulletproof, and frankly, the press is asking questions."

"I still think they were—are, maybe—in danger. Especially with Fredrik's murderer at large," Pippa said.

"Perfect."

"All we know, sir, is that the bomb on the train bears the same creativity as the bomb in the dirigibles. And that points to the Petrov Bratva."

"What about the nuclear waste?" Jonas looked at Fraser. "One of the canisters went missing."

"I think they're still looking for it," Fraser said quietly.

"Okay, so what we have is a lot of dodgy speculation and no real facts," Gunner said. "Most of all, what we're missing is motive. If we knew that, we might be able to piece this all together. But right now, it just sounds like you Marshalls have an uncanny ability to run into trouble. And now you've brought it here."

"Sir—" Fraser started.

Gunner held up a hand. "I know that sounds like blame, but I do see how you've tried to be on the right side here. Still, I can't let you run loose in my country. I really feel like you need to be on the next plane home."

"Sir!" Pippa stood. "I...I'm sorry, but if there's another bomb, we don't have the resources to disarm it—"

"We have an EOD expert on staff."

"From the Vietnam era. Sir!"

"Pippa—"

"No. Listen—what you're missing is that Princess Imani is still in danger. And we don't know why. And there are a hundred and fifty royals sitting in our dining room, and a fleet of tourists heading into our country to watch the charity football game in a week, and we need help!"

Gunner looked at her, and Fraser raised an eyebrow, looked at Jonas. Made a little bomb gesture with his hands. Yikes.

"Fine. They can stay. We'll book rooms for them at the Royal Dalholm."

"I have a place at the Queen Charlotte Inn," Fraser said.

Behind Gunner's glare, Pippa ran her fingers across her mouth.

"The Royal Dalholm has a private suite. I need you all in one place."

"Thank you, sir," Pippa said, and found her feet. "Now if you'll excuse me, I have a princess to go track down. Again."

Fraser glanced at Gunner, then stepped aside as she pushed past him, out of the room.

He followed her, however, into the hallway. "Not without me, I hope."

She gave him a long look, then finally smiled. "Don't get in my way."

"Or what?"

"I'll have to tase you."

"I would expect nothing less." He took her proffered hand and followed her down the hall.

AT LEAST HE WOULDN'T BE ARRESTED FOR A SECOND count of absconding with a princess, so maybe he could start taking full breaths again.

"Pippa said she and Fraser are on their way up. And so far, you're under the radar." Imani sat next to Creed in the Range Rover, leaning against him as heat poured out of the vents. He'd put his arm around her, woven his fingers into her other hand on his lap.

The driver—Griff—had to slow as they drove farther into the mountains, flurries starting just north of Dalholm and deepening, turning furious after they'd crossed the Highcrest Mountains pass.

They descended into an angry and lethal blizzard.

"The entire island is about three hours top to bottom on a sunny day," said Prince Xavier from the passenger front. "But winding through the mountains in a storm can take hours. I called ahead—the staff is clearing our drive. We'll be there in a jiff."

Hopefully before they ended up in a ditch or buried in an avalanche.

Imani had been cut off from her call by the interference of the mountain—he'd been hoping to get the lowdown on what had happened at the ball.

But as long as the queen's protective detail wasn't sending in the airships and armed military to hunt him down, and as long as Imani was safe, here, tucked against him, he could wait for Fraser's report.

Most of all, he wanted out of this silly costume, despite the warmth of the heavy jacket.

The headlights cut a swath through the night and the snow buffeting the windshield like they might be entering a Star Wars hyperspace. Around them, the forest cordoned the highway, now thick with snow, the evergreen heavy with white.

"From here, you can usually see the Haskell Ski Resort." The prince turned, his elbow over the seat. "Maybe we can take a run out to the slopes tomorrow."

Creed raised an eyebrow. The man had seen his cane, right? And frankly, what had seemed a run in his head had turned into a painful, wretched hobble. Pain burned up his leg, and really, he needed ice, maybe even a couple pain pills.

So, no skiing for him.

"Pippa will probably want me to go back to Hadsby," Imani said.

"We'll see," the prince said. He glanced at Creed. "We've got our own suite in the Haskell Ski Resort chalet. It's got a fireplace and plenty of hot cocoa." He smiled.

Creed managed something polite.

The prince turned back around, and Creed looked out the window. The guy probably didn't mean to be a jerk. After all, he hadn't even hiccupped at bringing Creed along on their great escape. He probably shouldn't assume Xavier was a villain.

Still, he'd seen the way the man looked at Imani on the dance floor.

Except, probably every man in the room had looked at her that way. Mesmerized. Taken by her beauty. So probably, Creed couldn't blame him for that either.

Griff slowed as they came to a side road, an overhead highway light flicked on, and he turned off and waited as a massive gate, held by two stone pillars, opened. They advanced through a recently plowed drive where shaggy pine trees lined the road, the drifts neat and groomed. Every ten feet or so, rustic timbers with lanterns lit up the night, illuminating their path further until ahead, the house—no, the lodge, maybe even the *castle*—came into view.

This was Xavier's *cabin*?

The place was a five-star hotel with a massive five-story A-frame central structure, lights beckoning from the floor-to-ceiling windows. A twenty-foot Christmas tree on the front deck glistened with lights, and a guard—or a footman—stood near the wide stone front steps that led to the timber-framed deck, all covered with a portico entry that jutted out over the drive.

Two three-story wings extended from the main lodge, with a dozen stone fireplaces jutting from the roofline.

They pulled up under the protection of the portico, and the sentry-slash-footman came down the steps and opened the prince's door. He stepped out, and Creed reached for his door while Imani's was opened.

He came around just as the prince was helping her out.

And he needed the help of the railing and his cane getting up the steps.

But Imani took his arm when they reached the top. "You okay?"

"Mm-hmm," he said, not quite sure how he felt, actually.

And he thought the Marshall family home was a palace.

They walked through the front entrance, and the prince shrugged off his jacket, then turned to his steward. "We'll also need clothing for Princess Imani and her friend."

The steward, a man in his mid-forties, maybe, bowed his head, glanced at Creed, maybe for a once-over for size, then smiled. "Very good, sir."

Another steward took Creed's jacket.

"Wow," Imani said as she followed the prince into the great room.

Indeed, to quote the English. A chandelier the size of a dining room table, made from birch branches and twined with golden lights, hung from the vaulted ceiling. A fire flickered in a stone hearth that could fit two sofas, the stone chimney rising all five stories. An enormous leather sectional that faced it was draped in sheepskin and wool throws. A coffee table that could have been cut from a redwood gleamed in the center of the sectional U.

On either side of the sofa, two more smaller chandeliers, these with three tiers of lights, hung over round tables with leather chairs.

Stairs on either side of the room led up to what he assumed were the bedrooms.

A light streamed out of a side room, and from it, a butler appeared. Bowed.

"Ehlers, this is Her Royal Highness Princess Imani from the House of Blue. And her friend, Creed..." Prince Xavier looked over at him and Creed had the crazy urge to blurt out *Crispin, Duke of Porto*.

Instead, "Marshall. I'm a Marshall."

For the first time, that felt almost insignificant. As if he hadn't been trying most of the last decade to fit into those words.

Ehlers bowed to Imani, then nodded his head to Creed before turning back to Xavier.

"Would you like a late supper, Your Royal Highness?"

"Actually, I think the princess would like to change into something more comfortable. And then, what do you think, Imani?"

"I'm starved." She looked at Creed.

"I could eat."

"I'll inform the kitchen," Ehlers said.

He'd *inform the kitchen*. Oh, just once Creed would like to *inform the kitchen*. His mother would probably throw a pot at him.

"Sir, can I show you to your room?"

It took a second, during which Xavier looked at him and raised an eyebrow, for Creed to realize that he was being addressed.

He was the *sir*.

"Yes, thanks," he said, and reached out for Imani's hand.

"Oh no, she's in the royal wing," Xavier said, and pointed up the other stairs.

Imani's eyes narrowed just a little, but Creed nodded, smiled. "Absolutely."

"I'll meet you back here in a bit," she said, then rose up and kissed his cheek.

Okay then.

He followed the steward up the stairs, albeit a little slowly, and then down the hallway to the first door on the left. "Clothing is in the wardrobe and bureau, sir."

"Just, Creed is fine."

"Very good, sir." He nodded once and left.

Ho-kay. Creed shut the door.

Outside the leaded glass, snow buffeted the small balcony, but inside the room was cozy, with a fire in a small hearth, an overstuffed white sofa facing the flames, backing up to a massive king-size bed with four posters and a decadent red brocade bedspread and overstuffed pillows.

A ten-foot wardrobe hugged the wall near the door, and a

bureau to match filled up the wall next to the bed. But it was the bathroom—er, ensuite—that drew him.

He toed off his shoes, not wanting to stain the plush white carpet of the bedroom, then stepped onto the flagstone floor of the bathroom, his feet warm on the stone. A piece of black granite, heavily veined with white and containing two sinks, spanned one side of the room, and a steam shower with an attached sauna spanned the other.

On the end, a small alcove hosted the massive claw-footed tub, with windows that looked out onto the darkened mountainscape.

He'd like to see what the *royal* suite looked like. Hello.

Closing the door, he stripped off the costume and cranked up the shower.

He didn't know how long he stayed under the heat, his arms braced against the travertine tile, but somehow, the knot between his shoulders released.

See, everything was going to be just fine. So what he was a fugitive? He had Imani, and he'd be happy to play along with Prince Xavier as long as the man kept his hands to himself.

And kept Imani safe.

Creed found clothes, just as the steward said, in the bureau— a pair of jeans, just faded enough but clearly freshly laundered, and a flannel shirt that felt right out of L.L.Bean and probably cost a fortune but that fit him perfectly, and even a pair of wool socks and leather slippers.

He slipped them on, decided he should probably call himself Crispin, and headed downstairs.

Empty. He stood in front of the fire a moment, staring up at a giant elk head that overlooked him from above, then moved around the room. A coat of arms hung on the wall near one of the tables, and beside that, a listing of the family tree.

Huh.

"Yes, that's fourteen generations, starting with young Horace Neville from Westmorland, son of Charles, who participated in the Northern Rebellion in England. He sent his son out of the country to secure a lineage in case things took a dive." Xavier looked askance at Creed. "Which they did, being patriots of Mary, Queen of Scots. Young Horace escaped to Lauchtenland, who wasn't involved, but the king needed funds for a standing army in the case of trouble, so he leased the tiny principality of Keswick to Horace with the agreement that it would be an independent principality for ninety-nine years. Since then, the lease has been renewed seven times, most recently in 1983. Unfortunately, Queen Catherine decided that the new lease would be for only forty years, but we are confident of renewal. After all, we are distant cousins to the House of Blue."

"Oh?"

"Yes. To ensure homage to Lauchtenland, the king at the time secured the bond by marrying his second daughter, Constance, to Horace." He then pointed to an oil of a couple, clearly set in the Renaissance.

"I didn't know the House of Blue was over four hundred years old."

"Older. Founded in the 1200s by a man named Thomas Wenton Blue, who came from Denmark with his family after a famine. He was hoping to land in England and found Lauchtenland instead."

Xavier had changed clothes also, now wore a pair of dress pants and a thick wool sweater, his dark hair wet and curly around his ears—so he must have showered too.

He walked over to a map hanging near the open doors of the dining room. "This is Keswick. About 180 kilometers long, and 90 kilometers wide. It takes an hour to drive from coast to coast, two hours north to south, and six hours around the entire country. We have one capital city, on the western shore. And here"—he pointed to a high point in the center—"is our state mine. My super great-great-grandfather Winslow found gold there, and since then, copper, zinc, silver, manganese, and salt. But mostly gold." He turned. "Because we're protected by two larger islands, we also have some beautiful beaches, both sand and

cliffs, and tourism is one of our main products. You should visit."
Xavier clamped him on the shoulder, his smile warm.

Huh.

"So, I need to ask," he said as he walked into the dining room.
A carafe with mugs sat on the sideboard. "How'd you hurt your
leg?"

"I was shot."

Xavier had picked up the carafe, started loosening the top,
and now turned to him. "Blimey."

"You shouldn't believe everything they're saying about me. I
saved Imani's life."

"Did you now?" Xavier picked up a mug and poured out hot
cocoa. "I'm impressed." He handed the mug to Creed.

Creed took it, his gaze on Xavier.

"She was single when we met in Peru. But she did tell me that
you were dating when we met a few days ago."

Creed didn't know why that felt like a punch in the sternum.
They'd corresponded for three months and she'd never told the
prince about him? Although, maybe he couldn't count sitting on
the sofa with his leg in a cast and playing video games dating.

"I can see why she fancies you. She's American, you're
American. And fit, I can see that." He had poured himself a mug
too. "And Prince John did break the writ—or rather, had it
changed for his purposes and married an American, so of course,
she doesn't consider our traditions a barrier." He took a sip. "The
reality of becoming royal hasn't been easy on her."

Interesting. "No, it hasn't."

"But she's here now and making a go of it, and I applaud her
for that. And she was lovely tonight, wasn't she?"

Creed took a breath. "Yes."

"It's too bad our dance got cut short—Imani, darling, you
look like you've recovered."

Creed turned, and she came into the dining room, her hair
still up, still wearing her makeup, but in a pair of stretchy yoga
pants and an oversized white fuzzy sweatshirt. "My sister Thea's

favorite. You look beautiful as ever." He walked over and, before Creed could move, bent and kissed her cheek.

"Hot chocolate, love?"

Then he winked at Creed and headed back to the side table.

And Creed suddenly had the terrible sense that he'd escaped the battlefield skirmish for the frontline war.

But as Imani came into the room, as she looked over and smiled at him, those beautiful hazel-brown eyes alight, yeah, he was ready.

Challenge accepted.

SIX

"I should have grabbed a hotdog."

Pippa glanced over to where Fraser sat in the passenger seat of the Ranger Rover she'd borrowed from the security garage. He'd changed clothes into a pair of jeans and a sweater after grabbing his pack—and Creed's—from the Queen Charlotte Inn, and if possible, looked even more handsome in the wan light, his hair a wreck, his blue eyes on the road, glancing at her sometimes.

Fraser. Here. In Lauchtenland. She just didn't know what to do with that.

Or the sense that something had shifted between them. It was one thing to be on security detail—if that's what they were calling it—at the Marshall family winery.

Quite another to have the former SEAL sitting in her Range Rover, his gear in the back end, getting involved in her real job.

The one where she was supposed to keep Princess Imani from danger.

Ho-boy.

But, "A hotdog?" she said now, because if she thought about the princess and the fact that she'd betrayed her, again, she might lose her focus on the road.

Which was becoming slicker with every minute the blizzard thickened.

"You know—one of those pigs in a blanket they serve as appetizers?"

The cold nipped at the windows, despite the heaters at full blast. "I don't think House of Blue is going to serve a pig as an appetizer."

"It's a hotdog in a biscuit."

"Disgusting."

"They're so good and I'm starved."

"Sorry, we're in the mountains now. You'll have to wait until we find Imani and Creed."

Which, in this weather and at this speed, might be early next week. They should have gotten started earlier, right after Imani called, not sat around for Fraser to unveil his conspiracy theory about Russia trying to bomb Lauchtenland. Absurd.

And she'd even *joined into his craziness.* She kept hearing her own voice, raised and not a little desperate in Gunner's office—*We need help!*

Probably she needed to eat, also, because maybe she'd been a little out of her head to yell at her boss, decorated officer, Sir Gunner Ferguson. Of Her Majesty's Security Detail. He'd guarded Prince John, for Pete's sake. Just about the *last* person who needed help.

And she'd shouted at him. Practically told him he was in over his head.

She wanted to cringe.

More, Gunner was *right.* The Marshall family seemed attracted to trouble like moths to a flame, and people around them tended to get burned.

Like Imani.

Or, if she wasn't careful, herself. And Pippa hated that she even thought that too. Because Fraser had risked everything to... what? "You really think the Russians are plotting an attack against Lauchtenland?"

He glanced at her, and his gaze burned her neck in her peripheral vision, but really—

"I don't know. Ten years as a SEAL told me to pay attention. Last time I didn't heed the clues, I found myself taken hostage and shot, so, yeah. Maybe."

She swallowed.

"But if I'm being honest, I came because I was worried about you."

She drew in a breath, glanced at him.

He wore an upturned eyebrow.

"What?"

"I know you're blaming the near bombing on yourself. And now Imani's gone, and...well, you haven't said two words since we left the Queen Charlotte Inn, and I know you're not thinking about food."

"I'm fine."

"You're white-knuckling the steering wheel."

"It's a blizzard outside! Do you want to go off the road?"

"No, I want you to take a breath and realize that this isn't your fault."

Her headlights carved out a wan path against the bulleting snow. She'd plugged in the GPS to Xavier's location, and it put them at least forty kilometers away, the snow having turned disastrous after they crossed the pass.

She downshifted into second as they descended the winding roads. The last thing they needed was to land in the ditch.

Silence pressed into the darkness as she tried to school her tone. No need to fight with him—he'd been trying to help—but, "If I hadn't kissed you, I'd have been in the room when the explosion happened. Imani would be with *me*."

He made a little sound, deep in his chest, and she could nearly see his blue eyes spark with disagreement. But his voice came out soft. "Maybe. Maybe not. You saw the rush of people. My guess is that you would have had a hard time getting to her. But, babe, Creed got to her. Creed will keep her safe."

CREED

"Creed is a fugitive."

"Creed is a Marshall."

She drew in a breath. "You're not the freakin' Avengers, Fraser. You get hurt. And you're not invincible."

"Well, that hurt."

She rolled her eyes.

"Listen. I might not be an Avenger, but I do know that you can't keep staring into the past rewriting it. You'll get stuck there. You have to shrug it off, thank God for the assist, and do the next smart thing."

"What is that, SEAL talk?"

"No. That's Garrett Marshall talk. SEAL talk goes like this: No plan survives first contact with the enemy. The plan is only on paper. But if you have the right people and the right training, you trust them to react inside the mission parameters. They don't panic. They stay the course. But you have to trust your team."

His hand slid onto her arm. "Pip. C'mon—that's what the last three months were about. Us becoming a team, right?"

She drew in a breath, for a moment her memories taking her back to so many nights hanging out in Marshall HQ, as he'd called it, watching monitors.

Watching each other. Oh, wow, he was right. She *trusted* him. But, "This isn't the Marshall family winery. This is...Lauchtenland."

"And here, you have eyes on you."

She hadn't exactly put a fine point on why her chest had thickened and stayed tight since the little chat in Gunner's office, but, "Yes. I'm supposed to protect Imani. But that's not all. This is the second time the team's been outwitted by an outside saboteur. This summer, we had an assassin try and take out one of our guests." She looked at him. "Your cousin's husband, York, actually."

She drew in a breath. Stilled. "Actually, they were aiming for your director of the CDC. York just happened to be in the way. I hadn't thought about that, but what if that's how they learned about our weaknesses, learned how to breach us?"

"Who is *they*?"

"The assassin was hired by Alan Martin. So him, and whomever he's working for."

"Like the Petrov Bratva." A beat. "Maybe I should call Logan."

Logan, the director of the Caleb Group, who'd helped them escape Europe with Imani and Creed the first time around. He had connections that went beyond borders. And, possibly, intel. "Maybe."

He pulled out his cell. "No signal."

They'd slowed to a crawl, no other cars on the road.

"My whole life people blamed my father for the attack on the king consort." She wasn't sure how or why that came out, but suddenly, in the darkness, with Fraser's words, bits of the past began to surface.

"The attack by Vogel, the RECOist—the one that killed him."

"Yes. He was exonerated, but public opinion crucified him. And yes, the queen made that right, but I still feel the sting sometimes." She touched his hand on her arm. "Princess Imani can *not* be hurt on my watch."

"I know." He squeezed her arm. "And Creed can't be arrested on mine. He's spent enough of his life believing he's a criminal— or comes from a criminal gene pool. He can't go to prison and prove himself right."

"It's hard to believe something else when you've told yourself one thing your entire life." She wasn't sure where the words came from.

"Like it's your job to redeem the family name?" Fraser said quietly.

She lifted a shoulder.

"Or maybe it's that your only purpose is to die in the line of duty," he said softly.

Her eyes widened. "I don't—"

"Don't you? Because we have another SEAL saying—All in, all the time. And if anyone is that, it's you, Pippa. Tell me this—have you given one thought to leaving Her Majesty's service?"

Maybe one. Or two. But, "Not...seriously."

Quietly, "Yeah. And I get that. And until I met you, I hadn't thought about it seriously either." He lifted his hand from her arm and moved his fingers. "But maybe we should. Maybe I did my part, you know? And you did yours. And you get to have a life of your own. Our own."

Her throat thickened. "Oh, Fraser—please don't—"

"This isn't a marriage proposal, Pippa, so don't panic. But you have to know that since you left, that's the only thing I've thought about. You and me. And what could be if we, you know, went all in, all the time."

Her eyes burned.

"I love you. And I thought maybe I could forget about that, let you go back to your life here, but clearly..."

"Please, Fraser. Stop. I..." She shook her head. "I...I don't even know what that looks like. I don't know who I'd be if I weren't just...well, Imani's protection detail." She drew in a breath. "Although, if I keep losing her, maybe that won't be an issue."

Silence.

"Then what?"

"What do you mean?"

"If it wasn't an issue...what would you do?"

"I..."

"What do you want, Pippa? Deep in your heart, what do you want?"

"I don't know, okay?" And maybe it was her emotion, maybe her frustration, but as they came to a curve, she tapped the brakes, a little too hard.

Way too hard.

The Ranger Rover started to fishtail. She whipped the steering wheel against the turn, and the car spun the other way.

"Don't overcorrect!" Fraser's voice, but she was already turning the wheel again.

The car kept spinning, around, around—

She held the wheel and slammed on the brakes, but it only locked them up.

"Hang on!" Fraser shouted as they careened down the road, the lights flashing against trees and rail. A terrible screech burned the night as the SUV hit metal.

The guardrail was rent asunder, and the Range Rover tore through, spun into the ditch.

And then they were rolling.

She didn't know how many times they banged the ceiling, her belt burning her into the seat. The airbag deployed, slammed her in the face, and she tasted blood.

Then the SUV stopped cold with a devastating crack.

She jerked, bounced back against the seat.

Silence.

"Fraser?"

No answer.

"Fraser!" She reached out and felt his body. "Fras—"

A horrifying crack sounded, like the earth ripping open, and then the tree trunk snapped. Thick, piney arms shoved into the broken windows. Snow fell, slamming into the hood. Then an avalanche of white and ice flooded the cab.

She stifled a scream as the snow encased them, her hand caught on Fraser's body.

It finally stopped, and she gasped, her body nearly buried.

"Fraser!"

Nothing but blackness.

And in that moment, she knew the answer to his question. *What do you want—*

"*Fraser!*"

She wanted to weep when his hand covered hers. "I'm here, Pippi. Take a breath."

She closed her eyes. Willed herself to do just that. Blood

heated her lips, and she put her hand up to close off her nose. The airbag was slowly deflating after impact. "I think I broke my nose."

"Get some snow on it."

Right. No shortage there. She scooped up some, her hand icy, and packed it into her nose. Already, the blood had stopped, so maybe she hadn't broken it.

"Are you hurt otherwise?"

"No." But she did a quick check, moving her limbs. "All intact. You?"

"Fine. But I know one thing."

A beat. "What?"

"I am definitely thinking that I should have gotten the hotdog."

What? Oh...no...and then she shook her head, trying not to laugh, because suddenly everything hurt. Her bones, her muscles, her wound from the train, her brain from overthinking, and most of all her pride.

She shoved her hand against the massive airbag, covered her eyes, and then...shoot, shoot—

"Pippa, are you crying?"

"No." Aw—

"Babe." He still had her hand, and now he released his belt and moved toward her, pushing away snow and finally putting his arms around her. He pulled her to himself, pushing more snow away.

And then, in his arms, she let herself unravel. Because yes, she knew exactly what she wanted. And it started with figuring out how to stay alive.

FOR A MOMENT, WHEN IMANI WOKE UP, THE SUN streaming through massive leaded windows onto the lush white

SUSAN MAY WARREN

carpet, the king-sized bed with scrolled posters, the white brocade pillows and coverlet, she couldn't place her surroundings.

Clearly not the charming and quaint Marshall family bedroom in the twin bed beside Pippa's, with the unused fireplace, the wood-planked floor, the eyelet curtains at the window. The place where she'd spent the past two-plus months hiding.

And not her bedroom at Perrigwynn Palace in Fressa either, with the arched windows under the shadow of one of the Gothic church towers. Not Hadsby Castle, with a view of the courtyard, the fountain in the middle, the lush flowers, at least in summer.

Most certainly not her old bedroom in the rundown but beloved farmhouse where she'd spent so many glorious years as Gemma's foster daughter, healing after the tragic loss of her parents, caring for refugee animals, building a small but perfect life.

No, here...was...

Opulent. Even decadent.

And then it came to her as she slid out of the bed, her bare feet finding the lush carpet.

Neville Lodge.

The getaway of Prince Xavier.

Pulling on a thick, plush bathrobe over the long T-shirt she'd found to sleep in, she walked to the window and opened the drapes.

Her breath escaped at the beauty. The blizzard had died in the night leaving a thick layer of crisp white frosting across the valley of the Haskell Mountains. The lodge overlooked Haskell Lake, now semi-frozen, a deep blue patch of water glistening in the middle and surrounded on one side by the village of Heath. A quaint ski town, with snow-laden timber roofs and smoke curling from chimneys. The Haskell Ski Resort rose from behind it, the runs cut neatly from the mountain like so many wide white rivers.

A glorious blue sky hosted a few high, wispy clouds, the storm having reaped its supply from the heavens, leaving it barren.

Neville Lodge sat on the side of a mountain, near the ragged edge of a cliff that fell into the valley of thick pine trees heavy with white.

Glorious.

She spotted her blue velvet dress draped on a hanger—clearly a housekeeper had entered, maybe even early this morning, to tidy the place. Her tiara, the one gifted her by Prince John when Gemma had adopted her, sat on a pillow on the bureau. She walked over to it. It always seemed a little ostentatious to her, but now she picked it up. Not a full halo—more of a half-circlet, with teardrop diamonds affixed to the filigree silver frame, a larger teardrop in the center. Not fancy, but elegant and simple.

She'd tied her hair back in a scarf and now undid it and put the tiara on her head, nestling it into the thick weave. Her hair hung gloriously long, past her shoulders, thick and shiny, and the tiara seemed the exact right accoutrement. She stared at the image of herself in the mirror, trying to align it with the woman she knew.

The woman who wore jeans and yoga pants and T-shirts, no makeup, who liked playing one-on-one with Creed. An orphan taken in by a small-town rescuer of refugees who became a princess and brought Imani with her.

Her words to Creed, spoken on the tarmac back in Tennessee, rushed back to her.

"I just...I'm not a princess, despite what you and Pippa and everyone else says."

"You are—"

"Fine. Yes, I am. Whatever. But I don't know what that means. I thought it meant freedom—but clearly not. And then maybe I thought it meant fun, but that feels wrong too. So I guess I don't know what it means."

"It means you get to go to a ball."

It had to mean more than that.

She headed to the bathroom and changed into her yoga pants and sweater from last night. Pulled her hair—the weave was heavier than she'd imagined—into a handkerchief back from her face, brushed her teeth, slipped into a pair of wool slippers, and headed out of her bedroom, down the hall to the gathering room.

She would have felt better if she could have just gone next door and knocked on Creed's door, but of course, Xavier put him in a different wing.

She hadn't missed the sparks between the two of them last night. She wanted to tell Creed that really, he had nothing to worry about, but she didn't hate the way he'd held her hand all night.

Still. Xavier was simply being polite. Sweet, even.

A fire crackled in the hearth, already stirred to life by the morning staff—although, how late was it? She looked around for a clock and found none.

And then it occurred to her.

Where was Pippa?

"Imani."

She spotted Xavier rising from where he sat in the dining room, the table laden with breakfast items—croissants, jams, jellies, breads, sausages, cheese, and even boiled eggs. Xavier wore a turtleneck and a pair of dress pants. "How are you?"

"I'm...fine—"

"Good. I was hoping we could hit the slopes today. Maybe get in a few runs before the locals ski away all the powder."

Her mouth opened. Closed. "Um, I..."

"I have skis. And boots, of course. You do ski, don't you?"

"Actually, no. I mean, I've been once, but...I...is Pippa here?"

He frowned.

"My personal security. When I talked to her last night, she was on her way up."

"Yes. I know to whom you are referring. I just don't know. I'll ring up Griff and see if he's heard from them."

"They didn't get in yet?"

"After we had our bite to eat and that lovely chat about American politics, I retired, just as you did." He pulled out his cell phone from his pocket and thumbed a text. "There. We'll see what he says. Maybe they stayed behind in the storm."

Maybe. She let out a breath. "Can I use a phone?"

"Of course."

He handed over his cell phone.

She opened the phone app and dialed Pippa's number. It rang, and rang, and finally Pippa's voice mail picked up. "It's Imani. Just worried. Call me."

She handed him the phone. "Thanks." Probably he was right—with the storm headed over the mountain, they probably stayed behind.

But that didn't *feel* like Pippa. The woman was a bulldog.

He pulled out a chair next to his. "Join me for breakfast?"

She walked to the table and sat down. "Creed can't ski. Not with his leg."

"Indeed. But we won't be gone long." Xavier sat down next to her. He smelled good—clean-shaven, freshly showered. "He's a good chap, that Creed. Is he returning to university?"

"I don't know. He had a track scholarship, but after..." She looked at Xavier. "He was shot. Because of me."

"I highly doubt you were the cause—"

"Oh no. There was an assassin who came looking for me. Attacked the house."

"Oh, love, you must have been terrified. They should have had more security."

She frowned. "I...yeah, it was terrifying. In fact, the last three months have been terrifying. Just...constantly waiting for something to happen."

She picked up a piece of spice bread. "I feel like that's been my entire life, though. Ever since my parents died, it's been...hard. My grandmother took me in for a while, but that was too much for her, so Gemma gave me a place to live. And then, of course, she met the prince and married him, and we moved to Lauchtenland. She adopted me, so then I became a princess. But that's not been..."

"Being royal has its challenges, for sure. Paparazzi, and of course—"

"No. I mean, yes, I don't love being on all the time, but...I don't know how I fit into this world. I'm not...I wasn't raised in the royal family. It doesn't feel real to me."

"But it is real, Imani."

"I know. Pippa reminds me of that every day. She's with me because...I'm a princess."

"You are a princess." He put his hand on her arm. "A beautiful princess. And this is your land." He turned her. "So I think you should go enjoy it."

She offered a smile. "I don't know. I feel like being a princess is more than that. More than just enjoying the title. I mean—yes, I like some of the perks, but..." She looked up at him. "Don't you feel like you should do something with your title?"

"I am very active in my father's business and our state charities."

"I'm sure you are. I just mean..."

He frowned.

"I guess I don't know how to describe it. Just this feeling that there is something more for me, but not knowing what it is."

He took her hand. "I'd very much like to help you find it."

She blinked, looked up at him. "Oh, X, uh..."

"Imani. I can appreciate how you care for Creed. Of course you do—he protected you as you fled from a terrible trauma. But consider your very words. Your future, Your Highness." He smiled down at her.

Oh. My.

His phone buzzed, and he picked it up. Frowned.

"What?"

"They didn't arrive." He got up and stepped away, and in a moment, was speaking with Griff.

"I can't get ahold of Fraser either."

She looked over to the door.

Creed stood there, leaning on his cane, his hair wet, wearing a hint of dark scruff on his chin, faded jeans, a thermal shirt that hugged his body.

She smiled.

He met it, but an emotion she couldn't place hung in his eyes. He glanced at Xavier as he came into the room.

"I see," Xavier was saying, his voice low. "Okay, well then, by all means, send out a search party."

She looked at him, her mouth opening.

"Yes, and keep me abreast. Very good."

He hung up even as Creed limped over to them. "What's going on?"

Xavier pocketed his phone. "Apparently, they did set out last night, but Hadsby Castle hasn't heard from them. They do have a GPS tracker that put them over the pass before it was closed, near about midnight. So—"

"So," Creed said. "Maybe they spun out and are in the ditch—"

"Or off the side of the mountain?" Imani set her spice cake down, suddenly not hungry.

"It'll be okay, Imani," Creed said. "We'll find them."

"Actually, I'm sending Griff and a team out as we speak." Xavier took the chair near hers again. "Let's have some breakfast, and then we'll see about getting you fitted for some ski boots."

She looked at him. "Wait—what?"

"My team will find them." He indicated a chair for Creed, across from them. "No need to waste a glorious day."

Creed just stood there, frowning. "I think we should search—"

"Exactly." Imani stood up. "I'm going with Griff." She started for the door.

"Your Highness!" Xavier stood, caught up with her and grabbed her arm.

She rounded, and his eyes seemed sharp. "Don't be ridiculous." His tone bore the edge of a man who knew his place.

At the top.

She stared at the two men in front of her. Prince Xavier, dashing and handsome and in command, looking very much a prince with his steely jawline, his perfect curly black hair, those sharp blue eyes. Creed, wounded, but resolute and fierce, his breaths rising and falling as he leaned on his cane, a common man who frankly seemed more a criminal than a prince, a sort of edgy, dangerous glint in his stormy brown eyes.

And maybe...maybe she was a little of both.

"Listen. This is my fault."

Xavier frowned. Creed drew in a breath, his mouth tightening.

"Darling—"

"No. If I hadn't talked Creed into escaping the night club back in Geneva, I wouldn't have been in the park. I wouldn't have seen a murder and gone running, been chased across Switzerland, and Creed wouldn't have had to rescue me. He wouldn't have been arrested in Italy, and Fraser wouldn't have had to spring him from the yacht."

Xavier's eyes narrowed.

"They wouldn't have had to hide me in Minnesota, where we were found and Creed was shot. I would be back here, getting ready to go to Haxton University, Pippa would have her promotion, and no one would be dead on the side of the road!"

Xavier's mouth pinched, and Creed opened his, but she wasn't done. "And yes, you're right, Xavier. If I'd been willing to accept the fact that I am a princess, maybe I wouldn't have run away from Pippa at all. I would have realized what danger I was putting her in, and... maybe tried to think of anyone but myself." Her eyes filled, her throat thickening. "In fact, maybe I've been thinking of only myself for the past two years." She wiped her cheek, hating that her voice shook.

"Imani—" Creed started.

"No. No, Creed. I stole your scholarship, your future from you, and if you get caught here...who knows what else. You should go home. And I should go back to Port Fressa. But most of all, I need to go find my bodyguard." She headed for the door. Paused. Turned. "Now, please point me in the direction of the search party."

"I CAN THINK OF WORSE WAYS TO DIE." FRASER WASN'T sure why he'd said that, but Pippa was turning so dark and morose, he was just trying to lighten up their situation.

"Seriously?" Pippa said. She'd just tried to use her cell phone, again, but the call wouldn't go through, and her battery life was at three percent, so there was that.

Not that she wasn't a little right. He'd managed to dig out most of the cab, including himself and Pippa, and create a sort of snow cave. The broken front window allowed some light and air, but the jagged glass kept him from wanting to attempt a climb out, especially in the dark.

But now that light seemed to spill in and illuminate the cab, maybe. Probably.

Because if they stayed here another night, no bets on not freezing to death. His toes already felt numb, his fingers thick. "Sure. Freezing to death is a soft death. You go to sleep. Wake up in heaven."

She just looked up at him, her golden-brown eyes containing a sort of horror. "What is wrong with you? Why would you even say that?"

He smiled. Attagirl.

"Oh, I get it. Reverse psychology." She fisted her hand, banged him on the chest, then settled back against him in their snow cave. "Sneaky." She had curled up with him, their bodies producing warmth as the night soldiered on.

"We will get out of this, Pippa. We'll figure it out."

She said nothing.

"You know, one of the great enemies of hope is forgetting God's promises."

"God promised to get us out of a snowbank?"

"He promised to always go with us. Never to leave us. And with God with us, there is always hope."

"Fraser, we're not just buried in here, but a tree fell on us. Even if we could dig ourselves out, how would we even escape from the truck? The back end of the Rover is crushed, the doors wedged shut, a massive trunk pins the roof and hood."

She did have a point. He'd retrieved his duffel bag from the back after an hour or more of digging. He'd found his Maglite and used that to assess their situation. Not great.

Then he'd dug Pippa free, shoving the snow into her space at the driver's side while he made a space for her near him.

He'd also kicked free his legs, and yes, their pocket was tight, but they'd survived the blizzard.

And that was step one.

As wan light bled into the cab, he made out their imprisonment, the bushy arms of the tree entrapping them, the heavy weight of the trunk pinning them. The tree cracked just above the roofline of the SUV. Any farther down and it would have crushed the cab—another miracle of God.

He was hoping for more. Lots more.

Like figuring out his own answer to his question to Pippa. *What do you want, Pippa? Deep in your heart, what do you want?*

Frankly, he'd been hoping, just a little, that she'd answer for him.

Then they'd hit the tree, and it'd become about right now, the future forgotten.

"My dad told me once that in every situation of life, God is always doing a thousand different things that you cannot see and you do not know. We might be stuck here, but He is not."

"No one even knows where we are."

He reached down and pulled her chin up. Met her eyes. "We despair because we look at ourselves, our own abilities, and we know we're not enough. And based on our own inferiority, we have doubts. But God says He will not desert us. That though life tries to shake us from His grip, Jesus will never let go."

She stared at him.

"What?"

"You remind me of him."

"Jesus?"

She laughed. "No—I mean, sometimes, maybe, but I was thinking about my dad. I think it's why I...why I..."

"Why you love me."

Her mouth tightened. She made a face and nodded. "Yeah. I love you, Fraser Marshall. And your unwavering loyalty. And your unfailing hope."

"Hope is...well, it's the byproduct of knowing God. God is not a joker—He doesn't do good to His children sometimes and bad to them other times. When things are dark, that doesn't mean God has stopped doing good. The devil wants to destroy our hope. To make God, and faith, look worthless. But He is not worthless, and hope is not empty, and God is for us and will rescue us, for our joy and His glory."

"That's deep stuff there, Captain America."

"That's my father. Regular sermons in the vineyard."

She laughed, and the sound of it seemed to loosen the terrible knot in his gut.

Hope. Yes. He needed that refresher too.

His arms tightened around her, and he closed his eyes. "Lord, strengthen our hope. Help us to see beyond ourselves to You. Build our faith. And we wouldn't mind being rescued too."

"Amen," she said.

Outside, a terrible crack sounded. The Rover shuddered.

Pippa pressed away from him. "What—"

"The car is moving."

Another crack, and again the car shuddered. "Hello! Anyone out there?"

Crack!

The Rover shifted forward. Fraser slammed his hand on the dash, his other around Pippa.

Then a terrible rending as the standing tree trunk ripped free of its roots.

Fraser threw himself over Pippa, waiting for the trunk to fall, to crush them.

Instead, the tree trunk dragged the car with it, the force wrenching it away from the cocoon of branches and breaking it free. It settled on top of the tree trunk, balanced there.

The snow on the hood fell away, clearing the view.

Fraser looked up and froze.

Pippa pushed up—

"Easy, babe."

She, too, caught her breath.

From what he could tell, the Rover sat on the remnants of the severed trunk, the back wheels caught in the uprooted roots.

And in front of them, nothing but air. He spotted a ravine dropping on either side of the hood, a cliff in the distance.

"I'll bet that's the Haskell River below us," Pippa said.

Another crack—

"Get down!"

The severed tree slid down over the top. Metal screeched as it crushed the back end against the roots of the tree.

Snow scattered, scrambling over the hood. The Rover shuddered, and Fraser waited for the inevitable crack that sent them over the edge.

Nothing. He lifted his head. "We're pinned."

She, too, sat up, looked at him, her eyes wide. "We need to get out of here before we go over."

"Agreed. Let's see if we can kick out this windshield now."

He leaned back, got his feet up, and she did the same.

"On three."

They slammed their feet against the intact edges of the glass, and the windshield shattered. He kicked it off in a sheet of webbed glass, then leaned up and pushed it away. "You first."

She was already on her feet on the seat and crawled out onto the hood. Stopped. "There's no way to get off. We need to—"

The tree trunk cracked, and he dove for her hand as the Rover tilted. Her legs slid off the front, into midair.

"Where do you think you're going?"

She glared at him.

"Too soon?"

"Just don't let go."

"Never." He pulled her back up, but the Rover kept creaking. "Grab the tree trunk! There's more weight holding it to the hillside."

She scrambled to her feet, then pulled herself up onto the broken tree. Her hand appeared, dangling down from above.

He swung his duffel on like a backpack, then scrambled out onto the hood.

Another crack, and this time, the Rover pitched forward.

He grabbed her hand, his other on a tree branch as the Rover slid out farther under the toppling trunk.

The branch broke in his hand. He jerked her, hard, his feet landing on the Rover.

It was just what the trunk needed, apparently, to topple forward.

He slipped on the hood, fighting for footing.

His grip broke away from Pippa. She screamed as he landed on the hood, even as the entire mess started to break free. He had a grip on the edge of the windshield, his feet fighting, and then—

Then he spotted the edge of an axe handle, shoved into his peripheral vision. "Grab on!"

What? But Pippa was clinging to the tree trunk, so far above he couldn't reach, so—

He grabbed the axe handle, one hand, then the next as the truck fell, careening out from beneath him.

The man on the other end jerked him away from the truck, the force so strong he flew off the hood into the snow, nearly on top of his savior.

Then, with a crack and a scream from Pippa, the Rover disappeared over the cliff.

"Pippa!"

He rolled over.

No. The trees branches entangled the Rover, and gravity fought the counterbalance of the tree, inching the toppled trunk toward the edge.

"Jump!"

This from their rescuer, a man dressed in a thick woolen anorak and a wide-brimmed hat. He held out his arms. "I'll catch you!"

Fraser fought the snow, trying to scramble up. The Rover jerked the tree trunk. "Jump, Pippa!" He didn't know why, but he believed the man.

But he did manage to find his feet.

Not before Pippa, however, jumped. She let out a scream, flung out her arms, cleared most of the piney branches, and aimed for the man.

She landed, and he caught her, pulled her down into the snow before the momentum could take her over. Fraser jumped on both of them and simply held on as the Rover took the tree trunk over, pulling it off the mountain.

Crashing sounded below, but he just lay there, the snow poofing up around them like fairy dust.

He could have stayed there all day, but suddenly the man pushed him away, rolled, then pulled her up. Grabbed his axe. "Run. Before the entire mountain comes down!"

Fraser looked at him, then up.

The ripping of the tree from the hill had left a scar of broken trees and tumbled snow in its wake. But yes, tiny rivulets of snow began to tumble down behind it. They'd slid maybe fifty feet or more from the side of the road, the torn guardrail evidence of the terror.

If the tree hadn't caught them—

Crunching. "Move!"

Pippa held on to the man's hand, moving behind him, and now turned to Fraser, held out her hand. The hill fought him, the steepness and gravity and slickness mocking him. He found escape in the wide steps left by the leather boots of the lumberjack. The man stopped behind a massive pine tree, its lowest arms maybe ten feet high, the snow lighter here, protected.

Fraser caught up, grabbed Pippa and pulled her against him, breathing hard.

Behind them, a shelf of snow broke free from the scar and thundered down the hill, casting out over the ravine and dropping.

"We would have been swept away."

The lumberjack leaned on his axe, glanced at them. "Naw. I wouldn't have let that happen."

Fraser frowned at him, then looked at Pippa. "You okay?"

"Yeah."

Shouts came from the road, and he looked up.

Two men stood there, waving their arms.

"We're here!" Fraser said, waving back. He stepped out from the tree. "Down here!"

Pippa grabbed his hand just as a woman joined the men. Dark hair spilled out of a white cap. She wore snowpants, boots, and a lime-green jacket. "It's Imani."

He looked at Pippa, and her eyes glistened. He pressed a kiss to her forehead, his heart still a hammer in his chest.

Thank you. Thank you.

He turned to thank the lumberjack also, but only the axe stood where he'd been.

"Mister?" He walked over and picked up the axe. Not heavy, but it had a worn handle, as if wielded often. "Hello?"

Nothing but forest around them.

And rescue coming from above.

SEVEN

Y*ou should go home.*
  Imani's words thundered, a hammer in Creed's chest as he stood at the massive window that overlooked the valley below Xavier's lodge, listening to the man talk on the radio in the next room.

Creed should have gone with her instead of staying behind, but with the limited room in the Range Rover, and with his leg aching, truth told him he'd only be in the way.

Xavier had also agreed to stay behind, to relay information from the searchers to Hadsby Castle, who'd sent out their own search party.

So there they sat, in Xavier's great room, the fire flickering in the hearth, safe and warm while Imani searched for his brother and her bodyguard.

The double doors opened, and Xavier came through. He walked over to Creed. "They found them."

"Fraser?"

"That's your brother?"

"Yes."

"Apparently, yes. Their SUV spun out, went over. But they're safe. I rang Hadsby Castle—they already have a chopper on the way. They want the princess back at the castle."

Right. Perfect.

Really, what had he hoped to accomplish by his bravado and idiotic idea of sneaking into Lauchtenland? Like he could protect her better than Pippa?

What. Ever.

I stole your scholarship, your future from you, and if you get caught here...who knows what else. So much agony in those beautiful eyes when she'd said that, her words dark and haunting, issuing from her in a sort of wretched truth.

Except she hadn't *stolen* anything—he'd freely given her... everything. The protection of his home and his family, and even his own person. And if he wanted to get technical, he'd been trying to save Fraser when he got shot, so...

Still, she was right. He had nothing to give her. No future, and probably only scandal if it got out he was in Lauchtenland.

"She didn't mean it, you know, mate."

Creed looked at Xavier. He looked very princely today, like he belonged on some royal reality show, in his turtleneck and dress pants. His fancy watch probably cost more than Creed's scholarship.

If he were his brother Spider, he'd be trying to snag it, figure out a way to pawn it. And the very fact that Creed thought that made him look away.

Maybe he did have criminal in his genes.

"What she said about you going home." Xavier sat on the leather arm of one of the overstuffed chairs that overlooked the massive picture window. "She has a serious thing for you. And I, for one, am grateful for all you did for her." He tapped his heart a couple times, then pointed at Creed. "She's got spirit, and my guess is that even if you weren't around, she would have figured out a way to ditch Pippa. She even did it once when we were together."

Creed looked at him.

"Not that we were *together*. Just friends." He held up a hand. "But, you know, she's also right about that. She is a princess, and she needs to start taking that seriously."

"Imani wouldn't be back in Lauchtenland if she didn't take her role seriously."

"You mean Her Royal Highness."

Creed considered him, the words he'd overheard Xavier say pinging back to him. *But consider your very words. Your future.*

And, as much as he'd like to tell himself otherwise, she was in danger, and he couldn't protect her.

Not anymore.

The radio crackled and Xavier got up, walked away.

And if Creed stopped to think about anyone but himself, he'd leave. The thought swept through him, brought him up.

"Very good," Xavier said. "See you soon."

He came back. "The chopper is arriving." He gestured out the window to where, on a lower jutting of the lodge, a flat area lit up with running lights. In a moment, a whirr shook the house, and a commando military chopper sped over the building, then set down on the tarmac. The door opened and a couple uniformed soldiers hopped out, dressed in body armor, black jumpsuits, armed.

Armed?

"What's going on?" Creed said.

"I dunno. Maybe something went down at Hadsby after we left. Stay here." He left the room, and Creed watched as another uniformed man got out, followed by an aid in fatigues. They stalked toward the lodge and disappeared out of view.

He had the sudden, inexplicable urge to run.

Behind him, the front door opened.

Imani—er, Her Royal Highness—came in, wearing a lime-green jacket, a wool hat, her cheeks flushed. And behind her—

"Fraser."

His brother seemed a little chilled but otherwise intact, no broken bones as he came in. But he supported Pippa, who wore bruises under her eyes. Dried blood stained her jacket, even as she shrugged it off.

"You okay, Pippa?" Creed limped toward them.

"Yeah. Fine." She touched her nose. "I don't think it's broken. The bleeding stopped. Airbag."

A steward had arrived to take their jackets, and now Imani, her boots off, simply walked over to him and put her arms around him.

Well. Okay then. He held her. "You all right?"

"Barely. They could have been killed." She leaned back. "We found where they'd gone through the guardrail and got there just in time to see an avalanche take out the path where they'd gone down."

He looked at Fraser, who came over with Pippa. "We hit a tree. And that tree finally gave way. But we got out in time." He exchanged a look with her.

Something more than that had gone down, clearly.

"There's some breakfast left in the dining room," Creed said, and it felt lame, but—

"I'm famished," Pippa said, and headed toward the dining room.

Creed slipped his hand into Imani's. She gripped it back, looked at him, those eyes so beautiful, so golden.

"I...I'm sorry about what I said before," she said softly. "I was just...worried." She put her hand on his chest. "I don't want anything to happen to you because of me."

"Babe. Everything is going to be fine." He tipped his forehead to hers. She met his eyes, smiled. Then lifted her face to his.

Why had he ever thought they didn't belong together—

"Get away from the princess!"

He looked up, froze.

Two soldiers advanced into the room, their weapons trained on him.

"What are you doing?"

Another man, the officer, simply came up, wrapped his arm around her waist, and yanked her away from Creed.

"Let me go!" She pounded at his arm.

"Get down!" shouted a soldier, and he lifted his hand.

"Hey! Let him go!" This from Fraser.

The other soldier turned his weapon on his brother. Fraser held a croissant in one hand and raised them both. "Hey, man, what's going on?"

"Sir!" Pippa came out of the dining room, stormed past Fraser. "Wait—what's going on?"

"Okay, okay," Creed said, his hand on the sofa as he tried to get down.

Next to him, Fraser hit his knees. "Get that gun out of my face!"

"Fraser, just calm down—" This from Pippa, who advanced on the man holding Imani. He released the princess into Pippa's arms.

"Keep her back."

"No! What are you doing?"

"This is Creed, right? Creed Marshall?" This from the officer.

"Yes," Imani said.

"Sir—" Pippa started.

"Did you know he was here, Miss Butler?"

"No—yes, not right away—"

Creed had lowered himself onto his stomach, put his hands back behind his neck.

"Xavier, what's going on?"

Creed looked over just as the prince entered the room, and his gut clenched as Xavier walked over and put his arm around Imani, pulled her against him.

What?

Imani shrugged Xavier away, put a little distance between them.

"Creed Marshall is under arrest on suspicion of the attack at Hadsby Castle," the officer said.

"Sir!" Pippa said, but managed to catch Imani, who whirled around.

"That's not true! He wouldn't—"

"He did not have anything to do with the attack," Fraser said, now also lowering himself to the ground. "We were there to protect Imani."

"Her Royal Highness to you, Mr. Marshall," said the man.

"Ferguson, c'mon. You know Creed is innocent," Fraser growled as he dropped the croissant and put his hands behind his neck.

"Stop talking. You were specifically told to stay in Dalholm. Not escape the city with Pippa."

"If he hadn't gone with me, I'd be dead right now, sir." Pippa held a furious Imani, who covered her face with her hands, shaking her head.

"Secure them," said Ferguson, and the soldier pulled Creed's hands behind his back, secured them with zip ties.

He did the same to Fraser.

Then the man pulled Creed to his feet. "Where do you want him, sir?"

"I have a place," Xavier said.

"Your Royal Highness, we need to leave," the officer said. "You're wanted back in Port Fressa."

Imani stared at the man. "I'm not going anywhere. Not without Creed!" She turned then and took two steps toward Creed.

The soldier stepped in front of her. "Sorry, ma'am."

"Get out of my way!"

Creed had leaned against the sofa, his leg on fire. "Imani—I'll be fine—"

"No. This is not right! I am...I am a princess of Lauchtenland. I demand to see him!"

The soldier looked at Ferguson.

"Let her say goodbye," the officer said.

Her jaw tightened as she walked over to Creed. Glared at the other soldier, who stepped out of the way also.

Tears ran down her face, her mouth a tight bud. She took his face in her hands, leaned forward, touched his forehead. "I'll figure out something."

He shook his head. "No, Imani. This is the right thing. I didn't do anything—and they'll figure this out. And then they'll deport me, and..." He swallowed, his eyes burning, his throat thick. "C'mon, we both knew it would end this way. I'm not... royal. In fact, probably this is exactly right."

"Creed—"

"No, Your Royal Highness. You are destined for bigger things than me. We had a good run, though, right?"

She looked up at him. Met his eyes, hers full. Swallowed. Nodded.

"Kiss me goodbye."

She closed her eyes, then stepped up to him, her arms around his neck. And then she kissed him. He tasted her heart, the person he'd known, who he'd run away with and spent the last three months with, the woman who'd made him laugh and healed him and made him feel, at least a little, like he deserved her.

And he kissed her back with everything inside his soul, all of himself wishing they could have had the fairytale, beauty and the beast. He memorized her smell, the taste of her, the feel of her tongue on his, the way she left him with pieces of herself.

And when she finally leaned back, he could nod. Could let her go. Could let the soldier muscle him to his feet.

"Careful! He has a bad leg."

Yeah, he could barely feel it with the open chest wound.

"This isn't over," Fraser growled to Pippa, who looked stricken as he followed Creed.

"Let's go," Ferguson said, and the last thing Creed saw was Imani standing in the great room, looking beautiful and wrecked and every inch the royal princess.

Xavier led them up the stairway, down the hallway, then up

another stairway, which Creed barely managed, and then finally to a small room at the end of the third floor. Octagonal, the windows looked out on all sides, upon the grounds in all directions.

"A car will come for them," one of the soldiers said to Xavier.

"Don't worry. I won't let them out," he said, and glanced at Creed and mouthed *Sorry, mate.*

Sure he was.

The door bolted behind them.

Fraser stalked the area, peering out of the windows, and as Creed sank to the ground, the rumble of the helicopter shook the walls.

Then Fraser let out a word, turned and looked at Creed, so much agony in his eyes Creed shook his head.

Sighed.

"What?"

A beat, and then Creed smiled. "I just knew we'd end up locked in a tower."

Fraser shook his head. "Yeah."

"Now, SEAL brother, how are we getting out of here?"

"You know he's innocent, Gunner! For the love—what—"

"*What* yourself, Butler. I know we're alone, but don't say anything you'll regret."

Gunner folded his arms across his chest, staring out of the window of his Port Fressa office located inside massive Perrigwynn Palace. The centuries old fortress of white stone and iron, the royal standard flying from the peaked rooftops and turrets, sat at the edge of the old city of Port Fressa. His window looked down upon the red-brick buildings and the modern skyscrapers that lined the blue-green water of Port Fressa Bay,

Parliament and the Clemency District, and most importantly, the six ancient cathedrals whose spiral steeples formed what looked like a heart. The royals and the locals of Port Fressa called it the Heart of God. Some said that the lights could even be seen from space.

And in this castle resided Queen Catherine, the king consort, Edric, Prince John, Princess Gemma, as well as Princess Imani, and even Prince Gus, Princess Daffy, and their baby girl.

So much responsibility, and since he'd taken the mantle of HMSD—Her Majesty's Security Detail—lines had become etched around his eyes, his handsome face.

Now, he sighed, turned. "Listen, I'm keen to believe you, Pippa. But we have footage of a man in livery fiddling with the heaters long before the guests arrived."

"Then it couldn't have been Creed and Fraser. They only arrived—"

"Twenty-four hours before the ball. We found their passport information. At best, they're here illegally, under false identities."

"Sir—"

He held up a hand. "Don't push it, Pippa. You're dangerously close to losing your position here. And frankly, you might be too close to the situation."

"Sir. I know Princess Imani better than anyone—"

"Agreed. And she keeps requesting you, so...for now, you're her detail. But go off the radar again and...well, I like you, you know that. You've earned my respect and that of the royal family. Don't jeopardize your future by aligning yourself with...well, with these Marshalls."

"They're not troublemakers, sir. Fraser was a Navy SEAL, and so is his brother Ned. And Jonas, he's...he's smart, and Creed—"

"Is a hoodlum."

"He's not, sir."

"Actually, Pippa, he is." He picked up a file on his desk. "I had my team vet everyone, and Princess Imani's friend has quite a background. His brother is in jail, as is his father. And he has a history of running away from foster homes."

She didn't know any of that, except, "That was a long time ago. Before he was adopted by the Marshalls. I promise, he's a good guy. And he loves the princess."

He dropped the file on his desk. "I just want to talk to him. No charges have been filed. But your friend Fraser broke laws also, and I can't make exceptions, especially for detail so closely attached to the royal family. As soon as we finish questioning them, they will be deported."

The word hit her like a punch.

"Sit down, Pippa."

He took his chair. Folded his hands on the edge of his desk. This office was larger, with a massive desk, but the same array of flatscreens hung on the walls. Outside the inner office, the larger space buzzed with two dozen techs watching every inch of Perrigwynn. Never would Creed have been able to sneak into the palace. Especially with the queen in residence.

In fact, he might have gotten shot. So, there was that.

She swallowed.

"I know you are loyal to the crown, Pippa. So I don't need to ask, but I'm going to—are you ready to defend the princess against every threat? Even if it might be...well, your boyfriend's brother?"

Her mouth opened. Closed. She swallowed, even as she nodded.

"Very good."

She closed her eyes, then opened them and looked out the window, fighting the burn in her throat. "Where are they now?"

"We're transferring them to the Port Fressa jail for holding. They'll be there in a couple hours."

Another knife in her throat.

"What about the Russian mob, and the bomb—"

"One crisis at a time!"

She looked up at him.

"Listen, with the charity football game this Saturday, we're completely focused on locking down Titus Stadium and keeping the royals safe. I've turned over the incident at Hadsby to the Lauchtenland Investigative Service."

"But what about the person who killed your brother? He's still out there—what if he's behind the explosion at the ball?"

"We have nothing, Pippa. Nothing. I've been through all the footage, all the visitors. No one visited him within hours of his death."

"No one. So, no leads. A ghost slipped in, dished up poison into Fredrik's porridge, and slipped out."

"Careful."

"I'd like to see the CCTV."

"Pippa."

"He's still out there. And who knows but he's after my princess. I need to know what's happening."

"No. You need to be alert, on the job, and not thinking about Fraser Marshall or his brother." He met her eyes.

She stared back. Right.

Except. Wait. *Brothers*. "Are Jonas and Sibba still here?"

He blinked at her. Then sighed. "I don't know. Are they the kind to go off on their own, disobey orders?"

"Um...well—"

"Blimey. Okay, I don't want to know. I want the entire lot of them on a plane and out of my country."

"You're deporting them also?"

He frowned. "No. Although my gut tells me to. Listen. I'm not ignoring what your friend Fraser said. But it's just pieces of speculation, Pippa. What I need are facts and hard evidence. And frankly, I'm just...very aware that where they go, trouble follows."

"Or trouble is thwarted. Don't forget Creed saved Princess Imani. Twice. And nearly lost his leg in the trouble. And Fraser was shot in the hand—"

"Because they kidnapped the princess on our watch!" He had hit his feet now, and she drew in a breath. "If they hadn't escaped the yacht—and don't tell me that you didn't have a hand in that, because I'm not stupid. But I am on your side, so..." He ground his jaw.

"I was afraid someone on the security team was a threat," she said quietly. "And I was right."

He drew in a breath. Ran a finger and thumb against his eyes. "Fine. Yes." Then he looked at her. "And because of that—and only because of that, and maybe because yes, you know Her Royal Highness so well—you're still on this detail. But, Pippa, you're too much like your dad."

She stared at him, blinking. "What did you say?"

"I just—"

"My dad gave his life saving the king consort because he knew there was a RECO plot and no one listened to him. He wasn't even *supposed* to be on that platform that day—but he knew that no one else would see what he was looking for. A traitor. And he gave his life for that hunch. And yes, maybe I have a hunch too. Something is brewing, and I know it in the bottom of my gut, and if that makes me like my dad, then...then...then good. Then you should listen to me!"

She stared at Gunner, realizing that she, too, had taken to her feet.

His mouth tightened. Then, finally, "Okay. I will ask the Lauchtenland Investigative Services to keep me briefed."

"And me."

He considered her, then, "Fine. But you have one job. One. Keep the princess safe. Leave the investigation in the hands of the LIS. Can you do that?"

"Yes, sir."

"Good. Now, how badly are you hurt?"

She blinked at him. "Sir?"

"You look like you were punched in the face."

"I was. By an airbag. And then I nearly slid off a cliff while being half frozen. But I'm fine, really."

"Okay, listen. The princess is safe, and for the next thirty-six hours, I'm assigning a temporary crew to her."

"Sir—"

"Take a break. Like a bath, and dinner. I don't want to see you back here until Tuesday morning." He raised an eyebrow.

Fine. "Yes, sir."

"Dismissed."

She closed the door behind her, aware of the glances she received from the crew in the security pit. But she ignored them and walked through the buzz of activity, out into the hallway.

Shut the door.

Creed and Fraser were in the jail. The same jail where Fredrik had been held. In a cell that had been breached.

Poison delivered.

And if an assassin could get to Fredrik, they could get to Creed.

And if they got to Creed, who knew what they'd do to get to Imani.

She walked down the hallway, her feet scuffing against the travertine tile. She still wore her boots, and yeah, her nose really hurt, and she could use a bath, her own smell a crime. But she took a set of stairs down, then walked outside and stood in an alcove in the cold.

Here, the snow only left a dusting, tiny crystals on the grass and covered roses. Overhead, however, the sky was turning to dusk, the oranges and reds bleeding out around the buildings, shiny on the glass skyscrapers.

She pulled out Fraser's phone, picked out of his duffel that she'd grabbed as they left Xavier's place, and dialed.

Because she'd had a feeling. The same feeling that told her that Imani wasn't safe, that something was brewing.

The voice on the other end picked up, masculine and deep. "Hey, Fraser, what's up?"

"Not Fraser. Pippa. Jonas, please tell me that you're in Dalholm."

"Pippa? Is everything okay with Fraser?"

"Not even a little. He's been arrested and so has Creed, and they're in trouble. Lots of trouble. And...how do you feel about a jailbreak?"

Silence. "Um. Well, I think we'll need some friends."

She sighed. "Sorry. I don't think we have any. Gunner Ferguson wants to deport them—and you guys."

"Then you probably need to come over."

Shoot! "I'm in Port Fressa. It'll take me a bit to get to Dalholm."

"You were right, Sibba!" He barely muffled the sound. Then he was back. "So are we."

A beat. "You're in Port Fressa?"

"You'll never believe it. But that's not all...there's something you need to see. And hopefully, we can solve your jailbreak problem. Because we have bigger trouble ahead."

EARN YOUR TRIDENT, EVERY DAY.

The phrase kept knocking around Fraser's head as he sat in the backseat of the Range Rover, hands cuffed behind his back, his legs also trussed. And yeah, it might take him two-point-three seconds to get out of the cuffs, another five to dive into the front seat, wrestle the wheel away, maybe ten to get the car to slow down.

Five more to kick open the door, spill out, roll, hit his feet and disappear.

But Creed sat next to him.

Also cuffed, hands and ankles. And that really didn't matter, because his brother couldn't run. Could barely walk, frankly.

And every single plan Fraser had devised over the past six hours had him rappelling a castle tower, or fighting free and running for the mountains, or even, as the car slowed as it came into the outskirts of Port Fressa, simply rolling through his most recent scenario and escaping through the alleyways of the darkening city.

Except, Creed.

Who looked at him with not a little disappointment when Imani's buddy, Prince Xavier, opened the door and let the dispatch from Her Majesty's Security Detail wrestle them to their feet and drag them down the hall, out to the waiting car.

Only two guys, so apparently the guys from Minnesota didn't pose a big threat.

Frankly, they were right, because Fraser had no doubt—okay, not a lot of doubt—fine, some doubt, but boatloads of hope—that they'd get this sorted.

If I get knocked down, I will get up every time.

Technically, he was still on his feet, but as he glanced at Creed, his brother seemed taken out at the knees, a grim look on his face.

"Sorry, bro," Fraser said softly.

Creed looked at him. Gave him a half smile. "It's okay. We said our goodbyes. It's better this way."

Of course his mind was on Imani. Right.

Fraser had barely given Pippa a thought except to run her stricken expression through his mind. That, and the look she'd given him when he winked at her, going up the stairs. Not sure what he'd meant by that wink except that he'd figure this out.

Frankly, it had been a little cocky, because now that he thought about it, chances were they'd throw them on a plane or a ship and he'd be headed stateside by morning.

That might be best case scenario.

"Where are we going?" he asked now as they drove toward the massive palace on the hill, the one with the towers.

As in, the Tower. And he'd thought Creed was being funny. Or ironic.

"No talking," said the man in front.

Right.

He leaned back, moved his hands. He'd managed to tighten

down the straps, hoping to break them, but since then they'd simply been cutting off the blood supply to his hands. Which did nothing for his damaged nerves.

He needed to get out of these cuffs, and pronto.

As for his feet, well, the zip ties were just silly. But he suspected Lauchtenland didn't contend with too many dangerous criminals, so probably he and Creed were a Big Deal.

But not so big they deserved a convoy. So, Medium Deal, maybe. "I'm hoping we can eat soon. I'm starved." He wished he'd hung onto that croissant.

The man in front looked at him. Fraser raised an eyebrow.

"You'll eat at the jail."

Aha. They were going to the city jail.

Shoot. Because probably, that had real bars, real security, and any hope of escaping had to happen right now. As they cruised through city streets, stopping at lights, signaling and driving through the warehouse and port side of the city.

A few blocks away, massive ships sat at dock, cranes silent as darkness fell. Only a few bright lights illuminated the dock area.

Not a bad place to get lost—

Stop. *Creed couldn't run.* But maybe Fraser could carry him— aw, not without backup. He'd get about a half block and the youngsters in the front seat would tackle them both.

Don't run to your death.

Right. Think. Knowing when not to act was as important as moving forward.

They stopped at a light. Here, lamplights buzzed overhead. A massive semi with a container strapped on the back moved into the intersection.

Stopped.

Fraser sat up.

The light remained red. The truck wheezed as if the driver fought the stick shift.

Wait—

Just like that, the back of the container opened. Figures jumped out.

No, men. Armed and armored up, faces painted black, and they ran for the Range Rover.

What—but in a second, Fraser brought his arms down and snapped the flexicuffs. Bent and pulled the end of the ankle cuffs to tighten them down.

Then he jerked his legs and they snapped.

Someone opened his door, but he turned to Creed.

The kid had broken free of his flexicuffs.

Right. YouTube.

Someone was helping him out, so Fraser scrambled out his side door.

The driver held up his hands, surrendering, and next to him, his cohort swore but released his weapon.

Poor guys. So much for Lauchtenland's standing army. But he wouldn't want to stand up to—well, whoever these guys were, either.

Seemed like American commandos, given the accent when they barked at the driver. "Get out!"

He got out, and they put him on his knees, then cuffed him and pushed him to the curb. "Don't move."

They put the other guy on the other curb, also facedown.

Then the soldier rounded on Fraser. "What does a guy have to do to not be bothered on his honeymoon?"

Fraser stared at him.

The man smiled. He stood eye to eye with Fraser, with thicker shoulders, dark hair, and blue eyes that sparked.

"Ned?"

He glanced at Creed, who braced himself on the car.

"What are you doing here?"

"Long story. Let's go." He walked over, put his arm around Creed's waist, picked him up, and together they hobbled to the truck.

Fraser hopped up on the bed, then turned and helped pull Creed in, assisted by a couple other men.

He glanced at the big man, his grip on Creed's arm. "Trini?"

"Hey, Fraser," said the man, his baritone rumbling through Fraser.

"Did you bring your entire SEAL team?" he said to Ned as his brother scrambled in.

"Hey, couz," said a voice, and he spotted a man climbing up behind Ned.

"Ford?"

His cousin held out a fist. Fraser met it. "What is going on? I thought you guys were tracking some rogue caesium through Russia."

Ned pulled the door closed while Trini banged on the front, and suddenly the truck lurched forward.

He collapsed onto a bench, holding on as they motored through the streets. Not far, because they stopped in a moment, then Ned opened the door again.

The harbor. A boat sat at dock, a driver standing at the helm. Fraser jumped out, and Ned helped Creed down.

"What happened to him?" Ford said, his other hand around his waist.

"Shot protecting a princess," Fraser said, and looked at Creed, who rolled his eyes.

"He has all the fun," said another voice, and Fraser spotted Riley McCord shutting the driver's door. He was married to the sister of the Kingston brothers, if he remembered right. He'd met him in Florida last summer.

Another man ran ahead and started untying the boat.

Fraser and Ford carried Creed down to the dock, the boat churning. So far, no sirens, so maybe they'd get this done.

He didn't recognize the man at the helm, but he'd retired before he could operate with Ned and his team. Still, the old juice sluiced through him. He lowered Creed onto the bench, then sat beside him, Ned sitting opposite.

"Casting off!" The SEAL tossed the lines in, then hopped in even as the captain backed the boat out.

"Hang on!"

The spray hit them, catching the lights of the city. Too loud to talk, but he kept looking at Ned. Crazy.

They rounded the port area and started around the southern end of the island, finally cutting the lights and pulling up to a dock that jutted out into the water. They drifted up silently, then Ford tied them off and helped Creed hop from the boat.

"I can walk!" Creed said, but Fraser stepped close enough to let him reach out for his shoulder now and again.

The house—no, mansion—sat back from the water, bright lights from the two-story window gleaming out onto the lawn. The place was easily ten thousand square feet, the land around it dark and secluded.

Trini spoke into his walkie, and the lights cut out.

"Where are we?" Fraser said.

"You'll see," Ned answered, then took off in a jog toward the house.

The rest of the team also ran ahead, and a light popped on in the house.

A figure appeared at the door.

"I think I got it from here," Creed said.

"Yeah, you do," Fraser said and started to run.

Pippa leaped on him in the darkness, her arms around his neck, her legs around his waist, holding so hard he staggered back.

"Pippi! Did you do this?"

She leaned back, met his eyes in the glow of the light, smiled, and his heart nearly exploded.

Oh no, no—what—

Then she kissed him. No polite, chaste kisses, the kind they could stop if his parents walked in. Or if Imani suddenly needed her.

All in. All the time.

Yes.

He held her tight and kissed her back, all the frustration of the past hour, and even the desperation of the last twenty-four hours pouring out in his touch, needing her with him, believing in him, claiming him as much as he wanted to claim her.

She tasted like home and adventure and strength and every tomorrow he'd always wanted but never realized until this moment.

Pippa.

She finally slowed her kiss, eased her touch and pulled back.

He swallowed. "I should break out of jail more often."

"Technically, you weren't in jail yet. If you were, that would have been much harder." She let herself down, but kept her arms around his neck. "I'm sorry Gunner arrested you."

"I did break into your country."

She nodded. "And now I think you need to break out."

"Yeah, that's probably a good idea."

She made a face.

"But not going to happen."

Her eyes widened.

"You want to tell me why Ned is here? With his team?" He raised an eyebrow. "Because as much as my brother is all in, all the time as a Marshall, he isn't going to talk his team into taking a detour from their hunt for a dirty bomb to rescue me and Creed from the terrifying clutches of the Lauchtenland royal guard."

"We can be scary."

"Oh, you, Pippa, are very scary." He kissed her forehead. "Are those guys okay? The drivers?"

"Yes. According to the radio chatter. HMSD picked them up while you were on your way here. Unfortunately, while they found the truck, they've lost track of the team that took you."

"Unfortunately." He put his arm around her. Worked his hand.

"How is it?"

"Could use some ice."

"Are you kidding?"

"Sadly, no." He opened the door and stepped inside.

Ford and Ned, along with the SEALs he didn't know, had shed their gear, some of them packing it into bags at a long table, others at an immense wet bar. Trini sat on an enormous blue U-shaped sectional, a flatscreen the size of a car on the wall.

Creed had made it inside, was also on the sofa, although he'd lain down on it, staring at the ceiling, an arm over his eyes, breathing hard.

Fraser recognized pain when he saw it.

The place had upscale beach vibe all over it, with overstuffed white chairs and nautical maps on the walls and a light oak floor covered in white woolen rugs.

"Nice digs. Who has the deep pocketbooks? Because this does not look like the work of the US government."

"That would be me." The voice came from the stairs, and in a moment, a big man—blond hair, built like an action figure—appeared.

"Hudson? Holy cow, what are you doing here?" Fraser walked over and met Hud's hand, then came in for a quick one-handed hug.

"We're here for the game." Iris, behind him. She wore her dark-blonde hair back, gave him a smile.

"The Vikings game?"

"We've been here since yesterday. We had a hotel, but when Jonas texted and said he was in Lauchtenland—and that's a scary story—we caught up with Shae and decided to rent something that could house our family."

"Or my SEAL team. Where's my wife?" Ned pushed past them, grease paint on his face.

"She's upstairs. Please keep it down," Iris said.

"I haven't seen her in a week, so no guarantees." Ned grinned and took the stairs two at a time.

Fraser shook his head. "That, I didn't need to hear. What is Shae doing here?"

"Photos, for the game. It's part of the social media package she was hired for," Iris said.

"Was that Ned?" Jonas appeared at the top of the stairs. "He's terrifying."

"You should see him kitted up," Hud said.

"I have. Hey, Fraser. So, how were the mountains?" Jonas came down and met his handshake.

"Zero stars, would not recommend."

Jonas gave him a grim nod. "Yeah, well, you won't like Port Fressa either." He walked over to the table where a map of the city lay rolled out.

He hadn't seen Sibba sitting there until then. The Slovenian wore her sleek brown hair back, studying the map. She looked up as he came over. "Hey, Fraser."

"What are you looking at?"

"Hiding places for nuclear waste. And locations Russians might want to bomb."

He stilled, looked at Jonas, then over to Trini, who sat on the sofa, working his phone. The SEAL team leader must have felt the silence, because he looked up over at Fraser. "What?"

"Who are you texting?"

"Logan Thorne." Trini said. . "He says that no one is going anywhere. So sit tight, because Logan and his team are on the way."

"Why?"

"Oh, because we tracked the missing caesium container here, and a dirty bomb is somewhere in this city."

EIGHT

S he should just go home.

Except, Imani wasn't sure where home was anymore.

Clearly, not Lauchtenland.

"If the internet is to be believed, I am singlehandedly responsible for the mess at the ball." Imani stood behind her mother at her desk in her office at Perrigwynn Palace, a beautiful room with a full sitting area, massive windows that overlooked the city with the clear blue sky and blue-green waters of Port Fressa Bay.

"It's just clickbait," her mother said as she closed the computer screen.

She stepped away and headed over to the sofa.

"All *Madeline & Hyacinth Live!* keeps talking about is the fiasco at the ball and how I ran away with Prince Xavier." She looked at her mother. "I didn't run away. X thought I was in danger—"

"But you did leave the castle and caused quite a ruckus for HMSD." Princess Gemma got up from her desk and came over to the opposite sofa.

A fresh vase of white poinsettias took up most of the glass coffee table surrounded by white leather sofas. A fire flickered in the marble hearth at one end of the room, and a white flocked tree held gold ornaments in the opposite corner. Along one wall, ancient books lined a built-in bookcase—probably put there by Prince John's previous wife, Princess Holland, who'd been killed early in their marriage.

By all accounts, and Imani remembered too, her stepfather had been wrecked by his wife's tragic death, although he'd managed to find his way back. But he had a country who loved him, whereas she was the pariah of Lauchtenland.

Imani picked up the daily *News Leader*. "Good thing they didn't find out about Creed." She dropped the paper on the table and sat down. "Who I haven't heard from since Xavier had him arrested. Arrested, Mom. For saving my life." Her eyes burned. "And Creed hasn't texted. Not once."

"Does he have a phone? Maybe the royal guard took it from him when they arrested him."

"I don't know. I don't know anything."

Her mother held up a hand, then got up and smoothed the elegant white dress she wore. Clearly she had a full social agenda today. "Prince John is seeing to the charges. I wouldn't be surprised if Creed and Fraser are already on their way home."

Now her throat tightened. But Imani nodded. Sighed.

"I know you're in love with him, honey. I'm so sorry—"

"No. It's okay. I was living in some sort of fairytale where I ended up with the hero."

"Prince Xavier seems like a hero." She raised an eyebrow, smiled.

"You and everyone else. Melissa Faris, the royal reporter on *The Morning Show*, had a ten minute monologue today about how I should marry Prince Xavier to preserve the line of succession. And Hamish Fickle was on *Tuppence Corbyn & Friends* again, preaching how he wants the queen to create a line of succession edict that, should Prince John die without a direct heir, the line of succession passes to Prince Gus. I thought he wanted to disband the monarchy. Isn't he with the RECO party?"

"Suddenly an interest in Lauchtenland politics?"

Only when people were trying to kill her.

But she didn't say that. Instead, she shook her head. "As if I would ever want to be queen."

Imani got up, walked over to the tray of coffee and biscotti. "X is great. It's just..." She lifted a shoulder. "He has everything. It means nothing for him to rescue me. But Creed...Creed risked everything, you know? And asked for nothing in return."

Silence, and after she poured herself a mug of coffee, she turned.

Her mother wore an expression she couldn't place. "That does sound like love to me," she said softly.

Imani nodded. "And now you're not helping at all."

"Sorry."

She sat down, set the mug of coffee and the biscotti on the glass coffee table. "When you first became a princess, did you...was it..."

"Overwhelming? Of course. But I believed it was God's plan for me. And I didn't need to have all the answers. Just today's steps."

Today's steps.

"But I do owe you an apology. When Prince John asked me to marry him, he promised that you'd spend your school years in Hearts Bend, at the farm."

"I did."

"Yes, but I know you weren't ready to say goodbye to that when you graduated. Which is why I agreed to your gap year, of course. But I thought when it was over, that you would be ready to move here, to start attending Haxton. But I can see now that maybe I dragged you into this life. It's not easy, and maybe it's not right for you, honey. And if not, then...you can always return to Hearts Bend and live with Memaw and Pops on the farm. Go to ETSU like you planned."

She didn't know why her mother's words tasted sour in her chest. "I...are you saying you don't want me around?"

A beat. "What?"

"I mean, I get it. The country thinks I'm usurping the crown, and I'm hardly what they'd think of when they think *princess*. I've spent the past year running, basically, and..." She looked at her mom, forced a smile. "Maybe you're right."

"Imani. No, I don't want you to leave. I just feel like you're miserable—"

"I'm miserable because I...because I feel like I've lost myself. And how selfish is that? An orphan becomes a princess. I am the fairytale, Mom. So what is my problem?"

"I know what your problem is."

The voice came from the doorway—a woman's voice, deep, commanding, and kind.

Imani stood up, as did her mother.

"Your Majesty," said her mother, and curtsied.

Imani did the same.

"Oh, pish-posh, you know you don't need to curtsy to me," she said, then turned to Pippa, who'd come in behind her, and nodded.

Pippa closed the door behind her as she left.

Imani started—she hadn't realized that Pippa was back.

But Queen Catherine—Grandmum, as she called herself to Imani—came into the room. Dressed in a light-pink dress, hosiery, wide-chunk heels, her dark brown hair perfectly coiffed, the slightest amount of makeup and lipstick...yes, this was royalty. Grandmum possessed herself—confident, charitable, wise. She didn't just enter a room, she graced it. Blessed it.

Imani could almost feel the sense of peace as she entered, as if everything might be put right.

No wonder they called the throne a divine appointment.

"I'm glad to see you're back safe from your travels, darling." Grandmum came over and pulled Imani into a hug.

Such a strange feeling to be embraced as a granddaughter to a woman she barely knew.

"I'm glad to be back."

The queen sat down, then patted the place beside her.

Imani sat.

"Are you?"

Imani frowned.

"Glad to be back?"

"Oh. I...I was just...I didn't mean—"

Grandmum put her hand over Imani's. "Shh. I understand more than you know." She sighed. "There are stories you will hear, if you live in the palace long enough, and one of them will be about my illegitimate daughter, Scottie."

She knew about Scottie—at least, knew that Scottie lived in Hearts Bend and was Prince John's older half-sister. But she said nothing.

"I fell in love with her father, Trent, back at university. I was young, had never been in love, and Trent was American and dashing and everything I wanted. I was the crown princess, but I foolishly thought that I wouldn't have to choose. Unfortunately, I did, and Trent and Scottie lived a life separate from me, in Hearts Bend. I married Edric, took the throne, and ruled Lauchtenland as I was intended to do."

"But didn't your heart break?"

"Of course. For over fifty-seven years. And then the Lord brought Scottie back into my life—okay, with a nudge from me, but we are healing." She squeezed Imani's hand. "It's terrible to live with your heart in pieces, in two places, isn't it?"

Maybe she did understand. Imani nodded.

"But I did what I thought was best. For Scottie, even if not for my heart. I knew she'd be ridiculed. Divided between nations. And maybe even in danger. But in His grace, God watched over both of us, despite the wounds."

She blinked, looked out the window, and in that moment, a cascade of years, even pain, perhaps, echoed in her countenance. Then she sighed and turned back to Imani. "Life, no matter what you choose, is not easy, darling. I grieved for my daughter. But I couldn't live with my feet in two places. I had to let Scottie go to embrace my life here. And yes, it was painful, but what I discovered in my grieving was that I had no one to lean on but Jesus. And that made all the difference.

"See, we often think that the deep well of our souls will somehow provide the strength we need to soldier on." She met Imani's eyes, hers a deep blue. "But the strength, even the joy, cannot be found within the well of our soul but by reaching up, to heaven. So, while the devil wanted to tell me that my life would never be whole again, God brought me out of the darkness, set me on solid ground, steadied me as I walked, and gave me a new song to sing. And through the grieving of my heart, my soul was strengthened. And now, sixty years later, I see what He has done and am amazed."

She squeezed Imani's hand.

"I know your past, Imani. And while you see brokenness, I see God preparing Lauchtenland for a princess who understands compassion, who embraces not just adventure but those who might feel like outcasts. I see a woman who God created to become more than she could on her own. You were swept up along with Gemma into this life. But it is time for you to find your footing as princess. For you to walk in the calling of the crown. To become an ambassador for the kingdom."

Imani's mouth opened, then she swallowed, glanced at her mother.

She gave her a thin smile, a wide-eyed shrug.

"If you're ready, I'd like you to have an investiture."

"What is that?"

"It's a ceremony, darling. Led by me, or Prince John, where you take the oath of Lauchtenland and are conferred with your official title as well as the formal duties of the office. For you, it would be Duchess of Dalholm. It's an official royal title, as opposed to an honorary title as you have now. Of course, you'd also still be a princess of Lauchtenland, but you would have royal duties and, of course, a royal line."

She patted Imani's hand. "But to do this, you'd have to take the oath of citizenship first."

"Become a citizen of Lauchtenland?"

"Officially, yes."

"Would I lose my American citizenship?"

"No. You could have dual citizenship. But to be the duchess, you would have to agree to keep your foot in Lauchtenland as your permanent home."

Permanent. But *home*. Oh.

"It's your decision, darling. But I do believe it might help solve not only some of the current unrest in Lauchtenland, but more importantly, the questions in your heart. You cannot live with one eye looking back into the life you long for. You will turn into a pillar of salt."

A pillar of salt?

"You must live in the life you've been called to. But only you and God will know what world that is." Grandmum stood up. "The other option, of course, is that you could decide to walk away from this world. We can remove your styling, and you can go back to being Imani Stone of Hearts Bend. American girl." She smiled. "And that is just fine as well. Gemma, will you walk me back to my office? I'd like a word."

"Yes, Mum." She got up and came around the table, glancing at Imani, eyebrows up.

Imani offered a thin smile.

The queen slipped her hand into Gemma's crooked arm and they left, Pippa again appearing at the door.

This time she closed it behind them, staying in the room. "Your Royal Highness, I have a note for you."

"From Creed?"

Pippa looked better today—but then again, she'd had thirty-six hours away from the palace. She wore makeup, probably to cover the terrible bruises on her face, but she seemed refreshed, as much in soul as in body. "Sorry, ma'am. I believe it is from Prince Xavier."

She reached out for the envelope. Her name was written in script on the front – *Her Royal Highness Princess Imani.* The back bore the stamp of the House of Keswick. "Very official."

"Indeed. By the way, I do have it on good authority that Creed is okay and out of HMSD's custody."

"Is he back in America?"

Pippa made a face. "Not...quite. But I believe that will all be sorted soon."

Imani studied her, but Pippa just folded her hands in front of her, her face solemn.

Hmm. She opened the envelope and pulled out a card. "It's an invitation to sit with Prince Xavier at tomorrow's football game."

Pippa swallowed.

"What?"

"I would feel better if you were in the royal box, behind the bulletproof glass."

Of course she would. Imani stared at the card. "You know if I accept, then we're practically engaged."

"Maybe not officially, but...I'm afraid you would be making a statement."

"Yes."

You cannot live with one eye looking back into the life you long for...You must live in the life you've been called to.

And maybe that included listening to her bodyguard. "Okay. How about if I invite him to join us in the royal box?"

Pippa smiled. Imani nodded, despite the pinch in her chest.

Tried not to think of Creed, on his way back to America.

"I'll pen him a note to send back. Make it official."

"Very good, ma'am."

She sighed. If Lauchtenland wanted an official princess, then maybe she'd give them an official prince as well.

JUST PERFECT. CREED WAS BACK TO BEING THE GUY ON the sofa.

He sat, his leg on a pillow, an ice pack on his thigh, the television on, listening to conversation drift down the stairs of the mansion.

And it didn't help at all that last night he'd woken again in a cold sweat, the dream—not a premonition—drilling him awake.

The darkness was back in his head, and he just couldn't shake it. But frankly, the very last thing he was going to do was share his little nightmare with his brothers, or their friends who were actually trying to *save the world.*

He'd spent not a little time over the past two days listening to the conversation about the missing caesium, the nuclear waste that would be the payload of any dirty bomb.

The team had pieces—like the blueprint of the Lauchtenland stadium that Iris had found. And the bomb that had detonated in Imani's train on the way to Dalholm. And according to the SEAL team leader, a big, dark-skinned man named Trini, they'd tracked the case via a tip from a man undercover in Russia, who worked loosely for the Caleb Group.

From what Creed could pick up, the Caleb Group was a sort of super-secret gray-ops group run by a guy named Logan Thorne, one of Fraser's spec-ops former-SEAL buddies who'd arrived yesterday along with a man named York. As in York who was married to yet another of the Marshall cousins, Ruby Jane.

Hard to keep them all straight, really.

Ford and York seemed to know each other well. Creed saw them catching up at the end of the table last night, eating pizza, laughing. York seemed guarded, his smile a little harder won. And Ford was an older version of Ned—tough, serious, and dedicated.

And not at all a weakling.

So, the house was abuzz with war stories and heroes while Creed succumbed to the pain, managed to clean out the meager supply of pain killers in the medicine chest, and kept his leg elevated.

A regular warrior.

Most of the guys had left earlier today, leaving Creed alone with Logan and York and Iris, who had spent most of the past two days at the stadium, getting ready for the big game. Hudson, too, spent his time with his team, the Vienna Vikings, although he wasn't playing, just coaching.

Creed had heard him talking about plans to retire after this season.

Interesting.

York and Logan had set up whatever they were into on the upper floor, off the kitchen area. Apparently no one—not Fraser nor his brothers, not the SEALs, not the Caleb Group, and especially not the Lauchtenland media—seemed to care about the two Americans who'd escaped custody. Instead, the media couldn't stop running the news about the upcoming charity football game and the fact that Princess Imani and Prince Xavier were sharing a box.

What. Ever.

Creed switched channels and found a soccer game, but really, what he wanted was to figure out how to get out of his own head.

He got up and walked to the door. Outside, the sky arched blue, but the air contained a crisp fall bite. Maybe that's what he needed.

He stepped outside onto the patio and then hobbled over to a chair. Gripped the back. Did a couple squats.

His leg burned, but at least he could move.

"Keep working it. Eventually it'll get better."

He looked over.

York closed the door behind him. The man wore a baseball hat over his dark-blond hair, a pair of aviator shades, black jacket, jeans, and boots. "I've been shot, more than once, and you have to fight through the pain. But you'll be back."

"I used to be a runner. I don't think track is in my future again." He did another squat, and a sound emitted deep inside. He blew out a breath. "I can hardly walk."

York came to stand beside him. He looked over at him. "Your brother told me what you did."

"Which brother?"

His mouth lifted up one side. "Fraser. Your story reminds me a little of how I met your cousin RJ. She was a fugitive in Russia."

So, he didn't mind terribly being compared to York. Except he wasn't a superhero or anything. "Yeah, well, you didn't end up arrested, a fugitive—"

"You don't know my story."

Oh.

"I was...let's say lost and confused, and wasn't sure what I was supposed to do next."

"I hate being dead weight."

"Spoken like a true Marshall."

Creed looked away. "I wish I knew what to do."

"Life is not a straight line, and it is certainly not a clear path. It's...messy. And confusing, and often the point of it is to show us that we're not supposed to have the answers. God doesn't just show up to clean up the mess—He's designed the mess to make us lean on Him. So He can reveal Himself through it. It wasn't until I was at the end of myself that He said, 'Stop trying too hard, York. Watch what I will do.'"

He stood, staring out at the sky, his hands in his coat pockets. "You need to get out of your own way, Creed. Let God have the helm, and you'll stop wondering if you're useful and you'll start *being* useful." He put a hand on Creed's shoulder. "Logan and I are going to talk to Gunner Ferguson."

Creed looked at him. "What?"

"He's a friend. Don't worry—your secret is safe with us. But Fraser said that you were on the call with Imani when the porter left the bomb in the train. Is there anything you remember about him that might help us?"

"I told Pippa everything. I didn't get a good look at him. He had dark hair, I think. And a scar on his neck. Like someone had knifed him, or wanted to." He put his hand under his chin, at the apex of his neck. "Sorry, that's all I know."

"Okay. Thanks." York clapped him on the shoulder and headed back inside.

Creed stared out at the choppy, dark sea, a few boats on the horizon. *God doesn't just show up to clean up the mess—He's designed the mess to make us lean on Him. So He can reveal Himself through it.*

For some reason his mother tiptoed into his head, her words right before he'd left Minnesota. *Don't you know that all heroes are just reflections of Christ?*

Maybe York was right. Maybe he was in his own way. Maybe it was time to stop trying to be in charge.

"There you are, bro." Iris had opened the door. "I'm heading over to the stadium to pick up some gear I left there. I need to wash it before tomorrow's game. Want to tag along?"

He looked at her. She handed him a baseball cap. "No one will suspect you there. I just thought you'd like to see it, since you can't go to the game tomorrow."

Right. But why not?

He pulled on the cap, then the hood on his sweatshirt, donned a jean jacket Jonas had loaned him and, leaning on his sister's shoulder, headed outside to her rental Jeep.

"The Vikings are done practicing, and Hud is spending the night at the hotel with the team, so the place will probably be empty." They drove along the seashore, then toward the city. "But it's pretty impressive right now, with the massive team flags hanging on each side, not to mention all the royal standards along the top of the stadium."

"Is it open air?"

"Oh yeah. Used as a futbol pitch for most of the year. Some polo matches, rugby, and cricket. It's the national stadium. But they have real grass, so that's cool. It smells amazing. It looks like the old Wembley Stadium in England, with columns and twin towers at the entrance. But inside, they're completely up to date, with a jumbotron and an amazing sound system. The game is going to be off the hook."

He glanced at her. He didn't know Iris well, but she was a Marshall to the bone—tough, dedicated, and fearless in her job as a football referee.

She turned off the highway and wove her way through busy streets toward the stadium, situated in the center of the city, behind one of the gothic churches. Two white towers rose from a platform in front of the entrance, which bore an immense neon banner announcing the game. On top of the cupolas, massive royal standards flapped in the wind. Arched entrances surrounded the oval building.

They drove around the parking lot to the back entrance, and she showed her pass, then parked in a gated section.

"C'mon, I'll show you around."

Lights cast puddles around the parking lot that led to the players' entrance, and they walked past a huge garage with grass grooming trackers and stripe painting machines.

"Hey, what's that?" He had ahold of her shoulder and now slowed.

She stopped and he pointed to what looked like a hot air balloon. "Looks like the Goodyear blimp."

"Yeah." It sat in the shadows, near the entrance of a closed door. "I always thought they were bigger." This one seemed about the size of a bus, however, so that felt big. A blue swash emblazoned the side with the words. *The House of Blue* written in gold.

Interesting.

They kept walking. "Looks a lot like the dirigible Jonas designed for his weather balloons."

"Really?"

"Yeah. He was home for a while before he went to Slovenia, working on his design in the garage. Oh, you can tell this is where the players hang out." He put a hand to his nose.

They'd entered the hallway to the locker room.

"In fall track we had to use the same locker room as the football guys, and it wasn't fun. They left their stuff everywhere, socks and pads and— "

"Oh, believe me, I know." She pushed into a room. "This is the refs' locker room. As you can see, there are vents." She pointed to one of the square vents by the door, then headed to her locker. She spun the lock, then pulled out a hanging bag, probably her ref's uniform inside. She held on to the hanger with two fingers and hung it over her shoulder.

"This is quite the place." He was looking at the whiteboards, names and plays written on them. Another door led to an inner office.

"That's where our lead ref has all our pregame meetings." She flicked on the light. "Just a boring office, metal desk. But you get called in here alone, you know you're in trouble." She flicked off the light. "That door leads to the training room, with the cold plunges and tables and lots of half-naked guys in pain. Want to see the field?"

"Yeah."

He was passing by the darkened training room, its door hanging open, when he spotted the crutch. Maybe he'd just borrow it for their looksee. He grabbed it.

"You look like you're walking better than the last time I saw you."

He leaned on the crutch, but yeah, it felt a little easier to walk. Maybe he would get there.

They came out of the tunnel and the field opened up, and he just stood there.

"Holy cow."

"I know, right? The smell."

It did smell like summertime, with freshly cut grass, despite the chill in the air. He stepped out on the sidelines and cupped his hand over his eyes.

"How many seats?"

"About a hundred and thirty thousand."

175

"That's a lot."

"And according to Hud, they're all sold out."

He scanned the seats all the way to the upper decks. A half roof covered most of the sides, open at one end where the jumbotron rose above the seats. A royal box with fortified glass jutted out over the field at the fifty-yard line.

From where he stood, he spotted the twin towers rising above the stadium. A balustrade encircled the cupola at the base, a walkway with a door. Maybe for security.

A glint caught his eye, the sunset catching something, and he winced, looked away.

"You okay?"

"Yeah." He looked at the cupola but didn't see anything. "Can we get up there?"

"The cupolas? I don't know. Maybe. Let's go see."

They entered the hallway again, then climbed up stairs and headed through the eerie empty interior walkways, past closed concession stands and arched entrances to the arena, past banners advertising Lauchtenland's futbol team, their cricket club, and a rugby team. And Andrea Bocelli was apparently having a New Year's concert here.

They reached the entrance where the towers stood, down at the lower level. Stairs with a railing in the middle led to the bottom alongside a stopped escalator.

She started down, but he went to the center banister, tested it, then hopped on, his arms out.

He rode it to the middle, then jumped off, landing on one leg.

"What are you doing?"

"It's a parkour move I saw on YouTube. This is a perfect banister."

"Oh my, you are such a Marshall."

He grinned at her. Yep.

This time when he hopped on, he slid down, balanced perfectly, and landed right. "Bam. That's how it's done."

"No more YouTube for you." She stopped in front of an

elevator. "Let's see where this leads," Iris said and pushed the button.

The lift hummed to life, and in a moment, the doors opened.

"I guess it's not off-limits."

"So far," Creed said and got on. She followed and pushed the button to the top floor. Folded her arms. "So, how is Mom?"

He frowned. "Fine, I think."

"No more episodes?"

"Like fainting in the kitchen? No. I think she was just tired."

Iris's mouth made a thin line, but she nodded. The elevator pinged at the second floor, kept going. She stared at the numbers. "It's good you're there. I know you don't want to go home, but having you around always seemed to make her smile. After we left, she was sort of...well, let's just say she had plenty of good mom left in her. You brought her a lot of joy, and for that, we're all grateful."

He had nothing at that.

She looked at him as they passed the third floor. "I know we can be sort of overwhelming as a family, Creed. And I know that taking Imani in sort of...well, it made you feel important."

He looked down at his shoes.

"And you were—but you already were, before that. Because... well, because you're a Marshall, our Marshall."

They rose past the fourth floor.

He took a breath, hating the heat in his throat. "I was kicked out of a foster home before I came to live with...you guys. I ran away, trying to find my little brother. I never did, but..." He looked at her. "I keep having this dream that Imani is about to be killed and I can't get to her. It's a nightmare. And it's not because I want to feel important but...I don't know. I can't shake it."

"But because you're that guy."

"What guy?"

"The guy who keeps promises—hey, did we stop moving?"

He stepped away from the railing. "We did." The Four light was still lit. He pushed the Door Open button.

Nothing.

She tried too.

Nothing.

She banged on the door. "Hey! Anyone out there?"

He pushed the Emergency Call button and the emergency buzzer began to ring.

She put her hands over her ears, made a face.

After a moment, he turned it off. "Let's try the door." He put his fingers into one door, she did the other.

Nothing moved.

And then, just like that, the lights winked out.

"Iris?"

"Yeah, Creed?"

"I think I'm done with the tour now. I don't need to stay for the game. I'm good."

"You're hilarious. I see you've got the terrible Marshall boy humor too." Iris pulled out her cell phone, her face illuminated by the screen. "No bars." But she turned on the flashlight and aimed it at the ceiling. It illuminated the entire box.

"We're in an ancient marble tower." He sighed and slid to the floor. Shook his head. Looked up.

And then, he just started to laugh.

"What's so funny?"

He smiled. "Gimme your dirty laundry. I'm going to get us out of here."

"No joy." The words issued from Fraser as he walked into the beach house, dropping the keys to the extended Range Rover onto the counter. Behind him, his cousin Ford did the same for the second vehicle, then began to peel off his body armor.

York and Logan sat at the long kitchen table on the upper

floor, computers in front of them. The smell of chili on the stove had Fraser heading into the kitchen for a bowl. "Who made this?"

"I did," Jonas said, coming out of his bedroom. "No caesium?"

"No," said Trini, coming in behind Fraser. "But it was definitely at the warehouse. We got readings on the Geiger counter that match what we picked up in Slovenia." He glanced at Logan. "Sorry. Any further email exchange from the courier?"

"No," Logan said, and closed his computer. "Coco said that the communication has gone dead."

"Probably got spooked after we landed on their doorstep."

Logan folded his arms. "Yeah. We're just one step behind." The sharp edges of his face betrayed the weight of his responsibility as head of the Caleb Group. "We met with Gunner today and briefed him. He's got his people checking passport control for anyone suspect."

"With the tourists here for the game tomorrow, that's no easy task." Roy had come into the room.

"When did you get here?" Fraser exchanged a look with him. He'd met the guy while trying to extract Shae from a Russian prison ship with Ned a few weeks ago. Roy, a former SEAL, was a sort of ghost, especially after he'd gone missing years ago with Logan after an op gone bad. He'd joined the CIA, and as fate would have it, began working again with Logan.

"I've always been here." Roy headed to the kitchen. "Haven't heard from our man on the inside, either."

"You have a man on the inside—of what?"

"The Petrov Bratva. He's been there a few years, laying low, listening. Feeding us information. Went dark about a year ago but resurfaced recently and gave us the intel about the caesium." Roy pulled down a bowl, then went to the pot. "Independent contractor, but reliable."

"I'm going to call Tessa," Logan said. "Then the president." He got up, grabbed his laptop, and headed into another bedroom. Shut the door.

Right. Just a casual chat with the president.

The rest of the SEALs had headed downstairs. Fraser pulled out a chair, leaned over his bowl. Worked his hand.

He had full feeling and could at least hold a gun now, but he was far from fully operational. York evidently saw the movement. "That from your excitement in Nigeria?"

He nodded. "How'd you know about that?"

"Logan. Who heard it from Ham, I'd guess. Small world."

"Getting smaller, it seems."

"You know that Abu Massif, the leader of the terrorist group who took you, was killed last summer. Boat accident."

"Yeah, I know. You behind that?"

"Could be."

Fraser nodded. Funny he didn't have bigger feelings about that.

Maybe because, despite everything, he hadn't been able to get Pippa out of his brain. Maybe if he'd actually been on the breach team at the warehouse, but no, he'd been designated driver. Sit in the cab and wait.

Which had given him plenty of time to remember the way she'd leaped into his arms. Kissed him. Lit a fire inside him that he couldn't seem to douse.

"You going back to Jones, Inc. when this is over?" York had closed his laptop, picked up a cup of coffee.

"Never left. Just on hold." But the question had been burning inside, too, for a while now.

What do you want, Pippa?

Maybe not fair to ask her that since he didn't know what *he* wanted either. Or maybe he did, just didn't want to admit it.

A fresh start. A life away from the darkness. He sighed and picked up his spoon.

"Yeah, I know what that feels like."

Fraser stopped midbite. "What feels like?"

"Feeling trapped in a life that you're not sure you want anymore."

Fraser blinked at him.

"Don't get me wrong—I like what I do. But I spent plenty of time wanting to walk away from everything. And maybe I did, for the most part. RJ and I are happy, expecting a baby, adopting a little girl. They're the reason I work for the Caleb Group. So that no one sneaks a dirty bomb into our country and destroys everything I love."

Fraser swallowed his bite, washed it down with a soda. "I miss being the tip of the spear, for sure. But..." He looked at his hand, flexing it again.

"You need to forgive yourself."

He looked at York. "What?"

"For getting caught. And for getting hurt. And even for not wanting to go back."

Fraser just looked at him. "I...I'm not angry at myself. It wasn't my fault."

York just took a sip of coffee.

"I mean, yeah, I go back and replay...okay, maybe I'm a little angry, but...Fine. Yes. I'm very angry that I messed up. And people died. And my hand got screwed up. But what am I going to do about it? I can't go back and fix it."

York set down the coffee. "Nope. But you can stop punishing yourself."

Fraser leaned back.

"Forgiveness is giving up the right to hurt someone for what they did to you." He leaned forward. "It's actually easier to do that for someone not yourself. Because we think we have the right—even the responsibility—to punish ourselves for our sins."

Fraser opened his mouth. Closed it.

"I don't know what you've heard about me and my past, but I didn't think forgiveness was possible for a guy like me. So God wiped my memory for a while and showed me exactly what it felt like to be forgiven. And it was...life changing. If God isn't going to punish me, what right do I have to punish myself? Even if I think I deserve it." He put down his coffee. "Grace says you get a fresh start. A new life. You don't have to pay for your sins."

Fraser stared at him. York met his gaze.

"Forgiveness takes courage. And forgiving yourself just might be your greatest mission yet." He got up. "I gotta call RJ."

Fraser nodded.

The house had quieted, settled, the guys probably heading to bed. Jonas had returned to his room. Creed was probably parked on the sofa.

A new life. But he owed God so much. He didn't deserve to walk away.

The thought caught him up.

What right do I have to punish myself? Even if I think I deserve it.

His breath caught. He got up, his chest tightening. And for some reason, words from Jonas, spoken while he'd been racing to find Creed and Imani in Europe, filled his mind.

Maybe this time-out God has given you is His way of showing you that you need Him more than you need a grand purpose.

He did, and he'd learned that. But maybe that wasn't a one-time lesson.

He closed his eyes. *Lord, I do need You. And I want to forgive myself, just as You've forgiven me. Help me to embrace grace. A fresh start, whatever that is.*

His phone buzzed in his pocket, and he opened his eyes to the empty kitchen and pulled it out.

Hudson.

HUD

Haven't heard from Iris. Is she back from the stadium?

Fraser stared at the message, then got up and walked down the hall to her door. Knocked.

No answer. Again.

This time at no answer he eased it open. "Iris?"

Darkness filled the room, wan light pressing in from the windows. "You here?"

He didn't want to turn on the light in case she might be sleeping for the big game tomorrow, so he turned on his phone light and flashed it toward the bed.

Two beds, twins—and that's right, she was sharing with Sibba. But both were made, no bodies in it. He flicked on the lights and went inside. "Iris?"

No adjoining bathroom, just the bedroom, and clearly empty unless she was hiding in the closet. Just to be sure...

Nope.

He knocked on Jonas's door. The light still pooled under it.

Jonas opened it. Sibba sat at a table looking at her computer. His was also open. "'Sup?"

"Have you seen Iris?"

"Not since she left for the stadium." He glanced at her door. Looked at his watch. "That was four hours ago. Did you text her?"

"No, but Hud did. No answer."

A beat.

"She took Creed with her. Maybe they ran into trouble."

"Creed?"

"I saw them leave," Sibba said. "He was wearing his hat and a hoodie. Definitely on the DL. But maybe stadium security saw him."

"Gunner has a BOLO out for him." Logan, now coming down the hallway. "Sorry, I heard your conversation. I talked with Gunner today—they are definitely on the watch, but with all the focus on tomorrow's game, I'm not sure how many resources he's allocated to the hunt."

Fraser stilled. "He doesn't know that we're still here, right?"

"Not from me or York."

Roy had also come upstairs. "What's going on?"

"Iris and Creed are missing," Jonas said.

"Let's see if we can get Coco to ping her cell," said Logan.

"Even if it's not on, she might be able to get a GPS signal." He pulled out his phone to send a text.

"I'm going to the stadium," said Fraser.

"Dude. You're *on* the BOLO." Logan looked up. "You should lay low and let us go."

"You do know I can't do that, right?"

Logan's mouth made a grim line.

"I'll go with you," Roy said. He picked up the keys from the table.

"Me too." Jonas went into his room and grabbed his jacket.

They headed out to the Range Rover. Fraser got in and texted Hud.

FRASER

Not yet. Will text when she returns.

Not a lie, just a creative answer. But the guy didn't need to worry—yet. He pocketed the phone and sat in the darkness, his jaw tight as they headed toward Port Fressa.

Hud replied.

HUD

I'll meet you at the stadium.

Oh goody. He liked Hud, but the man didn't have a stealthy bone in him.

"Maybe they went out for pizza," Jonas said.

Fraser glanced at him over his shoulder.

Jonas nodded and looked out the window.

Lights lit up the parking lot of the stadium. "Go around back to the players' entrance. We'll meet Hud there. Maybe he can get us in."

They pulled up and waited, the lights pooling around them until a little Panda Fiat Uber pulled up. How Hud fit into that car, Fraser hadn't a clue. But he pried his massive body out of the front seat and walked over to the Range Rover. "Let me drive. I'll get us in."

Roy got out and Hud took the driver's seat, then flashed his pass at the security guard. "Just checking on some gear."

The man flashed the lights into the car.

"Players. We promise not to cause trouble."

"It's after midnight, sir," said the guard.

"Can't sleep before a big game." Hud stared at him, flashed a blinding grin.

This would never work—

The gate opened, and Hudson pulled in, then parked beside what looked like Iris's rental car.

They got out and Hudson scanned his pass at the door. It unlocked and they entered the building.

"This is definitely a football locker room."

"Iris came to get her uniform. She wanted to wash some gear before the game." He walked down the hall toward a smaller locker room, opened the door, and flicked on the light. Empty.

"Weird."

Logan's phone buzzed. "Coco said that she got a ping from Iris's phone. It's on, even if she can't send a text or call."

"Where?"

"She dropped a pin." He opened it. "It looks like...here. Except maybe west a little, but still inside." He pointed, and they followed his lead down the hallway, up stairs, and then around the building, their steps echoing on the cement floor.

They came to the entrance of the stadium, under the shadow of twin towers. "She's not here," Hud said.

"Her phone is," Logan said and looked around.

Fraser also scanned the area. Empty concession stands, a couple bathrooms. "Hud, check the bathroom."

"The ladies' bathroom?"

He looked at him. Hud held up his hands. "Fine." He headed into the dark bathroom.

"What about the elevator?" said Jonas. He pointed to the lift.

Hud returned. "Empty."

Jonas had pushed the button on the elevator. It remained

dark. "The power's off."

"In the entire place or just the elevator?" Logan said.

"The exit signs are lit, so maybe just the elevator?" Fraser walked over to the door. Banged on it. "Iris?" He flashed his phone light between the doors, but couldn't see in. "Maybe it's stuck."

"Let's go upstairs," Jonas said, and headed up the flight. Fraser caught up in a moment, and there, too, the doors were stuck. But when he put his ear to the lift, he thought he heard banging.

"I think she's in there."

Hud looked at him, then turned and sprinted up another flight.

They found him on the third floor, fighting the closed doors.

"We need to turn the power back on," said Jonas. "The doors are closed mechanically—they'll only open with power. Or, of course, if someone pulls up on the lever that closes them."

Fraser looked at him. "How do you know that?"

"I don't know—I watched a documentary one night with Creed about perilous rescues. One was an elevator stuck fifty stories up during a fire. The fire department had turned off the power, so they had to manually open the door. It was cool. Creed watched all sort of crazy stuff when I was there."

"I know," Fraser said. Then he headed up another set of stairs.

The doors here were closed too, but even as he put his ear to the door, he heard voices.

Muffled, but definitely people inside.

Hud had joined him. "Let's get that door opened."

"It won't—" Jonas started when the door jerked and a gap appeared, only to close after a second.

A shout emerged from inside.

"Creed!" Fraser banged on the door. "You in there?"

A beat, then, "Fraser?"

"Yeah, we're out here!"

"Can you turn on the power?"

"How?"

A second, then, "I'm going to try and flip the lever again—grab the door and don't let it close!"

What? But he looked at Hud and got his hand into the door crack.

"Let me do that," Jonas said and pushed in. Got his fingers in the door. Hud had the other side.

Fraser stepped back, biting back a word. But shoot, he was right. Good way to get injured, again.

"Now!"

The door jerked again, a hiccup where it burped open. Hud and Jonas pulled, and then, just like that, it released and rolled open.

Iris stood in front of the door, having pulled it from the other side. Creed stood, his knee braced on the railing inside the lift, his other foot wedged into the electrical panel, now open, holding the wooden dowel of— "Is that a hanger?"

"Yeah." He lowered himself down. Grunted. Then he pulled the dowel out of a hole at the top of the elevator box. A wire came out with it. "We've been trying to get the door open for the better part of two hours. I knew if I could wedge in something to lift the mechanical arm that held the door, I could get it to pop open, but just when I'd get it up, the wire would slip and the stupid doors would close again."

Iris was in Hud's arms. Jonas turned to Creed. "Brilliant." He fist-bumped Creed.

"Yeah, well, we would still be in there if you hadn't come along. Iris couldn't hold it open. We needed four hands plus mine and...anyway, I'm starved."

He was so nonplussed, it reminded Fraser of the stories his parents told of when they'd found Creed and his track team after a tornado took out a neighboring town. They'd been trapped for nearly a week afterward...and Creed had helped keep them alive.

The guy had operator written all over him. That or team leader.

And it hit him that he sort of wanted to be the guy to help Creed succeed.

Huh. "YouTube?"

"Yep."

He lifted his fist. "Smart."

"Thanks." Creed bumped it.

"What are you guys doing over here, anyway?" Logan said.

"Creed wanted to see the tower," Iris said.

"Actually, I thought I saw something, but I think it must have been just the sun. I think all your conversations about terrorists were in my head. Especially after seeing the dirigible."

Fraser stared at him.

"What dirigible," Jonas said.

"We saw a Goodyear blimp in the garage on our way in," said Iris. "Creed said it reminded him of your design."

"It had a big blue swash on it with *The House of Blue* written on one side. Must be for the game. Maybe for an aerial shot?"

Jonas looked at Logan, back to Creed. "Where was it?"

"The garage," Iris said. She held Hud's hand. "I'll show you."

But when they arrived at the garage, the doors were closed.

"Hud, get the security guard," Logan said. "But you two better make yourselves scarce." He pointed at Fraser and Creed.

Right. They got into the Range Rover and watched as Hudson fetched the security guard, fed him a story, and then got him to open the garage.

But his stomach turned into a fist, his chest tight, when the team emerged, something stricken on Jonas's face, a grim look on Logan's.

They got into the car.

"So I guess that means it's gone?" Fraser said.

"Let's not jump to conclusions," Jonas said quietly.

Then Logan hit the steering wheel and let out a word.

So that was a yes to panic.

Fraser looked out the window. "I think it's time to tell Gunner that we're still in town."

NINE

Despite her smile, Imani was nervous. Pippa saw it in the way she fidgeted with the tassels on her leather gloves, the way she looked at Prince Xavier.

She was trying, Pippa had to give her that.

The royals had all turned out for the game, Gemma and Imani bringing American style to the event with a couple of sleek blue hoodies, a puffer vest and leather jackets, and black jeans over tennis shoes. Xavier looked like he might be attending a polo match, in pressed dress pants, a pullover sweater, and a puffer jacket.

Prince John even got into the mood with an open-neck sweater, a pair of dress pants, and a black wool jacket. He also wore a blue scarf with the House of Blue crest.

So, not anything like the football game attire she'd seen at the Marshall family home, but it was a good try. A shot and a miss, but still a shot.

Princess Imani stood in front of Prince Xavier, smiling even as he put his hand on her shoulder.

Or maybe she wasn't acting. Maybe she simply was accepting the next chapter of her life.

Still, it brushed all the hairs the wrong way on Pippa. Something about him...

Aw, she was just biased toward a certain hero that deserved to be here with his princess.

The paparazzi finished shooting, and the family gave a final wave before heading to their box. She hustled beside Imani, a few steps back, her gaze on everything—the crowd, the security ahead, and around, the roar of the crowd filling the stadium. Thirty minutes to kickoff and the place buzzed with fervor. Not a few tourists from over the pond had arrived. They stood at the ropes cordoning off the royal entrance, dressed in garish purple and yellow, a couple with face paint, one wearing a helmet with horns.

Ah. Vikings, right.

In fact, the Vienna Vikings had been patterned off the Minnesota Vikings, in part, with similar uniforms, colors, and horns on their helmets. They'd wear purple on the field, with the Vikings from Minnesota in winter whites.

Iris would already be on the field, as one of the seven-person referee team, and Hud apparently would stay on the sidelines, officially a player, but now in a coaching role.

They'd seemed happy, those two, when she'd talked with them at the house so many days ago. And now her mind went to Fraser and the way he'd held her, the way he'd kissed her, the fact that she had broken the law to keep him in country.

And didn't care.

That part had her a little worried, maybe, but she was right to keep him here. Especially with so many pieces still unsolved.

And now they were entering the box and, oops, she hadn't been paying attention for nearly three minutes.

No more thinking about Fraser. Not until after the game, and the princess was safely tucked back in the castle.

Then she'd call him and maybe figure out...

Oh, she wanted a tomorrow with him. But he was a fugitive and—

"Pippa, I see Iris," Imani said, and again, Pippa jerked herself back to now. Stepped up to the glass and looked down to where Iris stood on the sidelines, her ponytail extending from her black official's hat. She wore the black-and-white striped zebra uniform.

"Get something to eat," Imani said. "I think they're serving nachos!"

Pippa frowned at her. Shook her head.

Imani made a face. "Someone has to eat. I'm starved, but Mom says I can't eat until after the game."

"Do you want the front page to be a picture of you eating a hotdog?" Princess Gemma asked. Prince John and Princess Gemma sat in the middle seats. But she smiled, and in fact, seemed in good spirits today.

Maybe because she missed America as much as the princess did, and today, a little of that had arrived in Lauchtenland. And really, they *were* safe. Gunner and his team had constructed a ten-inch bulletproof glass case around the box, which extended into the stadium twenty feet to accommodate five rows of seats and a reception area. The entire box connected to a private, secure area for the royals, with thick reinforced doors and an exclusive elevator that exited down to the main floor and out a secured back tunnel.

"Hudson isn't out yet—the team went back into the locker room. I think they'll burst through that arch." She pointed to a papered arch, the Vienna Vikings logo and name, along with a few key players, imprinted on the massive entry.

Of course, Hudson's form stood in the middle of the pack, dressed like a modern-day gladiator, with his short blond hair and intense blue eyes.

He'd make a good personal security agent.

So maybe she could breathe a little, let herself wonder—

"And look at that. Is that the Goodyear blimp?"

Imani pointed to the sky, and in the distance, over the sea, floated a large dirigible.

Pippa just stared at it.

"I didn't know you were bringing over a blimp, Xavier," Prince John said. "Good show."

"Actually, I had it repainted for the game," Xavier said. "It has the updated House of Blue logo on the side."

"Really." Prince John seemed impressed, glancing over at Xavier.

Wait. What was she missing? She stepped back and spoke into her microphone. "Sir, what does Prince Xavier have to do with the football game?"

Gunner had personally decided to helm today's security, and now his voice came through her earwig.

"Prince Xavier is head of the charity arm of the game. He's organizing the charity gala in Minnesota that will happen in a couple weeks."

"So, he organized this event?"

"His team worked with both the NFL and the ELF to put this together."

"So he's in charge?"

"Overall, yes."

"Thank you." She stepped back and melded into the wall when the door opened and in walked the prime minister, Hamish Fickle.

A younger man, mid-forties, elected out of the Midlands, Fickle had stirred up trouble with his RECO party and the Writ of Succession. But today, apparently, it was all smiles and polite faces for the good of the children, because Prince John rose and greeted him. Hamish bowed to the royals, then took his seat beside Prince John. His complement of security lined up opposite Pippa.

She couldn't get her gaze off the dirigible, the way it niggled at her.

And then... "Sir, did you know there is a dirigible heading over the stadium?"

A beat of silence, then, "Repeat that, Butler?"

"A dirigible, sir. The Goodyear blimp. Except it's painted blue. Prince Xavier commissioned it."

"The stadium is a no-fly zone," said Gunner.

"I thought so."

"Very good, Pippa. We'll get back to you."

Imani turned and looked at her. She smiled at her.

But her mind was chewing over the fight in Gunner's office, so many days ago.

All we know, sir, is that the bomb on the train bears the same creativity as the bomb in the dirigibles. And that points to the Petrov Bratva. Her words, and now she went cold, especially remembering Jonas's follow-up.

What about the nuclear waste? One of the canisters went missing.

But it was Fraser's reminder that had her reaching for her cell phone.

I think they're still looking for it.

Um, guess what...

She stepped back and pulled out her phone. Oh, Fraser had texted.

She thumbed it open.

FRASER

911. Tried to contact Gunner—he is out of pocket. Call ASAP.

She thumbed back a response.

PIPPA

In the royal suite with PI. I see the dirigible. ???

She waited, but the text remained unread.

Maybe they were all jumping to conclusions. What would a dirty bomb be doing floating over Lauchtenland? There were no terrorists in Lauchtenland.

Except.

She walked to the back of the suite and pulled out her cell. Dialed Gunner's number.

He answered on the second ring. "What are you doing?"

"Sir. I wanted to keep this off our channel, but I have a bad feeling about this blimp. It feels too...out of place. I think we need to evacuate the royal family."

Silence. "That's a big move, Butler."

"I know, sir, but if this is really what we think it is, it could be catastrophic."

"I know, Pippa. Fraser is standing in my office right now. We're assembling a search team, but for now, yes, secure the royal family. I'll relay this information to Ethan on Prince John's detail."

"I think we need to leave the premises, sir."

"Get them in the bunker. Oh, and Pippa, you do understand that this is not the end, right? I know you had a hand in his escape."

She drew in a breath. "Yes, sir. Can I talk to Fraser?"

His voice came over the line. "I'm so sorry, babe. But we had to go to Gunner. The safety of the royal family—and Lauchtenland—is on the line. I'm going to try and find the operator of the dirigible. But get away. Far away. I love you."

She closed her eyes to his words. Nodded. "Me too. See you soon."

Across from her, Ethan was nodding, listening to his earwig. He looked up at her, his mouth a tight line.

She headed down the steps. "Your Royal Highness, we need to leave." Standing at the end of the row, she gestured for guests, including Hamish Fickle's entourage, to move to the side.

"What?" This from Prince Xavier. "What's going on?"

"Nothing to worry about, sir, just a...small hiccup in the plans." She held out her hand to Imani. "Your Royal Highness?"

Imani got up. Across the row, Prince John and Princess Gemma were already leaving their row. Ethan held a hand up to Hamish, who had risen. He sank back down into his seat.

Pippa cut between Xavier and Imani, gesturing her up the stairs.

"Hey!"

His security, Griffin, waited at the top of the stairs. She held her hand up to him, then walked past him while Ethan opened the doors to the bunker. They went inside, followed by Prince Xavier and his man.

The prime minister joined them, along with his detail.

The door closed behind them.

Prince John turned to Ethan. "Can someone tell me what is going on?"

Ethan looked at Pippa. She clasped her hands behind her back. "We think Lauchtenland is under imminent danger from a dirty bomb, sir."

Prince John just stared at her. A half minute went by, then, "And my people. Are they safe?"

"We're trying to assure that, sir," she said.

"We can't cause a panic. And there are too many people here to evacuate." He looked at Ethan. "I'm going back to the box. But I want you to take my wife and daughter home."

"John!"

He turned to Gemma. "Hamish and I need to stay. And probably Xavier, since he is the organizer. We can't abandon our people. But you, darling, need to leave."

She took his hands, bowed her head. He kissed her forehead. Then he looked at Pippa. "Keep them safe."

"With my life."

He looked at Ethan, then Hamish, and they headed back out of the room. Xavier came over to Imani. "I'll see you after the game."

She closed her eyes as he kissed her forehead.

Then, to Pippa, "I'm going to ask Griff to make sure you get home safely." He looked at Griff, who nodded.

"Not necessary, sir," she said.

"For me it is." Then he exited the room.

"Your Royal Highnesses. Let me call the car, and then we'll go down the elevator." She keyed in her mic. "We need transport, asap, from the dove's nest."

"Affirmative," said a male voice.

"Let's go," Griff said, and punched the key to the elevator.

They got on and took it down to the tunnel under the stadium, got off in the semidarkness, and headed toward the exit. She walked ahead of Princess Imani, behind Princess Gemma, Griff behind all of them.

A car had pulled up outside, and a man got out, opened the door. Big man, his suit seemed to pull around his waist. Disheveled for a royal chauffeur.

Something about it raised the tiny hairs on Pippa's neck. It felt...not...

"Your Royal Highness," she said, hissing to Gemma as she reached for her Glock, inside her jacket in her underarm shoulder holster. "Stop, please—"

It happened so fast. The man stepped out from the car and raised a weapon.

"Run, Imani!"

Pippa pulled off a shot, then leaped for Princess Gemma. More shots echoed.

Heat burned through her. She cried out. Then all she heard was screaming, in her head, in the tunnel, and footsteps as darkness took her under.

Run, Imani. *Run.*

HE KNEW IT'D BEEN A BAD IDEA TO TALK TO GUNNER. Because now Fraser was stuck in an office overlooking the field, listening to the raucous noise behind him while he watched the dirigible float nearer the stadium.

And here he stood, not handcuffed, but he felt like it, with

Logan and York and Roy out there with the security team, trying to evacuate the prince and princesses from the event.

Never mind the one hundred and thirty thousand fans packed into the stadium. He could see Iris on the field below, her ponytail sticking out of her black cap as she took the field in the umpire position.

His chest filled every time he saw her on the field—half pride, half fear.

But he spotted Hudson also, wearing Vienna Vikings gear, standing on the sidelines, legs braced, arms folded, his gaze not on his players but the woman he loved.

So maybe Fraser could just calm down about Iris and focus on taking down the dirigible.

He looked at Jonas, who was on his computer, his gaze hard on the screen. "Are you sure you can't get control of this thing, drive it back out to sea?"

"Trying."

Sibba stood behind him. "This is a bad idea." She walked to the window and picked up the binoculars. "It's too far to see, but if it were me, I'd put a failsafe on the signal, so that if it was hacked, the bomb would detonate."

"It scares me to think how your brain works."

She looked at him. "Ten years in EOD. Nothing is beyond a depraved mind."

Yeah. And that's why the world needed guys like Fraser in the game.

Maybe a fresh start wasn't on the horizon. Ever.

He glanced at the guard by the door. Securing him, probably, although Gunner hadn't exactly said not to leave.

Just to stay put.

Which were completely different things.

He picked up his walkie. "Any progress?"

"We're still searching." This from Ned, who was out of uniform and not a little angry that the SEAL team wasn't allowed weapons.

In fact, Gunner had come close to simply arresting all of them.

You have a lot of hubris, Marshall, to show your face here. Gunner's words after Fraser, Logan, York, Roy, and a US Navy SEAL team had marched into the stadium office this morning. Even if they had put most of the pieces together—the dirigible, seen by Creed in the garage, only to have him and Iris trapped in the elevator. Not an accident, confirmed by Gunner's team when they investigated the lift motor, turned off in the elevator room in the basement of the stadium.

What you're missing is motive, chaps.

Again, Gunner's words, and now they churned inside Fraser. Why would the Petrov Bratva send a dirigible over a football game to release a dirty bomb?

He stood, arms folded, jaw tight, eyes hard on the floating weapon. "Can't they shoot it down?"

"That's a great idea. Over the stadium? Never mind the falling debris—"

Fraser held up a hand to Sibba's words. "Sorry."

"Our only hope is to find the driver, get control of the device, land it, then let me deactivate it."

"Just that."

He scanned the stadium. The teams came out for the coin toss in center field. He glanced at the royal box, located a few sections down. Prince John and PM Fickle stood, watching.

"What is the crown prince still doing here?" Fraser said. "Are they not taking this seriously?"

"Maybe they didn't want anyone to panic," Sibba said.

"I'm panicked!"

Jonas looked up. "I think I have a source of the signal. But it's...it's coming from above the stadium."

He pointed to a dot above the stadium, almost on top of them.

Fraser stepped closer. "I don't understand..." Then he looked at Jonas. "Last night. The elevator. We assumed whoever shut it down wanted to stop Iris and Creed from letting the information leak while they evacuated the dirigible. But what if..." He lifted the walkie. "Ned. Where are you guys?"

"Level two, uh...section 135. We split up—Trini and his team are in the lower decks, and Marsh took his guys to the main floor. This is a regular Charlie Foxtrot if you ask me."

"Roger. Can you get to the towers? The ones at the entrance?"

"Yeah, but it'll take some time. We're across the stadium."

"I'll meet you there."

He pocketed the walkie, glanced at Jonas, then at the guard.

Jonas gave him a look, a shake of his head.

Yeah, well, the shadow of the dirigible drifted across the far end of the stadium.

"I'm sorry, man, I gotta go," Fraser said, and turned to the guard at the door.

A young guy, and Fraser had him disarmed in a moment, his Glock 17 in his grip, the man on the floor.

Sibba pressed her hand to her mouth, her eyes wide.

Jonas was on his feet. "Is he dead?"

"That was a sleeper hold, so no." He pulled the walkie out of the soldier's belt. Tossed it to Jonas. "Channel thirteen."

Jonas followed him. "Get control of the device. If you shoot him—I don't know how this thing detonates, so be close enough to catch it."

Right. "Stay on that signal!"

He lit out into the hallway. Third floor security, best view in the house, with the exception of the royal box.

And the tower entrance was just down the busy hall.

The place buzzed with the announcement of the players, the crowd lit up with cheers. Lines formed in front of concession stands, the air heavy with the greasy scent of french fries, and grilling hotdogs.

He spotted the tower where he'd rescued—okay, *Creed* had rescued—Iris and Creed today. Smart kid.

Fraser ran up to the lift, hit the button. Nothing.

Right. Because if someone was up there, they'd turn off the power. Again.

But maybe he could get to them from the other tower. He ran down the hall, found the twin, and slammed the button.

The lift hummed to life.

The doors opened and he got on. No fifth-floor button. But it did have a service button, accessed by a fireman's key.

Aw, why did this have to be so hard?

He got out and stuck his foot in the door. Searched the wall— yes, a KnoxBox.

He just needed to get inside to the fireman's key.

The elevator was dinging, but he spotted a fire cabinet across the hallway, near the entrance. Reaching in, he turned on the emergency stop, then scooted across the hall and broke the glass with the handle of the Glock.

Pulled out the axe.

Then he broke the KnoxBox off the wall and retrieved the key.

The alarm had attracted attention. Good. He inserted the key and activated the maintenance access.

The doors closed and the elevator rose.

Breathe.

The doors opened. When he stepped out, he found himself standing at the base of the cupola, a railing encircling it, the view casting out over the stadium.

The dirigible had nearly crossed the stadium threshold. Now the teams had lined up on either side in anticipation of the Lauchtenland national anthem. Fraser looked over to the other tower, and his heart nearly stopped.

A man, dressed in the attire of stadium security, crouched behind the railing, holding what looked like a game controller.

Gotcha. *Get control of the driver.* Shoving the gun into his belt, he lifted the axe, Jonas's words in his head.

He didn't have a clear shot anyway.

Fifty feet spanned the towers, and between them, a narrow

ledge. He climbed over the edge and let himself down onto it, grabbing the wall before he went over. Maybe a foot wide, so this would be fun.

Except, now the balloon's shadow moved across the grass, toward the middle.

The announcer asked the audience to rise for the anthem.

C'mon, Marshall—

He held the axe out, like a balance beam, looked ahead, eyes on the driver, and started walking. Steady, quickly, and his brain harkened back to the muscle memory of the balance logs back at the obstacle course at Coronado.

He picked up speed as he went and hit a near run by the time he launched himself up to the railing.

He hurtled himself over.

The man hit his feet, gaze casting from Fraser to the dirigible.

Then, he smiled.

Fraser swung the axe, let it fly, and dove for the box.

The axe hit the man, full chest and Fraser followed it, grabbing the controller as the man's hands slackened.

He didn't even watch the man fall, just stepped away, breathing hard, and yanked out his walkie. "Jonas?"

"You got it?"

"Yeah." He moved to the edge. "What do I do?"

The blimp was over the stadium, the crowd singing the words to the national anthem.

"Sibba says to get it away from the stadium. Turn it south."

He looked at the controller. "Um, I'm not the video game guy."

"Okay, the right stick controls the heading, or movement. Up is forward, down is backward. Then left and right. Got it?"

"So, like this?" He pushed the drone hard left, and it began to move south, toward him.

"That's it...keep going—oh no."

He never liked *oh no*. "What?" The blimp had started to move over the far edge of the stadium. C'mon.

"I don't know what you did, but the device has activated a self-destruct."

"What?" He looked at the driver. The man held something in his fist, even as he lay prone, the axe embedded in his chest.

He bit back a word.

"There's a countdown," Jonas was saying. "Looks like five minutes."

"A countdown." Sheesh, this thing moved like a turtle in the air. "Can we get everyone out?"

"They'd be in the parking lot."

Silence on the other end.

"Okay, Fraser." Sibba's voice now. "The greatest danger from a dirty bomb is usually the explosion from the blast rather than the material. In this case, the amount of caesium in a closed space like the stadium would cause fallout. Our best chance is to get it someplace where the explosion can't hurt anyone and to eliminate the concentration of the fallout—"

"Speed it up, Sibba."

"Get the blimp over the shipping yard to the south, headed back to sea. Most of the buildings there are empty, warehouses and metal ships that will be protected from the blast. That's the shortest and best route to safety."

He looked up as the blimp passed overhead, and his heart chilled a little at the contraption affixed to the bottom. It looked like a helium machine, ready to disperse gas.

Except in this case, nuclear waste.

He rammed the control up, moving it forward. "Any way to make this thing go faster?"

Jonas now. "Sorry. It was a weather balloon design. It's supposed to linger in the area, gather data."

"There's no way we're going to make it."

"Put it down, Fraser." Sibba, again on the line. "Get it into the parking lot—I'll defuse it."

Get it down? They didn't have that kind of time—"I'm going to shoot it down."

He pulled the Glock from his belt, aimed, and pulled the trigger.

It hit, but the blimp barely moved. He hit it again, but again, nothing.

"C'mon!"

"Fraser." Jonas's voice, through the walkie at his belt. "The dirigible is filled with helium—but there are four balloons inside the frame that contain the gas. You have to hit each of them to get it down. You need to guide it down so it hits the parking lot and not any of the buildings around it. And don't let it crash. It could release the caesium."

Oh, sure, no problem. He'd used at least eight rounds, if the guard had a full clip.

"Fraser!" He looked up. Ned stood at the parapet, along with Gunner's security team.

Yes. "Ned!" He pointed to the dirigible. "Shoot it down! Hit the balloons inside!"

Ned looked at him, as if trying to sort out his words, rounded, put hands on one of the security guards and relieved him of his Glock.

Then he stepped up to the rail, aimed, and fired.

A terrible pop sounded, and the balloon jerked. Fraser picked up the controller and directed the dirigible toward the service area of the parking lot.

Another shot, no joy, but the balloon began to descend.

Ned got another shot off with another soul-satisfying pop. The balloon cleared the public lot, and with another two shots, finally began to fall.

Fraser held it over the loading area and spotted a figure, running.

Sibba. And right behind her, Roy.

The thing had to weigh a couple hundred pounds. Please let it not land on her.

Jonas appeared behind her, and with him, Logan and York. The balloon landed, and they grabbed it and rolled it.

And then Sibba disappeared under the folds of the construction.

Please.

Fraser set the device down, not sure what to do with it, and realized his body shook, covered in sweat.

He looked over at Ned, who lowered the gun, then met his eyes.

A long, terrible moment passed, just his heartbeat hammering in his chest.

Then, "All clear."

He picked up the walkie. "You guys okay?"

"Sibba disarmed it before it could deploy."

Fraser leaned over, his head in his folded arms on the railing, still breathing hard.

"Logan says he's sending a man up to you."

"Roger."

He picked up the controller, then turned it off. Walked over to the driver. Stared at him. He wore a baseball cap, the blue uniform of HMSD, dark hair, and matching stubble on his chin. Built. And an axe, dead center in his chest.

The elevator behind him dinged, and the door opened.

Ned ran out, followed by the guards. Fraser backed away, hands up. "Self-defense of the kingdom, guys."

Gunner walked out last. "Put your hands down, Marshall."

Ned stood over the body, frowning. "I know this guy." He looked up at Fraser. "I met him on a ship in Siberia. Lukka Petrov, son of Arkady, head of the Petrov Bratva. I thought he was dead when the ship got blown up."

Gunner was looking at him. "The Russian mob is behind this?"

"We did mention that possibility a few days ago."

Gunner just blinked at him. Took a breath. "Right. But why?"

"Dunno, sir."

He drew in a breath. "Okay, I'm going to need statements

from both of you."

"Would sure like to catch the game." Fraser lifted an eyebrow.

Gunner considered him. "You can watch from my office." He was turning when he stopped, froze, then looked back at Fraser.

And there was just something about the expression, the way that he blinked, swallowed, then nodded, that turned Fraser cold.

"Okay, find her. And lock down the stadium."

He turned to Fraser.

"There's been a shooting, and Princess Imani is missing."

He opened his mouth, closed it, and darkness speared through him at Gunner's next words.

"Pippa is down."

AND NOW HE WAS STUCK IN THE CAR. AT LEAST HE could hear the game on the radio, but maybe it was still better than being back at the house, watching the game on the telly, pacing, or maybe just throwing something at the screen yelling—so, yeah.

Sitting in the cab of the Range Rover like a ten-year-old was ever so much better. He stared out the window toward the entrance to the players' area, right where Iris had parked yesterday, listening to his words to Fraser.

Check the tower. There was someone in the tower.

Who knew his brother actually listened, so consumed was he with the fact that he was with his SEAL bros again, he and Ned back in action, saving the world. Even Jonas was in on it.

Because they were real Marshalls.

And Creed was just the fake.

What. Ever.

He leaned his head against the glass, hearing York. *Let God have the helm and you'll stop wondering if you're useful and you'll start being useful.*

No question as to the answer there. Not useful.

He'd memorized every car in the lot, watched a few stragglers enter the stadium, and stared at the sky, the car parked facing the massive entrance.

Occasionally, his gaze went to the towers, remembering his efforts in the lift. Even Fraser had seemed impressed, given his fist bump. *Smart.*

Maybe. Or just one of thousands of useless facts in his head.

Creed had been watching a limousine near the entrance for a while. It had pulled up to a doorway, and a man had gotten out, dressed in a uniform.

He would have liked to see Imani one more time before he left. But really, what was he going to do? He wasn't a prince—she probably needed to be with a guy like Xavier, really.

And he needed to get on with his life. His rehab. Whatever future lay out there for him.

Suddenly, the chauffeur ran into view, around the limo, got in, and as Creed sat up to watch, the limo kicked up gravel and sped away.

Well, that was weird. And he didn't know why he opened the door—a gut feeling, maybe, or maybe it was an echo from his past.

Running. Gravel spinning. People—

Screaming.

He stilled, then took off, half running, half skipping, past the entrance gate, around the inside of the perimeter.

"Help! Someone!"

The voice was high, panicked, and when he hit a fence, he climbed it, barely aware—not even, really—of his leg. Just vaulted over the top, landed, and took off again.

Rounded the entrance, into the shadows.

And stopped.

His breaths caught on each other, and now he pulled off his jacket, advancing on the two women on the ground.

Imani's mother, Gemma, kneeled, her hands over a wound in

Pippa's abdomen, her hands bloody as Pippa writhed, grunting, trying to breathe.

"Oh no—no—" He came over, jacket off, then pulled off his sweatshirt and wadded it up. "What happened?"

"I don't know—I don't know!" Princess Gemma was shaking. Pippa grabbed his wrists. "Princess Imani—you gotta...find..."

"Okay, okay." He looked at Princess Gemma. "Did you call for help?"

"With what? Her earwig is wrecked."

He found the device a few feet from her, as if it had been torn off.

"Okay—where is Imani?"

"I don't know!" Gemma stared hard at Creed. "I don't know what happened—just that someone shot at us, and then—oh, Pippa!"

Her eyes closed. "C'mon, Pip. You're tougher than that—stay with us!" *Okay, YouTube, don't let me down—* "Let's get her feet up. Get all the blood to her heart." He looked around, then grabbed Princess Gemma's shoulder. "Sit down. You're going to hold her feet on your lap. C'mon. Against the wall."

He pulled Pippa over, and Gemma sat and pulled up her knees, and he put Pippa's legs on her. "Now I need you to hold my sweatshirt on the wound."

She nodded. Pressed her bloody hand onto the cloth.

He wadded up his jacket and put it under Pippa's head. Checked her pulse. "I'm going for help. Pippa. Don't you die. Don't you die!"

He turned.

A fist came right at him. It hit him so hard, he spun, then hit the cement.

Princess Gemma screamed.

What—

But he rolled into a ball just as a foot landed in his gut. He tightened up, grunted.

"Stop! Stop!"

No—

But he looked up to see Imani, full speed, swinging something at his assailant.

She connected, and the man grunted. Then he rounded and slapped her so hard she went flying.

But the weapon clattered next to Creed's head.

A weight bar.

Attagirl.

He scooped it up and aimed for the ankles. Cracked one, and the man howled but stayed on his feet. Reached down to grab Creed's jacket.

Scars. On his neck.

The porter on the train.

Creed shoved the bar up and kicked at the man. Then he rolled, and all those squats had helped, because he practically bounced to his feet.

The man had also rebounded and now took out a gun.

"Griff—no! He's not the shooter!"

What?

He looked at Imani, who had gotten up, her nose bloody.

Wait. No, this wasn't right.

He swung with everything he had, and the gun went off, just as he knocked it from Griff's hands.

Then he rounded, grabbed Imani, and ran. Sort of ran. His was a limp-jump-hop-run sort of thing, but it got the job done.

Griff shouted after them, but a glance back had him limping—so Creed *had* struck an ankle bone.

Which helped distance them. He found a door at the end of the hall and opened it.

It came into the players' area.

"C'mon, Imani!" He scooted down the hall, then pushed her into the refs' locker room.

Turned off the lights.

Then he shoved the bar against the door and the handle.

"We need to call for help."

Imani was breathing hard, looking at him, wide-eyed. "I don't—I think Pippa is hurt!"

He grabbed her shoulders. Pushed her against the wall. Then he held her face with his hands. "Yes, she is. And she needs help. But Griff isn't the guy you think he is—he's the guy from the train."

She just blinked at him. "What?"

"The porter, who left the bomb. It was him. I recognize him."

"Oh, Creed...no...no...that—he was with us in the hallway. Someone tried to shoot us—he ran after him—"

"No, he didn't. I saw the guy who tried to shoot you—I was outside. Griff wasn't chasing him. I think he was looking for you."

She stared at him, then her breaths started to hiccup, and her eyes filled. "Oh..." Her hands covered her mouth. "Pippa?"

He pulled her close then and just held her. "Shh. I dunno. Gemma is with her."

"We have to go back—"

Pounding on the door. Griff, shouting, fighting the wedged bar.

Creed took Imani's hand, then went to the office and closed the door. "Stay in here. Get under the desk, and no matter what happens, you don't come out. Not until you hear me—or Fraser, or maybe your stepfather, okay?"

She looked at him, then grabbed his shirt.

And then she kissed him. Hard and sure, and this, this was the woman he'd met in Switzerland. This was the woman he'd give his life for.

She let him go. "Don't die. Because I have big plans for you."

"Under the desk. And pray."

As she climbed under the big metal desk, he flicked off the light and closed the door.

Then he quietly let himself into the training room and found the crutch he'd returned. He slid to the door.

Griff had his back turned to him, talking on the radio.

Yeah, well, here went nothing. He stepped out quietly, then

charged.

He hit Griff in the back with the pointed end of the crutch, and the man went down.

And that was the end of his plan. So Creed pounced on him, his arm around his neck, the other catching his hand, pulling.

He'd seen Fraser do it, once upon a time.

Griff elbowed him, but he hung on, his legs entwining Griff's, even when he hit his hands and knees. Creed put his legs around his waist. The man was a bull.

He stood up and slammed Creed into the wall.

His breath huffed out, his grip broken, and he dropped.

Griff spun away, breathing hard.

What had he been thinking? He wasn't Ned. Or Fraser or—

The vagus nerve.

Creed scrambled for his crutch, scooped it up, and as Griff rounded, charged, he swung it at the man's ear with everything inside him.

Griff got a hand up, so no joy, but the movement made him slip—

Creed leapt for the training room and shut the door. Locked it. Crawled to the locker room.

So, that wasn't great. He opened the door to the office. "Imani?"

"I'm here!" He heard the chair push out, then, as he leaned against the frame, she fell into his arms.

"Are you hurt?"

"No—I mean—"

Banging on the door made her jump.

"Creed Marshall! We know you're in there!"

She stared at him.

"This is Gunner Ferguson. Please don't hurt the princess. This has gone far enough."

Aw. He met her eyes. "They think I kidnapped you. Again."

"And again," she said in a thin voice.

He nodded, then shouted at the door, "I agree with you! And

I would never hurt Imani!"

"Come out, Creed! We don't want you getting hurt."

She palmed his chest. "Creed?"

His jaw tightened at the fear in her face.

"This won't help you, Creed," the voice shouted again. "You know that we'll do whatever we have to in order to keep her safe."

He drew in a breath. "If they come in here, there might be shooting. I don't want you to get hurt."

Her eyes filled.

"But I think this is it. I don't think there's any coming back to Lauchtenland after this."

She swallowed. Nodded. "But I'll find you. I know where you live."

Yeah, she did. He wrapped an arm around her, pulled her to himself, his throat filling.

Then he kissed her. And not a fast, desperate kiss, but the kind that told her that the last three months had changed him, that *she'd* changed him. The kind of kiss that he'd hang on to and cherish, the taste of her lips on his, the smell of her, the feel of her hair between his fingers.

"Creed!"

He finally let her go, met her beautiful eyes in the wan light. And said, "I love you, Imani."

Her eyes filled. And she nodded. "That was the exact right thing to say."

Then he winked and let her go and hobbled to the door.

He undid the pole, unlocked the door, and opened it.

Hands reached out and pulled him to the floor, a knee in his back—

"He saved my life!"

He heard Imani but couldn't see her as they handcuffed him, this time with metal cuffs. They pulled him up, and then Gunner got in his face, his eyes dark.

"I doubt that, Your Royal Highness. Because he's under arrest for the murder of Pippa Butler."

211

TEN

Pippa wasn't dead.

Just in critical condition.

Just like Imani's heart, but that was vastly less important than both Pippa and Creed's future.

Imani stood in the surgical waiting room of the Port Fressa Hospital, surrounded by Gunner and half his staff, still covered in blood—mostly her own, but also Pippa's, because by the time she'd run back to the corridor, paramedics had been packing her up.

Her mother then grabbed her in a hug that nearly crushed the life from Imani, and thus, spattered her with Pippa's blood too.

So yeah, she was a mess, and her mascara bled down her face, her stomach emptied after watching them drag Creed away, maybe for the last time, hand and foot like he really was a criminal, and—"He didn't kidnap me. He was trying to save my life!"

"From whom, Princess?" Gunner kept his voice low, but he was a menacing force, his hands on his hips, his dark eyes searching hers. He seemed almost as confused as she was.

Almost.

"Because according to Griffin Hoff, he saw Creed standing over Pippa's body, covered in blood, his hand around her neck!"

And she had nothing for that, because she didn't know what had gone down. "All I know is that Griff was kicking him, and for all I know would have killed him—"

"He was resisting arrest!"

"He was saving Pippa's life! Ask my mother!"

But her mother wasn't here. She'd been taken back to the palace, where the royal doctors were looking her over, treating her for shock.

Yeah, well, Imani was in shock. Breathing hard, sweating, feeling nauseous—

It couldn't end this way.

She shook her head. "Listen. Here's how it went down. We were coming out of the elevator and walking down the tunnel, and this limo pulled up. A guy got out, and suddenly Pippa was telling me to run, and she was leaping on my mom, and there were bullets flying and I...I ran. I ran because Pippa told me to run, so I did, and I found myself in the players' weight room." She sat down on the sofa, a leather sectional that ran the length of the room. "And I thought—what if Pippa's hurt or my mom is hurt and I'm hiding? And I realized...I don't hide well. I've never hidden well. I'm a doer, and sometimes that means running away, but sometimes that means running *to* danger, and the past three months were...frustrating, and maybe, okay, a little awesome because I was with Creed but, I just...I couldn't hide anymore. So I found this bar and headed back. And I saw Creed standing over Pippa, and there was so much blood—so much blood, and then—I don't know where he came from, but Griff was there, and he was attacking Creed, hitting him, and he kicked him, and I just....I knew Creed wouldn't hurt me. Or Pippa or my mom, and..." She stared up at Gunner, who seemed to not have moved this entire time. "Griff hit me."

Silence. "Clearly he thought you were someone else."

"Seriously? He was the guy on the train, Gunner. He was the porter with the bomb."

Gunner just frowned.

"Creed saw him that day—we were on the phone, and he said he recognized him. And...I believe him. I mean, I don't know how or why, but he's not going to lie to me—"

Gunner narrowed his eyes, took a breath.

"Creed is not a murderer."

"He loves you, Princess. Enough to take out your guard and your mother and—"

"You've got to be kidding me."

She stilled and looked past Gunner to the man who'd just walked into the room.

Fraser. And he stood with Ethan, her father's guard, who came in a step before—

"Mom!" She ran to Princes Gemma and flung her arms around her.

Then Prince John walked into the room, and everything went quiet.

Gunner bowed his head. "Your Royal Highness."

Her stepdad walked over, gave her a long look, then turned to Gunner. "Gunner, what's going on here? And start with an update on Pippa."

"She's still in surgery, sir. They think the bullet nicked her kidney, and there was a lot of internal bleeding."

Fraser swallowed and walked to the window. Hung his head.

Behind her father, Jonas and Sibba had entered as well as Ned and Shae. Now Jonas walked over to Fraser and stood beside him.

Her eyes filled again.

Prince John turned to her. "Prince Xavier is outside also. He's worried about you."

She didn't know what to do with that. She nodded, but turned to Gunner. "I don't trust Griff. And you shouldn't either." Then she walked out of the door.

Ethan followed her, and she got that.

Xavier stood at the end of the hallway, his back to her, his hand around his neck. The wing had been cleared of all other visitors, and now he turned to her. His expression looked stricken. "Darling, please tell me you aren't hurt."

He came up to her, hesitated, then reached out to pull her into a hug.

She let him. It wasn't his fault his bodyguard was a brute. "I'm okay."

He let her go. "Creed—"

"Is innocent. He didn't shoot Pippa. And he tried to save me..." She stopped then, because, well... "From Griff."

He frowned, then shook his head. "Griff wouldn't hurt you. According to him, he saw Creed trying to strangle Pippa."

She stepped away. "No, that's not—"

"Okay." He took a step toward her, grabbed her hand. "Okay. Clearly Griff was distraught and maybe read into things. We'll get it sorted."

She searched his blue eyes and saw nothing but concern. "I need to go back in with the family." Her family.

It only hit her then that...yes. The Marshalls had become as much of a family to her as the Stones—Gemma, and Memaw and Pops—and maybe even more than the House of Blue.

And most of all, Pippa. Who wasn't her bodyguard but maybe her older sister.

Oh.

"I need to be there...waiting."

"Of course you do." He leaned over and kissed her forehead. Met her eyes again. "I'll be in touch. And I'll get this bit with Creed cleared up."

Her throat thickened. "Thank you, X."

He nodded, winked.

She left him in the hallway and walked back to the room.

PM Hamish Fickle had joined them, which felt weird, but maybe he was here to check on Princess Gemma.

Or to find out, first, the story behind the dirigible.

He wasn't getting it from Fraser, clearly, who still stared out the window, his shoulders stiff, but Jonas and Ned had started to explain the pieces that seemed to fit together.

"So our team tracked the missing caesium here," Ned was saying. "And for the past few days, we've been trying to find it."

"Did you know about this?" Prince John said to Gunner.

"I did, sir."

Hamish made a sound, shook his head. Oopsies. Maybe, but really, what were they going to say—there's a dirty bomb in your country? The shutdown of the game would have been a financial fiasco.

On the other hand, if Fraser and the rest of the team hadn't stopped the bomber...

Prince John nodded, clearly processing the events. "So how did you connect the nuclear material to the dirigible over the stadium today?"

"My sister Iris, and Creed, spotted it in the garage of the stadium yesterday. It was the same design as the dirigible that was stolen and used to deploy a dirty bomb in Slovenia a couple months ago. My design."

Her stepfather raised an eyebrow.

Jonas continued. "They were locked in an elevator for their efforts, but Creed figured out that the driver might have been hiding on one of the towers."

See, he's not a villain, Imani wanted to shout, but maybe her stepfather was already figuring that out.

"And the man you intercepted today?" Prince John asked.

"Was the son of Arkady Petrov, who runs the Petrov Bratva," Ned said. He had ahold of Shae's hand, his fingers wrapped into hers. "They were the ones who kidnapped Shae in an effort to reclaim the missing caesium."

There were a few details left out, but Imani just nodded.

"So my question is...why would the Russian mob want to detonate a dirty bomb over Titus Stadium? We're a small country with a small military, and we have almost nonexistent relations with Russia. Our closest allies are the North Sea states."

Silence.

"And that isn't even formal yet," PM Fickle said. "Not until Lauchtenland joins the North Sea Alliance." He raised an eyebrow at Prince John. "Which might a good idea, sir, given the ruckus. We'd at least have the protection of the North Sea states should we get in a tussle with Russia."

"We're not getting in a tussle with Russia, Hamish," Prince John said quietly.

Hamish made a noise in the back of his throat.

"Who was the man in the tunnel who shot Pippa?" her mother asked. "Why would someone still be after Imani?" She held Prince John's hand but looked over at her daughter.

For a second, the flash of gunfire in the tunnel, the scream in the direction of her mother, had turned Imani to ice.

Then Pippa had said run, and her reflexes told her to obey.

"Maybe it's because she's an American." This from Hamish Fickle. "What if, and stay with me, sir, this was a Russian diversion? To take our attention off the bombing at the stadium and—"

"Hamish. Why would the Russians want to bomb us or shoot my stepdaughter?"

"I don't know, sir—maybe to draw America into a war?"

The air left the room. Even Fraser turned around.

Hamish shook his head. "Princess Imani is an American. It stands to reason that if something happened to her, America might get involved."

"I'm not that important," Imani said.

"You undervalue yourself," PM Fickle said.

"That's absurd," said Imani. "I'm more likely to be killed by a RECOist than a Russian."

Hamish frowned.

"Aren't the RECOists against the monarchy? Aren't they the

ones who brought up the old writ about succession? Maybe my mother was the target—she's American."

"She took the oath of Lauchtenland when she became queen consort in waiting," Prince John said.

She glanced at her mother.

"As long as an American stands to take over the crown, I'm afraid there will be unrest in this country, sir. And not just by the RECOists. Citizens of Lauchtenland want to see their own on the throne."

He looked at her. "Of course, you could marry. Prince Xavier, for example?"

She met his gaze.

"My daughter isn't marrying anyone. Especially not for political reasons."

There was another way..."I'll take the oath. And accept the investiture."

Her mother looked at her. "Formalize your role as a working royal? Imani—what about college, and your plans—"

"If I take the oath, will that satisfy the Writ of Succession?"

Hamish's mouth tightened around the edges. "Yes."

"No," Prince John said. "We're not forcing Imani to do anything—"

"Will it stop the unrest?"

Hamish drew in a breath. "Probably."

"And then whoever is trying to kill me for being an American won't have that power."

"We don't actually know if that's true," said Jonas.

"But it could be. And I'm tired of running and hiding. It's time to stand my ground, and if this how, then...yes, I'll do it." She again locked eyes with Hamish. "But only if Creed is released, all charges dropped."

"Ma'am, with all due respect, he broke numerous laws. Kidnapping, fraud, escape from custody, assault of an officer of the queen—"

"All to save my life." She looked at her stepfather. "Send him back to America. Ban him from Lauchtenland—whatever. Just let him go."

Her stepfather took a breath, then turned to Hamish. "I'm amenable to that, if the government of Lauchtenland agrees."

Hamish's jaw tightened, but he looked at Imani and slowly nodded. "The press doesn't yet know of his involvement. Perhaps...perhaps this is better. No need to stir up more anti-American sentiment." He gestured to Fraser. "And this one?"

The look on Fraser's face could level a man. "I'm not leaving Pippa."

Yep. No one was going to argue with him.

"Fine," Hamish said. He looked at Imani.

Then he bowed.

She watched him leave.

Her mother walked over and put her arm around her. *You cannot live with one eye looking back into the life you long for...You must live in the life you've been called to.*

"Sir," Ethan said. "The surgeon is outside. She'd like to talk to you."

Prince John nodded, and the door opened. A surgeon walked in, her hair in a cap, wearing scrubs and booted shoes. She curtsied to the royals.

"Thank you, Doctor. How is she?"

Fraser had stepped up to stand beside the prince. Taller, grittier, he lacked her stepfather's polish, a warrior to her father's regal state.

But both of them fierce in their own ways.

"She is still critical. We were able to save her kidney, and she lost a lot of blood. But she is still with us, sir."

Fraser's breath shuddered, and he turned away, his hand over his eyes.

Yeah, her too.

"The next twenty-four hours is crucial. I'd suggest prayers."

"Can I see her?" Fraser had turned, his eyes reddened, his voice a little shaky.

"You're Fraser? She was asking for you before surgery. Said she had something to tell you. I'll let you know when she's ready to see you."

She left then, after another curtsy, and Fraser just stood there, looking hollow, as if his world had turned to glass under his feet. And that at any moment it might crack, and he'd go through.

Imani knew exactly how he felt. In fact, she was already falling.

THEY SURE WERE IN A HURRY TO GET CREED OUT OF the country. They hadn't even bothered to change his passport. He was back to being Christofer Bento as HMSD marched him through security and to the gate of United flight 249, nonstop to NYC, where he'd then get on a flight to Minneapolis.

All there, on the printout of his ticket, and apparently, they weren't taking any chances that he'd cut and run, walking him all the way to the gate bridge and watching as he boarded the plane.

Just when he'd been making himself comfortable at the city dungeon. At least they'd let him shower and given him a change of clothes—jeans and a hoodie—maybe so he didn't scare the other passengers.

What he didn't get was a goodbye. A glimpse of Imani, and update from his family.

Who had abandoned him.

Okay, that might be overstated, but...

"Welcome aboard." The flight attendant, a woman in her thirties, dressed in the blue uniform of the airline, handed him a goodie bag of toiletries and earphones.

He checked his ticket. All the way in the back of the plane. Figured.

He bumped his way back, glancing out the window as he went. Night had fallen.

Better than being shot at dawn, probably.

No, definitely.

He bumped past the exit row, all the way to the back, then found his seat by the window. Just one seat beside him, so maybe he'd get lucky. He picked up the pillow from under his seat, unsheathed it from the plastic bag, and shoved it under his head. *But I'll find you. I know where you live.*

He closed his eyes. Yeah, well, it didn't matter.

Because he wasn't a fool. He'd never thought it would end any differently than this.

Aw, he was a liar.

He'd totally thought they'd figure a way out. He leaned back, stared at the ceiling. What. A. Fool.

He wasn't a prince, and there was no happy ending waiting for a criminal of Lauchtenland.

"I think I'm here."

Creed looked up to see a man checking his ticket. He wore a pair of canvas pants, boots, a flannel shirt, vest, and a backpack which he swung up into the compartment above. Brown eyes, dark brown hair cut to just below his ears, and he wore a scrabble of whiskers on his chin. Most of all, he exuded the presence of a warrior—big shoulders, strong body—and it reminded Creed a little of his siblings.

"Going home?" the man said.

"Yes."

"Were you here for the game?"

"Um, sort of."

"Good game. The Vikings nearly squeaked by."

"Which ones?"

"Good one." The man laughed, and it was full and robust and sort of unwound something inside Creed.

Creed wasn't entirely kidding. "I actually didn't see the game."

"Oh?"

"I, uh...got a little tied up."

221

The man had warm eyes. "I see. A bit of trouble?"

Creed looked over him. "Why would you say that?"

"Because you keep cracking your knuckles. Like you'd like to punch something."

Creed looked down. Oh. He opened his hand, but offered a nod. "Maybe I do." He took a breath, looked out the window. He spotted the palace, on a hill above the city, all lit up. "Maybe I do."

"I know that feeling. A little trapped and angry and misunderstood, and...it just sits right here, you know?" He touched his chest. "Like a piece of coal."

Creed considered him. Then, "Yeah. I guess so."

The flight attendant came on with instructions, and the man seemed to listen, nodding along. Then the plane spooled up for takeoff.

Creed sighed.

"You don't seem all that excited to go home."

"Oh, uh. It's just that...I...so, I sort of thought my family would be here to say goodbye to me. And they weren't." And just saying that aloud made the coal burn deeper. Maybe they didn't even know he was being ousted.

"So, you're leaving them behind, in Lauchtenland?"

"Yes—no. I don't know. Actually, they're not really my family. I'm adopted, so..."

"So?"

Creed frowned. "So I guess it's not surprising that they all..."

"Abandoned you?"

"They didn't *abandon* me."

"It sounds like they did."

"No—they...so, my brother's girlfriend was shot, so they're probably all at the hospital."

"Oh no, is she okay?"

"I dunno." He looked out the window as the plane took off, at the lights of Port Fressa spilling out across the horizon. As they rose higher, what looked like a heart formed from the six cathedral towers. "That's cool."

The man looked at him. "What's cool?"

"The churches make a heart, see?"

The man leaned over, out the window. "No matter how many times I see that, I love it. It's called the Heart of God."

He sat back. "Can't see it from the ground, though. You need to get higher, see it from a different perspective." He looked at Creed. "Did I see you walk in with a couple of HMSD guards? Are you royalty or something?"

Creed laughed. "Would I be sitting in steerage if I were royalty?"

"Depends on the situation. Maybe. Jesus sat in steerage when he came to earth."

Creed raised an eyebrow. "Right. Well, no, I'm not royalty. Actually, to be honest, I was under arrest."

"And now you're not."

"Nope. Just evicted from Lauchtenland." He glanced again out the window. The plane was just rising into the clouds, the island disappearing. He sighed.

"I was in prison once."

Creed said nothing.

"But sometimes the prison isn't just physical, you know? It can be in our heads. Like anger, or rejection or helplessness."

"I'm not angry."

Silence. Creed looked over. The man was looking down at Creed's fists.

Fine. "Sometimes I'm angry. Like..." He shook his head. "I do everything to prove that...that I'm a good guy—I *am* a good guy—and it just sort of...backfires." He sighed. "It's no big deal."

"It is a big deal if the anger sits inside you. It's like a weed. It affects what we believe and how we think and what we do. It makes us afraid, or jealous, and even believe that we are worthless."

Creed stared at him.

"Chris, I'll bet you didn't start out angry. None of us do. But something happens in our lives that feels out of control, or hurts us, and that anger lands in our heart and starts to become barbed wire."

The pilot came on to announce cruising altitude.

"Chris?"

"Your ticket, man." He pointed to the boarding pass, half tucked into the seat in front of him.

"That's not my real name. It's just...my name is Creed."

"Nice to meet you, Creed. My name is Judah." He shook Creed's hand. Then he reached for the blanket under his seat. "I don't know what it is, but I can't seem to get warm." He undid the plastic and pulled it around him.

But Creed's mind buzzed with his words. *You didn't start out angry.*

"When I was eight years old, my sister was killed by a drive-by shooting, and I knew it was it was going to happen."

Judah looked at him. "What?"

"I don't know where that came from. Sorry."

"No, I mean—how did you know it was going to happen?"

"I had a dream. A nightmare. My brother was in a gang, and my dad—he was real rough on us. Beat my mom. So maybe I just let all my fears dream it up. But then it happened, you know? And I..."

"You felt guilty."

He nodded.

"I'll bet that made you angry."

Creed looked at him. The man's eyes were gentle.

"Yeah. Yeah, it did. I even told my mom about it before it happened, but she didn't listen." He shook his head. "I don't blame her. She was a mess too. I would wake up at night and hear her screaming. And my brother—he tried to do something about it but couldn't, and...anyway...yeah. Maybe I've been angry a long time."

"And helpless. And grieving. And, given your words about your family abandoning you, rejected."

"I *was* just kicked out of a country." Creed smiled.

Judah didn't.

Fine. Creed's throat tightened. "I guess so. I mean, yeah. You haven't met my family—my adopted family, the Marshalls—but they're all overachievers. And sometimes I feel like I don't belong."

"Yep. That's one of the devil's favorite lies. That you don't belong. That you'll never be accepted. It makes people do crazy things. And keeps them trapped in the cycle of trying to be loved. And even if those things are good things, one wrong word from someone can trigger more and more lies. And it all begins with the anger in your heart, from your childhood. But here's the truth, Creed. Even before you were born, God was thinking of you. Thinking of your life and the man you'd become. He was thinking of all the ways He loved you. And the great plan He had for your life if you let Him."

"I don't know. I feel like I'm way off the map here."

"We were created to be fruitful, to be used by Him beyond our wildest imaginations. But to do that, we need to be set free. Healed. And empowered with truth. So don't let your lies keep you from that. It's time to be set free."

Creed leaned back. "I don't even know how—"

"You start with confessing your anger. And then you forgive the people that hurt you. And then you tell the devil to leave you alone, because you are a child of God, and that means you *are* a prince of heaven." Judah smiled. "I knew I was sitting with royalty."

Creed laughed. "Lucky me, I get the comedian. Are you here the whole flight?"

Judah smiled. "The whole ten hours, man. I have all the time in the world to listen." He pulled up his blanket. "So, how did you end up in HMSD's custody?"

Creed ripped open the plastic on his blanket and also tucked it around himself. "Have you ever heard of Her Royal Highness Princess Imani of Lauchtenland?"

Pippa, please wake up.

Fraser stood at the foot of her bed, watching as the nurse again checked Pippa's vitals. The heart machine played out a steady rhythm, and the oxygen mask had been replaced with a cannula.

And still, she slept.

Beautiful in her sleep, her dark hair splayed out over the pillow, her eyes closed, more peace on her face than he'd ever seen, really. A tube ran from her arm to an IV bag on a stand affixed to the bed, her hand still curved where he'd been clutching it most of the night.

The sun sprayed into the room, the early morning light cast with gold and reds and oranges. He'd spent not a little time last night staring at the lights of the city, the glow from the six cathedrals of Port Fressa.

Praying.

Please. Don't take her from me.

It was just that simple.

Because he'd made a decision in the night.

He didn't know how, but he wasn't going to leave her ever again.

The nurse finished taking her pulse, then lowered her arm and recorded the results on her tablet. Looked at him. "Would you like me to order breakfast?"

"I can't eat."

"You should get some sleep."

He gave her a look.

She gave him a closed mouth nod, then left the room.

He walked over to his chair and sank into it, took Pippa's hand again. Soft and limp in his. Lowering his head, he pressed it against his forehead.

Please, Lord. Bring her back.

Footsteps into the room, and he looked over to see Jonas walk in. And with him, Ned. And finally Iris.

They looked as rough-eyed as he felt. Jonas wore a pair of cargo pants, a pullover sweater. Ned, too, although he wore a black sweater. Iris had on a pair of jeans, a Vienna Vikings hoodie, her dark-blonde hair pulled back.

"Anything?" Jonas said as he put a hand on Fraser's shoulder.

"She's still with us."

"That's something," Ned said, walking over to lean against the window ledge. He crossed his ankles and folded his arms. He hadn't shaved, maybe for a week, because he sported a thin beard.

"Where's Shae?"

"She's at the Delafield Hotel with Sibba."

He glanced at Iris, who sat down on the chair opposite him, across the bed. "Hud is seeing his team off. He'll be over soon."

"You guys don't need to stick around," he said. "I got this."

Silence.

Jonas walked over to the wall, leaned against it, arms folded.

He looked over at Ned, who was shaking his head. "Really?"

Right. His throat filled.

He cast his gaze back to Pippa. "When I was in captivity, there was this other spec ops guy on Ham's team who was also with me. Colt Kingston. Tough son-of-a-gun. And every day, he'd sort of get into it with the guards. I don't know how many times they beat him until he passed out. They'd drag him back to where I was, sitting there with my broken arm, and I'd think, *This time he's not going to wake up.* The thing is, I...cared about Colt. Of course I did. But seeing him wrecked is nothing compared to seeing Pippa lying there."

His eyes burned. "I sort of spent the past two months thinking—even behaving—like we were teammates. And we are, but...." He shook his head.

"You don't need a teammate," Jonas said quietly. "You need a wife."

The word tackled Fraser, grabbed him up, caught his breath.

Then, slowly, he nodded. "I love her. But..." He flexed his hand. "I always thought I'd be going back to the Jones, Inc. team as soon as I got this sorted."

He looked at Ned. "If you hadn't shown up, I'm not sure I would have been able to bring down the dirigible. I don't have the aim I used to."

Ned nodded, his mouth a grim line.

"But...then what? I go back to the winery? Help dad with the vines?"

Iris raised an eyebrow. "Seriously?"

"I don't know..."

"Our best hope in the middle of confusion and chaos is not to try and solve our problems ourselves. We just have to remember whose we are and who we hope in."

Fraser looked at Jonas.

"Dad said that, remember? When I got back from Slovenia?" He looked at Ned. "Right after Shae was taken."

Ned nodded slowly. "'Come to me all who labor and are heavy laden. I will give you rest.'" He pointed at Fraser. "You said that to me, right after you came back from the dead."

Iris's brow went up. "You were dead?"

"Mostly dead." He gave a small smile.

"You told me that I didn't have to carry the answers, or even the troubles," Ned said.

"What in your life requires you to trust God, Fraser?" Iris, pulling up one leg and wrapping her arm around it.

He frowned at her.

"Mom asked me that. She said that I choose the comfort of the known instead of the freedom of trusting God."

"My lifestyle is hardly comfort."

"It is to you," Jonas said. "You're a warrior. That's known. Putting down your identity... now, that's hard."

"I..." He drew in a breath.

"You told me once that feelings aren't facts. That God loves you and is doing something good in your life."

Pippa lying in a hospital bed struggling to live didn't feel like God's good.

"Your soul might be shaken, Fraser, but you will never be forsaken."

He looked at Jonas. "Dad?"

"No, that's all me, bro." He winked. "But maybe it's time to shrug off your fleshly identity and embrace your heavenly identity. You don't have to be a spec ops guy to be a warrior for the Lord."

"It's time for you to walk in that grace you keep preaching to us," Iris said. Smiled.

He smiled back. "So basically, you all stuck around to harass me into what? Proposing?"

Jonas's eyebrow went up.

Ned grinned at him, winked.

Iris made a sort of face.

"What?"

She shook her head.

"What?"

"I think Hud is going to propose. When he packed up his gear in the house, I saw...a jewelry box."

"I was thinking about maybe proposing to Sibba once we get this thing with Jones, Inc. sorted," Jonas said.

"Don't wait," Ned said. "Trust me on that."

Fraser laughed, and okay, maybe he didn't hate them sticking around.

A moan from the bed, and he looked over to see Pippa's eyes blink open. Her gaze went to Fraser with a frown. Then Jonas, and finally Ned and Iris. Back to Fraser.

"What's...happening..."

Fraser stood up. "Pip. You're okay. You're in the hospital. You got shot."

Her eyes widened. Then— "Imani?"

"She's fine. You saved the life of Princess Gemma too."

She took a breath, then seemed to sink into the bed, the pillow.

"But don't think you're going anywhere," he said, his crazy eyes filling. "Because you still need to save my life."

She stared at him.

"Oh, no, I was just being...you don't...I'm fine."

Her eyes narrowed, then she smiled. "Yeah, you are."

He pressed a kiss to her forehead. "Jonas, can you go tell the nurse that she's awake?"

Jonas left the room, and Fraser reached for her glass of water, the straw, and gave her a drink.

She closed her eyes, leaned back. Sighed. "I hurt."

"I know. You lost a lot of blood." He gripped her hand again, squeezed. "You'll be okay." He breathed out, the words finding a secure place in him. "You'll be okay."

She nodded, her face a little white. "Who shot me? Did they catch him?"

"No. We're still trying to sort that out. But the nurse said that you wanted to talk to me—that you needed to tell me something, right before you went into surgery. Do you remember what that was?"

She swallowed, shook her head. "The last thing I remember was watching Princess Imani and Prince Xavier take pictures at the game—no, wait. A dirigible. I remember that."

"We shot it down. It's sorted."

Her gaze stayed on him.

"I promise I'll tell you everything. But think, babe. Something...you wanted to tell me something."

Her eyes softened. "Maybe it was...I love you."

Oh. Well. "I love you too."

The nurse came in, followed by her doctor, and he had to step back as they ran more vitals on her, checked her pupils, then her wound.

He stood by the wall, arms folded, his gaze on her. Maybe he *should* propose. His prayer in the kitchen of the house settled over him. *Help me to embrace grace. A fresh start, whatever that is.*

Maybe this was it.

Maybe this was what forgiveness felt like. God's. His.

Yes. He most definitely was proposing.

The nurse left, and Fraser caught a glimpse of Jonas standing in the hallway, on his phone. His expression sent a chill through Fraser. Something grim and fierce.

Jonas turned away as the door closed.

When he turned around, Ned, too, was on his phone, frowning as he read a text.

"What's—"

The door opened and Jonas walked in. He was pocketing his phone, even as he took a deep breath. His gaze landed on Ned, who leaned up from the window.

"—going on?"

"That was Dad," Jonas said.

It took a second. "It's three a.m. in Minnesota."

"Mom's in the hospital. And it's serious. He needs us to come home, right now."

Fraser looked at him. "All of us?"

Jonas nodded.

"Why?"

"He wouldn't tell me." Jonas's eyes glistened, his jaw tight.

Oh.

Fraser walked over to Pippa, sat down. Took her hand. "No." He met her eyes. "I can't leave her."

Silence.

Iris was looking past him to Jonas. Behind her, Ned was nodding.

Jonas put a hand on his shoulder, squeezed. "Dad will understand."

"No," Pippa said. "No, Fraser. I'm fine. All I'm going to do is lie here in this bed for the next week and...what if it's serious?"

"Sounds serious," Jonas said. "But I agree with Fraser. We can't leave you alone."

"Pippa's not going to be alone."

Fraser looked over, and Imani stood in the room, wearing her backpack, a pair of jeans, sunglasses, and a white puffer jacket. She looked at Fraser, then the rest of them. "Sheesh, guys. You're freaking me out. What's going on?"

"My dad called. Something happened to Mom—she's in the hospital. He needs us to come home."

She dropped her backpack on the floor. "Then you should go."

"Imani—" Fraser started.

"Hey. I'll have you know I'm a fantastic bedside nurse. I'll change the channel and yell at her for not eating her Jell-O and make sure she doesn't harass the nurses." She walked over to Pippa, opposite Fraser, and took her other hand. "I'm not going anywhere."

Pippa smiled at her, tightened her hand in hers.

"I don't..." Fraser shook his head.

"Fraser. Go home. Your family needs you."

"I need you."

"I'm not going anywhere either."

He looked at her, then Imani, and back. "I don't trust either of you."

Pippa grinned. "Yeah you do. Because we know wherever we go, you'll just follow us."

He braced his hands on either side of her pillow, leaned down and touched her forehead. "And don't forget it." Then he kissed her. Sweetly, softly, lingering just a moment before he leaned away. "I'll be back, Pippi."

ELEVEN

C reed really didn't expect anyone to pick him up. Especially since he didn't have a cell phone or a way to call home.

So in the end, he paid a taxi driver a good chunk of his checking account to drive him all the way to Chester, Minnesota.

The house sat quiet under the bleeding dawn, the snow thick, the drive plowed, the family truck parked outside the garage. His breath caught in the air as he got out and paid the driver.

He needed food, a shower, and sleep, maybe not in that order. Still, as he opened the door to the house, the creak breaking the quiet morning, his heart deflated a little that his mother wasn't sitting in her chair by the window reading her Bible, a fresh basket of muffins on the island.

Instead, the chair was empty, wan light softening the night's edges in the great room. He toed off his boots, then dropped his jacket onto a hook and headed inside, right to the fridge.

Leftover lasagna. He wanted to weep. He pulled out the glass container and peeled off the plastic wrap. Let the smell fragrance the air.

Pulling out a knife, he cut a large piece and put it on a plate. Slipped it into the microwave over the stove.

Stood, watching the plate turn.

A creak sounded from the den. Maybe his father was up, working.

He walked over to the hallway.

Stilled.

The man stood in the semidarkness, dressed in a white T-shirt, jeans. A thin scrape of dark whiskers, dark curly hair cut short, and eyes that could turn Creed cold.

He didn't realize he held the butter knife until the man's eyes flicked down at it.

He held it up, a ridiculous move given the man's history, and probably skills, but—"Spider. What are you doing here?"

He still wasn't walking well, and fourteen-plus hours in an airplane had turned him achy, but every cell lit when Spider took a step toward him. "Hey, Creed."

Creed took a step back.

More light on his face now, and a scar over his eye made him seem tough. Or tougher.

The microwave beeped.

His brother was big—not tall, but like a truck. Clearly he'd spent time working out in the prison gym. Or his cell. Or on other people. "What are you..." Creed's breath caught. "Where are my parents? Do they know you're here?"

Spider held up a hand. He wore a tattoo on his forearm. "They're at the hospital. And yes."

The word—*hospital*—strummed through Creed, and a tightness gripped his chest. "What do you mean—hospital? *What did you do?*"

"Nothin', man. I didn't do anything." He took another step, and Creed did too.

"Dad?" He lifted his voice, his gaze hard on Spider.

"Not here, bro. Like I said, they're at the hospital. Some checkup or something."

"Get out. Right now—get out."

Spider now held up his hands. "No can do, bro. I'm supposed to be here."

Creed just stared at him.

"Garrett sent me back here to wait for the family. Said he texted them, that they're on the way home."

The words simply did not settle. "My dad...what? I—"

"Listen, you gonna get that microwave or just let it beep?"

Creed had nothing.

Spider kept a hand up but now walked over to the microwave and pulled out the plate. "Hot." He nearly dropped it on the island. "Jenny makes some killer lasagna."

Again, most of the words just sort of skipped against his brain, bounced off.

Still... "What?"

"Her lasagna. Almost as good as her good morning muffins." He went to the fridge and pulled out a gallon of milk.

For a second, a blink, it felt like he might be having an out-of-body experience, seeing himself, so many years ago when he'd first arrived at the Marshalls'. Spider, although bigger, tougher, angrier, making himself at home. Trying to believe...

"What is going on? What are you doing here?"

Spider screwed off the top of the milk, then reached for a glass.

At least he wasn't drinking out of the carton.

He poured himself a glass of milk. Then he pushed it to Creed. "You still like milk?"

Creed nodded.

"Put the butter knife down, bro. Sit down and eat something. You look like you haven't eaten in a week."

A beat, then, "Not until you tell me why—how—you got here."

"Jenny invited me." Spider reached for a plate also and cut off a piece of lasagna. "I've been here for about four days. Waiting for you." He put the plate into the microwave. "But, you know, helping around the vineyard too. Garrett is a real taskmaster."

He leaned a hip against the counter and folded his arms. Smiled at Creed.

It didn't feel like shark teeth, but... "You've been *here*?"

"Yeah. Didn't you get my letter? I wrote to you and told you I was getting out. I wanted to see you."

"I tore that letter up."

Spider's smile dimmed. "What?"

"I don't want to see you. Ever." He put down the butter knife and pulled the plate of lasagna toward him. Yeah, hot. He picked up the glass of milk, his eyes hard on Spider. "I threw the letter away. I'm done with you."

For the first time, Spider seemed less. As if Creed's words took the air right out of him. He swallowed, nodded, and turned away, gaze hard on the microwave.

Please. "You seriously thought—what? You'd come out here and we'd be a family? I have a family, Spider. A real family who loves me. They adopted me. I *changed my name*."

Spider nodded, his back still to him.

Oh brother. "What?"

"Nothin'. You're right." The microwave beeped, and Spider opened it. Took out the plate. Set it on the counter. Braced his hands on the island. "I just thought...maybe...you'd forgiven me."

The air left the room. Creed sank onto the stool.

Silence fell between them, and in it, of course, Judah's voice lifted inside. Creed had left the guy at JKF when he'd switched planes, but...yeah, their conversation had found soil.

Now, *You start with confessing your anger. And then you forgive the people that hurt you. And then you tell the devil to leave you alone, because you are a child of God.*

Weird. Like Judah knew he'd come home to face Spider? Yeah. Whatever. But as Spider stood there, unmoving, the words wouldn't subside.

Confess. Forgive.

He swallowed. "I'm angry at you, Spider. Because of you, Janelle is dead and Mom is dead and...Apollo is gone and..." His eyes filled. "Man. You have no right to come back here and mess up my life again."

"I know." The words emerged soft, a little broken. "I know." His eyes were wet. "I was scared. Really scared. Dad was...a...he was—"

"A monster."

Spider nodded. "So I thought, you know, I'd get with some brothers. Learn how to keep us safe. But it all blew up, and then J was killed and, yeah, it was my fault." He closed his eyes, looked away. "Sometimes I can still hear Ma screaming."

Creed couldn't speak.

"I know it's my fault. And you have every right to be angry at me." Then he opened his eyes and looked at Creed. "But look at this life. This—family that...that God gave you. He rescued you, man. Can't you see that?"

Creed's mouth tightened, a tight tangle of words caught inside. But he nodded. Because right then, standing in the kitchen, the sun stretching across the great room, he saw it. God had taken an angry kid and given him more than he could ever imagine.

I'm sorry, God, for my anger.

Maybe, in fact, Spider needed what he'd been given. Grace. A new identity. Belonging. Who...and whose.

Spider looked away, shook his head, then back to Creed. "I came here because your mom started writing to me. In jail. Right after you arrived, and she...she told me how you...you were like this gift or something to her. I didn't write her back. I figured I had no claim on you, you know? But then she just kept writing and telling me about your life and how you turned into this track star and went to state. She told me that God had a plan, for you and for me. She told me how you rescued all them kids after the tornado. I ordered the newspaper. I cut out the article and hung it up in my cell." His gaze fixed on Creed. "I'm so proud of you, brother."

You're not my brother. The words pulsed inside him, but staring at Spider, the wretched look on his face, his dark-brown eyes filled with tears, something inside Creed broke.

"She told me that God had a good plan, even though it looked pretty dark where I was sitting, and...finally I started writing back. And then one day, she and your dad came to see me and everything changed."

"They came to see you?"

"Told me that I could be forgiven."

What? "They never mentioned it to me."

"I asked them not to." He made a face, and a tear crashed down his cheek. "I didn't want to mess up your life any more than I already had."

Aw...shoot. He stared at Spider, his chest hammering. "I forgive you, Spider."

Spider stilled. "What?"

He took a breath, this time louder. "I forgive you." Simple words, but weirdly, with them a terrible knot, deep inside his chest, simply gave way. And with it, a strange fullness, a painful rush of compassion swept through him. He saw not only the scars on Spider's body—the prison tats, the scars on his arms, his shoulder, his face—but the ones inside.

Saw Spider, then, as a child, hiding with him and Janelle under the bed.

Spider, holding his hand at night, Ma screaming in the next room.

Spider, telling him that everything was going to be okay right before he slipped out the window.

"I forgive you, brother."

Spider covered his face with one hand, and then his shoulders started to shake.

Creed had nothing to stop the burning in his eyes, the tears that came. Oh, it hurt, but the groan that twisted through him sent him off the stool and around the island.

And then Spider turned and threw his meaty arms around Creed, crushed him to himself.

And wept.

Creed closed his eyes and let himself feel the strength of his brother's sorrow, and as Spider wept, he released his grip on his own. The anger. The guilt. The grief.

And somehow, in its place, a wholeness swept over him.

Even peace.

Spider eased his grip, and with a shudder, let him go. Stepped back. Met his eyes, his own reddened. Nodded. Then, "The lasagna is getting cold."

Right.

He hobbled back to his place, pulled the plate and milk to himself. Spider sat at the other end with a fresh glass of milk, diving in.

Silence, but it didn't hurt.

Finally, "So, you've been here for four days?"

"Yeah. But yesterday, your mom had an episode or something. Garrett drove her to the hospital and told me to stick around. Wanted me to watch over the place." He shook his head. "Pretty brave."

"No. My dad knows people." He looked up, and Spider gave him a half grin. "Wait. You said yesterday?"

"Yeah. I'm supposed to bring you guys to the hospital when you show up."

Creed put down his fork. "You just might be the worst messenger ever. Get dressed. We're leaving now."

Spider picked up his plate, shoveled in the last of his food, and set it in the sink.

Creed went up to the bathroom, splashed some water on his face, brushed his teeth, then eased his way back down the stairs. Better. He was definitely healing.

Spider stood at the bottom of the stairs, frowning. "What happened to your leg?"

He hit the landing. "Got shot saving the life of a princess."

Spider gave a laugh. "Yeah, right."

Creed said nothing as they went outside and climbed into the truck.

"Does this have anything to do with her collapse last month?" he asked as they pulled out.

"Dunno," Spider said. "I do know that your dad told her it was time, or something like that when they left."

Creed let that roll around inside him. But yeah, it was time. He could feel it, like a charge about to go off inside him. *We were created to be fruitful, to be used by Him beyond our wildest imaginations.*

He looked at Spider, sitting at the wheel of the truck, something solid and resolute on his face, a peace in his countenance.

Yeah, God was definitely up to something.

The sun had cleared the eastern horizon, bright upon the city as they entered Waconia. Spider had filled him in on his life at the prison and what he knew about Apollo, who had written to him once, many years ago.

"We'll find him," Spider said, and looked over at Creed. They pulled up to the entrance. "Hop out and I'll park."

"Thanks." Creed slid out of the truck and headed inside. Gave his name at the entrance, and they issued him a badge and his mother's room number. Took the elevator up.

The floor was quiet, a reception desk right outside the elevator door. He flashed his badge, then headed down the hallway.

The door to his mother's room hung half open, and inside, a male doctor stood at the foot of her bed, writing in his tablet.

Creed half knocked, then came in. The doctor looked up. "Can I help you?"

"Yeah. I'm Creed Marshall. That's my mom."

Maybe. Jenny Marshall lay in the bed, her skin dusky, almost yellow, looking fragile and fading. He stared at her, a fist punching through him. "Mom?"

"She's sleeping. I'm Doctor Gregg." He held out his hand.

"Where's my dad?"

"Stepped out to get coffee. Are you ready to get started? You're over eighteen?"

Creed shook his hand. "Twenty."

"Good. I'll have a nurse come in soon to get your consent, then run through the procedure. We'll need blood tests, a chest X-ray, an EKG, and an ultrasound of your liver. If all that looks good, we'll do a CT scan to make sure your liver is big enough to donate a piece."

The words fell through him, and he processed them slowly, until, "My mom needs a liver?"

The doctor frowned. "I thought that's why you came. Your father said the family was on the way."

Oh.

"It's just me for now. Um..." He looked at her. Then, why not? "Where do I sign?"

The man smiled. "You father did say that all his kids wouldn't hesitate to help."

His kids. Well, count him in. He nodded, and the doctor left.

He walked over to his mother's bed, her blonde hair splayed on the pillow, her skin thin, almost translucent. He leaned down and kissed her forehead.

She didn't rouse.

The nurse came in with a tablet, then had him sign. "Let's bring you down to phlebotomy to get your blood panel drawn. Then we can start with the other tests."

He stood up, looked out the window. *Even before you were born, God was thinking of all the ways He loved you. And the great plan He had for your life if you let Him.*

Okay, then. Let's do this.

He followed the nurse down to the lab. Then he donned a gown for his chest X-ray, and then sat for an EKG. And finally, lay on a table for the ultrasound.

An hour later, he made his way back up to her room.

His father stood at the window.

"Hey, Dad."

He turned around. Oh, his father had aged a year in a week, lines around his eyes, his hair graying. The man looked exhausted. "Creed." He walked over. "I'm so glad you're back." He enfolded him in a hug.

"Got in this morning. Spider brought me over."

His father let go, his hands on his shoulders. "Sorry. We should have told you." He made a face. "Your mom got sick so fast, I sort of forgot..." He pressed a hand to his mouth.

"What's going on, Dad? Why does Mom need a liver transplant?"

He sighed. "Your mom has liver damage from all the cancer treatments."

"Oh."

It was then his father looked past him, to the hallway, back to him. "Where are your siblings?"

He shrugged. "I don't know. HMSD sent me home alone."

"HMSD?"

"Her Majesty's Security Detail."

His father raised an eyebrow.

"It's a long story, Dad. But don't worry. I took the panel."

His father nodded but wore a strange expression.

"What?"

"Nothing. It's just...um...well, probably the match will come from a biological child, Creed."

Oh. Sure. He cleared his throat. "Yeah. I knew that. I just...I wanted to help."

His dad clapped his hand around his neck, then lowered his forehead to his. "I would expect nothing less from my son."

"Just keep smiling, honey. You're doing great."

Princess Gemma held up a freshly wrapped gift and smiled as

the photographers snapped another shot of her wrapping toys for the annual holiday Port Fressa Children's Hospital visit.

Imani and her mother had spent the morning cutting and wrapping and posing, and frankly, if this was what royal service was—

"Okay, I think we have enough," said Beatrix, her mother's secretary.

Tamsyn, her new, rather grumpy, all-business security detail ushered them out. Oh, how she missed Pippa.

Pippa would at least have a smile for her, maybe a wink.

Pippa would ask her how she's doing, and maybe even tell her that she found a cool pizza place that delivered to the palace's secret entrance.

She hadn't realized how much she needed Pippa in her life.

Staff swooped up to the table and began to wrap the rest of the gifts as her mom pushed her hand into the crook of Imani's arm. "You okay to go to the hospital with me tomorrow?" They walked out of the waiting room with the tall golden panels and into the hallway where the ancestors of the House of Blue watched their conversation.

"Yes, of course. I made a promise. I'm in this. Gifts for kids. Two thumbs up."

Her mother gave her a look. She looked tired today, her hair back in a bun, elegant in a pair of white pants and a red sweater. But ever since the nightmare at the game, she'd seemed...overwhelmed.

Imani squeezed her hand. "I can even go alone, you know. I got this."

Her mom stopped her in the hall, right in front of a window. The sunlight striped the parquet wood floors, and tiny winter fairies danced in the light. Outside, one of the church bells rang— noon. "You don't have to do this, you know."

"Go to the hospital?"

"Take the oath of Lauchtenland, submit to the investiture. Become a working royal."

Oh.

"You had your whole life planned out, and then...I went and married a prince."

"Just happened to marry a prince, like, oops, tripped, and there he was."

"Actually—"

"I know about the three-legged race and the burlap sacks, Mom. I was there. But you make it sound like I'm a victim here."

Her mom drew in a breath.

Imani held up a hand. "And I get that. I sort of acted that way too. For far too long. And because of it, people got hurt." Her eyes burned. "Pippa got hurt."

"Oh, honey, Pippa getting shot was not your fault."

"I know."

"She was saving my life, if you'll recall."

"Yeah, I...don't remember much, actually."

"Me either. I blame it on pregnant brain."

Imani froze.

Her mom smiled.

"What?"

"Yes. We're expecting. Again. But it's still early, so..." She put a finger to her lips. "The doctors found out when they were checking me over after the incident."

"Oh, Mom." Imani threw her arms around her neck. "I'm so happy for you."

"You don't mind having a sibling?"

"Are you kidding me?" She stepped back. "Dibs on teaching them the jump shot."

Her mom laughed. "Okay. You can have that one."

"So, actually, Pippa saved two lives."

"Yes, she did." They kept walking. "How is she doing?"

"Recuperating. You know her—she's already up and taking walks. Said she was trying to get CCTV footage of the attack at Titus Stadium so she could figure out what happened. I do think she feels weird to be back home with her mom in Dalholm."

"She doesn't have a place in Port Fressa?"

"She has a room here, but...I don't know. She wanted to go home. I'm not sure why. But now she misses the palace. I think she'll be back soon."

"Has she recovered her memory of what happened?"

"No. And without her testimony, no one believes Creed about Griff."

"Do you believe him?"

They'd reached her apartment. "I...yes. But you know, I can't believe that Prince Xavier would have someone so close to him who would try and kill me."

"Because Prince Xavier is in love with you."

She shrugged and opened her door.

"I can see it. He dotes on you." Her mom pointed to a massive spray of lavender roses on Imani's bureau.

"I think I'm a long way off from...well, falling in love with anyone."

"You need to get over Creed first."

She nodded, her throat thick. "I wish I'd been able to say goodbye to him. I might have been able to explain, or even just... you know, thank him. Maybe it would help us both to move on. Although..." She shook her head, shrugged. "He hasn't called, so whatever."

"Oh, Imani. Sweetie. You could call him."

"I don't think...I...I'll just drag him into trouble by his heart. I can't do that to him. Besides, with his mom's illness, I think maybe I should stay away."

"His mother's illness?" She'd sat on the settee near the hearth, the fire now at a low crackle.

"Yeah, his dad called all the siblings home to get tested for a donor liver match. His mom had cancer years ago, and now her liver is failing."

"Oh no."

"When I talked to Pippa yesterday, they were still waiting on the results. Apparently it takes a couple weeks to get all the labs in, but...yeah, they're hoping someone is a match."

"With that many children, I'm sure..."

"Maybe. Otherwise she goes on the donor list."

Her mom looked at the fire. "You just never know what life is going to throw at you. How and where you're going to end up. The journey you'll take." She looked at Imani. "Your mom and dad would be so proud to see how you ended up. You're so brave and compassionate, and you believe in justice." Her eyes glistened. "You deserved a better journey, Imani. Parents who didn't die suddenly, a grandmother who wasn't overwhelmed—"

"And then I wouldn't have gotten you and Prince John." She walked over, sat next to her mother on the settee.

"He wouldn't mind if you called him Dad, or Papa, or...Father?"

She laughed at the way her mother said it. "Give me time. I'm still getting used to being a princess."

"Which brings me back to the investiture. You don't have to do it."

"Oh, but, Mom, I do. And it's not just about a promise. It's about...me. Yes, I offered it in a moment of panic, as leverage, but as soon as Grandmum suggested it, I started wondering if maybe that was the point of all this. I'm not sure the old Imani, who set out on her walkabout, as you put it, would have said yes to the impact she could have on the world.

"I once told Pippa that I didn't want to be a princess anymore. And it wasn't about the weight of it—it was because I didn't feel like a princess. It's not a title...it's a state of being. It's being set apart to do good things. And, yes, I wanted to do something great...but I wanted to do it on my terms. It wasn't until I was with Creed and his family that I realized that surrendering is the key to doing something great. To living the life that stirs you deep inside."

"There's something in the Bible about that. Losing your life to find it." Her mom winked.

"Yeah. I know. And maybe I forgot that a little, but these last few months have reminded me of it. I think being the Duchess of Dalholm is my *calling*. And now that sounds weird."

"Or, spoken like a true princess of God."

"You aren't disappointed?"

"What, that you're not going back to America where I could lose you to some college? Never. As long as you're happy." She slipped her hand into Imani's.

"I...am."

Her mother looked at the fire, then at Imani. "So, John and I were talking, and we were wondering if you'd like to go to Hearts Bend for Christmas."

Imani stilled. "Spend Christmas with Memaw and Pops?"

"Yeah. But first, see, there's this charity event for the International Children's Cancer Fund."

"Oh yeah. The one with the Minnesota Vikings...really?"

"Yes. I was thinking that you could represent the crown at the event."

"Aren't you going?"

"Yes. Prince John and I will be there, but there is a small speech that must be given, and...I think you should be the one to give it."

Her mouth opened. Closed. Then, "I think I'll need a date."

"You most likely will."

A beat. "Prince Xavier will be there."

Her mother raised an eyebrow. "Is that...your chosen date?"

She shook her head.

Her mother sighed. "I know I should warn you. Say things like...guard your heart. And remember, he can't return to Lauchtenland. And most importantly, don't hurt this man, after all he's done for you. But I have a feeling he'd be throwing caution to the wind too."

"He's a lot like me."

"This is both the trouble and the reason why we like him." She smiled.

Imani gave her a sad smile. "Maybe I should just...let him go. Forget him."

Her mom pressed her arm. "You never forget your first love."

And then, for some reason, Penny was in her head. *It's the way he makes me feel—like the sun rises inside me, into a new day. When I'm scared or alone or even angry, he's the one I want to talk to. He believes in me, and around him I'm braver, bolder, smarter, prettier....yeah, he's the one.*

Yes. Yes, he was. "He wasn't my first love. Creed is my *true* love."

Her mother said nothing, and they sat in front of the fire, watching the flames die, turn to embers.

"What's this?" Her mother got up and lifted a gauzy white feather off the mantel. Wispy and light.

"Oh, it was on the floor of my room when I got home from the hospital." She took it from her mom. "Maybe it was from one of the maid's dusters."

Her mother made a sound, then put it back on the mantel. "Interesting. You know there's a fairytale about a feather that appears to the royals of Lauchtenland when they've found the one."

She drew in a breath. "I know the story. But I don't quite fit the fairytale."

"Or maybe you do."

Hmm.

"Would you mind if Pippa came with us to America?"

"Oh, I'm not sure she'll be ready for HMSD service."

"Off duty. As a friend. As a...sister." The word felt a little clumsy, but then right as it settled in her heart. "She's seen a lot with me."

"And you're both in love with Marshall men."

There was that.

"She's put up with an awful lot. Maybe it's time I give her a thank-you."

"If she'll let you. Pippa is pretty by-the-book." Her mom got up. "You know, I know what the crown and common sense tell you to do. But then...there's the happy ending that God wants for you."

"How do I know what that is?"

"You don't. You just follow His leading, one step at a time." She leaned over and kissed her forehead, then walked out of the room. Imani got up, lifted the feather from the mantel, and walked to the window, looked out at the festive lights of the castle grounds, the tree bedazzled with gold ornaments, the wispy blue sky.

And ran the feather through her fingers.

TWELVE

C'mon, brain, remember.

Pippa heightened her pace as she walked up the hill to her family home in North Dalholm, a paper bag in her hand, sweat along the brow of her wool cap.

She'd thought the fresh air and home might jog the memories loose, the twelve hours that included the attack that seemed to have been scooped from her mind. But two weeks later, the memory remained embedded, a sliver, painful and pulsing, festering.

She just needed to extract it. Because answers came with it.

Like, who had shot her?

She rounded the stone fence that belonged to the Mullinses. A hundred more meters to her house. But first she stopped and stared back at the village. The mountains rose to the northeast, white-capped and gorgeous against a pale blue sky. The old town, the north of Dalholm, scattered below her, a cluster of stone houses huddled together, winding roads skirting between them. The vast North Sea Channel to the west churned, white caps upon pewter. And in the far-off distance, the island of Keswick, where Prince Xavier held court. Beyond that, out of reach, Scotland.

And set up on a hill on the western edge of the village, the stone castle of Hadsby.

"Pippa, is that you?"

She looked over to see Nan Mullins coming out of her house. The older woman wore a pair of woolen pants, a thick knitted sweater, a farmer's cap. She walked over to a small pen and opened the gate. Chickens began to cluck for their breakfast.

"It is, ma'am," Pippa said.

"I see ya stopped at the bakery. Bringing some meringue to yer mum, are you?"

She laughed. "Maybe for me."

"That's good. Ya look too skinny." She pointed at her. "I saw ya on the news, with the princess. Made a name fer yerself. The girls down at Hove Grammar still remember ya. Couldn't keep a dress clean to save yer life."

"Still can't." She tossed her away with a wave and a smile.

"Glad to see ya home, missy!" Nan waved, then headed to the feed bucket.

Pippa headed up the hill. The wind whipped down from the mountains, found the spaces in her puffer, and blew her tracksuit against her legs. So much for the sweat.

But at least she could walk without assistance, and soon, she'd put a run back into her schedule, get back in shape so she could...

What? Return to service? It seemed like the right answer. So why did it sit at sharp angles in her heart?

She entered the gate to her mother's house, the one she shared with her husband, Basil Cliffe, the other barrister at Cliffe and Butler. She'd kept her deceased husband's name even after the marriage.

But they seemed happy, melding together in this life.

Boxes covered the roses that lined the stone house, and the walk had been shoveled, everything tidied for winter. But in summer, her mother's English roses bloomed white and yellow, thick and fragrant. It reminded Pippa often of her childhood home Wython, in the north, back when life felt simpler. Waiting for her father to arrive home after his duty at Perrigwynn. Her mother working in a local law firm. She'd had easy dreams then.

A home. A husband. A family.

Then her father died, and things got complicated for a while, at least in her heart. Until they didn't.

Follow her father's footsteps.

Done.

"Mum?" She came in, took off her boots and coat, then walked into the kitchen and dropped the bag with the meringue onto the round wooden table. Sunlight streamed into the kitchen windows over the sink, across the granite countertops, over the tile floor, and more windows pooled light into the cozy sitting area with the whitewashed hearth. The main room connected to a den-slash-guest room where Pippa had set up shop.

Hours, so far, watching different angles of Titus Stadium, trying to spot her assailant.

She'd also requested CCTV footage of the visitors at the Port Fressa jail, where Fredrik was killed.

Turning on the kettle, she found the basket of teabags and opened the fridge to the bowl of lemons. She cut herself a slice, put the tea bag into a cup, then cut herself a piece of meringue. Because yes, she should be getting back in shape, but she also loved meringue.

But something else warred inside her that she couldn't put a finger on.

The water boiled, and she poured it into her teacup. Picked up the saucer and a spoon and headed to the den.

Her father's den, even though her mother had moved in, replaced pictures, cleared his desk. But somehow, the memories remained.

Her father, sitting in his tweed chair in the corner, reading the papers. Or a book. Putting it down when she came into the room to climb onto his lap. Pictures of their life hung on the walls— Pippa and her dad at the seashore, the whole family in the shadow of Hadsby Castle in the early days after their move here.

His books still cluttered the shelves of the built-in case. But as her gaze fell on it, she noticed a weathered orange oversized album. She took it down and sank into the tweed chair and opened it.

Her drawings. Huh. Some of them on coloring pages, others on blank paper. Crayon and marker, and pencil as she got older.

She turned the pages and stopped on a drawing of a giant tree, fairies dancing around it. A castle behind it.

"I remember that one."

She looked up, and her mother stood at the door. She wore black wool pants and a white blouse, a scarf, her dark hair pulled back, neatly coiffed. Maybe on her way to work.

"You drew that one for the queen."

Huh. "Yes. She came into Dad's office once when I was about twelve and saw me drawing. She told me that fairies lived under the big linden tree near the castle, and that if I wanted to, I could watch over them someday. I told her I wanted to be a royal guard."

"Of course you did." She made no move to walk in farther, just folded her arms and leaned against the frame. "She gave this back to me at your father's funeral. Said that she hoped one day you'd find your way back to this."

Pippa frowned. "Back to what?"

"Dreaming?" Now she came in. "The day your father was shot changed you, Pippa. I hate that you were there, that you saw it. I think for a long time you thought it was your fault."

Her throat tightened. "I know it wasn't. Dad chose to be there. I'm proud of him."

"I'm proud of you."

She looked up.

"Your father's death took out both of us. I threw myself into work, and that wasn't the right thing."

"Mum. You did what you could."

"Yes. And you did too. But when I married Basil, he reminded me that we have seasons. And my season of grief was

253

over." She offered a smile. "I still miss your father. He was my first love. And I have you because of that. But he wasn't my only love."

Pippa looked up. "For a barrister, you are taking a long time to get to the point."

Her mother gave a small laugh. "Very good. Well, I suppose I'm saying that there is a season for everything. And maybe the fairies miss you."

Pippa looked at the picture again. Maybe.

"I see how much time you spend with your man, Fraser, on video chat, and then the long blank stares afterward. Your heart isn't here, Pip. It's over there."

"It's here. Too." Maybe that was the problem.

"How is he?"

"Worried. His mother is home from the hospital, but they're still waiting on the results of the donor tests. All the kids took them, but they're not sure who might be a match."

"Is he coming back to Lauchtenland?"

That was the question, wasn't it? "I'm not sure yet."

"Or are you going there?"

She made a face. "My world is here."

"Is it?"

She studied her mother. "You just can't escape the hard questions."

"I'm a barrister." She winked. "And your mother." She glanced at the array on the desk. "What are you working on here?"

"Oh." Pippa closed the scrapbook. "I'm trying to see if I can jog my memory loose. I can't remember the events around the shooting, so..." She lifted a shoulder. "I got access to the CCTV at Titus Stadium, and I'm just trying to see if I can figure out what happened."

"But this is a view of the Port Fressa jail visitor inspection room."

"Yeah, it's not very helpful. You mostly get the backs of people."

"You have the wrong CCTV file. You need to request the file on list of persons who signed in."

"Gunner gave me that. So far no one has checked in to visit Fredrik the day of his murder."

"Perhaps you need the photo scan."

"What's that?"

"It's a photo they take of everyone entering." She turned to her. "I can get it for you. It's an easy request, although it takes a day or so."

"Yeah. That would be great."

Her mother headed to the door. "On one condition."

"Oh no."

"Oh yes. I just want you to ask yourself what you really want."

Fraser's words, and now they struck her, stilled her.

"Pippa?"

"I...I'm not sure we always get what we want."

"True. Often, instead, we get what we need."

"Maybe I don't know what I want. Or need."

Her mother had stopped by the door. "Yes. But God does. He knows even our unspoken desires. You might start by asking Him."

She stared at her mother.

"Pippa Fay. God isn't done with you yet. Or have you forgotten the verse your father prayed over you every time he left."

No, no she hadn't. "Isaiah 43:1."

"Yes. Your father didn't leave you—or me—destitute. He left us in the hands of our Heavenly Father. You are His. And He loves to delight in His children. Is that meringue I see?"

"Knock yourself out."

An eyebrow rose.

"Blame Princess Imani." Pippa grinned.

Her mother left, and she got up, then sat down at the desk. Stirred the tea, then squeezed the lemon in. Stared at the still picture of a man emptying his pockets. She pushed play.

The ridiculous camera angle only got his wide back,

shoulders, dark hair. Into the tray he dropped sunglasses, pocket change, a car key, then he took off a ring and a watch from his wrist.

She hit pause, then picked up the tea.

What do you want, Pippa?

Easy. Because there was nothing like waking up in a hospital bed to see the answer looking at you with delicious blue eyes, so much love on his face that it swept away any pain, any fear.

Any doubt.

But it was like the fairies, a dream.

She belonged to the House of Blue in Lauchtenland. And he belonged to the House of Marshall in Minnesota. And she simply didn't know how to bridge that gap.

She looked out the window, at the stretch of sky and ocean. To the tiny island of Keswick, a steppingstone between the two.

Wait. Turning back to the video, she enlarged the shot, then again, and again, until only the contents of the container filled the screen.

She knew that watch. *Prince John* had that watch. Eighteen carat gold case, with a blue face, gold hands. It featured a perpetual calendar with smaller orbitals for days of the month, day of the week, and the month of the year.

It had been designed by the House of Schaffhausen, long ago, for the House of Blue, and official members received it upon their investiture.

No. That couldn't be right...

"Pippa, darling, you have a visitor."

Pippa set her tea down and got up.

She'd have to call Gunner, who would call Ethan and—

Her Royal Highness Princess Imani stood in the kitchen. She wore a pair of jeans, Uggs and a white puffer jacket, a headband, and that long weave still in her hair from the ball. Even dressed down, the woman was gorgeous, but something about her seemed changed. Different.

Her mother stood at the sink, just rising from a curtsy. Pippa stared at her, then curtsied.

"Please, Pippa. C'mon. It's me."

Pippa stood. "I see that, ma'am."

Tamsyn, Pippa's replacement, for now, stood behind her and nodded to Pippa. Tamsyn had been on Princess Daffy's detail until recently, when Daffy had moved officially to Hadsby. But Daffy, who'd grown up in the palace, her mother one of the servants, was a far cry from Imani.

Lace up your running shoes, Tas, Pippa wanted to say.

Instead, she nodded back.

"Stop with the ma'am, also. Listen. How are you feeling?"

"Healing, ma—Princess."

"You just can't break it, can you?" Imani grinned at her.

"I'm sorry, but...I'm afraid not." Oh yes, she missed standing behind, in front of, and around this woman.

"Feel good enough for a trip?"

"I...maybe. Depends. Where are we going?"

Imani waggled her eyebrows. "Do you trust me?"

She looked at her. "Oh no."

Imani grinned. "Oh yes. Do. You. Trust me?"

Pippa looked at her mother, who shrugged. Fine. But it wasn't a hard truth. "Yes, Princess, I trust you."

"Good. Get your stuff, we're leaving."

"To where?"

"First stop—the Vintage Shop. You're going to need a dress."

"So, what are you going to do?" Ham looked over from where he was stringing the lights on his over-large Christmas tree. It towered nearly thirteen feet and took up half the great room of his remodeled 1970s home, but it filled the vaulted space with cheer and a piney smell, and most of all, his nearly teenage daughter Aggie couldn't stop grinning.

So yeah, Fraser didn't hate the distraction of the past few hours, using his truck to meet Ham at the Chester Christmas tree farm, help Aggie find the perfect tree, load it into his truck, and help Ham haul it into the house.

Now, Fraser was a light dispenser, feeding Ham the untangled white and red lights that he wound like a surgeon through each branch, then around the trunk and back out. "I'm going to unbox more lights. For cryin' out loud, you have enough here to go twice around the world."

Ham looked down, laughed. "What my princess wants, my princess gets."

Aggie beamed at her dad, looking up from where she sorted ornaments.

And of course, for a second, the word brought him back to Lauchtenland, to Imani, then Pippa and the last time he'd held her hand. The ache pulsed, a fresh shot to his heart.

"Ham, you're going to spoil her!" The shout came from the galley kitchen where Signe was pulling out fresh-baked rolls. The house smelled of cinnamon and brown sugar and stirred up memories of Christmases at the Marshall house.

Not this year, although everyone, especially Sibba and Jonas, was throwing in to help with the baking and Christmas prep, only four days to go.

But despite the festivities at the homestead, he couldn't shake the doom that gripped his soul.

Mom. Pippa. The war inside himself. But maybe, today, he could wage one battle. Find a win.

"Actually, I was hoping to talk to you about that," he said, looking up at Ham as he fed him the last of this strand of lights.

"Oh?" Ham pointed to a bag, and Fraser walked over, found it full of more boxes of lights. He pulled one out and opened it. Unwound the string.

Then he returned and handed up the lights. "Yeah. I was...I think..."

"Oh," Ham said, stilling. "It's that talk."

Fraser swallowed, and Ham climbed down the ladder. Glanced at Aggie, then Signe, who still wore her hot pads. She looked domestic, but she'd spent years undercover with the CIA, so, yeah.

Reminded him a lot of Pippa, really. Beautiful. Unflappable.

"Let's go outside," Fraser said. Maybe he needed the brisk chill of a Minnesota day to gird him up. *You're a warrior. That's known. Putting down your identity...now, that's hard.*

Maybe not as hard as it might have been three months ago. Still.

Ham handed him his jacket, and they stepped outside. Ham led him toward the fire pit, shoveled and freshly used.

He loved Ham's backyard, the wide, flat meadow that led to a sloping hill that fell to the lake below, now thick with ice and snow. They'd played football in this yard only four months ago, and Fraser had practically begged to join the team again.

The Jones, Inc. team. His life. His world. Until...

"I think I'm...out."

Ham had picked up wood, secured under a waterproof tarp. Now he set the wood in the firepit, making a tent with the three logs. "Yeah. I was waiting for that."

Fraser looked at him. Ham wore a hard-edged look in his eyes as he stared out toward the lake.

"Ham?"

"It's all good." But he blew out a breath. "Orion and Jenny are moving back to Alaska, permanently. He's going to help out Air One Rescue there."

"I met them. Moose Mulligan's crew."

"Yeah. And"—he grinned, cast a glance at Fraser—"Jake is taking a timeout as soon as the baby's born."

"Stay-at-home dad?"

"Maybe. For a while. Aria's got that offer on the table to head up the Children's Cardiothoracic Department at Texas Children's Hospital in Houston."

"You're losing the team?"

"No. Skeet and North are out on a detail right now. And I still have Scarlett on tech, but she asked for some PTO."

"Oh?"

"She and Ford are taking a page from Ned and Shae, I think. Last I heard, they were heading to sunshine." Ham added kindling and paper to the tepee. "But, yes, it seems like I'll need to do some recruiting."

"I heard you're thinking about recruiting Sibba."

"Yeah. I'm in a dogfight with Logan. He got a whiff of her skills in Lauchtenland—"

"More than a whiff. She saved the entire freakin' country."

"Yep. So he wants her for the Caleb Group. And he's got some sort of meteorology job lined up for Jonas in Miami. Monitoring hurricanes."

"Oh, you're cooked, man."

"I know." He sighed, and that triggered all Fraser's tripwires.

"Maybe I shouldn't..."

"Nope. We're good here." He lit a match, and the fire caught on the paper. Then he tossed the match into the kindling and stood up. "I remember standing almost right here a few months ago telling you that God has a plan. And that He'll tell you when you're ready to get back in the game."

"My hand...it's getting better. And I feel ready. I don't know. I feel bad walking out on you."

"Just because our feelings tell us something doesn't mean it's the plan. You need to ask God what He wants. That's your answer."

The flame had started to flicker, to grow.

"I know I'm supposed to be with Pippa. I can't imagine my life without her. I just don't know how." He looked up. "But it can't be with me involved with Jones, Inc., leaving for months on end. I...I want a different life, Ham." He glanced toward the house. "Your life. And Jake's life. The life I see my parents have."

"I get that. By the way, how is your mom?"

The fire had started to nip into the logs, crackling, sending up black curls of smoke. Fraser stuck his hands in his pockets, warming them.

"It's serious. She should have told us earlier, so I'm trying not to be angry about that. But she needs a liver transplant. All of us got tested." He gave a chuckle. "Even Creed."

"Who knows, right? I've heard stories of entire families not matching and a wildcard donor steps in."

"Thanks for that." The flames snapped and popped.

"Sorry. I'm sure one of you will match. I'll bet your mom likes having all you home."

"It's loud, for sure. Hud and Iris are big into the college playoffs. And Ned and Shae keep talking about their amazing honeymoon. Jonas and Sibba have taken over Christmas dinner duties, so that's a production."

"Jonas never does anything small."

"Or without way too much research. So it's just Creed and me sort of wandering around the house."

"That sounds bonding. How is he doing?"

"Not thrilled about being deported from Lauchtenland, but it was the only move. His brother Spider was at the house when he got home."

"Spider? That's a name."

"I think it's a nickname. But he's interesting, at the least. He was in prison, and of course my mom decided to write to him. And somewhere along the way, he found Jesus. My folks invited him to visit, but he's sort of unpacked."

"That's your parents, for sure."

"I know. Creed seems okay with it, though. Spider has a cot in the garage, and they spend a lot of time working out. Creed's getting stronger. He's walking better. Doing a lot of extra PT, volume up high in his earbuds."

"Reminds me of someone," Ham said, glancing at him. "You sure he doesn't have spec ops in him?"

"He might. He's smart, though. And resourceful. And tough. So, I guess, yes?"

"Or he goes to college and gets a degree and does something where he doesn't have to leave behind the people he loves."

Fraser looked at the flames again, now blackening the wood, turning them to char. "You need me, ever, for something...off-books, you call."

Ham nodded, also staring at the fire. "So, what's your next move?"

"I don't know."

"You going to ask your dad to help with the winery?"

"I'd rather run naked across shards of ice, but...maybe. Dad built a good life. I'd have to get Pippa on board, though, so..."

"Have you talked to her about it?"

"Can't figure out the right time. She's back on her feet and has been working hard on trying to remember who shot her. I remember what that's like, to be obsessed about something. It's consuming."

"What if she never gets it back? She'll have to learn to let go."

"She doesn't let go easily."

"You're right. She's a perfect fit for you."

Fraser laughed. "I'm learning."

His phone buzzed and he pulled it out of his jeans pocket. "Dad says the doctor is going to call in an hour. Wants us all on a Zoom call. I need to roll."

Ham turned to him. "God loves you and is doing something good in your life. Don't forget that." He held out a fist.

Fraser met it, then headed to the truck.

The sun had fallen across the horizon on the backside of the day by the time he pulled into his parents' plowed drive. He sat for a moment in the truck, watching the simmer of orange through the dormant cottonwoods on the far side of the property. Snow topped the barn roof, and every vine slept under a blanket of pristine white. Magical in its stillness, waiting.

And then he could almost hear his father's voice lifting over the vines as he held up a ripe grape. *Hey, Fraser! Isn't she a beauty?*

Yes, Dad. Yes.

So maybe sticking around didn't have to dig out his heart. Maybe, in fact, like his dad had when he'd returned to help Granddad, he'd find it.

He got out and headed inside.

His siblings sat or stood around the island, his dad's laptop open. Creed was working the mouse. "We'll figure it out, Dad."

"What's going on?" Fraser said.

"Dad's trying to figure out Zoom," said Iris, and only then did he realize—

Iris wore an elegant, one-shoulder-exposed black gown. The other sleeve was puffy with a wide cuff. The dress dropped to the floor, exposing her rather toned leg.

"What did I miss? You guys going to a party? And Iris, are you sure you're allowed outside the house in that? Dad? Where's Hud?"

Iris gave him a look, but then he winked. "You look great."

"We're going to the Vikings charity event," Hudson said, walking in behind him from the guest room down the hall.

The man wore a tux. And well.

"Those are some fresh threads, Hud."

Hudson was affixing a pair of cufflinks. "Thanks."

"Sorry, but he doesn't compare to a Navy SEAL in dress blues," said Shae as she came down the stairs. She wore a deep-green sequined gown, boat neck, with open sleeves, her hair up. Behind her came Ned.

"I have a monkey suit like that," Fraser said.

"Probably doesn't fit anymore." Ned raised an eyebrow. "All that civvy weight you've put on."

"Nice chest candy. Is that a combat action ribbon? *Wow.*"

Ned rolled his eyes.

"So, you're going to this gig too?"

"Shae's taking pictures, so yes, we got a golden ticket."

"Sibba and I are going too," said Jonas. He was at the counter, wearing royal blue suit pants, a white shirt, and a silver tie. His jacket hung over a counter stool. "Prince Xavier sent us the invitation in thanks for what Sibba did."

"What Sibba did?" Fraser looked at him. "What am I, Casper the ghost? I figured the entire plot out!"

"Dunno, buddy. I feel like maybe you've got a whole Criminal of Lauchtenland vibe going." Jonas made a face, then looked past him to Sibba, now coming down the stairs.

Oh man, the guy was totally moving to Florida, given the look on his face. And why not? In her curve-hugging, deep-V white dress, the waistline ribbed in gold metallic thread, Sibba practically looked like a bride. Her dark brown hair was down and wavy, pinned back at the top. An exotic European model.

Jonas just grinned. What a goofball.

"I got it. The video is loading," Creed said, and Fraser walked over, stood behind his brother. Their mother sat on a chair, an afghan around her shoulders. His dad stood behind her, his hand on her arm.

Dr. Gregg, the transplant nephrologist, appeared on the screen. He'd blurred out his background, but leaned in, peering into the screen. "Hello, Garrett. Jenny. How are you?"

"Fine," said his mother.

"Worried," said his father.

"Well, I have good news, and first I want to say thank you to everyone for taking the tests. I know the blood panel and chest X-ray and the EKG and the ultrasounds and the CT scans all seem like overkill, but we need to make sure your body, as well as your mom's, is ready for this. A liver transplant is no small ordeal, and for the donor, it can mean four to six weeks of recovery time, and even more to get back to your regular life. Eventually, your liver will regenerate, but it takes a while."

"But it can save Mom's life, right?" Jonas, his hand in Sibba's, from the back.

"Yes. If all goes well. We'll remove her liver and transplant the piece from the donor. And eventually, it will grow into a full-size functioning liver. You should know, however, that there is a thirty percent mortality rate for live liver donors."

Fraser had been watching his mother, and now she flinched.

"But without it, she dies," Ned said.

"Yes. And soon." He shook his head. "Her steatosis has advanced more rapidly than we'd hoped. And it's not responding well to treatments. If...if the donor agrees, I think we're looking at a transplant not long after the new year."

"A week, then?"

"Maybe two. But soon."

"So, Doc, give it to us. Who's gonna give Mom their liver?" said Iris.

"The good news is that a male to female donor has the highest rate of success."

Fraser eyed Iris, whose mouth pinched at the sides. Yeah, well, he got that. They all wanted to help.

"Your mother has type A blood and your father type B. So, there were two matches—one type A and the other type O. Both excellent, one scoring just a little higher than the other." He paused. "Ned. You have type A blood. You're the strongest match for your mom."

Ned drew in a breath. Swallowed, then nodded. "Right. Okay then, I need to get some leave from—"

"No."

Even Fraser stared at his mother, nonplussed.

"Do you know how hard it is to get into the SEAL program, Doctor? Ned has worked for four years to become an active duty SEAL." She looked at Ned even as he stared at her, words forming, given his expression. But she might be the only person who could stare him down. "No. What if there are complications? Or...what if they don't let you operate again?"

"Mom—"

"Who is the second?" This from Jonas.

And for a moment, Fraser actually hoped it might be Jonas. Because he had...space. And time. And with all his brains, he could probably figure out—

"Creed."

Silence.

Then, from their dad, "Say again?"

"Creed. He's got type O blood, and he's RH-negative, like Jenny. He also has the healthiest liver—"

"I have type O. What about me?" Fraser said.

"Sorry, Fraser, your blood pressure came in a little high."

He gaped. "Of course it was high. I had to leave the woman I love in the hospital to get on a plane to save my mother!" He rounded on his brothers. "Why wasn't yours high?"

"I'm just calmer than you," Ned said. Smiled.

"I chase storms for a living, bro," Jonas said.

"What. Ever."

"And you're RH-positive, like your dad," said Dr. Gregg.

Figured.

"So I'm a match," Creed said quietly. He looked at Ned, then his mom. "I'll do it."

"Creed—"

"Mom, you're right. Ned is...a superhero. And I'm just a guy."

"You're more than just a guy," Fraser said quietly. "You're like...I dunno. A little bit of all of us, maybe."

Creed offered a tight smile. "Yeah, right." He turned to his mom. "I want to do this, Mom. For you. Please?" He put his hand on hers, squeezed. "Don't you know, it's supposed to be me."

Her eyes filled. Then she nodded. Leaned up, put her arm around him, and gave him a kiss on the cheek.

He hugged her.

Okay, fine. Maybe Creed was even right.

Supposed to be him.

Creed turned back to the doctor. He was giving him instructions on how to prepare when a knock sounded at the door.

"I'll get it," Fraser said.

No one moved, listening to Dr. Gregg.

Ho-kay. He went to the door, opened it.

Froze.

What?

Pippa stood with Imani on the stoop, both holding a hanging bag over their shoulders.

He had nothing.

She wore her hair back but loose, a long white wool coat and boots. Almost, well, regal.

"It's cold out here," Pippa said, her eyebrow rising.

"Right." He opened the door and stepped back, not sure— "What are you doing here?"

Pippa came in. Imani walked past her.

He heard Creed call her name, but his gaze was only for Pippa.

"Seriously? What kind of hello is that?"

He took the bag from her hand, hooked it onto a coat hook, turned to her and trapped her against the door, his hands braced over her shoulders.

"I can do better."

Then he pulled her into his arms, and he didn't care why she was here, because in this moment, everything suddenly felt right and whole and unbreakable.

Please.

He finally, reluctantly, let her go. "Now, what's going on?"

She was grinning, something new and fresh in her beautiful eyes. "We've come to take you to a ball." She picked up the hanging bag. "Suit up, Captain America."

THIRTEEN

He was probably in the wrong movie. Because last time Creed looked, he wasn't a prince. But when Imani burst through the door of his parents' home, carrying a tuxedo, grinning at him as if he was her long-awaited knight in shining armor, yeah, he'd dive into the fairytale, if only for a couple hours.

Besides, as it turned out, he looked good in a tuxedo. And it wasn't just the mirror that told him that but the look on Imani's face as he came down the stairs. She'd changed, also, into a dress fit for a princess—sleeveless, with a shimmer of gold in the wispy fabric that overlaid her blue dress. All she needed was some fairy dust.

He didn't miss the small tiara she wore, tucked into her hair at the crown. The rest of her dark hair fell loose to her waist.

Yes, he might be in way over his head, but he was all in as he gave her his arm and escorted them out to the limousine.

Sibba and Jonas also joined them.

Hud and Iris, along with Shae and Ned, had left earlier.

Fraser and Pippa climbed in and sat on the opposite seat. She'd also dolled up in a blue evening dress with puffy sheer sleeves and embroidered flowers on the front. She'd tied up her dark hair, but not quite as severely as usual. He didn't see a gun on her—hard to hide it in that silky dress. But she had mad martial arts skills, so maybe she didn't need it. Still, "Are you armed?"

She looked at him. "I'm always armed, Creed. But in case you get out of hand..." She opened up a pocketbook and showed off her taser.

"Please do not use that on me," Fraser said.

She laughed. "Don't give me a reason."

"Is that a thing?" Sibba said.

Fraser looked at Creed, and even Creed smiled.

Then Fraser took Pippa's hand, held it, and seemed unable to take his eyes off her.

Creed knew the feeling. He caught Imani up on the last two weeks, the conversation with Spider, his mom's condition, and then the news.

"You're going to donate part of your liver? Is that possible?" She had woven her fingers through his on her lap as the limo drove them into the city.

"Yes." He explained the details that Dr. Gregg had told him. "I'll probably be back on my feet by this spring. Maybe even running again."

She'd gone quiet at his explanation. Offered a tight-lipped smile.

"I'll be fine, Imani."

"I know." She looked away. Then back to him. "For the record, I don't know what God has planned for us, but I couldn't get past the idea I was supposed to invite you to the ball tonight. It might be our last outing, however. Because I'm going to be an official royal after this."

Oh.

And, "You're upset."

Yeah, he was, the last thread of hope for them snapping. "I'm just glad to be here with you. Right now." He didn't let his thoughts spool out past that. But yes, he was all in for trusting God. As if there was any other choice.

They pulled up to the venue. "This looks like a palace."

"It's a mansion," said Imani. "It's an old, elegant mansion, built in the late 1800s. Apparently it has the largest ballroom in all of Minneapolis. Three floors and a dressing area, and the royal entourage is staying next door in the carriage house. It's quite gorgeous. Xavier picked it because it had a regal feeling. You know him."

He held his words.

"Wow," Fraser said, looking out the window. "I feel like I'm back in Lauchtenland."

Three stories of stone, all lit up with blue and gold lights. It had a sort of Italian Renaissance kind of feel to it, with pillars and a red-tile roof. White flocked Christmas trees flanked the doorway of the expansive, covered front porch. Limos pulled up before a grand staircase with pillars, but their driver continued under an archway around back to a courtyard, shoveled and lighted, and let them off under the scrutiny of security.

Another woman, dressed in a black suit, followed Imani in. "I'm at the head table," she said to Creed as they entered the house.

The entry hall was large enough to host a small army, and here guests entered, shedding their coats. The dark mahogany wood was richly shined and glowing under a bright chandelier. A blue carpet led up two floors of a wide staircase with sturdy scrolled banisters. He could look all the way up to the third floor.

Security had stopped the influx of guests so Imani and her entourage could take the central stairs up. Three flights, all the way to the top floor, but his leg was a champ, and he barely felt the burn.

And then he forgot it as the stairs opened to a grand, elegant ballroom. Chandeliers lit the room, casting a glow upon the arched ceiling. From the floor, blue lights turned the walls a royal blue. Gold chairs encircled round tables with more gold candles flickering and white and blue roses at the center. And at the front, a long head table with a podium.

He spotted guests already assembling—cousins, the QB of the Vikings, and one of the running backs, as well as Hudson and his coach from the Vienna Vikings. Iris had spiffed up, left her zebra stripes long behind in that exotic dress. No wonder Hud kept looking at her as he held his glass of champagne.

"I have to leave you," said Imani then, and kissed Creed on the cheek. "But only until after the speech. Then, I want a dance."

"You bet."

She left him with Pippa and Fraser, and that's when he figured out that Pippa wasn't on duty. In fact, she sat down next to him, between him and Fraser at a table in front, near the podium.

"What's going on?" he said. "Were you fired?"

She shook her head. Glanced at Fraser and smiled. He grinned back.

Seemed they had something cooking. Especially when Pippa leaned up to Fraser and pointed toward the side door.

He followed her point, and his chest tightened.

Griff, standing at parade rest, watching the crowd. Next to him, in a black suit, Imani's female protection officer.

Ignore him. Creed wasn't going to let the man destroy his night. Although, for a second, he had a very real memory of the man's hands around his neck.

Shake it off. Clearly, he'd been wrong about Griff and his involvement in the bombing. Maybe he *had* just been trying to protect Imani and her mom.

Hud and Iris came over and introduced him to a player from Hud's team, a guy named Felix.

Shae was taking pictures, moving around the room with her phone.

Ned came over looking splendid, of course, and Fraser saluted, mocking his medals.

Ned laughed and looked over at Jonas, who'd also joined them and was now rolling his eyes.

And the strangest feeling of...camaraderie, maybe, swelled through Creed. This was his family. *It's supposed to be me.*

He didn't know why, but as soon as he'd said those words, a peace had swept him up, like the wind, or maybe a wave. But even as Dr. Gregg had outlined the dangers and his diet changes, any fear vanished.

He was made for this.

An orchestra had played during the welcome reception but now stilled as—of course, Prince Xavier took the mic at the front.

"I'd like you all to rise for the entrance of our guests of honor—His Royal Highness Crown Prince John of Lauchtenland, Her Royal Highness Princess Gemma, and Her Royal Highness Princess Imani."

Creed found his feet and couldn't help the strange ping that hit him when Imani came in, regal and perfect, and immediately found him in the crowd. Bam.

He couldn't wait to see her invested as a royal princess and Duchess of Dalholm. Because although she'd explained her upcoming investiture to him at the house, it'd taken until this moment for his heart to explode with joy.

The Duchess of Dalholm and Her Royal Highness Princess Imani of the House of Blue couldn't be with an American nobody.

He'd tried, though, to shrug it off. But now...now he saw it. Saw *her*.

Because she was also made for this.

It didn't even matter that she took a chair next to Prince Xavier. Her parents sat on the other side. He'd been loved by her, and that was enough.

The crowd bowed or curtsied, and Prince John took the podium.

He had a deep, regal voice—a good looking guy, really. "We're so glad to be here to celebrate the success of the Viking face-off in Lauchtenland, to support the International Children's Cancer Fund. With your help"—he looked at Xavier—"and Prince

Xavier's hard work, we raised over eight hundred thousand dollars."

Clapping.

"Tonight, we celebrate. Let's give thanks, and then Princess Imani will give some remarks on behalf of the House of Blue, and we'll raise a glass of champagne."

He nodded to a chaplain, who rose from his table, took the mic, and prayed.

Creed bowed his head but kept his gaze on Imani, who stood next to Prince Xavier.

A server walked over during the prayer with champagne flutes. As he watched and the rest of the room prayed, Prince Xavier reached out and picked up two flutes by the rim. One he set down in front of Imani's plate.

The other he put back on the tray. Then he picked a new one, by the stem.

The server continued down the row to the Prince and Princess. Gave them glasses from the tray, one of them the one touched by Xavier.

Something about it felt...off.

The chaplain finished and the assembly sat.

Creed couldn't get his gaze off Imani's glass.

Iris was sitting behind him, and she leaned forward. "Did you see that?"

He looked at her. "Xavier, switching the champagne flutes?"

"No—yes, but first, he put something in those flutes."

He looked at her, and her mouth tightened. She looked at Pippa in front of him.

Right.

He tapped her and she glanced back. Imani was just taking the podium. Smiling out into the audience.

He met her eyes, smiled back. *You can do this.*

She took a breath, and he leaned in to Pippa. "Xavier put something into the champagne flutes."

Pippa just blinked at him, then frowned.

He nodded. *C'mon, Pippa, trust me.*

"I'm so delighted to be here today to say a few words on behalf of the House of Blue and Her Majesty Queen Catherine," Imani said.

Pippa leaned over to Fraser, spoke into his ear. Fraser was sitting with his legs crossed, his hands folded. He didn't move a muscle in his body, just gave the smallest nod.

"Imagine your child in terrible stomach pain. He's crying and screaming, and you don't know how to help him. After countless trips to the ER, you finally get an MRI and are told the worst. Cancer. He's given hope—through chemotherapy—but even after months, the pain increases."

Pippa got up, ducked, moved away from the table, and headed over to the side.

Creed's gaze had moved back to Xavier.

Who was staring at him, eyes dark.

He lifted his chin. Xavier's jaw tightened. So, they weren't friends. No surprise there.

"There's nothing they can do, and not long after, your child passes away in your arms. Excruciating. And yet, this happens every single day to over two hundred and fifty children across the world and over four hundred thousand children a year, globally."

Pippa had walked up to a man standing beside Imani's guard, a male. Probably on Prince John's detail.

"Many of these children live in low- and middle-income countries, where treatment is costly and sometimes not available, and the survival rate is as low as thirty percent. Sadly, childhood cancer is not rare, but funding to eradicate this disease is far behind that of breast cancer and leukemia and even melanoma. And yet this is the number-one killer of children in America. Eighty percent of children, by the time they are diagnosed, are already at stage four. And one in five children will die."

Creed's gaze stuck on Griff, whose attention was fixed on Xavier.

Then Griff nodded.

Huh.

Back at the podium, Imani said, "But together, we can help. Because of people like Prince Xavier and his team, and athletes like the players of the Minnesota Vikings and the Vienna Vikings, awareness is rising."

Pippa motioned to a nearby server.

"The House of Blue is proud of the ICCF for their work in investing in health care and treatment in remote areas, training, and research of innovative treatment that includes earlier screening and support."

Creed stilled as the server moved behind the table to remove the flutes.

Prince John glanced up as his was removed, frowned, and looked over.

His bodyguard simply nodded.

"So, in gratitude, we'll raise a glass—" Imani looked over, hesitating. "Or actually, let's just give them a round of applause."

She stepped back and turned to Prince Xavier, clapping.

Creed stood, clapped.

The prince came to the podium, and she held out her hand. He took it, bowed. Waved to the crowd, then moved into the mic. "Let's eat, shall we?"

Imani sat down.

Good job, Creed mouthed, and winked.

She grinned, practically glowing, and winked back.

And it didn't even matter that Prince Xavier put his hand behind her chair and leaned over, speaking into her ear, because her eyes were on Creed.

And maybe, in the moment, yeah, he was a prince.

MAYBE IT HAD BEEN OVERLY CAUTIOUS TO REMOVE THE champagne flutes, but as soon as Creed had whispered what he'd seen into Pippa's ear, Iris's story of the poisoning of her fellow football referees stirred and lit a fire inside her.

Probably it was overkill, but just in case...

Because the last thing Pippa needed was something to make her second-guess her decision.

Somewhere over the Atlantic, Pippa had known the truth—she wasn't going back to Lauchtenland. At least, not in Her Majesty's service.

You are His. And He loves to delight in His children.

Maybe it'd happened when she'd tried on the dress down at the Vintage Shop. Despite Princess Imani's over-the-top joy at getting her in a dress, even Pippa appreciated the way it turned her curvy, even elegant.

And she might never forget the look in Fraser's eyes when she'd exited the bedroom and come down the stairs.

Almost as good as the expression on his face when he'd opened the door. Those blue eyes shining with disbelief, then a deep stir of desire.

And the way he kissed her, there went her doubts.

He cleaned up well, too—shaved, and filled out the tuxedo perfectly. She'd been a little worried about the size, but Imani had asked Gemma for Prince John's size and compared Fraser to him.

Although honestly, the comparison stopped there. Where Prince John was refined and proper, Fraser had a barely reined-in edge that completely undid her. Even now, as he sat at the table, his gaze on her, sitting casually, she sensed something just simmering under his smile.

Yes, they only needed one proper *t*'s-crossed-and-*i*'s-dotted person in the family.

Family. Yeah, she was going there. If only she could figure out the words for Princess Imani. *I resigned the commission...*

They stuck like a burr in her throat.

Especially now, as she stood beside Tamsyn, watching the princess as she talked with Prince Xavier.

Ethan came back to stand beside her. "Prince John expects a briefing later."

She nodded, kept watching Prince Xavier. He wore a suit tonight, looking dapper and polished, nothing odd about his behavior.

Except, of course, for Creed's accusation.

No. She believed Creed. In fact, it was about time people started believing Creed. He'd proven himself enough.

Her gaze went to Prince John, and with it, the conversation with Fraser in the dining room as they'd waited for Imani back at the Marshalls'.

"Any memory of the event?" Fraser had said as she'd stood in front of him, tying his bow. Oh, he smelled like the north woods, and for a second, she was in the Range Rover with him, his arms around her. She took a breath and shook her head.

"Nothing." She stepped back and flattened the bow. "Nice."

He caught his reflection in the mirror. "Where did you learn that?"

"My dad. I used to tie his ties when he had special events at Hadsby. I spent hours on the footage from Titus Stadium. Every angle simply has the limo pulling up and a uniformed driver getting out, but then he disappears into the tunnel."

"And nothing from the limo camera."

"It wasn't registered. We pulled all the limo footage, but none of them caught it."

He handed her a cufflink and held up his wrist.

"Fingers still a little tight?"

"Or I just like you fussing over me."

She affixed the cufflink. "I did pull the CCTV from the Port Fressa jail where Fredrik was killed. No visitors logged in to see him the day he died."

"They might have logged in to see someone else. Who did he share a cell with?"

"I checked that too. A man named Percy, who was picked up for petty theft."

"Strange cell mate for a political assassin."

She looked up at him. "Yeah. I hadn't thought of that. But Fredrik was just in a holding cell overnight. He was supposed to be arraigned the next day. I think Percy was actually moved that night, before Fredrik died."

"Would he have had time to poison him?"

"I don't know. His visitor met him in the morning. So maybe. But Fredrik didn't die until nearly midnight, long after dinner." She stepped back. "You look like trouble."

"Really. The right kind I hope." He leaned close.

She stepped back. "I have makeup on. Do not mess it up."

He grinned, and she nearly changed her mind, but then he'd reached into his pocket and pulled out his watch. Handed it to her and pulled up his sleeve.

She put it on. "The crazy thing is, I think I saw Prince John's watch in the CCTV footage."

The clasp snapped, and he shook his wrist, moving the watch. "Really?"

"Yes. It's a certain design, made for the House of Blue. But certainly the man wasn't Prince John. There's no way he would have visited Fredrik, and if he did, Fredrik would have been brought to him. So I must have mistaken it."

Fraser pulled down his cuff. "Maybe have Gunner take a closer look at this Percy fella."

His suggestion had sat inside her the entire ride into Minneapolis, until she'd pulled out her phone and texted Gunner. He had arrived days before and already set up shop in the security area of the mansion. She hadn't really expected a response, and by the time she'd gotten to the event, had largely forgotten it.

Except, something was stirring inside her as she stood watching the crowd. Waiters had started to serve bread on tables while the crowd, maybe two hundred and fifty, by a loose count of the tables, broke into their salads. A few waiters also refilled wine glasses. Others gathered up empty champagne flutes.

She could probably return to her seat, but...

"I'm going to have a word with the princess," she said to Tamsyn, who nodded.

She walked over to Imani. Prince Xavier had his arm over the back of her chair, leaning in to talk to her.

Pippa crouched behind her chair. "Your Royal Highness."

Imani turned. "Everything okay?"

It was then that Prince Xavier removed his arm.

And everything simply whooshed out of Pippa, her gaze on his watch, still exposed as he reached for his glass of chardonnay.

"Pippa?"

"Prince Xavier has a House of Blue watch," she said, the words simply slipping out.

"Oh." Imani looked at his watch, then back to Pippa. "He got it from his father when he turned eighteen."

The Prince now looked at her. Then his watch. Frowned. "It's adapted from a House of Blue design, but I can assure you, it's from the House of Neville."

"Yes, Your Royal Highness. It's quite handsome."

Prince Xavier smiled. "Can we help you?"

"Uh, I just wanted to congratulate Her Royal Highness on her speech."

He lifted his glass to Imani. "She will be well suited for her role as Duchess of Dalholm."

Pippa looked at her. Imani made a face. "I was going to tell you. I made my decision. I'm taking my oath after the new year."

Pippa nodded. "Very good, ma'am."

Imani narrowed her eyes. "Ma'am?"

"You should get used to it. Because after the investiture, there is no going back."

Prince Xavier made a noise. "Why would she go back? She's going to be officially a princess, with land and title and legacy." He grinned at Imani. "May the House of Blue rule forever." He took a drink.

Huh. "Indeed," Pippa said and stood up. Then she walked back to Tamsyn. "Keep an eye on the prince. He's drinking a lot."

"Yes, ma'am."

Then she caught eyes with Fraser.

Oh, she loved this man. He hadn't taken his gaze off her. She glanced down at her wrist and tapped it. Then looked over at Prince Xavier.

Fraser frowned, then put his hand to his watch and covered it. She nodded.

He turned his gaze to Xavier, and something dark flickered in it. See, she didn't even need comms to communicate with him.

I go down, you go down. She didn't know where his voice came from, but there it was, deep inside her heart. Because she wasn't in this alone.

And she'd never felt that more than right now.

He knows even our unspoken desires.

Yes, He did.

All in, all the time.

She lifted her phone and texted Gunner again.

PIPPA

Any info on Percy?

Nothing.

She looked up.

A server was clearing away the champagne flutes at the Marshall table.

Everything froze inside her.

Because in that moment, she was in a tunnel, staring at a chauffeur, a burly man with dark hair and a gun pointed at her.

The recognition shook through her. It was *him*.

Except, the shot had come from behind her.

And then she remembered. *All* of it.

Imani shouting and Pippa diving for Princess Gemma, and then the terrible burn through her body.

Then Griff, standing over her, his Glock out.

She took a breath, her hand pressing against her stomach. She was going to be sick. Still, she tightened her jaw and glanced at Griff.

He saw her, his mouth tightening, and his eyes narrowed.

No.

Then she simply rounded, headed for Imani.

Run.

FRASER HAD KNOWN SOMETHING WASN'T RIGHT THE minute he walked into the mansion. His gut started to churn, the tiny hairs on the back of his neck rose, and the cells right under his skin buzzed.

Just like Nigeria, when he'd walked into a village filled with dead people and an ambush for the living.

But what was he going to say? Security packed the place, and why not? The royals were in town. Besides, the mansion wasn't a hotel, with numerous entrances—the place had been buttoned down by Gunner's team.

So, just calm down.

Instead, he'd been trying out words in his head.

Pippa, please don't go back to Lauchtenland.

Pippa, I know in my heart we're supposed to be together.

Pippa, you are...well, so many words. Gorgeous? Breathtaking? Courageous?

How about, *Without you, I can't breathe.*

No, no, that felt too much.

Maybe just, *Will you marry me?*

The words had nearly tipped his lips as she'd been helping him dress in the dining room. She smelled so amazing, and he'd wanted to capture one of those wisps of dark hair and run it through his fingers.

Don't mess up my makeup.

Fine. For now.

Maybe the churning in his gut came from the sense that if he didn't propose, and now, they'd miss it somehow.

That he had to capture this moment before it slipped away.

So yeah, he'd been thinking about proposing all the way until Pippa had leaned over and said, "Keep your eyes peeled. Something's afoot."

Aw, see, he knew it.

What he hadn't expected was for the champagne flutes to be whisked away from the head table. That was weird. He'd even glanced over at Creed, and the expression on his kid brother's face said it all.

Princess Imani was still in danger. Or at least, Creed and Pippa thought so.

So yeah, then he'd started paying attention. Quietly.

As Pippa tiptoed up to the table to talk to Princess Imani, he sized up the security, especially Ethan, who seemed to be talking to someone, quietly, in his earpiece near the door.

His gaze went to the woman who'd replaced Pippa. Her gaze scanned the room, looking for threats.

Then Griff, who seemed to stare out at nothing, his face blank.

So maybe they were all over-reacting.

But then Pippa returned and motioned to the watch, and then to Xavier, and now his brain was ticking on that information, remembering their conversation, trying to focus on it instead of the overwhelming need to take her into his arms.

Focus.

A waiter came and set a basket of bread on the table. Frankly, Fraser had no appetite for the peach and arugula salad, but he pulled his napkin onto his lap.

Shae had joined them at the table, next to Ned, who sat between them. "That was weird, right? The champagne flutes?"

Fraser looked at her.

"It's because Xavier put something into Imani's glass," Iris said, leaning in, cutting her voice low.

"What?" Fraser said.

"Yeah. I saw it too. During the prayer," Creed said. He hadn't turned to eat, his gaze still on Xavier. Yeah, well, Fraser might wear that expression too if some guy was getting handsy with his girl.

He cast a glance back at Pippa. She was on her phone.

A waiter came by and lifted the empty champagne flutes onto a tray.

And next to him, Ned froze.

He looked over. Shae had a grip on Ned's arm, her eyes widened. "That's Zurab."

Ned put his fork down. Picked up his napkin to wipe his mouth.

"Who is Zurab?"

She leaned in, her voice low. "He was in the prison camp with me and Vikka."

Poor Shae had turned a little white.

He got a look at the guy. Built like a buffalo, hair, with trees for forearms. Yeah, he had Russian all over him.

How did he get past security, unless....

Prince Xavier. Fraser glanced at him, talking with Princess Imani.

"He's up to something," Creed said softly. "He's slippery, like a snake."

And that's when he spotted Pippa's expression.

Something wasn't right. Something—

She took off for Imani.

He hit his feet.

Zurab dumped the flutes. They crashed to the floor, glass shattering, and the room hushed. But Fraser's gaze was only on the man's napkin-covered hand and the weapon in his grip.

He *knew* it.

Pippa was already in a run, but he was closer. He launched himself at the Russian.

A shot went off. Screams.

Please, God, don't let Pippa have been hit!

Zurab had staggered back, barely tackled, but Fraser snagged his shirt and slammed him into a table.

Dishware scattered. Fraser picked up a fork even as the Russian slammed the butt of his gun against Fraser's head.

His vision spun, but he shook it off and viced the man's wrist. Another shot, this one to the ceiling.

More screams.

"Everyone stay where you are." Xavier had gotten up, grabbed the mic.

The Russian hit Fraser again, a fist to the jaw, but Fraser got his arm up, deflected.

But his grip wasn't what it used to be, and the Russian jerked his wrist free. Slammed his hand into Fraser's jaw.

Heat exploded, and he slipped.

But not before he jammed the fork, with everything he had, into the man's neck.

Zurab roared. Stood up and kneed Fraser in the jaw.

Fraser staggered back, caught himself, and—

And Ned was right there, along with Jonas, and Hud, who had the girth to match Zurab. Ned kicked out his legs, then they wrestled him down—Hudson on top of him, blood saturating Zurab's jacket where the fork had dislodged.

Felt a little like they might be in a bullfight.

He searched and found the handgun, dropped by Zurab. Scrabbled for it.

But before he could turn and point it at Zurab, before he could find a shot, Sibba stepped in and stabbed the taser into Zurab's neck.

The others fell away as he yelled, but she held it until he lay, undone, still breathing but briefly paralyzed.

Yeah, Fraser knew exactly how that felt. Not so fun, big guy.

Sibba stepped back, held up the taser. "I like this thing."

"Oh, you scare me," said Jonas.

She grinned.

Fraser looked up and spotted security leading people out a

side emergency exit, HMSD creating a corridor of armed protection.

Attaboy, Gunner.

A couple more security stepped in and cuffed Zurab. Fraser got up, breathing hard.

He spotted Pippa at the other side of the room, her arm around Princess Gemma. Tamsyn followed with her gun drawn, all moving toward the far exit.

And then he saw it. Pippa standing up, turning, her eyes wide— "Imani!"

He followed her gaze and spotted Prince Xavier, Imani in tow, disappearing out the side door.

But before he could turn and take off to intercept, he spotted Creed, just steps behind, running out after them.

All he could think as he untangled himself from the clutter of security and bodies and finally took off after him was—*Don't get shot, kid!*

"LET ME GO! LET ME *GO*!" IMANI FOUGHT WITH Xavier's hand on her wrist as he yanked her down the hallway outside the third-floor ballroom. "X! Stop!"

"No, Imani. That's enough." His voice sounded almost angry, even as pulled her to himself, then pushed her, hard, against the wall. "You are so...infuriating."

She stared at him, her breath caught. His jaw tightened.

"I'm just trying to keep you alive."

No, no, he wasn't. And for a second, just to be sure, she spooled out the events.

And here she'd been thinking everything was perfect. Creed, looking incredible in his tuxedo, the way he'd scooped her up at the house. He hadn't kissed her, but probably that was okay.

Or not. Because with everything inside her, she longed to be in his arms, dancing, or just sitting under the stars under a blanket. She'd forgotten how much she loved the sound of his voice, so caught in it during their limo ride into the city.

That and the way his brown eyes had turned rich and deep when he'd spotted her coming down the stairs, dressed in her blue ballgown.

Then he'd mouthed her the words *good job,* his expression gleaming, and she knew…she couldn't let him go.

Which meant what? That she stayed, gave up the duchy?

Became just plain ole Imani Stone?

And right in the middle of that thought, even as Prince Xavier was leaning over—she couldn't even remember what he'd been telling her—she spotted Pippa running for her.

Pippa, with such a stricken look on her face that Imani stood up.

Pippa tackled her, slamming her right into the ground, even as a shot went off.

A beat, and then Pippa got up. "I'm sorry, Your Royal Highness—Imani—are you okay?"

"Yes, I'm fine."

Pippa found her feet, grabbed her hand. "Follow me."

Tamsyn appeared right behind her. "Princess Gemma!"

Imani turned, but her mother was crouched behind her chair, Ethan having pulled her down.

"I'm fine!" her mother said.

"She's pregnant!" Imani said to Pippa. "Get her out of here."

Pippa's eyes widened. Then, "Stay behind me."

Maybe Tamsyn thought Pippa was talking to her, because she was on Pippa like glue as Pippa wrapped her arms around Princess Gemma and headed toward the side entrance.

Imani had turned to follow.

A hand on her wrist stopped her, and for a moment, a split second, she'd hoped—

No. Not Creed. *Xavier.* "Come with me."

She paused. Then, "Not this time. I'm following Pippa."

"Now!" His face had darkened then, even as another shot went off. Then he'd pulled her toward the opposite door, Griff leading the way.

So no, he might be trying to keep her alive, but not on her terms.

"Let me go," she said again now, in the hallway.

"No," he said, and grabbed her arm, then shoved her in front of him.

"X!"

"That's Prince Xavier, darling." His jaw had tightened, his eyes flashing. "Even in exile."

What? But, "I know what a prince is, and you're not it."

Griff stopped at a side door, then flung it open.

Stairs. Griff headed down.

"Hurry up!" Xavier barked.

"Hey! I'm in heels here!" She picked up her skirt and held the railing.

"Faster."

"He's going to find you, you know." She looked at Xavier.

"Who? Your skinny American boyfriend?"

He wasn't *skinny*. Far from it.

But she was thinking Fraser. And Pippa. And most of all, "Prince John."

He laughed. "Prince John is an idiot. He has a coup happening right under his royal nose."

"What?"

"No one wants the monarchy anymore."

"But you're—you're in the House of Blue."

"I'm in the house of broke, bay-bee."

They hit the landing and Griff tried the door.

Locked.

He turned. "We'll take her out the front. Security has the rest going out the emergency exit."

"And the royals?"

"Probably already in their limos." He stepped out into the hallway, gun out, and then motioned for them to follow.

She had no idea what Xavier was talking about.

"What are you going to do? Hold me for ransom?"

"Are you kidding? You are nothing but trouble." He grabbed her elbow, trying to hurry her along.

They passed in front of the grand stairs.

"Imani!"

Xavier turned, stopped.

Creed stood at the top of the landing, breathing hard.

Creed. Of course he'd come after her. Armed with nothing but his bare hands and a limp, ferocity in his eyes. Her love for him caught her up, swept over her, stole her fear.

This man. Yes, this man was worth giving it all up. The title, the duchy, the royal lineage—

Because this was it. The love her mother had found when Prince John came to America to propose, for the second time. And probably the love her parents had had, throwing caution to the wind to marry so young, so penniless.

This was the true love of the white feather, the one of Lauchtenland lore.

Creed is my true love.

She belonged with Creed. And that had never been more obvious than right now, when he looked at her like a man on fire.

Griff aimed his gun at Creed.

"Don't, Griff!"

Creed raised his hands, shook his head. "This is not going to end well for you."

"What? You're a mind reader?"

A shout from above, and Creed looked up, then he smiled and looked at Griff. "No. I'm a Marshall."

And in that second, she recognized the look on his face. The one that had made her take his hand in a park so many months ago, trusting him with her life.

Then one that said *Let's do this.*

He took two steps, then landed on the railing, sliding—

She rounded on Xavier, ripped her wrist from his grip, slammed her heel into his foot.

A shot went off just as a body landed on her, taking her down, then bracing himself over her.

She clung to his shirt, staring up at him. He met her eyes. "Going somewhere?"

"Not without you."

Then another body landed over them, crouching, arms down to brace himself, protect them. "Stay down, bro," said Ned.

"What are you doing?"

"Gotta protect the liver!"

Creed shook his head. Then he looked at Imani and smiled, and for a second, again, she thought he might kiss her, but of course, not with the shouting, so many voices. She looked up to see Griff on the entry floor, bleeding, Fraser over him, still holding a gun. He kicked away Griff's gun. It went spinning toward the fireplace.

Then Xavier lit out for the door.

In a second, Hudson Bly, wide receiver, barreled out after him.

Creed shrugged Ned off him, sat back. Imani scrambled up beneath him.

"Aren't you guys going after him?"

"Nope," said Ned. "But I do wanna watch." He got up.

Creed also got up, then pulled her up, then they watched as the big man took down Xavier with a flying tackle.

They landed in the snow with an *ooof* that made even Creed wince.

Xavier was swearing as Hud hauled him up, his arm wrenched behind his back.

Jonas came down the stairs, breathing hard, looking at Fraser, then at Hud. "I miss all the fun."

"Get a medic. Griff's bleeding pretty badly here," said Fraser, who had taken off his bowtie and wrapped it around Griff's leg.

He writhed in pain, and even more so when Fraser motioned for cuffs from security.

"Want me to tase him?"

This from Sibba, who had followed Jonas.

"No. Put that away," Fraser said.

Then the air in the room seemed to still. Fraser looked up. Ned turned and also stiffened. And even Jonas and Sibba, who put the taser behind her back.

Creed slid his hand into Imani's, gripping it.

Prince John stood with her mother, his hand in hers, alongside Gunner, Ethan, and Pippa, and not a small contingency of HMSD officers. "Can anyone tell me what in the blazes is going on?"

Silence. Imani looked at Fraser, who was blowing out a breath, and Ned, who made a face, then Jonas and Sibba, who looked away, and finally Creed. Who just stared at her stepfather, unflinching.

"I think I can, Your Royal Highness," said a voice.

She looked up, and Shae was coming down the stairs, Iris behind her. "I think, actually, we all can. And it starts with this guy right here." She held her phone up. A man's picture showed on the screen. "His name is Alan Martin, and he's a rogue member of the CIA who just walked out of here with two hundred and fifty other hungry guests."

A beat. Then Prince John turned to Gunner. "Lock down this place. No one leaves until we have answers." He looked at the crew. "Please start at the beginning."

"Oh, sir, I'm not sure you have time for that," Fraser said.

A moment, and then a smile cracked her stepfather's face. "Try me, Mr. Marshall."

A few other smiles lit.

"What do you want me to do with this?" Hudson stood at the door with Xavier, roughed up, his nose bloody.

Prince John motioned with his head, and Gunner stepped

forward along with a couple other officers and took Xavier into custody.

He looked at Prince John, shaking his head. "This isn't over."

"Yes," said her stepfather. "It is."

A siren sounded and Fraser handed off Griff to one of the other security officers, who came armed with a med kit. "The paramedics are on the way."

Fraser looked at the prince. "Would you mind terribly, sir, if I went upstairs and finished my salad?"

Prince John gave a small smile. "Good idea. We have a lot of food up there." He headed upstairs.

But Pippa came over to Imani. "Are you okay? I thought you were right behind me."

"I tried—I'm sorry—"

And then, crazily, Pippa pulled her to herself, crushing her hard, holding her.

Imani wrapped her arms around Pippa's waist and held her back. A sigh finally went out of Pippa, and she unwound her arms, put Imani away.

"Your Royal Highness. I have to tell you something."

Imani raised an eyebrow.

"I quit."

What?

She looked at Fraser, then back to Imani. "I mean, with your permission, I hereby resign my position as your personal security."

"Of course." She looked at Creed. "I'm in very good hands."

He looked down at her, something in his eyes as Pippa walked over to Fraser.

"Yeah, you are," Creed said. Then he pulled her into a nearby cloakroom.

Shut the door.

Braced his hands on either side of the wall, right above her shoulders. Looked her in the eyes. "Don't you dare give up your title. Because I really, really love kissing a princess."

"Are you sure?"

"Don't worry, babe. I know how to sneak into a country."

And then he kissed her. He tasted of adventure and fun and joy and belonging and everything a fairytale ending should have.

"Ma'am?" A knock sounded at the door. Tamsyn.

He lifted his head. Grinned, a sparkle in his eyes. "Should we run?"

WHERE IT ENDS . . . FOR NOW . . .

"You sure he's gone?"

"Searched the whole house, sir. He left with the crowd."

The man on the other end of his earpiece sighed. "Months of surveillance, and at no small cost—"

"We'll get him, sir. I promise."

Another sigh.

"And anyone get hurt?"

"A couple injuries, but all alive."

And bouncing back, given the conversation around the two tables pushed together. Prince John and his crew had shown up first and secured the room, then pushed tables together for the families.

Ethan had asked the kitchen to bring up dinner, and while everyone finished off the salads, they started to unravel the story.

Starting with Imani and Creed, who arrived after a heartbeat, all smiles.

"So this man, Vogel, who killed the nuclear physicist, was the son of the RECO man who killed your father, Pippa?" Prince John leaned forward, his elbows resting on the table. He looked every bit as regal as he should tonight, a true king-in-waiting.

"Yes, sir, as was the man who tried to kill Iris on the field. They were brothers."

"And they were behind the poisoning of Iris's referee team?"

"Maybe," said Fraser. He looked a little roughed up but sat with his dress shirt unbuttoned at the collar, his arm stretched out behind Pippa's chair. Kept looking at her with a happily-ever-after expression.

Yeah, they'd make it. He knew warriors like Fraser. He'd pour everything he had into being a husband, maybe even a father.

"But since it was Vikka who tried to poison her at the end, we feel like the Petrov Bratva was behind that too."

"The same guys who were behind the bombing attempt at Titus Stadium," Princess Gemma said. She was slowly eating her mashed potatoes, little sips of water between each bite. Right. The royal baby-in-waiting.

"So it was the Russians behind tonight's attack," said Ethan.

"Yes," said Shae. "I can't believe I didn't recognize Zurab sooner."

"You were taking pictures, honey," said Ned. He also leaned forward, elbows on the table. "I'm just glad you got a shot of Alan Martin."

"Yeah, well, I wouldn't have know it was him except Iris said something."

"He was just standing in the back, dressed like a waiter. Crazy."

Nope, not crazy. Because evil liked to blend in, make itself seem normal.

"I saw him, and then something just clicked, and I looked again, and I think he saw me. But that was right after you tackled the Russian guy, so people were exiting out the back. I grabbed Shae and asked her to take a picture of the guy so I could be sure." Iris leaned back, looked at Hud. "I'm sure."

"What was he doing here?"

"Making sure that I was killed?" Imani said.

"Except Zurab wasn't aiming at you," Jonas said quietly. He

then pointed to a shot in the wall, right behind where Princess Gemma had sat.

Princess Gemma set her fork down. Looked over at Pippa. "If you hadn't started running for Imani, I would never have gotten down. I was already on the floor when Ethan dove on us."

"Sorry," Ethan said.

"Ethan. For Pete's sake, you can't be omniscient," Prince John said.

"I am trying, sir."

A few smiles.

"And this leads us back to the Russians. Why try and hurt the royal family?" said Prince John.

Silence.

He sat back. "PM Fickle has been trying to get me to sign the North Sea Alliance for a while. But I've done that math—if I sign it, then we'd be aligned to the North Sea countries, who are aligned with NATO. And any attack on our country would pull all the NATO nations in, by proxy."

"An attack like the death of your wife?" This from Sibba.

He looked at her. "It does seem like the Russians are after the royal family."

"So, the Petrov Bratva threatens the kingdom of Lauchtenland with a dirty bomb," Sibba said. "Dirty bombs, especially that one, are meant to frighten more than inflict damage. And at a very public event, national pressure to align with a nation—or nations—that have great military flex might be exactly what they were hoping for." This from Ned. "And maybe that's the reason why. So that eventually America might be drawn into a scuffle between them, you, and Russia."

"We have had quite the blowback in the paper," said Gunner, who'd walked in about halfway through the conversation. "PM Fickle is very keen to have us sign the alliance. Do you think he's behind these attacks?"

"That would be quite the accusation," said Prince John.

Silence.

"By the way, Prince Xavier is buttoned up, sir, and being flown back to Lauchtenland."

"Why would he want to hurt Imani?" asked Princess Gemma. "I thought he was in love with her."

"I know the answer to that one," said Creed.

Attaboy. He knew Creed was the dark horse.

"It's because the lease on Keswick has run out."

Prince John just frowned at him.

"Yes, the land is only leased from the crown. It's not owned. And apparently the queen might not renew the lease."

"Which means what? It goes back to the crown?" Jonas asked.

"I don't know. But I did some YouTube research after I came home—"

"Of course you did," Fraser said, grinning.

"Yeah, well, you should try it. Because according to a couple YT royal conspiracy theories, Xavier has been auctioning off Keswick to the highest bidder. His so-called magnesium and gold mines have dried up, and he's deep in debt to his English cousins, the Percys, back in Northumberland."

"Where's that?" Imani asked.

"It's near Scotland."

"And he owes them money?" Prince John said.

"Apparently."

Gunner looked at Pippa. "Percy."

"Yeah," she said. "A guy with that surname was in jail with Fredrik. And I think Xavier went to visit him."

"So, did Xavier poison him?" asked Imani.

A beat. "We're looking into that," said Gunner.

"While you're at it, take a closer look at Griff and his involvement with the bombing on the train." Creed's dark gaze landed on Gunner.

"Yes," Gunner said. "Very good, Creed. I'd like to apologize for not listening to you."

Creed nodded and took Imani's hand.

"So, is Xavier a RECOist?" asked Pippa.

Jonas stood behind Sibba's chair. "Maybe. Because if Xavier takes down the monarchy, maybe the debts are canceled. Maybe he thought he'd walk away from the chaos with his country."

"Or he sells out to the Russians and gives them a foothold in the North Sea," said Pippa.

"Or he marries Imani and gets his land given to him as a dowry," said Sibba.

"Yeah, that's not happening," said Imani. She grinned at Creed.

"And the dark ending has the Russians invading Lauchtenland and dragging the US into a war," Iris said.

"All at the design of this guy," said Shae, again holding up the phone. "I'd like to know his story and why he hates the US so much. And why Arkady Petrov wants a war with America so badly."

"Greed? Revenge? Pride? Pick an evil." Gunner stood up, folded his arms, his face grim.

"My head hurts." Hud made a face.

Iris gave him a look. "Please don't say things like that."

He held up a hand. "Kidding. But it's all very tangled."

"No, it's all very simple," said Prince John. "At the end of the day, I'll do anything to protect my family. Even give up my kingdom. But that is the *only* way I'd give up my kingdom. So, at the heart of this is the RECO movement, and it all goes back to Vogel and the murder Imani saw in Geneva."

He looked at Pippa, then Imani. Then, finally, Creed.

"My nation owes you a debt of gratitude that I'll never be able to repay, Creed."

Silence.

Creed swallowed, then, "If I could come and visit Imani once in a while, I'd call us even."

Prince John smiled, something that felt not just from his heart but from the future throne. "I think I can do better than that."

"You still with me?" The voice in the man's ear brought him back.

"Yes, sorry, sir. All sorted here." He headed for the door.

"And they didn't recognize you?"

"I'm not here to be recognized."

"Are you wearing a mask?"

"Me?" He walked out into the hallway, then down the side stairs, peeling off the nose, the eyebrows. He could hardly breathe in that stuff. "It wouldn't do any good for them to know I've been following them."

"But good idea. We nearly got him."

He stepped out into the cold, brisk night, the array of stars cascading over him, so many eyes, so many yesterdays.

So many tomorrows.

"The hunt isn't over, sir. There are plenty more good men out there."

"Yes, there are, Lion. Yes, there are."

He hung up.

Then Judah stuck his hands into his pockets, hunched over, and headed out into the cold.

EPILOGUE

No matter what happened, this would be Jenny's happy ending. Sitting in the Marshall family room, cluttered with wrapping paper and bows and cardboard boxes, the tree lit but empty at its base, the gifts having been given, the love having been shared. From the kitchen, the smell of fresh cinnamon rolls lingered, now being replaced with the scent of the Christmas Day turkey, roasting in the oven.

She'd gotten up early, expecting to have to stuff it, put it in the oven, start baking the rolls, only to find Iris heading up the kitchen duties, applying her on-field skills to the current players—Hudson, Jonas and Sibba, Fraser and Pippa—who made coffee, stuffed the turkey, baked the rolls, and even whipped up a massive pot of scrambled eggs for breakfast.

"Never in a thousand years did I imagine seeing you stuff a turkey, Jonas." She'd sat on the high-top stool, cradling her cup of coffee, wearing her bathrobe and wool socks—she couldn't seem to get warm—grinning at the way he took orders from Sibba, like she might be telling him how to defuse a bomb.

Creed had come down the stairs then, showered and dressed and looking nothing like the boy who'd come into their lives, broken and scared, so many years ago. He'd shaved and smelled good, and it probably had something to do with the fact that Imani and Pippa had shown up last night, fresh from Hearts Bend, where they'd gone after the charity event.

Really, in all her years, she'd never seen Fraser so happy. The man wore his emotions close, but seeing the way he'd come up behind Pippa and put his hand on the small of her back or share a look with her...yes, finally Fraser had come home.

And not just Fraser, but Jonas, too, had found a woman who could keep up with him, both physically and intellectually. Sibba had beaten him in a game of Mastermind last night, and Jenny couldn't get past the way he kept looking at Sibba, as if trying to figure out how he'd managed to talk her into his life. But then again, Jonas never understood his own charisma, the weatherman who was, under it all, a storm chaser. And he'd found his own beautiful, intriguing storm in Sibba.

She'd had to laugh when Hud and Iris got in a tussle over how to scramble eggs, Iris bumping the big wide receiver away from the stove with her hip only to have him pick her up and walk her out of the work area.

And Jenny had been privy to the conversation Hud had last night with Garrett in his study. She'd gone looking for her husband while the kids played a rousing, cutthroat game of Sorry, only to find Hud asking Garrett if he could marry their girl.

While she was there, she'd given him her blessing too. Because she'd never seen Iris light up like she did around Hudson. Never met anyone who could stand up to her like Hudson did. And she'd never thought Iris would ever consider giving up football.

But today, after they'd finished unwrapping gifts, Iris said it... "I'm thinking of coming back to America."

That turned everyone quiet. Even Ned and Shae turned around from where they were headed up the stairs to go pack for their drive to Montana.

"What?" Pippa said. She was sitting next to Fraser on the sofa, her hand woven into his. Imani sat on the floor, legs crossed, leaning against Creed.

"Yeah," Iris said. "Hud's been given an offer to coach in the US. But...we're not sure what we want to do." She sat next to Hudson, curled up on the other sofa, his arm around her. "Maybe we're done with football."

"Then what are you going to do?" Fraser said.

Iris looked at Hudson. "Hud once dreamed of being a farmer. Or a rancher. So...maybe he'll take up wine-making."

To Jenny's shock, Fraser's mouth opened, and he looked at Garrett. Who was sitting on the rocker, just watching, something enigmatic on his face.

"I thought you said I could run the winery."

"You want to run the winery?" Ned said then, coming back down the stairs. "What about Lauchtenland?"

Fraser gave him a look. "Um, newsflash there, Ned, but Creed and I are still enemies of the state."

"I think that's overstated," Imani said, and reached up to catch Creed's hand. "Methinks there's a pardon, or more, coming from the queen."

"Yeah," said Jonas. "Where's the guy who thought his brain was going to atrophy last fall as he babysat the wine. Something about watching paint dry?"

Fraser gave Jonas a look. "Listen, I know you and Sibba are headed down to Florida for all the fun and games with Logan and the Caleb Group, but frankly, maybe Pippa and I want something different."

Even Jenny wasn't buying it. "Fraser. Son. I'm with Jonas on this one."

"And me," said Ned.

"And me," added Creed.

"I love you, son. But I agree." Garrett, finally, his voice soft. "Wine-making is a long game. Are you sure this is the life you want?"

"Besides, just because you're the oldest doesn't mean you automatically inherit the winery," said Iris. "Maybe some of us want to live off the land. Raise a family here."

And now the room went quiet.

Fraser raised an eyebrow.

Hudson smiled. And then, "Okay. Yep. I asked. She said yes."

Iris then lifted up her hand, and clearly she'd just put on the massive diamond ring, because Jenny would have seen it earlier. Probably.

Imani screamed and hit her feet, and then Shae came down the stairs, and all the while, Hudson just smiled and looked over at Garrett.

He met Hudson's eyes and winked.

"Fine," Fraser said and got up. "I'll arm wrestle you for it."

"I'm not dead yet," Garrett said, but everyone ignored him as suddenly Jonas walked into the fray and started to clear away the wrapping paper, pulling out the ottoman.

Jenny looked over at Garrett and smiled at him.

He got up and walked over to her. "You look tired."

She sighed. "Maybe a little."

Across from her, she felt Creed's gaze. She looked over at him. He wore a look of concern on his face. She winked at him.

He nodded, winked back.

This last man-child had been the biggest surprise of all. In her heart, in her life. But it didn't surprise her at all that the princess had chosen the man with the heart of a knight.

She got up and let Garrett put his arm around her as Hudson got on his knees in front of the ottoman.

Fraser faced him, the opposite side.

Jonas crouched over them as they both slammed their elbows on the ottoman. Clasped their hands.

Jenny stood at the stairs, looking over at her raucous clan. Pippa stood beside Fraser, giving him a ring-side peptalk. Ned stood with his arms around Shae, her back to him. She looked different since the honeymoon, and Jenny had a sneaking suspicion why. Shae nearly glowed with the look of expectancy.

Sibba knelt opposite Jonas, clearly the other judge, and of

course, Iris had lit into the rules. "To win, you have to bring the opponent's wrist all the way down to the pad."

Garrett took Jenny's hand, helping her up the stairs.

Imani had gone to sit next to Creed, her gaze on him, so much love in her eyes Jenny wanted to forbid Creed from the procedure ahead of them. But Creed had told her, when Spider left, that she'd given him a sort of fresh start by bringing his brother to the house. "I always had this dream that I wasn't enough. But Mom, let me do this. Let me be enough for you."

And what was she going to say to that? Especially when Imani agreed.

So, there was that.

"Ready?" Jonas said.

Already, the shouting began. Iris stood behind Hudson now, rooting for him.

Pippa gave Fraser a kiss. "C'mon, Captain America," she said.

Iris looked at her. Then took Hud's face, turned him and kissed him, hard. "Thor, Son of Thunder, don't let me down."

Laughter, and Ned was shaking his head, Jonas grinning.

Creed had his arms around Imani. Yes, he'd be just fine.

It hit her then—this was right. This was wholeness. The crazy chaos of their home, their lives, their futures. And despite the struggles, the fears, the challenges, if it happened with these people, on this foundation that God had built around her, she could face it. Endure it.

Even find joy in it.

"They remind me of us," Jenny said to Garrett as they reached the top of the stairs.

"Which one?"

"All of them."

He laughed, then reached down and pulled her up, into his arms. "Garrett!"

"Jenny, my love. Trust me, you weigh nothing. And in my arms is exactly where you belong."

As the laughter and shouting lifted from below, he carried her into their room and shut the door.

NOT QUITE READY TO SAY GOODBYE TO YOUR FAVORITE family?

Download the secret Bonus Epilogue via the QR code!

WANT TO KNOW WHAT'S NEXT FROM SUSIE MAY?

USA Today Bestselling Author Susan May Warren pens a tale of rescue and romance set in the wonderful wilds of Alaska.

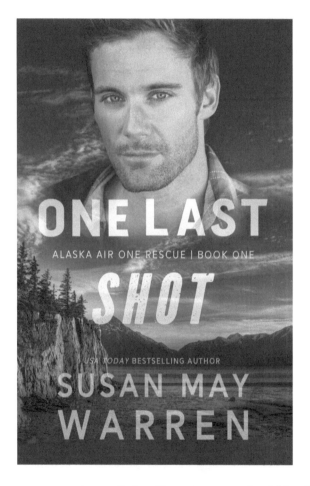

When country music star Oaken Fox joins survivalist Mike Grizz's new adventure show in the Alaskan wilderness, he just wants to boost his fan base. But when tragedy strikes, and Air One Rescue must save them, Oaken just wants to quit. Too bad his producer has other plans—signing him on with Air One Rescue as a recruit and making a reality show...

EMT Boo Kingston did not join Air One Rescue to train a celebrity. But she's a rookie to the team, so yes, she'll train Oaken and keep him alive and not for a minute pay attention to his charm...

And then five women go missing from a resort during a bachelorette weekend gone south. Now, Air One and the rescue team will have to use all their skills--and manpower, including Oaken--to find them before a blizzard settles in. But can they work together before tragedy strikes?

Exclusively available in the Susan May Warren Fiction Store in February 2024.
Releasing March 2024 at all other retailers.

Want More Like This?

Meet the Montana Marshalls, a family with Big Dreams, and Big Trouble, under the Big Sky, and cousins to the Minnesota Marshalls!

A cowboy protector. A woman in hiding. Forced proximity might turn friends to sweethearts if a stalker doesn't find them first...

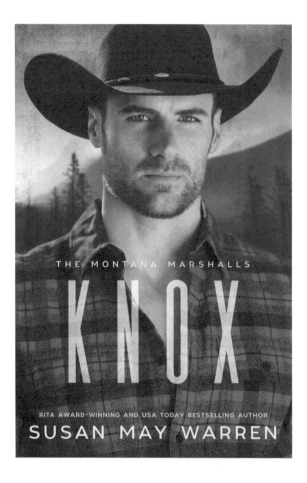

Montana rancher Knox Marshall's danger years are behind him. A former bull-rider, he now runs the Marshall family ranch, raising champion bucking bulls for the National Professional Bullrider's Expo (NBR-X). Wealth and success are his, and he's not looking for trouble.

But trouble is looking for county music star Kelsey Jones. Onstage, the beautiful rising star of the Yankee Belles becomes the person she longs to be - vivacious and confident - burying the brokenness she carries from a violent assault. But her attacker just might be on the loose...

Knox and Kelsey's paths collide when an explosion at an NBR-X event traps them in the rubble, igniting Knox's obsession to find the bomber and protect Kelsey...no matter the cost.

Start the epic romantic suspense today!

Would you like news on upcoming releases, freebies and sneak peeks from Susie May?

Sign up for updates at susanmaywarren.com, or scan the QR code!

THANK YOU FOR READING

Thank you again for reading *Creed*. I hope you enjoyed the story.

If you did enjoy *Creed*, would you be willing to do me a favor? Head over to the **product page** and leave a review. It doesn't have to be long—just a few words to help other readers know what they're getting. (But no spoilers! We don't want to wreck the fun!)

I'd love to hear from you—not only about this story, but about any characters or stories you'd like to read in the future. Write to me at: susan@susanmaywarren.com. And if you'd like to see what's ahead, stop by www.susanmaywarren.com .

And don't forget to sign up to my newsletter at www.susanmaywarren.com.

Susie May

ABOUT SUSAN MAY WARREN

With nearly 2 million books sold, critically acclaimed novelist Susan May Warren is the Christy, RITA, and Carol award-winning author of over ninety novels with Tyndale, Barbour, Steeple Hill, and Summerside Press. Known for her compelling plots and unforgettable characters, Susan has written contemporary and historical romances, romantic-suspense, thrillers, rom-com, and Christmas novellas.

With books translated into eight languages, many of her novels have been ECPA and CBA bestsellers, were chosen as Top Picks by *Romantic Times*, and have won the RWA's Inspirational Reader's Choice contest and the American Christian Fiction Writers Book of the Year award. She's a three-time RITA finalist and an eight-time Christy finalist.

Publishers Weekly has written of her books, "Warren lays bare her characters' human frailties, including fear, grief, and resentment, as openly as she details their virtues of love, devotion, and resiliency. She has crafted an engaging tale of romance, rivalry, and the power of forgiveness." *Library Journal* adds, "Warren's characters are well-developed and she knows how to create a first rate contemporary romance..."

Susan is also a nationally acclaimed writing coach, teaching at conferences around the nation, and winner of the 2009 American Christian Fiction Writers Mentor of the Year award. She loves to help people launch their writing careers. She is the founder of www.MyBookTherapy.com and www.learnhow-towriteanovel.com, a writing website that helps authors get published and stay published. She is also the author of the popular writing method *The Story Equation*.

Find excerpts, reviews, and a printable list of her novels at www.susanmaywarren.com and connect with her on social media.

facebook.com/susanmaywarrenfiction

instagram.com/susanmaywarren

twitter.com/susanmaywarren

bookbub.com/authors/susan-may-warren

goodreads.com/susanmaywarren

amazon.com/Susan-May-Warren

The Marshall Family Saga

THE MINNESOTA MARSHALLS

Fraser

Jonas

Ned

Iris

Creed

THE EPIC STORY OF RJ AND YORK

Out of the Night

I Will Find You

No Matter the Cost

THE MONTANA MARSHALLS

Knox

Tate

Ford

Wyatt

Ruby Jane

Also by Susan May Warren

SKY KING RANCH

Sunrise

Sunburst

Sundown

GLOBAL SEARCH AND RESCUE

The Way of the Brave

The Heart of a Hero

The Price of Valor

MONTANA FIRE

Where There's Smoke (Summer of Fire)

Playing with Fire (Summer of Fire)

Burnin' For You (Summer of Fire)

Oh, The Weather Outside is Frightful (Christmas novella)

I'll be There (Montana Fire/Deep Haven crossover)

Light My Fire (Summer of the Burning Sky)

The Heat is On (Summer of the Burning Sky)

Some Like it Hot (Summer of the Burning Sky)

You Don't Have to Be a Star (Montana Fire spin-off)

MONTANA RESCUE

If Ever I Would Leave You (novella prequel)

Wild Montana Skies

Rescue Me

A Matter of Trust

Crossfire (novella)

Troubled Waters

Storm Front

Wait for Me

MISSIONS OF MERCY SERIES

Point of No Return

Mission: Out of Control

Undercover Pursuit

TEAM HOPE: (Search and Rescue series)

Waiting for Dawn (novella prequel)

Flee the Night

Escape to Morning

Expect the Sunrise

NOBLE LEGACY (Montana Ranch Trilogy)

Reclaiming Nick

Taming Rafe

Finding Stefanie

THE CHRISTIANSEN FAMILY

I Really Do Miss your Smile (novella prequel)

Take a Chance on Me

It Had to Be You

When I Fall in Love

Evergreen (Christmas novella)

Always on My Mind

The Wonder of Your

You're the One that I Want

THE DEEP HAVEN COLLECTION

Happily Ever After

Tying the Knot

The Perfect Match

My Foolish Heart

The Shadow of your Smile

You Don't Know Me

A complete list of Susan's novels can be found at susanmaywarren. com/novels/bibliography/.

Made in United States
Troutdale, OR
02/28/2024

18038927R00202